MW01598300

Prospector's Run

Artifact: Book 1

Kevin W. Bates

Nuova Aurora Press

For David my life long friend. Thanks, buddy—
without that receipt this book would not exist.

CONTENTS

CHAPTER 1

Analysis complete, Holtz, er, Captain Mitsumi. We have no sign of activity within the five thousand year time horizon." On the main screen, an orange and brown sphere turned, set against a black velvet backdrop just visible at the screen's edges. Doom was written at the bottom of the screen.

"Thank you, Gwilim. I can still read." His lips compressed into a flat line, Mitsumi closed his eyes, shutting out failure, struggling to keep his head above a rising tide of disappointment. This was simply not possible. Everything he had, and a good slug of credits he didn't, rode on this.

Mitsumi opened his eyes and riveted them on the unnamed planet's surface, willing the telltale impact craters into existence. None appeared. On the screen's lower section, the glowing text remained stubbornly unchanged: "GV332195093:P4G-Negative for recent strikes."

Suspended next to his pilot, Holtz Mitsumi was unwilling to admit that his last chance had come up empty. *This can't be it*, Mitsumi thought. *What will I tell my backers?* Through the tumult and nastiness, they'd stuck with him, taken his side even, and given him this last run. They deserved better than utter failure; they merited at least some success, even if it wouldn't repay them entirely. How could he face them empty-handed?

But the prospect of facing his backers paled beside the ultimate horror. What if his ex-wives found out? He cringed,

1

blood flowing to his cheeks, their jeers and mocking laughter, imagined in exquisite and all too realistic detail, echoing in his head.

His information source had been so confident. Yet, at planet after planet, the computer had thrown the same words in his face: "Negative for recent strikes." And this was it—the last stop.

Something *had* to be there. Mitsumi ran a hand along his smoothed jet black hair and grabbed the knot of hair at the back of his head thinking of possibilities. The ship's processor wasn't infallible. "Perhaps the computer missed something?" he mused, his voice tailing upward in hope.

Pim snorted in disgust. Mitsumi lowered his hand. *I get it, Pim*, he thought. *But I need a break and the universe owes me one.*

"It tests at—" Gwilim began.

"Ninety-nine percent accuracy," Mitsumi finished, acknowledging how unlikely his speculation was. Ninety-nine percent. Almost impossible odds. Similar though to the odds against his advancement in the navy from Training Cadet to Second just below Captain, and he'd made that happen. "I get it. Still ..."

"Still what?" Pim demanded, his face set in defiance. "Nothing's there, Holtz. It's time to go home."

Mitsumi eyed Pim. *When the crew uses your first name, you have lost your command.* And *that* was something he was familiar with. So, Pim didn't want to waste any more time and resources on a one-in-a-million bet on either a computer error or being the first exception to the rule. "Gwilim?" Mitsumi said, addressing his pilot. "Should we drop down the well, look for ourselves?"

Gwilim flicked his eyes at Pim and licked his lips. "Well, I suppose it wouldn't do any harm—"

"Oh, come on, Gwilim," Pim demanded, throwing his hands in the air. "You can't be serious. A year we've been out here chasing Holtz's leads."

"That's Captain Mitsumi," Mitsumi said, allowing his

irritation to show.

Pim sneered, ignoring Mitsumi. "Solid leads he told us. Finds as spectacular as Sundered's, he said. Well, that worked out, didn't it?"

Eyes fixed on the screen before him, Mitsumi set his face, forcing disappointment from his mind. He refused to admit defeat. His source *had* been impeccable and *had* promised decent, if not spectacular, finds on this run. Perhaps he'd raised unreasonable expectations, but he couldn't go back empty-handed until he'd explored every avenue. "Okay, say the computer's right," Mitsumi gestured toward the screen, "no recent strikes. But maybe the pattern won't hold. This might be the exception."

Gwilim sighed and lowered his head, clearly embarrassed at Mitsumi's suggestion.

"Oh, here we go," Pim said.

He knew how it sounded. Odds weren't good betting on an exception that had for twenty years been an unbroken rule. Still, the "rule" wasn't a fundamental physical constant —it was just a statistic. "It's possible," Mitsumi said, desperate to make his point and convince Gwilim to vote to stay and investigate. "We've discovered only ten dead First Civ planets in the twenty years since Sundered's find—"

With an incredulous look on his face, Pim shook his head as soon as Mitsumi spoke. "And they all fit the pattern, Holtz —significant impact cratering within five thousand Uniform Federation Years. Not to mention the two hundred explored planets without cratering and with no First Civ traces. And where would you look, anyway? That's a whole planet down there. We can't—"

"Uh, Hol—I mean Captain Mitsumi," Gwilim nodded at the screen. The text superimposed on the planet had changed. "GV332195093:P4G —Anomalies detected: 40.234, 119.345; 42.342, 118.481."

Mitsumi's heart beat a little faster; this might be it. Maybe the pattern didn't hold; maybe his luck *had* changed.

3

Anomalies. Those might be First Civ remnants despite the craters' absence. "Let's start there," Mitsumi said, indicating the screen.

"It's just alien ruins," Pim scoffed. Mitsumi's shoulders slumped and his spirits sagged. Pim was almost certainly right. Since venturing out again among the stars at the end of the Great Dark, human beings had never found aliens, only their fallen civilizations' ruins, and no one had recovered anything useful from those ruins.

"Look," Pim said, "we can sell the location. An institute will pay us. It'll net less than our costs. The trip's still a loss. But let's not hang around and make it bigger."

Deflated, but not willing to give up, Mitsumi considered the image on the screen. Pim had a point, but Mitsumi wouldn't surrender while hope glowed on the screen: "Anomalies found." He clenched his jaw, preparing himself for the reaction. "We should investigate," Mitsumi said, trying to force steel into his voice. "We might find something worth more than the location. You never know, and we're here."

Pim shook his head in disgust. "I vote no."

"Gwilim?" Mitsumi asked, still staring at the screen, resisting the urge to cave to Pim.

Pim glared at Gwilim, daring him to disagree. "I don't know Ho ... Captain. I think Pim may be right."

Mitsumi lowered his head, his resolve softening as disappointment and despair made an unwelcome reappearance. Pim and Gwilim were right—nothing was there. Perhaps that was for the best—give up the impossible dream. Face his backers' disappointment, find an anonymous post on a freighter and disappear. It would be another rung down as he descended the ladder of success. But hey, he was looking at it wrong. To be positive, he was climbing, making his way up the ladder of failure. Should he feel better being an accomplished loser?

He might as well skip the next few steps and go straight to the part where he was planet bound, starving and alone.

Of course he could always go home, live off one of his siblings or his parents. Unable to shift his eyes from the view screen, he marveled at the thoroughness of his reversal. Everything had been clear space and tight jumps only a few years ago. He'd been Second on a Federated Worlds' Star Ship married to the gorgeous love of his life on the brink of a brilliant career. Now, he was a forty-year-old failed prospector staring at a "Welcome Home, Son" sign strung over the steps to his parents' basement. It hadn't happened all at once. First there had been the fiasco with his wife that ended his marriage and his stint in the navy. So he had started over—new marriage, new career in the commercial ranks only to have both end the same way. What were the odds?

Among his earliest memories, he couldn't have been more than five at the time, he stood in a park on the city's outskirts staring through half-closed eyes as shuttles from the spaceport speared into the cloudless emerald sky on blinding flame to the tune of deep, rolling, shaking thunder. That had been his dream—riding that flame and jumping to the stars and, for a fleeting, sparkling moment, he'd made it. But now as the power guttered out, he felt himself falling down the gravity well.

"Wow, anomalies, but no recent craters so ... aliens, right?" Kalal Deo drifted across the access tube to the bridge, his observation dragging Mitsumi from his morass of self-pity.

"We're leaving," Pim said, glowering at Kalal. "We'll sell the location and recoup part of our losses, but we're leaving now; that's what we decided, right, Holtz?"

With a skeptical look, Kalal considered Pim then turned to Mitsumi. "Is that right, Captain Mitsumi? Is that your decision? 'Cause I'd like to see alien ruins up close and personal."

Uncertain now, Mitsumi glanced from Kalal to Pim. Kalal's enthusiasm thinned Mitsumi's disappointment—the chance to explore actual alien ruins *was* enticing. Pim was right though, every minute they spent here increased their losses, and the odds of uncovering anything of value in alien ruins were long. Mitsumi dithered, indecision paralyzing him.

Kalal tapped his chest. "*I* think we should visit these sites." He shrugged. "But if you tell me we're leaving—well, you're the captain, so I guess we'll leave."

"We've decided—" Pim began. Kalal cut him off with a gesture.

"Captain Mitsumi?" Kalal said.

Mitsumi nodded at Kalal, acknowledging his lifeline. "It seems we're at loggerheads," Mitsumi said. "I *would* like to stay and explore as you suggest, but Gwilim and Pim want to leave so …"

"So, you're the captain," Kalal said, fixing his eyes on Pim, "in charge of this expedition."

And that is true, Mitsumi thought. Although at times it hadn't felt like it, and he hated making decisions that upset anyone. But he'd upset *someone* no matter what his decision. Gwilim and Pim might be right, but he couldn't bring himself to concede defeat yet. Mitsumi reached deep inside and hauled up what courage he found there as a bulwark against Pim's anger, even as he was upset at his weakness.

"We're staying and exploring," Mitsumi announced with as much force as he could muster, hoping his cringe wasn't as obvious as it felt.

Pim smacked his console in disgust. "You're insane," he said. "That's not a rational decision."

Kalal smiled and nodded in approval. "I'll prep the shuttle."

He should take the victory and walk away, but he couldn't do it. "It won't take long, Pim," Mitsumi said, attempting to placate Pim, repelled by his need to do so, "a few days at most."

"Fine," Pim spat, "but the extra cost is coming from your pocket."

At touchdown, the shuttle's fusion drive kicked up huge

dust clouds before they were close enough to fuse the soil. Analysis from orbit had shown the atmosphere's composition lacked sufficient oxygen, but was of adequate pressure, and the temperature was at the higher end of acceptable, so a breathing mask covering his nose and his mouth were the only accommodation required on the surface. New high-end models, the masks were a permeable material that passed nitrogen and oxygen in the correct levels while excluding anything else—one technology derived from a recent First Civ find. *Why couldn't I have* their *luck,* Mitsumi thought putting on his mask. *Those guys made out like bandits.*

The outer airlock door opened, and they descended the ramp to the surface. They had landed at the first set of coordinates the computer had identified as containing an anomaly—regular patterns on the surface indicating artificial rather than natural formations. That put them in a broad valley between low rounded hills. Flat, brown, and gray, the valley was unrelieved by anything suggesting life. Ruins, brown and gray matching the colors in the valley, lay in front of them. The planet's star, a red giant taking up a good chunk of the sky, hung overhead. Two of the planet's three moons floated, silhouetted against the star's surface. The sky, a blue green dome, stretched cloudless from horizon to horizon. A stiff breeze blew through the valley, hissing along the ground. Occasional stronger gusts swirled up dust and grit and sent it whipping through the air, layering his exposed skin with grime, stinging his hands and arms and drawing tears from his blinking eyes. The wind pushed traces of atmosphere around an imperfect seal at one of the mask's edges. Sulphur-tinged air wrinkled his nose and a few dust motes almost prompted a sneeze. On the plus side, the breeze cooled Mitsumi, evaporating sweat that had sprung up the moment he set foot outside.

Kalal strolled toward the site. Mitsumi followed along with Gwilim, enjoying the powerful sensation of walking on a world with gravity a touch lower than Newome, his birth planet. Pim hung back flaunting his lack of interest.

Kalal surveyed the buildings, eyes squinting in concentration. "They're Caliban," he said, "not Noric or Hental." Mitsumi noted the similarity now that Kalal mentioned it. "It's the style that tells, not the colors because the colors vary with the planet's soil composition," Kalal added. He had walked up to a building and was rubbing his hand along a wall's surface.

In front of Mitsumi, structures curved up from the ground as if they had grown from the soil. The outlying formations were the height of a human two-story building. From the soil, the walls curved outward then back together stopping well short of meeting again at the top. They then rose straight for a meter. On top of that structure rested a cube whose outer walls reached the limit of the curved walls below. The result looked like a box on top of a sphere. The surfaces were pitted and worn from age, but at least half the buildings were complete, the others having fallen in on themselves through the eons.

Caliban ruins—so-called because humans first discovered ruins of this type on Caliban's World—had been catalogued on ten different planets. As far as any one had discovered, the Caliban had left nothing significant behind, only these oddly shaped buildings. Exploratory expeditions had recovered only bits and pieces of metal, ceramic or other commonplace materials with un-guessable functions. Other than a few unfathomable symbols, no writing, sculptures, pictures, or anything resembling art had ever been discovered. The same was true of the older ruins of the Noric and Hental, even older civilizations named for their discoverers. Whatever had befallen the Caliban, Noric, and Hental differed from the human First Civ's fate. Whoever or whatever had pounded the first human stellar civilization into oblivion had left precious few ruins standing.

"You know," Kalal said, laying his hand flat against a wall, "no one's figured out what they did to the soil to form it into such a durable material. If these are Caliban, they date from a million UFY ago."

A million years, Mitsumi thought. No one in the Federated Worlds built anything that would last even fifty UFY without constant maintenance.

Kalal ducked into the structure he'd been examining. Mitsumi turned away and ventured ahead deeper into the site among the buildings. He couldn't see Gwilim. He activated the com in his ear. "Gwilim?"

"Yes, Holtz?"

"Just checking in," Mitsumi said. "I lost track of you."

"I'm in a building, haven't seen anything yet."

"Okay, let me know if that changes."

Past the outer circle of low level buildings, the ruins added another sphere on top of the cube, increasing their height to a three-story human building. As Mitsumi explored the buildings, a million years settled on his shoulders, slowing his steps despite his resolve to remain unaffected and concentrate on the task at hand.

He wandered into an alley, reaching out and tracing his fingertips along the walls to either side of him. Shadow slanted across the alley. With his head in the sun, the shadowed side was almost impenetrable. He felt the rough wall on his fingers, but could barely make it out. Who had lived here? What had the Caliban been like? In his mind's eye, as if the walls called them forth, alien children, small five legged beings with tentacle arms, chased each other ahead of him flashing in and out of the sun, their alien laughter echoing down the alley. No one had any idea what they'd looked like of course, but that meant his guess was as good as another's. He had expected sterile age from the ruins. But they weren't sterile. Ancient? Certainly. But sterile? Millennia had degraded but not eliminated the life impressed on the walls. Immersives he'd run on other Caliban ruins failed utterly to convey the sense of the place. When he was growing up on Newome, his father would take their family on camping trips to the wild places—places of sheer cliffs and sudden peaks where just under a layer of green life, the Horde's destruction was still raw. There, after nightfall in the flickering firelight, his father would tell old stories—stories from the Great Dark that spoke of spirits lingering in places they had known in life. He stopped, pressed his hand against one gritty wall, and wondered if the beings who built this place told similar stories out in the wilderness, in the dark.

A crunch came from behind him. He whirled, hand scrabbling for his flechette gun and pointing it at—nothing. But there on the ground, he saw a chunk of wall material. It looked like a piece from high above had separated and hit the ground. Embarrassed at his reaction, he scanned the alley, making sure no one had seen the spectacle, and hit his mask as he tried to wipe sweat from his upper lip with the back of a trembling hand. Even more chagrined at having forgotten about the mask, he holstered his weapon.

Mitsumi shook off his nerves and proceeded farther into the ruins. Mitsumi wandered through the least damaged buildings into various sized rooms with ceilings of different heights. Standardized interiors hadn't seemed to be a priority to the Caliban—a room with a ceiling well over two meters tall adjoined one with a one meter ceiling. On staircases, the rise from one tread to another varied at random. These discrepancies made what at first could appear normal human structures completely alien. He stopped again and reveled in the strangeness surrounding him.

This was why he wanted to be among the stars. Nothing on his home planet Newome compared to the feeling of discovery when he made planet and, under a strange star's spectrum, his skin glowed aqua and the air smelled of ripe peaches and mold; where under a different gravity your entire body thrummed with the knowledge you didn't belong. Once on leave at home before he'd married, he'd tried explaining the sensation to Saeko, his older sister. But holding a year-old daughter on her hip, she'd smiled and rubbed his navy reg baldness. "I know I used to tease you for your dream of exploring the bright dark.

I don't understand and it's not for me, but I'm glad you made it out there." Only Tuan his younger brother had understood his dream. Tuan who was now irretrievably lost. Grief at the loss knifed into his gut.

A gust of wind threw more grit into his eyes and brought him to the present. After clearing his vision, Mitsumi surveyed his surroundings. Based on the view they'd had approaching the site in the shuttle, he estimated he was close to the center of the rough circle of structures they'd observed.

"Gwilim, Kalal, you seen anything?" Mitsumi sent as he turned to the left.

"Nope." "Nothing." Gwilim and Kalal said at once.

"How about you, Captain?" Kalal asked.

"Nothing here," Mitsumi said, trying to keep disappointment from his voice.

"Haven't you guys given up yet?" Pim said. "Why don't you admit defeat? C'mon, let's lift and jump."

"If you've nothing to add, Pim," Kalal said almost growling, "shut up and leave us be. We'll go when we're finished, not before."

"I *am* contributing," Pim said. "I'm contributing sense to this ridiculous search."

Mitsumi wandered through the site along broad avenues that connected to narrow passages, always moving toward the site's center, without success. From one of the narrower alleys he'd encountered, Mitsumi emerged into an open space he would have called a plaza in a human city. An intact, single story building stood in the center. Straight walls emerged from the ground capped by a dome. The walls and roof were a dark gray and smooth with no evidence of weathering as on the surrounding buildings.

In front of him, the doorless entrance to the building revealed only impenetrable black from the darkened interior. The darkness was so profound it seemed palpable as if he might grab handfuls of the stuff.

Wind moaned and whistled through the abandoned

structures, raising the hair on his arms and the back of his neck. A tremor of fear wracked his body. With a sudden gust, the wind seemed to push him toward the entrance's tangible blackness.

Irritated at himself for anthropomorphizing an atmospheric temperature differential and a simple absence of light and allowing it to spook him, Mitsumi shrugged off his apprehension and approached the building, moving with caution despite his attempts at enforcing calm. Really, he told himself, the structure wasn't the least menacing. True, it was unlike everything surrounding it, but that didn't make it dangerous. Maybe his luck had changed at last and inside he'd find a fabulous life altering treasure. That would be good.

Another wind gust wailed through the surrounding buildings and forced him to step forward and catch himself.

He stopped, eyes fixed on the darkness, heart suddenly hammering his chest. But the difference in appearance between this and the other structures might be bad. Its unique design could be purposeful, tagging it as off limits because it housed an evil presence that had escaped and annihilated the entire Caliban race beginning right here. He lifted his hand, smoothed his hair, and gripped the hair knotted at the back. While trying to work saliva into his cotton mouth, he lectured himself. *Get a grip. Are you listening to yourself? You sound insane.*

With an effort, he forced thoughts of supernatural aliens aside. He had faced the unknown before without any such qualms. Mitsumi took a step forward, then another, advancing toward the entrance while fighting an increasing dread weighing his limbs and slowing his steps. For a moment he considered calling the others to him, but he didn't want to admit that he was scared for no reason.

"C'mon," he said out loud. "There's nothing here. It's just an empty building like the others." His courage fortified somewhat, Mitsumi advanced until he stood before the entrance. He had expected light reflected from the outside to illuminate the interior, but the darkness was complete. Maybe a profoundly black door blocked his view of anything inside. It didn't look like a door—it looked like empty space, but more completely black than anything he'd ever experienced aside from founder caves. Heart in his throat once more, Mitsumi lifted his hand to test his theory and paused. In his mind, he recalled entertainments where some unlucky shlub found an unknown substance and, uttering the fateful words "I wonder what this is?" touched the substance only to suffer a slow screaming death. With caution, he withdrew his hand. Instead, he flicked on his handheld light and raised it.

At the touch of his light the blackness split in the middle from top to bottom and parted, like a curtain opening, absorbed into walls. With the blackness gone, his light revealed a hallway extending about five meters and ending at a wall. Tension wringing his muscles, Mitsumi peered down the hallway. No terrors lurked, but at his light's touch the blackness had withdrawn, inviting him in.

To a trap? Perhaps once inside would the blackness snap back imprisoning him with unknown horrors.

To fabulous wealth? He might find untold riches inside. The unadorned walls gave no clue.

Steeling himself for an attack, he stepped into the passageway and stopped, prepared to leap backwards at the first sign of the blackness' return. The entrance remained open and unobstructed behind him. Inside the passageway, shielded from the wind, the heat was stifling. Heat and fear prickled sweat from his forehead. It trickled down his face around his breathing mask. With the palm of his hand he wiped away the sweat as he crept down the hall, heart thudding with each step.

At the hall's end, a doorway opened to his left. Stepping through, he shone his light into a large room. With nothing threatening in sight, he stepped through the doorway.

No beams lashed out, no projectiles pierced his body, no creatures pounced, but a soft light came up illuminating the interior. As his heart stopped pounding and his breath slowed,

Mitsumi surveyed the space. The interior was one large chamber with blank walls empty save for a plinth sitting in the middle.

Knee high, the plinth was of the same material as the walls. As he stared at the plinth, a powerful light snapped on from overhead illuminating an object sitting on its surface.

Cautious again, Mitsumi circled the plinth. Each of the four faces of the stone contained the same symbol—the galaxy as seen from above the plane of the ecliptic looking down at the center. A point at the center of the disk glowed brighter than the rest of the representation. From this center point, faint rays emanated spreading throughout the disk. An unmarked rectangle, five centimeters wide, ten centimeters long and a half centimeter thick with the appearance of a diamond, glittered on top of the plinth.

Excitement bubbling, Mitsumi took out his camera and recorded the plinth and the object from every angle. With this and the power source for the lights in the room, things changed. The symbol on the plinth transformed this find from trivial to significant, perhaps enough to put the expedition in the black. And who knew what the object on the plinth would yield? Visions of wealth and vindication danced before his eyes. He'd pay his backers in full, taunt his detractors with success, and prove the skeptics wrong.

With the objects recorded, Mitsumi reached to open communication with the others and inform them of his find, but his hand stopped short of the com button as a thought wormed its way into his mind. He should pick up the object. He frowned. That was wrong. Its value was tremendous in situ where experts with great care would measure, probe, and scan the object and the plinth across the EM spectrum.

And yet.

Again the thought intruded, thrusting beyond his attempts to see reason. He must pick up the object. Puzzled, he resisted the notion. But the idea persisted, growing stronger and breaking down his reticence. A force drew him to the rectangular object, pulled him closer to the plinth until, reaching down, Mitsumi picked up the oblong object.

Light flashed from the plinth where the object had rested. Under his hand light, the object gave no hint it was more than a rectangle of grown diamond, common even among the Federated Worlds—there were no markings on it, and the transparent interior bore no signs of having a hidden function.

As he peered into its transparent depths, the diamond clouded then silvered, its surface now a reflector showing him his face. In the mirrored reflection his mask disappeared. Next, each layer of skin peeled back revealing facial muscles and eyes naked in bony sockets. His eyes peeled back and layers of bone removed until his brain, channeled and crenelated, lay exposed. As he watched, his brain vanished layer by layer drilling down through the thalamus, hypothalamus, midbrain, cerebellum, and stem.

Without warning, the chamber disappeared, and he floated in space without a suit.

Panic seized him. Without a suit, he had mere seconds to live. But those seconds passed—his heart still beat, he was warm, his lungs still swelled with breath. If this was a simulation, it was more realistic than any he'd experienced. With the notable exception of not having a spacesuit, this felt as real as any other occasion he'd drifted in the void. As he relaxed into the sim, he marveled at the expanse before him. Below, the galaxy lay suspended in a frozen pinwheel. Ahead, a cluster of stars hung above the bulging galactic center tagged with symbols glowing in a notation he didn't recognize. He knew somehow that the symbols were the coordinates for the globular cluster.

His eyes fixed ahead on the cluster; it grew brighter. He had no sense of movement, but the cluster soon resolved itself into individual stars and then a single star with more symbols in that alien notation. He rushed toward the star but, before smashing into it, he came to an abrupt halt floating over a planet, again with symbols suspended above it. Zooming closer still, he saw a single green continent split by white-capped mountains dominating the planet's upper half.

Now he plummeted toward the surface heading to one of the mountain chains. Mammoth snow-covered peaks flashed by him and he cringed awaiting the impact. When none came, he opened his eyes. He stood on the planet's surface facing a shear rock face on which—either projected or etched—was the symbol from the plinth. Turning from the rock face, he surveyed the valley in which he had landed. It stretched before him, green with unfamiliar grasses and bushes to a broad river bisecting the valley. Beyond the river, the greenery stretched to the foot of a tremendous peak rising from the valley floor to snow-capped heights. A light, cool breeze redolent with the scent of water and life rustled the grasses. He shivered with a chill, wondering why he would feel cold now when he'd been comfortable in absolute zero a few moments before.

As he turned back to the rock face, the rectangle in his hand grew warm and glowed. Out of the corner of his eye he saw an answering light on the rock face. Certainty sprang into his mind: the diamond rectangle belonged in the light at the rock face and he had to place it there. Something waited for him on the other side of that action. It came to his mind. Power. Power to do anything he wanted. Power beyond his wildest imaginations was his and this diamond rectangle was the key. Impelled by that conviction, he strode through the grass and brush to the light and raised the diamond to meet it. Snatched from his hand, the diamond flew to the light on the rock face, melded with it and the scene disappeared.

He returned to himself in complete blackness holding the diamond rectangle. After waiting a few moments to see what new wonders awaited him, he clicked on his hand light and surveyed his surroundings. He stood next to the plinth. Disoriented, Mitsumi swept his hand light through the room. He saw nothing to explain his experience. To no avail, he replaced and retrieved the rectangle twice, hoping to replicate the phenomenon—if not his fantastic voyage at least the room lighting.

Nothing worked. Had he imagined the whole bizarre experience? But even as he posed the question he understood the Artifact had shown him something real. That star and that planet existed in an extra galactic globular cluster and the diamond in his hand belonged there. Ultimate power resided there. As the diamond weighed heavy in his hand, another extraordinary certainty settled into his mind—that power must be his. If this power was what it purported to be, he could save Tuan. After ten years, countless hours, and hundreds of credits to no avail, it would take that kind of power. And if he could help Tuan, he had to. He needed to discover the cluster, the planet, and the rock face, return the Artifact and claim his prize.

Well, he thought, *I'm not sure how that'll happen. I need to see the alien symbols again and interpret them...and raise credits for a ship and a crew and supplies.* And besides was it really possible that he had discovered the key to absolute power? The idea was ridiculous. As if in response to his thought, the urge to return the Artifact and assurance the offered power was real forced itself into his mind. *Okay, Okay*, he thought, *I'll see what I can do.* Once again he tried to retrieve the sim moving the Artifact around and on the plinth, setting it down again and picking it up. Nothing worked.

"Captain?" Kalal said over the com, interrupting his thoughts. "Have you found anything? I've met up with Gwilim and we're ready to move to the next site."

Now, there was a good question. He'd found several things, hadn't he? But which of those things was he willing to disclose and discuss? The power source for the room's lighting would be worth plenty, if he could convince anyone it existed and if it even still functioned. The plinth's symbol would be worth something—alien symbols were rare. As for the Artifact...well, he'd realized two things. One, he'd started of thinking about the Artifact with a capital A, and two—he couldn't give it up. Although it might be worth something, it had wormed its way into his mind such that he now identified with its purpose and the prospect of obtaining the offered power seized him. Even though it meant possibly giving up his dreams of vindication, he couldn't let it go. He had to keep the Artifact and find the mysterious planet. That decision warred with his every instinct to openness with his crew and his backers but, when he even considered letting it go, he was almost physically ill. Things would have been easier if he could have kept his ship and enlisted his crew to help him. But the ship belonged to his backers and they would not look with sympathy on a proposed voyage without a destination or prospect of reward but with unknown expenses. And his crew would expect to be paid. No, as much as it pained him, he had to keep the Artifact secret for now.

"Captain? You there?"

"Yes, Kalal, I hear you." He slipped the Artifact into a pocket. "I've found something. Head toward the center of the site and look for a domed building with four straight sides. I'm in there."

"We're on our way. What did you find?"

"A symbol. It doesn't look like much, but it may be worth something."

Minutes later, Gwilim and Kalal showed up inside the building. Mitsumi pointed his light at the plinth, the symbol glowing with reflected light.

Kalal gave a quiet whistle. "I think you might have just saved the expedition. I'm sure the Alien Institute folks will pay a pretty credit for access to this site. Have you recorded it yet?"

Mitsumi slid his hand into his pocket and felt the Artifact. All the images he'd taken showed the Artifact on the plinth. "No, not yet, I was waiting for you and Gwilim. You're better at that than I am." Kalal cocked his head, puzzled. Mitsumi groaned inside—no one had recorded anything planet side yet on this voyage. "At least, I'm sure you must be better, because I botch every recording I try, and this needs to be good." Gwilim was slowly circling the plinth by all appearances oblivious to this exchange.

With narrowed eyes, Kalal appeared to consider whether to question Mitsumi further then shrugged. "Whatever you say, Cap'n."

They spent the rest of a standard day wandering through the site without success, repeating their search the next day at the second site and coming up empty there too. "Well," Kalal said in the shuttle on the way to their ship parked in orbit, "I count that a win. We saw alien ruins and found an ancient alien symbol. We might even come out ahead on our trip."

Pim snorted. "That location's next to worthless. If we come out ahead, it'll be by decicredits. I should've hired on a tramp freighter for a year or even signed on with the Consortium."

"Quit whining, Pim," Kalal said. "You knew the risks before you joined."

"Yeah, talk to Holtzie here about that," Pim said. "You heard the same pitch I did: solid coordinates for pristine First Civ sites with tech not seen since Sundered's treasure." Pim lapsed into sullen silence. Kalal didn't rise to Mitsumi's defense and, not for the first time, Mitsumi regretted his overly confident sales pitch when recruiting his crew.

As they approached the ship, Gwilim floated the shuttle into its bay. When the airlock doors had closed and atmosphere was restored to the bay, Pim was first to the shuttle airlock. He paused with his back to the others. "I've laid in the jump durations and coordinates for our return to Support," Pim said. "I'll be in my quarters if you need anything from me before we arrive." Pim pushed off and disappeared into the ship.

Gwilim licked his lips. "I'm sure he can handle any systems problems from his cabin access. We'll be fine?"

Kalal clapped Gwilim's shoulder. "No sweat, Gwilim," Kalal said smiling. "You just follow those times and locations. We'll be back, ready for another adventure. Right, Captain?"

Mitsumi pasted a smile on his face and said with forced cheer, "Right you are."

She leaned against the door to her cube breathing hard, tensed against the prospect of a signal requesting access. Gradually, her breath evened out as no notification sounded. After a moment, she pushed away from the door and issued a command extruding sanitary facilities. In the mirror above the sink that formed itself from the wall she stared at her image searching again for any trace of the person she had been. She found none, as she'd found none the other million times she'd looked. No one would recognize her. Short blonde hair, high cheekbones and a long slender nose was the last thing someone looking for her broad nose, flat cheeks and long curly red hair would expect. That glint of recognition from the man in the pub was her imagination working overtime— again. If she didn't stop fleeing to her cube every time her fancy constructed someone who had sussed out her real identity, she'd call attention to herself. The opposite of her goal. Besides, in addition to an altered facial profile, her light, almost translucent skin and the two inches the Adapter had shaved off her height would fool anyone. She'd paid the Adapter way too many credits, but couldn't argue with the results.

Thinking of credits, she consulted her assistant, wanting to confirm what she remembered—yeah, enough to keep her in consumables for another two weeks. She had allowed herself three standard months to find a posting—plenty of time. In hindsight, she had overestimated the need for pilots with no experience and sketchy qualifications. In two weeks, without a posting, the Station's management would ship her down to Support. Not the end of the world, but it would be harder to reach her goal. Lips compressed into a grim line, she vowed that wouldn't happen—she'd find something.

Calling for a desk and chair, she pulled up her assistant again and checked for the latest crew listings. Only one or two fit her profile. She pulled up the applications for those and, calling up her virtual input board, typed out of habit. Fal—no, that was wrong. Mei, that was her name now. She'd practiced it enough. It should have been second nature to her—Mei Ricci.

The return voyage to Support was uneventful if uncomfortable. Pim stayed in his cabin and ate at off hours to avoid the rest of the crew. Gwilim lapsed into an uncommunicative funk. Only Kalal remained social, but not even his relentless cheer penetrated Mitsumi's gloom.

Within a day after jumping into Support's system and beginning their normal space boost to Support, Mitsumi had completed negotiations to sell the alien ruins' location.

"So it didn't work out," Kalal said hours before completing their return voyage to Support. "You're not quite broke. Your backers recouped their costs, and you ended up with a few credits."

Under acceleration from their jump point to Support orbit, they sat at a table in the mess which doubled as the ship's lounge. Mitsumi gave Kalal a sidelong glance. He'd never met the engineer before signing him for this voyage, but he'd developed a fondness for his optimism. For decades after Sundered's find, each member of the crew contributed a share of the costs for a percentage of the profits on prospecting voyages. That model had changed as it became evident that Sundered's accomplishment had been exceptional. Now, backers sponsored voyages, and the crew hired on. But for this venture the find had been so sure, his funding had been ... unconventional. His backing had been insufficient to engage a ship and pay for supplies. He had had to work hard to convince his crew to contribute the required balance in exchange for a share of profits.

"Yeah, well about that." His eyes fixed on a point in the distance, Mitsumi sighed. "You thought you were sharing the costs according to the share of profits we agreed to, but I took on more than my share of the cost because I didn't think I could put a crew together otherwise and I was so sure ..."

Kalal frowned. "So we made money but you ... ?"

"I'm deep in the hole. My backers didn't recoup their costs. I sunk every last fraction of a credit I had in this venture. I sold everything and gambled it all."

Kalal shook his head in sorrow. "Sorry to hear that, Holtz." They sat in silence for a moment. "Your backers," Kalal said. "They're not the shady type are they, the kind who'd take a loss hard?"

Mitsumi stared at his hands clasped before him on the table. "It's worse than that Kalal," Mitsumi said and sighed. "They're my ex-wives' siblings."

Kalal gave a puzzled frown. "Why would your ex-wives' family get involved?"

"I don't want to talk about it now," he said. In point of fact he'd rather burn in pain for a thousand years than talk about it.

Kalal studied Mitsumi. "Okay, Holtz. Confession is good for the soul, but it's your choice."

Mitsumi nodded, thankful Kalal hadn't tried to pry more information out of him.

"I've enjoyed this trip," Kalal said. "It didn't work out how we wanted, but I saw ancient alien ruins and one of the few evidences of aliens' attempts at communication. That was worth the price of admission." Kalal paused, lowered his eyes to the table, then fixed them on Mitsumi. "A few words of advice for you, Holtz." Mitsumi groaned inwardly and almost raised his hand to stop Kalal. Mitsumi needed more "advice" like he needed an untraceable atmosphere leak. But Kalal had been kind to him and they would not likely meet again, so Mitsumi let him counsel away. "When you're in charge, be in charge. Decide and stick to your decision. You can consult others, but only if you show you're looking for advice and the ultimate decision is yours alone. You may not feel confident in command, but you do everyone in your charge a disservice if you don't act like a leader."

Desperately resisting the temptation to roll his eyes, Mitsumi attempted a smile. Kalal held Mitsumi's gaze, seemingly oblivious of Mitsumi's reaction, then smiled himself, reached across the table and grabbed Mitsumi's forearm. "You're all right, Holtz. You'll be just fine. Don't worry about what's coming." Kalal rose from his seat. "Well, I'm off. I have to be ready to disembark as soon as we dock." Kalal rose and left the lounge.

With Kalal gone, Mitsumi considered his words. It wasn't anything Mitsumi hadn't heard before. "You're a great Second," his superiors had told him before the incident that led to the end of his career in the navy, "but as for a command..." His evaluations at Holman Starlines had been even less enthusiastic before his abrupt termination. Mitsumi still blamed losing both those positions on his exes' behavior which, Mitsumi noted with chagrin, his exes attributed to Mitsumi's fecklessness. So, Kalal had tumbled to the obvious. But Kalal was late to the party, and Mitsumi didn't see how Kalal restating the obvious was any help. What was he going to do now?

From his pocket, Mitsumi pulled out the Artifact and turned it over in his hands. It had displayed no unusual characteristics since he'd picked it up and had that ... vision. His shipboard analyses revealed it to be an ordinary industrially grown diamond with no signs of alien manufacture. No matter what he'd tried, he hadn't been able to replicate the sim that was still so vivid in his memory.

At the first opportunity, he'd tried to duplicate the symbols he'd seen over the globular cluster, the star, and the planet. The urge he'd felt to discover their meaning, return the Artifact and access that power had steadily grown and now sat like a constant pressure behind his eyes.

With a sigh, he stood, replaced the Artifact in his pocket

and quashed the feeling. *You'll have to wait*, he thought, *I'm not going anywhere until I'm back on my feet.*

Hours later, Mitsumi floated alone on the bridge as the ship maneuvered itself to dock at one of the five stations surrounding Support. The screen showed the docking sequence coming to completion. The new owners would be on board within minutes. His backers had sold the ship while Mitsumi had made the transit from the jump point, its price together with Mitsumi's share of the proceeds from the sale of the alien planet's location didn't come close to recouping their investment.

Someone popped up through the access tube. "Holtz Mitsumi?" he said. Mitsumi nodded.

"I'm Darron," the man said. "This will take but a moment and you're on your way."

Wonderful, Mitsumi thought. *I can't wait.*

After a quarter hour Darron rotated toward Mitsumi. "It all checks out, Hode. You're free to go." Mitsumi didn't bother correcting the man. He made his way toward the connecting air lock. He'd transferred his meager personal items to temporary storage on the station. From the air lock, Mitsumi emerged into a corridor and floated toward the main hub. At the hub others floated past on their way to or from the transports to the habitable part of the station. Notice of an incoming communication beeped in his ear. He pulled out his assistant knowing what it would show and dreading it. It was Corban, his (ex) brother-in-law and one of his backers.

Mitsumi stared unseeing at the passersby, the beeping increasing in volume and frequency while his thumb hovered over the accept icon. He lowered his thumb.

"Holtz," Corban said. "Welcome back."

"Thanks."

"We're ready with the final accounts. You should have the address now. See you soon."

Mitsumi checked his assistant for the location and pushed himself toward the transports. He hoped his ex-wives Riga and

Cala wouldn't be there to gloat. It would be bad enough seeing Cala's brother Corban and his other backer, Riga's sister Jonta. Eventually, as much as he'd dragged his feet, he found himself in front of the door to the apartment Corban had directed him to. It was on the top floor, of course, nothing but the best for Corban.

Mitsumi stood before the door, head down and leaning with one arm against the doorjamb fighting the vertigo centripetal force always induced in him. Thoughts turning toward the Artifact in his pocket, he wondered how soon he could finish this and get on with his life. He had to find work and raise credits. After a moment, he straightened up and raised his arm to the door signal when the door whisked open revealing a taciturn Corban. They stared at each other. Corban pivoted and walked into the room. Mitsumi trailed behind him.

Mitsumi scanned the room and groaned inside. Dressed in a skin-tight, glittering jumpsuit that even while covering her, elicited a blush from Mitsumi on her behalf, Riga lounged on a sofa to his right. Arm extended in languid ease along the back of the cushions, she drummed ring-encrusted fingers and grinned at him like a Kelta spying a juicy meal. Cala, ramrod straight in an uncomfortable looking chair next to the sofa, wore modest business attire. With a satisfied smile, Cala eyed him, her eyes glittering with triumph. Riga's sister, Jonta, reclined in a chair next to where Corban stood in front of the reading chair. *At least their husbands aren't here*, Mitsumi thought.

"Ah! Look! Our *hero* has returned," Riga sneered, eyes fixed on Mitsumi. "Empty-handed," she turned her head to Jonta. "As I predicted."

Jonta held up a warning hand. "Don't start, Riga. Don't make me regret allowing you to be here."

Riga eyed Mitsumi. "Oh, you couldn't have kept me away, sis." Cala nodded agreement, her smile twitching wider. "You wouldn't listen to me," Riga continued, "your own sister. I told you he was a failure. Always was; always will be." Riga sniffed. "Ophan sends his greetings, by the way. And our son is doing well."

Stung by the insult, Mitsumi fought his tendency to accept her characterization. He wasn't a loser, despite the expedition's failure and her taking their son, abandoning Mitsumi for his erstwhile boss. She'd always had that effect on him, even though he knew she said it to trigger his reaction. "It's good to see you again, Riga," Mitsumi said, trying to keep emotion from his voice and almost succeeding. "You too, Cala."

Cala twitched her head to the side. "You never disappoint, Holtz."

"If we're quite through with the pleasantries," Corban said. "Let's get down to business. Holtz?" Corban indicated the chair in front of him.

Mitsumi walked forward and sat in the chair facing Corban. A screen appeared behind Corban displaying readings from sensors in Mitsumi's chair. A green strip extended across the screen below the readings, a strip that would turn red if his account of the voyage varied from the truth as he understood it.

"I'm sorry about this, Holtz," Jonta said. Riga snorted. Jonta shot a sharp look at Riga then turned a sympathetic face to Mitsumi. "It's just business."

Corban remained impassive. "From the beginning, please," he said.

Mitsumi started from the date they undocked and recounted the voyage in as much detail as he could remember, careful to leave out the Artifact and his vision.

When he had finished his account, Corban studied him for a moment. Steeling himself for this next part, Mitsumi fought to relax, only to end up with more knots than he'd had to begin with. Circuits in the chair sniffed out deception by measuring his brain's electrical activity so the anxiety twisting his guts shouldn't lead to false positive readings, but a formal report's examination portion always left him uneasy, feeling as if the examiner were trying to trap him.

"When you came to us with the leads wanting our support, did you have any idea the leads would prove fruitless?"

His nerves quieted at this straightforward inquiry. He could hear Riga dictating this question which had the subtlety of a null matter bomb. It was just like her to all but accuse him of outright fraud. He looked Riga square in the eye. "No."

"Did you visit any worlds other than those you've told us about today?"

His anxiety ticking up a notch, Mitsumi sensed Cala's influence and wondered if this might be a trap. "Assuming you mean to limit this question to those planets I visited on the voyage I described in this report, no." Sure enough, so fast that Mitsumi almost missed it, Corban's eyes flickered in Cala's direction. Cala narrowed her eyes, but didn't raise an objection.

"Are you in league with the Consortium or any Consortium member?"

Whoa, where did *that* come from? Riga, Cala, and their families had heard him rail often and at length against the Consortium's activities. If Corban dove into that singularity, they'd be all day. "No," Mitsumi said, spitting the word.

"Have you ever been in league with the Consortium or any Consortium member?"

"No."

Corban's questioning went on in this vein for what seemed an eternity, trying to make sure Mitsumi hadn't cheated them. The examination ended with the question Mitsumi had been dreading, the one for which he had prepared his mind, convincing himself that his answer would be truthful.

"Did you recover anything of value you have failed to describe to us?"

Mitsumi stared at Corban, willing himself to remember that the Artifact was a plain grown diamond and with nothing to show its alien origin was worthless. and convincing himself that what he had thought the Artifact had showed him was merely a halucination. "No," he said, and somehow kept his

27

eyes from darting to the screen to see whether the reader had accepted his answer.

Corban tapped a finger on his assistant and the reading screen went dark. He sat back satisfied, or at least as satisfied as someone who was out half a million credits could be. Cala was less so.

"I still think he's hiding something," Cala said leaning forward, her eyes boring into Mitsumi.

Mitsumi held Cala's eyes for a moment then swept his gaze across the others. "Is that what you think?"

Riga sat up straight on the couch and yawned. "This is tiresome," she said. "Holtz is broken." With her eyes fixed on Mitsumi, disgust saturated her voice. "I never have to see him or hear from him again." Mitsumi stiffened in the chair. Frequently having been the target of Riga's disdain, Mitsumi expected the familiar guilt and shame at failing to meet expectations to put in an appearance; their absence was a surprise, but left him quite relieved. Riga looked pointedly at Jonta. "Right, Jonta? You won't fall for any more of my very ex-husband's schemes, will you?"

"I already told you, Riga," Jonta said. "I went to Corban and suggested that we approach Holtz after you dumped him to see if we could help soften the blow." She shook her head. "I'm your sister and even *I* couldn't stomach how poorly you treated him. He was the best thing you had, and you tossed him like a broken toy when a shinier trinket appeared. He explained his plans, and we agreed to help."

Riga cocked her head. "Go ahead, scoff at my taste in companions, Jonta, but Holtz has proven me right." She narrowed her eyes. "So, no more then?" Jonta held Riga's eyes for a heartbeat then looked away. "That's good." Riga rose from the couch and stood in front of Mitsumi with a cold smile, one hand on a cocked hip. "Ophan will spread word of your adventures through the commercial ranks and investment community. You should consider a different job."

As he fought to keep his expression neutral, he cringed

inside. Ophan, the man Riga had left him for, had extensive connections in the shipping community. Ophan's badmouthing might make work in space hard to find. His failure to advance his career had disappointed her, but her animosity seemed to have ratcheted way up since he'd last had contact.

In the glare of Riga's cruel, tight, little smile, Mitsumi felt something inside him loosen. When they were first married, Riga had teased and cajoled him to be more assertive, to stand up for himself. Later, viewing her efforts as unsuccessful, she had graduated to pointed barbs and humiliation culminating with her betrayal with Ophan. In a moment of blinding clarity, he saw her—grasping, vicious, concerned only for herself, interested in others only to the extent they helped her. Now, seeing her take such pleasure in his failure, he wondered why he wanted to please Riga. She'd been different once, in the beginning. In the chair, he straightened and returned her gaze without flinching.

After holding his eyes for a moment, Riga dropped her gaze, turned and strolled from the room. Cala stood from her chair and smoothed wrinkles from her business attire. As she considered Mitsumi, her expression softened. "For what it's worth, Holtz, this wasn't as enjoyable as I thought it would be. I only wanted you to step up and be more..." Cala gestured vaguely, searching for the right word.

He understood. It had been a constant refrain the last year of their marriage. But apparently she found the phrases she'd used so often too harsh for the occasion. She thought she was inviting his sympathy and, in times past, he would have let her off the hook and smoothed her difficulty. But his flash of understanding Riga also illuminated Cala. Not as intentionally or openly cruel, Cala had only loved him, not for who he was but what he could provide her. No, he wouldn't help her now. He'd give voice to what she was thinking. "Like Darmat?" Mitsumi said.

Cala stiffened, her face hardening. She opened her mouth

29

and with a visible effort closed it again. She turned away from Mitsumi. "Corban, may I assume that you will have no further dealings with Mr. Mitsumi, that all our ties are now severed? Because news of this little venture was quite a shock." Corban remained impassive and nodded once.

"Good, give my love to mother when you see her today," Cala said and, with a last cool glance at Mitsumi, followed Riga out of the room. When the door slid shut, Corban's shoulders slumped, and he sighed.

"Look, I'm sorry, Holtz," Corban said. "When Cala discovered our arrangement, she insisted on a formal winding up and, with family money involved, putting her off was not possible."

Mitsumi waved off his apology, relieved that Cala's animosity hadn't rubbed off on her brother. "I imagine she didn't take the news well," Mitsumi said. "And I assume it was worse with Riga."

Corban nodded. "I wasn't there when Riga found out, but Jonta tells me you're right."

"Smashed tableware, threats of violence?" Mitsumi said, looking at Jonta.

"Weapons purchases," Jonta added.

Mitsumi's eyebrows rose in surprise. "Do I need to...?"

"No, no," Jonta said quickly. "That's been sorted."

Mitsumi lowered his head and stared at his hands. "Listen, I'm sorry this happened. I was sure my sources were reliable. I had no idea that..." Mitsumi raised his head.

Corban rose from his seat, stepped to Mitsumi and placed a hand on his shoulder. "I know what Jonta meant when she said you were the best thing that happened to Riga. You were that for Cala as well. You didn't deserve how she treated you."

Mitsumi stood, grasped Corban's arm and looked at Jonta. "Thank you—both of you." He released his grip on Corban and let his hand fall to his side. "I learned something here today, something that's taken me a long time."

Corban and Jonta looked at him curiously.

"You're both right," Mitsumi said and with a grin added, "They didn't deserve me."

Jonta smiled and Corban chuckled. "That's the spirit, Holtz," Corban said.

Sobering, Mitsumi said, "I will pay you back though." Pressure behind his eyes increased. It was the Artifact reminding him of a more important goal. Mitsumi reached into his pocket and gripped the Artifact as if to reassure it that he had not forgotten. "I have business to resolve first that may take me away for a while, but I *will* repay you."

Corban and Jonta remained silent without meeting Mitsumi's gaze—embarrassed disbelief plain on their faces. "Sure," Jonta said, condescension leaking into her voice, "you'll get the money somehow, but what will you do now? Even before this meeting Riga had Ophan putting the black mark on you with commercial lines; you'll never get a passenger or freight run in the Federation again."

His vision of earning enough credits to sponsor a voyage to the Artifact's world evaporated, and Mitsumi's shoulders slumped at the reminder of that wrinkle.

"And where Ophan can't reach," Corban said, "Darmat can. Was that last crack necessary?"

Mitsumi slid his hand down his face. "No, Corban," he said. "You're right. I should have just ignored the fact that the woman I married felt sorry for me because I couldn't measure up to the man she ran off with." They sat for a moment in embarrassed silence. "As to what I'll do," Mitsumi said, "I don't know. I'm flat broke at the moment. I can't even pay for consumables and I'll need at least a few days to put something together." As he described his circumstances out loud, a few more drops of resolve leaked out. "I don't suppose you could see fit to…"

"I can't," Corban said shaking his head. "Cala made sure of that. The family's involved now and while I in theory have complete autonomy over my portfolio, in practice the family frowns on debacles like this rather severely, hence my meeting with Mother later today. Normally, I could find petty cash for you, but the scrutiny is too intense now."

"I might be able to help," Jonta said. "I can get you twenty credits without anyone knowing. Riga would have my head if she found out, but…" She shrugged.

"Thanks, Jonta. I understand, Corban. It's my fault I put you in this position. I should have been more careful. I shouldn't have fallen for the con. In my defense, I can only repeat that I served with Fai during the Neopa campaign. He was a standup guy with impeccable integrity. He assured me the coordinates were high quality First Civ sources. I should have been more skeptical with the back-up material."

"Ah," Corban said, "we evaluated everything along with you, so we're also to blame."

With a glance at his assistant, Mitsumi confirmed he had received Jonta's twenty credit transfer. Eyes fixed first on Corban then on Jonta, Mitsumi said. "I meant it; I'll pay you back. Next time I see you it will be to pay you back with interest." Turning on his heel, he marched from the room.

CHAPTER 2

Back in the orbital's corridors, Mitsumi considered his position. Twenty credits meant a week's maintenance on the orbital or a shuttle to the planet and two months expenses on the surface. It'd be more difficult to connect with a crew planet side though and, despite the prospect of Riga and Cala's current husbands' poisoning the ears of prospective employers, their reach couldn't be comprehensive. He took out his assistant and searched for a cube, choosing the cheapest bare minimum accommodation he could find—an enclosed bed and sanitary facilities and nothing else—and routed his personal items to a nearby storage unit. After the purchase of a week's consumables, Mitsumi had one credit and change. His physical needs taken care of, Mitsumi instructed his assistant to pull up a list of contacts. He started at the top.

Six days and twenty-two hours later, Mitsumi, long hair pulled back in a loose tail in the station's spin gravity, stared into his drink wondering when the "but" would appear. Just now, Hentac Zaming, a buddy from his navy days, was waxing nostalgic recalling an eventful tour to Fit where they'd helped to root out a tenacious criminal enterprise that had associated with the Consortium.

"Remember that ship they had?" Zaming said. "The one with the shielding no one had seen before?"

Mitsumi lifted his head and nodded with a wan smile. How could he have forgotten that Zaming had been on that cruise?

"Cap'n wanted to take it head on, didn't credit the reports

or the evidence right in front of him."

Mitsumi maintained his smile with difficulty, waiting for the punch line, willing to endure the reminder once more, on the off chance that "but" wouldn't appear. The iron determination with which he had begun his search had rusted away as lead after lead had failed.

"And you wanted to draw the bad guys out and try something new, a 'jump implosion' you called it." Zaming stared off into the distance, lost in the memory. "The Cap'n refused until we'd lost five decks and twenty men and were down to our last four missiles, and he gave you the con." Zaming shook his head, mouth and eyes wide in amazement. "You made history that day calculating four precision HE jumps to within a thousand meters of their shields and timing the missile launches so the warheads detonated simultaneously triggering an overload!" Zaming took a long pull at his drink and wiped his mouth with the back of his hand. "Pustulating Cap'n took the credit though, didn't he? Claimed it was his idea, blamed you for the losses. Altered the logs and threatened the crew. Is that why you quit the military?"

"It's a little more complicated," Mitsumi said, awed at his understatement's vast scope. A million lifetimes ago on the third day aboard the Federated Worlds' Annihilator class warship *We Won't Tell You Twice*, Mitsumi's inaugural voyage as a Second, a different captain had tasked Mitsumi with quelling a disturbance that had grown to involve two subgroups and their commanders. The details of the dispute had long ago faded in the haze of memories, but what Mitsumi had done and the result remained to this day crystalline in its clarity. He'd always been uncomfortable with the rigidity of military hierarchy and, as a newly minted Second, had determined to demonstrate a different way.

As it turned out, bringing the two groups together and encouraging them to air their grievances was not the optimal approach, and he had watched in horror as heated words escalated to shouting and quickly to blows. The captain had intervened and confined the lot of them to quarters, threatening prison and worse if they didn't bury their dispute and do their jobs. While not comfortable, the resulting atmosphere was at least functional.

Later, the captain had explained to Mitsumi that the crew didn't have to like each other, but they had to do their jobs, and understand that if they didn't do their jobs serious consequences would follow. He had tried to learn that lesson but, in the end, Mitsumi could not assert command, feeling that his view should not be privileged and that everyone should engage in discussing decisions until they reached a consensus.

That attitude had not served him well on subsequent postings, and then came the fiasco with Captain Darmat Notil taking credit for Mitsumi's success, falsifying logs so the navy blamed Mitsumi for Notil's screw up. Shortly after, Cala, his wife at the time, had started an affair with Notil and left Mitsumi. At that point, he'd seen the writing on the wall and quit the military.

Zaming paused, looking thoughtful. "Didn't I hear Cap'n Notil and your wife…" Zaming's voice trailed off and he gave Mitsumi a sidelong glance. Mitsumi stared straight ahead. "Yeah, Darmat Notil, what a diseased piece of slime he was. I can't believe he's an admiral now." Adam's apple bobbing up and down, Zaming drained the rest of his drink. As he lowered his glass to the bar, he continued. "Anyway, look. You were a great officer, wonderful with me and the men, brilliant, resourceful—all those great things. And it's a shame you're down on your luck now. I wish I could help—recommend you for a post, put in a good word." Mitsumi's shoulders slumped— here it came. "But the word's out on you. I don't know what you did. You must have torqued someone hard. Was it Notil?"

"I'm not sure," Mitsumi lied, shrugging his shoulders. "Might have been."

"That's bad," Zaming said with sympathy. "Look, if I were

you, I'd drop to Support. There're lots of opportunities on planet. I just don't think you'll work in space again." Mitsumi stared straight ahead. Zaming rose from his stool. "Thanks for the drink, Holtz. I'm glad we did this." He clapped a hand on Mitsumi's shoulder. "Think on what I said, Holtz. Lots going on down the well." Zaming walked out of the bar.

Futile as it was, Tai Quest began another database search with different parameters—"male between twenty-five and thirty-five standard years ago, arrival by ship shuttle, unaccompanied." Before his eyes, the words hung in space, and he wondered without hope whether this would be the time. Over the years he had searched, he had tried thousands of combinations. Even though he had no memory of this identical search-term mix, he was certain he'd tried it before. He punched "search" on the 3-D display hovering over his table. There was nothing like a central database on Support, so he had used a service that would crawl every known database containing records for off planet arrivals.

While waiting for the results, he sat back in his chair, idly surveying his surroundings and trying to stifle the inevitable rising anticipation from starting another search —they were always fruitless. He sat on the edge of the only open plaza on Five Station, keeping a practiced eye on the other people scattered around the plaza and on the steady stream of pedestrians. Overhead, suspended from the only vaulted ceiling on the station, enormous hydroponic containers overflowed with plants, giving the plaza light a distinct greenish cast. Despite the greenery and a well maintained filtration system, with each breath he drew humid air and smelled the musk of humanity packed together in what amounted to an airtight can.

A return to Support—even to one of the high stations— wasn't how he planned to end his latest engagement. But the masters of the good ship *Forever Hyperbolic* hadn't asked his opinion when they'd dumped him here. No matter. Even after all this time, he had contacts on planet, and they reported no one interested in his whereabouts. Of course he had changed his name and his appearance so the odds of anyone locating him were remote. Still, it was nice that no one cared.

With a soft ping, his assistant announced the results of his search. Having to squelch another rising hope, he began tracking down the names, and one by one eliminated them as candidates. Hours later, stiff from sitting in one spot, he ruled out the last one. Disappointed, he closed his assistant's virtual terminal and stared unseeing at the ceaseless peregrinations across the plaza. He'd been right. There was nothing here for him.

Tomorrow. Tomorrow he'd search for a spot on another crew.

Mitsumi lowered his head. He hadn't told Hentac, because he didn't want to sound too desperate, but in two hours he would use up the consumables he'd purchased. Then, Station management would ship him to the planet whether or not he wanted to go. His last credit would buy a few more hours of air and water, but what good would that do? He'd exhausted his list of contacts. Ophan and Darmat had been more thorough than he'd believed possible. No one would hire him; no one would advance him any credit. Two choices remained: drop to Support and give up his quest to find the Artifact's planet for years and abandon the only work he'd ever known or try the Consortium. In his mind the two choices almost balanced out, dropping to the planet maintaining a slight edge.

Established ten years ago with the expressed intent to systematize exploration for First Civ worlds, anonymous backers sponsored the Consortium and rumors of less than savory activities swirled around the organization. In the past

37

few years, the Consortium had ramped up efforts to control the exploration trade; he'd heard rumors of convenient deaths among prospecting crews who'd reported having leads on promising finds after which the voyages had departed under Consortium sponsorship. That should have been another red flag for his lately concluded failure—no one from the Consortium had approached him. The Consortium wasn't picky who they hired, so he ought to be able to hitch onto a crew and make a decent living, but...the sour taste in his mouth at the prospect was not just the result of too much liquor consumed too fast. Besides, working for the Consortium for paltry wages, he wouldn't be able to put together the funds for his voyage to return the Artifact and relieve the increasing pressure.

Without work, though, he was down to his last credit and no prospect of gaining any more. One credit. Enough to get plastered before they took him away. Downing the drink in front of him, he motioned to the barkeep for another. The bartender walked over and poured his drink. "I couldn't help overhearing your conversation," he said.

Mitsumi lifted the glass and tossed back its contents. "Yeah? Then you know I'm a loser, blackballed from ever working in space again unless I sign on with the Consortium, and I'm not desperate enough for that."

The bartender gave Mitsumi a sympathetic look. "A guy's been coming in every so often. Been making the rounds trying to put a prospecting crew together. Can't seem to interest anyone so far."

Mitsumi had scoured the boards and was sure he had contacted any paying jobs around. This guy must be trying to round up a crew the old-fashioned way—no pay, just a profit split. Mitsumi couldn't play that game anymore. "And?" Mitsumi said.

"He's sitting at a table over there." The bartender nodded his head at something behind Mitsumi. Mitsumi turned. A small, pudgy, shabby man sat at a table by himself staring at an old battered assistant. In his late thirties, hair graying at the temples and receding from his forehead, he rubbed a small diamond stud earring in his right ear as he studied his assistant. To Mitsumi the lines on his forehead and around his eyes appeared to be recent, and his face sagged with fatigue. With a frown at his assistant, he laid it on the table in front of him and hung his head.

Mitsumi turned back to the bar and his empty glass. The bartender had moved along serving another customer. Mitsumi tried to catch his eye. He needed a drink, not conversation with a down-and-out prospector; he already knew one of those. The bartender remained stubbornly unaware of Mitsumi's efforts to snag his attention. Mitsumi glanced at a mirror behind the bar. The prospector rubbed his eyes and raised his head, catching Mitsumi staring. Mitsumi averted his eyes, but the damage was done. A chair squeaked on the floor. Someone sat on the stool next to him.

Mitsumi ignored the new addition, relying on custom to keep from being disturbed unless he expressed interest.

"Excuse me, sir," the prospector said. Studiously keeping his eyes forward, Mitsumi hoped a lack of response would send his message.

"Excuse me, sir," the prospector said again, this time plucking at Mitsumi's sleeve. The silent treatment hadn't worked which left him with three choices—take off without speaking, tell the man to bugger off, or engage. Option one was out—he wanted his remaining credit's worth of alcohol. Option three wasn't attractive either—he wasn't in the mood for conversation. Much as he disliked being rude, this last week had absorbed all his patience. He turned to tell the prospector to walk out the nearest airlock. The man's head lay on his arms. He snored softly.

The bartender arrived at that moment. "What'll it be?" he said in a loud voice.

His head jerking up at the sound, the prospector looked around in confusion. "Ah," the man said, "I'll have, uh," his eyes flicked to the glass in front of Mitsumi, "what he's having and...bring him another one?" The prospector turned to Mitsumi with his eyebrows raised in a question. Mitsumi closed his eyes in defeat and inclined his head in assent. It was an offer he was powerless to refuse.

Mitsumi stared ahead in silence while the bartender poured their drinks. He had accepted the man's offered drink—an implicit agreement to interact. But that didn't mean he had to be chatty. The prospector raised his glass. "Cheers," he said looking at Mitsumi, waiting for a response. Mitsumi continued to ignore him, raised his glass and downed the contents. The stranger sipped his drink. "I'm Aber Chandra." Chandra extended his hand. Mitsumi ignored it. "Yes, well anyway I'm, uh—"

"You're from Dell," Mitsumi said, examining his glass without looking at the prospector. He didn't need to look. The man was as common as paper; his story as familiar as failure. "And you've found information guaranteed to lead to the biggest find of First Civ tech since Sundered, and all you need to recover this once in a lifetime treasure is a crew, a ship, and provisions. You can't pay for any of it, so you need the crew to advance costs, but, hey, everyone will be rich as Sundered so what's a little risk?"

"Well, that's...not quite... How'd you know I'm from Dell?

"Your accent."

"I don't have an accent."

He should ignore the man, let him discover for himself the reality of the statistic Mitsumi had snubbed—ninety percent of exploratory voyages either yielded enough to break even or nothing no matter how "reliable" the information was. But he couldn't, partly because he couldn't bear to see another thousand credits wasted and partly because his darker side wanted to pop the man's bright bubble of hope. "Listen, Able."

"That's Aber."

"How many sure-fire, can't miss, one hundred percent gold-plated leads are out there, do you suppose?"

Confusion crossed Chandra's face. "Um, one or two?"

Mitsumi snorted. "Thousands. Tens of thousands. Everyone's got one. In fact, I just returned from chasing down several myself." As he stared into his empty glass, Mitsumi shook his head recalling his excitement when he'd made the first jump on that expedition. What an idiot he'd been. "I came home empty-handed. Spent my last credit on that dream." Mitsumi stared at his hands. "Well, not quite my last credit. That's going to," Mitsumi raised his voice, "another drink!" He signaled the bartender.

Chandra shook his head. "I *am* looking for a crew, that's right. It's been difficult, impossible in fact. My time and budget are almost exhausted. So, do you know of anyone who might crew my ship?"

With a shake of his head, Mitsumi wondered at the man's obtuseness in ignoring the voice of bitter experience. But through the building alcoholic haze the man's words penetrated. "You've got a ship?" Perhaps he'd misjudged the guy. He had a ship. That meant he had credits. That meant he could pay.

"And supplies and fuel, but I need a crew."

Even with his buzz, Mitsumi's ears pricked at this and hope floated through his mind. This prospector had credits but needed crew, and he was crew who needed credits. "The crew's the easy part. Lots of qualified pilots, astrogators, and engineers around. In fact, I'm between gigs at the moment. I'm available to captain—for the right price, of course." *Yeah*, he thought, *any price.*

"But I can't pay them."

Of course not. Mitsumi closed his eyes and cursed himself for allowing hope into his mind once more. The temporary lift it brought was never worth the bitter price of dashed expectations. "Yeah, that's a problem." The bartender arrived and poured more liquid into Mitsumi's glass.

"It shouldn't be. I have this—"

"Absolute, rock solid, indisputable lead, yeah, I got it."

41

Mitsumi raised his glass ready to down its contents. He was only two drinks shy of spending his last credit.

Chandra laid a hand on Mitsumi's arm preventing him from downing his drink. Mitsumi glared at Chandra. "I found data on some paper," Chandra said.

Roundly cursing the idiots in charge of hiring for the *Keep It Together*, Sentaa Koning stabbed her assistant and the holographic display winked out along with the rejection notice. *Who needs those morons anyway?* she thought. *I can do way better than a routine cargo haul between Support and Fit.* Or, a little voice in her head reminded her, Galaxy Starlines, or Nebula, or Federated or Geodesic or Planet Bound, or Interstellar—or the Consortium.

She snatched up her assistant and stormed from her cube into a man walking along the corridor. The assistant he'd been staring at flew from his hands and slammed into the corridor wall. Forced backward by Koning's impact the man pinwheeled his arms trying to maintain his balance, then thumped on his rump. "Hey," he yelled at Koning. "Watch where you're going." Embarrassment drove away her anger.

"Oh, I am so sorry," she said, reaching a hand to help him up. The man glowered at her, refused her hand and pushed himself to his feet. "I don't need your help. What I *need* is for you to remember the rules and look before you barrel into someone else."

"Right," she said "I know the rules...it's just..." She waved her hand at her cube not sure how to explain what had happened. The man ignored her, picked up his assistant and stomped off. *Well, okay then*, she thought, *don't accept my apology, jerk*. Still irritated at the man's abrupt dismissal, she made her way down the corridor to a cheap eatery and found a seat. With the menu pulled up on her assistant she input her table number and ordered a basic yeast steak. It was the cheapest thing on the menu and had been her staple these last two months while she looked for a crew and watched her declining credit balance.

After ordering, she pulled up crew requests and perused the list. Something was bound to turn up.

Mitsumi lowered his arm to rest his glass on the bar. "That's impossible," Mitsumi said. "No one's ever found anything on First Civ paper." At every discovered First Civ site along with the occasional valuable technological marvel dug from a world wrecking bombardment, prospectors and explorers had found pieces of thin flexible sheets of what looked like paper. Analysis had actually revealed them to be single atom layers of graphite sandwiched between single atom layers of silicon. Further experiments had yielded no clue as to their function or purpose. It turned out you could write on the material with a pen or pencil and because of this quality, its appearance and its ubiquity it had become widely referred to as paper.

"Turns out, it's quantum memory."

"I've heard the speculation, but no one's ever proven that's what paper is."

"I did."

Mitsumi doubted that was true, but Chandra's simple declaration penetrated his alcoholic haze. He spoke with confidence without bluster or exaggeration. Mitsumi could easily verify or falsify such an unqualified assertion. "Show me."

Chandra lowered his head and shifted in his seat without responding.

"That's what I thought." Mitsumi lifted the glass to his mouth.

Chandra grabbed his wrist. This time drink sloshed from the glass onto his arm. "It's my life and yours if anyone finds out I've done this."

Running a hand through his hair and grabbing the back of his neck, Viram Mantor released a breath puffing his cheeks. From his assistant's holographic display, the eval from his last ship's captain stared back at him burning into his mind. It was unfair. Four years he'd run with that crew heading their engineering, four years in which his engines had functioned flawlessly and no system had failed for more than a standard day. And they did this to him.

He tried to draw more anger, but that well was dry—he only had annoyance at the moment. Now he'd have to be ready to reassure prospective employers he was capable and that the problems recited there were no concern.

Brushing away the offending report, Mantor tapped into the section of the Station's data net reserved for matching vessels with crew. It might take time, but he'd find something suitable.

On the way to Chandra's cube, Mitsumi removed a tab from his pocket, placed it in his mouth and let it dissolve. By the time they reached Chandra's cube the effects of the alcohol had disappeared from his system, which had its plusses and minuses. In the plus column, with a clear head he'd be able to see through Chandra's deception right away. In the minus column, with a clear head he recognized he'd been an idiot thinking there was anything to this.

Chandra's setup was the same as his—four walls from which he could extrude sanitation facilities, a chair or a bed, but only one at a time. At the moment, the cube was empty. A black, worn valise sat on the floor. The door to the room slid shut. Chandra pressed the privacy button. He dug his assistant from a pocket, fiddled with it, then passed it over himself and the walls of the room. He looked at Mitsumi expecting Mitsumi to submit to the same nonsense. Mitsumi rolled his eyes and nodded. Chandra was one of those—convinced his secret information was so important that all the Federated Worlds were after him. With his assistant raised, Chandra approached Mitsumi and moved it around him front and back.

"A little paranoid, aren't we?" Mitsumi said.

"It's not paranoia if—"

"Oh, please," Mitsumi said. "Just get on with whatever magic act you've planned, so we can both be on our way."

Chandra looked hurt at that, but he shoved the assistant back in a pocket and bent over the valise on the floor. "You've seen a piece of what's called First Civ paper before, yes?" Chandra said, straightening up holding a glass case. A bit of paper five centimeters square with ragged edges rested on the bottom of the case. He offered the case to Mitsumi for his inspection.

Mitsumi accepted the case and examined its contents. "Sure, that stuff was all over the ten First Civ finds. The best and the brightest think it's a memory medium, quantum-level, trapped-particle, spin-state, First Civ wizardry, but it's only speculation; at the limit of our abilities, we can only examine the stuff to see what it's made of. Nobody's ever pulled anything off of one of these." He handed the case back to Chandra, who took it with a smug smile. "Except you, it seems." Mitsumi said dryly.

Chandra lowered himself to the floor cross-legged next to his valise. Mitsumi joined him. After rummaging in the suitcase, Chandra pulled out a rectangular board with electronic components attached to it. A small screen was fixed to one of the board's short ends. At the other end was a flat square with raised sides from which hair-thin wires protruded.

"I stumbled on this by accident." Chandra moved the valise to the side and placed the device on the floor with the screen facing them. "I've been fascinated with paper ever since I start

—for years." Chandra removed a pair of tweezers from his valise. He examined the paper in the glass case, turned the case one hundred eighty degrees and, using the tweezers, eased the paper from inside.

"One day I was inspecting this sample and noticed that those edges that look ragged appeared to have sections in a recurring pattern." He leaned over the device on the floor and placed the material inside. "Under the most powerful microscope I could access, the pattern was obvious."

Chandra tapped a button and sat back while the screen displayed the boot sequence for the board's brain. "The existence of the pattern was unique among all the samples of this stuff I'd examined or researched. So I assumed the pattern was an access point and played around with it trying to attach different-sized wires with varying voltages and resistances until one day by accident, I dropped it into a test setup I hadn't yet completed and," the screen sprang to life, "I got a signal."

On the screen a standard star map popped up. It depicted the arm of the galaxy containing the one hundred light-year volume encompassing the Federated Worlds inside a red translucent sphere. Scattered over a much larger area, twenty stars were labeled in an unfamiliar language. One star had a few lines of text below the label. At the sight of the foreign script, Mitsumi's pulse quickened, but on further examination, the characters bore no resemblance to what he'd seen in the sim.

"What is this supposed to be?"

Chandra's face shone with excitement. "It's a star chart." Mitsumi gave Chandra a don't-plague-me-with-the-obvious look.

"A First Civ star chart. Those are First Civ worlds. And that one," Chandra pointed to the system with the extra lines of text, "is our first target."

Mitsumi leaned toward the screen and studied the chart. Various theories floated around to explain and predict the location and distribution of First Civ worlds. None of them predicted the chart on the screen.

"What are those thin lines connecting the labeled stars?"

Chandra's voice dropped to a reverent whisper. "That showed the Underground. It was real."

Mitsumi sat back with a deep sigh. He should have known better. Had his recent experience taught him nothing? Yet, here he was, sucked in once again.

"You almost had me there, Aber. I nearly fell for the whole thing." Mitsumi pushed himself to his feet. "I won't waste anymore of my life chasing Andacks." At a soft beep from his assistant, Mitsumi took the device from his pocket. His consumables had expired. Nothing on the station was free, that included air and water. He had paid for a week's worth and that week was up. Station management frowned on overstaying consumable payments. Officers were on their way to escort him to a shuttle.

Chandra scrambled to his feet. "No, don't go. I understand your doubt. I shared it."

Mitsumi turned to leave. Chandra grabbed Mitsumi's arm and swiveled him back. "I can prove it to you. I recovered one other bit of data from the memory store—a video file." Chandra squatted in front of the device on the floor, fiddled with it, then beckoned Mitsumi to join him. Mitsumi considered walking out the door, but decided it didn't matter where the officers found him so he might as well take a look. He squatted next to Chandra and stared at the screen. "What you're about to see is a spaceship using the underground to travel from the galaxy's rim to its center instantaneously."

In the infinite night, stars glowed in unfamiliar formations. Without warning, a uniform grayness replaced stars and blackness. Superimposed on the gray, a red bubble depicting an outline of a strange spaceship came into view on the outskirts of a star system. Faint lines extended from the red bubble to other star systems. In the video, a finger appeared, touched the symbol representing the ship and moved it along one line into a red bubble near another star system close to the galaxy's center. The finger then moved the ship symbol outside the red bubble. The light from a million suns at the galactic core burst into view replacing the uniform gray and almost obliterating the blackness of space.

Chandra looked at him, waiting for his reaction. Weary of this charade, Mitsumi snorted. "That's a nice trick, Aber," the screen blanked to gray again, "but anyone—" His mouth gaped open as he was unable to complete his thought, his mind in turmoil.

On the screen the galaxy in miniature floated in the air as seen from above the plane of the ecliptic, looking down at the center. A point at the center of the disk glowed brighter than the rest. From this center point faint rays emanated, spreading throughout the disk. Mitsumi went cold, recognizing the symbol on the plinth from which he'd recovered the Artifact.

CHAPTER 3

At Chandra's door, the emergency override alarm sounded. It slid open revealing two bored officers in the hall. One of them looked at something in his hand. "You, uh, Holtz Mitsumi?" he asked, nodding at Mitsumi.

Hardly hearing the officers, Mitsumi compared the video's last image, still burning in his mind, to the image he'd found on the stone plinth. It couldn't be a coincidence —they were identical. The video, the plinth and therefore the Artifact in his pocket all belonged together somehow—a thought confirmed by sudden return of the Artifact's pressure. Chandra had discovered something incredible that could fund his expedition, but he couldn't afford any more time to check into it. "I'll do it. But I'm out of consumables and broke so…"

Chandra pulled his assistant from his pocket. "Sure, send me your transfer codes, and I'll advance you a week. That should be enough shouldn't it?"

Mitsumi pulled out his assistant and transferred the codes to Chandra. "A week?" Mitsumi frowned. "Not possible. More like two."

Chandra shook his head. "I can afford a week; that's it. The Station should have recorded the purchase, Officers."

The officer who had spoken poked at his assistant. "There it is. Next time," he glanced at his assistant, "Holtz, don't make us come after you. Show up at the collection point like a good boy, okay?"

The door slid shut. Mitsumi turned to Chandra in disbelief.

"We can't get a crew together in a week."

Chandra shrugged. "I told you, I can only afford a week and, besides, I can't stay. We have to leave by then because…" he fiddled with his assistant, eyes darting around the empty cube. "We just have to."

Mitsumi was already wondering what he'd gotten himself into. Aber was out of his depth.

"What did you mean advance?" Mitsumi asked.

"Like I said, I can't pay a crew up front. Your only compensation is a share of the profits from our voyage. Profits —that's gross receipts minus costs and the extra consumables I bought you are now part of your costs."

That was irritating. He'd forgotten the arrangement Chandra had proposed at the bar. Mitsumi's annoyance subsided as the screen on the floor drew his eyes, holding him in thrall. It glowed with the galactic core's exploding light. "What was that?" Mitsumi pointed at the screen.

Chandra stepped toward his valise and the device he had used to read the "paper," squatted and began to disassemble his setup. "You've heard people speculate about the Underground?"

"Speculation is the kind word for it; I've heard more fitting descriptions like 'wild fantasy.' C'mon, who buys into the idea that a billion years ago mysterious aliens built an instantaneous transportation system between stars with handy jumping-off and re-entry points like stations on a rail line and left it lying around for anyone to use? Who were these fabulous old ones? How does it operate? How did they build it? I've never read even wild speculation on how it might work. But more to the point—where are the old ones now? What happened to their mystical transport system? Was it set on a timer?" Mitsumi glanced at his wrist, mimicking looking at a timing device. "Oh a billion years gone? Well, times up! Take it down, boys!"

Chandra gestured with a hand holding the bit of paper now back in its glass case and raised his voice. "But what else can explain the simultaneous founding of First Civ worlds two hundred light years apart? Somehow the founders of those worlds arrived at the same time."

"Well, the HE drive for one."

Chandra shook his head once and frowned, placing the glass case and the circuit board back in his valise. "But they didn't have—"

"How do we know?" Mitsumi said, cutting him off. "We only have small fragments of First Civ tech, but those fragments are developments five hundred years ahead of our time. Why wouldn't they have had the HE jump?" Chandra opened his mouth. Mitsumi held up a hand, forestalling Chandra's comment. "And before you say it, I'm familiar with the 'system-trap' theory and I don't buy it."

Chandra stood, folded his arms, cocked his head and said without heat, "Then where is everyone? If First Civ people could jump out of their systems as the Horde slaughtered them in their trillions and pounded their homes to bouncing rubble," Chandra threw his hands in the air, "why didn't they? And if they did, where are they?"

Well, he had a point there. Although the idea of an ancient magical, alien interstellar transportation network had always been tough to swallow, alternate explanations for the facts on the ground were equally debatable. If the inhabitants of the First Stellar Civilization could jump away from the danger, wouldn't they have returned at least to see if anyone had survived? And finding those survivors, his ancestors, wouldn't they have offered help? "They'd be fools to return to the scene of destruction since they were incapable of preventing it in the first place," Mitsumi said gamely, not wanting to concede the point.

"What you saw there," Chandra said stubbornly, waving at the screen, "was video of the Underground in action—a ship transported instantly from the galaxy's edge to its core."

"Or a simulation manufactured by one of the ancient alien conspiracy groups."

Chandra cocked his head and considered Mitsumi. "Then why did you agree to help me after you saw the video?"

Mitsumi put his hand in his pocket and rubbed his thumb along the edge of the Artifact; it remained cold and unresponsive as it had since his "vision," but the lure of unthinkable power and the pressure to find the vision planet and return the Artifact remained. That symbol appearing on the plinth where he'd found the Artifact and the video was a tenuous connection, but it was something and he had nothing else. "Let's drop it, okay? We need to find a crew."

CHAPTER 4

"So, Tai, tell me again why you were kicked off the crew of the *Philosopher's Stone*?" Mitsumi dropped his eyes to his assistant, "the *Razor's Edge*, the *Happy Coincidence*, and the, uh, *Just in Time*?"

Tai Quest, bright blue eyes in a dusky face, jet-black hair neatly arranged, impeccably dressed, stared unblinking at Mitsumi. After a minute of silence that seemed to stretch for hours, Quest responded. "Incompatibility with the crew."

Mitsumi skimmed the summary report on his assistant with the highlighted words "uncooperative, abrasive, not a team player, and reclusive" along with the conclusion, "piloting skills barely adequate." Next to the report, a counter showed five hours left before the consumables Chandra had advanced Mitsumi ran out, and they had to depart in the bucket of bolts Chandra laughingly referred to as a ship. Why was he engaging in this charade? Although they had rounded up an astrogator/communications specialist, an engineer, and one pilot, they needed another pilot and Quest was it.

"And you're aware of the arrangement? No pay unless we succeed, and then it's a share of the profits after costs."

It might have been Mitsumi's imagination so slight was the movement, but Quest's head appeared to lower. Mitsumi took that as a yes; after all, they'd gone over the arrangements before and he'd offered no objections.

"Well," Mitsumi smiled, stretching out his hand, "welcome

aboard the *Are We There Yet*? We'll see you at docking bay Q-23 in three hours."

As he gripped Mitsumi's hand, Quest effortlessly—and Mitsumi hoped unintentionally—crushed it in a grip that was more hydraulic press than handshake. Quest rose, his squat form reaching only to Mitsumi's shoulder, and left the room.

"Well that went well." Chandra's voice came from the tiny speakers in Mitsumi's assistant.

"Not the word I'd use," Mitsumi mumbled. As the week had progressed and they'd picked up members of their crew, Mitsumi had grown anxious. Potential crew members had been as thin as intergalactic gas, and the best candidates had other more attractive alternatives. But they could do nothing now. They'd done their best.

"You're on your way then?" Chandra asked. "Because the others are arriving, and I'm a bit uncomfortable."

By "others" Chandra had apparently meant Mei Ricci, the number two pilot who, when Mitsumi floated onto the bridge of the *Are We There Yet*?, had strapped into one of the pilot acceleration couches and was holding up her assistant, shifting her attention between the information device and the controls. Raised on Neopa, a lower gravity world, she was almost too tall to fit in the couch and certainly too tall to be comfortable. She was tall even for a Neopan. Her short blonde hair had formed into a fuzzy ball in the zig, having apparently attracted static electricity somewhere along the way. Dressed in a close-fitting stylish jumpsuit, light years from the usual dowdy attire common among a tramp prospector's crew, she appeared to be puzzled.

Mitsumi floated closer. Ricci peered at the control panel on her right. With hesitation, she reached toward the panel, extending a finger to press a red button. Mitsumi coughed. Startled, Ricci jerked her hand back and twisted in her couch.

He tried to remember Kalal's advice. Shoulders straight, he attempted to arrange his face into a "look of command." "I'm pretty sure," Mitsumi said, "we're not in a position to execute an explosive docking release just now, what with both airlock doors being open to the station connection and all."

Ricci frowned and consulted her assistant, taking her lower lip in her teeth before turning bright red. After a moment she assumed a look of haughty confidence and raised her eyes from her assistant. "I was brushing up on the controls. These old model Sunchasers can be tricky."

"Yes they can," Mitsumi said, equably. "Especially when the controls are still in their original configuration as I mentioned in our interview." He hoped he wouldn't regret his decision to take on Ricci. Although the girl had valid licenses, she'd received her training from a somewhat shady remote learning outfit and had zero experience.

After a flicker of doubt, her face returned to lofty assurance. "Yes, I was confirming the old configuration."

Mitsumi glanced around the bridge. Dull gray walls hadn't been painted since the ship had been commissioned. The couches at astrogation and command were as worn and patched as the pilot's. The view screen had a sprinkling of dead pixels. Exposed wiring floated in places from the ceiling and the walls. Discolored patches at the pilot, astrogation and command stations told of damage and slapdash repair. A faint whiff of sewage in the stale air evidenced an ineffective recycling system.

"And found them as old as everything else, I assume?"

Ricci nodded once. "Just so."

"I'm afraid the only accommodation to the modern world aboard *Are We There Yet?* is a command neural interface."

Arrogance faltering, her forehead wrinkled in confusion. "A command neural interface? That's a nice feature, but what good would that do you? Don't you have to have an implant for the interface?"

Mitsumi considered Ricci, waiting for the light bulb. Yep, questionable training and no experience.

"Oh," Ricci said after a moment, "you have an implant? I thought those were expensive and provided to captains of large passenger liners, freighters and..." Ricci's eyes widened. "Were you a navy captain?"

"Not a captain, no. I was a Second. The navy in its wisdom thought they should equip me to command in the event something happened to the captain."

"Huh," Ricci said, "I wouldn't have taken you for a naval officer. You seem too..."

Only too aware of where this was going, Mitsumi waited for Ricci to complete the thought. She appeared to consider her options and, evidently deciding that there were no good ones for ending that sentence, remained silent. Instead, she resumed her aloof certitude—an attitude inconsistent with her obvious inexperience. With a snap, Ricci released the constraints and floated above the couch. "I must return to my cabin and finish stowing my gear." Ricci pushed away from the couch toward the passageway to the rest of the ship. She stopped herself before entering and turned back to Mitsumi. "We are still expecting a 1500 departure?"

Mitsumi nodded. "If everyone's reported and our supplies have arrived."

Ricci inclined her head in acknowledgement and pushed herself along the passageway followed by the sharp sound of a collision and imaginative swearing. "If we haven't blown ourselves up," Mitsumi muttered. Idly, he reached back and gripped his hair knot, back in place now that he was in the zig and swept his eyes over the controls assuring himself that Ricci hadn't put their lives at risk. An alert from his assistant informed him that Viram Mantor had showed up with his kit.

When Mitsumi arrived at the main passenger airlock, Mantor hung in the air slack-jawed, staring at a bulkhead. "Viram," Mitsumi said, wondering whether more than his engineer's body was present, "welcome aboard." Mantor's jaw snapped shut and his face became more animated.

"Thanks, Cap'n Mitsumi." Mantor dragged his hand across his face. "You want to show me where I'm bunked so I can store my stuff? Then I want to get a look at my engines and HE drive."

With a neutral expression, Mitsumi studied Mantor. Even as long as it was, his tight-knit, kinked hair didn't float in the zig causing issues, but it was weirdly distorted like he'd been tearing at it. His eyelids drooped as if he were struggling to stay awake; large dark circles under his eyes accentuated that effect. He was thin to the point of emaciation, but skin hung from his bones suggesting recent significant weight loss. Deep lines on his face belied his youth. Mantor smiled weakly. "I need to review the maintenance logs and run diagnostics before we can leave."

Mantor's appearance didn't bode well, but he'd sworn he was clean no matter what his prior crew had said, and his tests had come up negative and they couldn't travel without an engineer. "This way." Mitsumi showed him to his quarters and directed him to the engineering level. As he entered the engineering compartment, Mantor's eyes lit.

"It's true," Mantor said reverently. "I thought you were joking. No one flies with an original Sunchaser Mark I fusion in-system propulsion and," Mantor floated to the HE interface panel, "a third generation HE drive." Mantor stroked the panel. "How'd you find this, and how do you keep it up? I mean parts for this baby must be impossible to come by."

"I'm glad you're pleased, because the prior owner didn't have much good to say about this tub. It wasn't my choice to fly an antique. This is the best ship within our sponsor's budget. Its previous owners certified its soundness, verified by our third-party inspector. Their reports say we're stocked with replacement parts and communication drones. Would you check their results?"

Mantor nodded absently and tapped on the HE interface board. After a few moments, Mitsumi turned and floated out of the compartment. At least he seemed to know what he was doing. Mitsumi made his way to the main airlock to await the remaining two crew members. A few minutes later, a loud voice echoed down from the station.

"You're a fool if you think this is anything but a chance for free consumables until something real comes along. That's why I'm here. I had lots of opportunities, of course, but nothing that was right for my skill level. But this 'expedition' has zero chance of success."

Sentaa Koning drifted through the airlock with her personal kit in tow, looking back at whoever she was talking to. She too was Neopan, not as tall as Ricci, with short black hair in tight curls. Her brown eyes were close-set and intense. She couldn't have been above twenty-two standard years old. Inexperienced, her previous engagement with Nova Starlines had not gone well. Nova's records reported that on her first run, the one that had brought her to Support, her jump calculations had landed the ship perilously close to Support's star. If Nova hadn't gone bust, she'd have been fired. In light of this information, Mitsumi sensed an unpleasant odor wafting from her Astrogation Certificate. Others must have agreed, because despite her comment just now, she'd been stuck on Support Five Station for months unable to land a berth.

Koning turned her head. Her eyes widened at the sight of Mitsumi hanging in the air, but she smiled, projecting confidence. "Hello, Holtz. Nice to see you again. We weren't expecting a personal greeting."

Mitsumi shifted his eyes from Koning. Tai Quest followed Koning through the airlock.

"I was just telling Tan here how much I'm looking forward to this voyage and how excited I am to share in new and profitable discoveries."

Quest's eyes flicked from Mitsumi to Koning and back to Mitsumi. His expression unreadable, Quest pushed away, gliding toward the hatch leading to the crews' quarters. Koning's eyes followed Quest. "That's the way to the quarters, is it?" Koning said.

"Yes," Mitsumi said. "I sent everyone a schematic."

"Right, I remember. But I have a hard time with those things. Kinda ironic for an astrogator, huh?" Koning pushed off in the direction Quest had gone.

Mitsumi gathered the crew in the mess before their departure. Everyone oriented themselves right-side up, treating the deck below like the floor as if under acceleration, except Ricci who stretched out sideways a meter off the nominal "floor."

"I thought we ought to formally introduce ourselves before we started," Mitsumi said. "As I told you in our interviews, we've planned to be out a standard year, we have twenty targets to investigate, unless we strike it big in our first visit, then it'll only be a couple of months and we'll be rich." Mitsumi smiled. With varying degrees of boredom, except for Ricci who grinned with excitement, the crew remained silent.

"So, why don't we start with—"

"Who's he?" All eyes turned to Quest, who nodded at Chandra.

Mitsumi eyed Chandra, wondering what he'd say about his background. "Sure we can start with Aber, he's our sponsor. Aber?"

Chandra's eyelids fluttered as if he was surprised anyone noticed him. "I'm Aber Chandra," Chandra said slowly. "I'm from Del and—"

"You're the one with the coordinates?" Quest said.

Chandra licked his lips and hoisted a smile on his face. "Yes, that's right I—"

"Where did you get them?" Quest said. Koning's expression had changed from boredom to mild interest. Mantor's light year stare was unchanged. Ricci switched her orientation to align with everyone else.

Mitsumi wondered how Chandra would answer. So far, Chandra had refused to say where he had found the quantum memory store and had made Mitsumi promise not even to disclose the store's existence.

"I uh," Chandra said, "I, um, can't say where the information came from."

Boredom returned to Koning's face. Ricci allowed herself

to drift sideways again. With a micro inclination of his head Mitsumi interpreted to be a nod, Quest pushed off heading out of the mess.

"Wait, Tai," Mitsumi said. "We haven't finished our—"

"Just shoot us everyone's profiles, Holtz," Koning said, following Quest. "We'll figure it out. And we've a year to become better acquainted."

"I'm sorry that wasn't how you'd planned it, Captain." Ricci shrugged and pushed off after the other two.

Without speaking, Mantor continued to stare for a moment then shook his head as if trying to rouse himself. With a wan smile, he said, "I'll just, uh, be in...you know, uh, making sure we're ready." Mantor headed toward engineering.

"What a marvelous crew," Chandra said beaming. His smile turned into a frown, and he pulled his assistant from a pocket in response to an unheard alert. Chandra's eyes widened and his mouth sagged open in horror at whatever had appeared on the screen.

"Aber," Mitsumi said drawing his name out, "what's going on?"

Chandra raised his head and snapped his jaw closed. Eyes wide and skittering around the mess as if looking for a way to escape, he stammered, "Nothing. Could we advance our departure, do you think?"

"Why?"

"Oh, no reason," Chandra said, attempting but failing to feign unconcern. "I can't wait to be on our way, that's all." Chandra smiled weakly and glanced at his assistant. His smile faltered. He reached up and fiddled with his earring. "Please," he wheedled, "as quickly as possible."

Mitsumi considered Chandra. Something had changed, but in Mitsumi's limited experience with Chandra he was unlikely to extract more information from him and, with everyone on board and the supplies delivered, there was no good reason to postpone their departure. In fact, given Chandra's obvious discomfort, it might be in everyone's interest to leave now.

He made a mental note to discuss this further with Chandra. Mitsumi drifted to a com panel to communicate with the crew.

"Viram, how long until you've prepped our engines for departure?"

Silence stretched for a good ten seconds. Mitsumi opened his mouth to repeat the question. "We're ready now, Captain." Mitsumi closed his eyes and, with a slight shake, lowered his head.

"Sentaa, do we have a course for our first destination?"

"We do."

"Tai—"

"Ready," Tai said.

Mitsumi opened his eyes. Chandra stared at his assistant, then raised his head desperation plain on his face. Mitsumi sighed inside. He hoped he wasn't making a huge mistake.

"Mr. Koning," Mitsumi said, invoking the formality that by tradition began each voyage, "please give our compliments to station guidance control and request separation vectors."

"Vectors received and plotted," Koning said after a moment's hesitation. Mitsumi relaxed a hair. Chandra's behavior had raised the specter of a hold order.

"Mr. Quest—" Mitsumi began and felt the subsonic rumble of clamps unlocking and the engines powering up. "Undock, separate, and proceed to our jump point," Mitsumi concluded uselessly. "Don't mind me," he added under his breath. "I'm just the captain."

CHAPTER 5

Records, requisitions—performance reviews! Never in her wildest imagination had Dominica Fylan pictured herself heading the Federation Worlds' most successful criminal enterprise, yet drowning in endless forms, reports, and spreadsheets.

With a sigh, she tried to focus on a financial spreadsheet, but her eyes glazed. Back in the day, seeing the fruits of her labor had brought her pleasure. A murder here, a beating there, some light torture—a good day's work was hands-on. She missed that—being able to point to a mangled corpse with pride and see the tangible result of her accomplishment. That was, she admitted to herself, in part because the Consortium's criminal aspects remained hidden behind nominally legitimate activities, all of which required hated administrative crap. On the other hand... Wiping away the forms projected from her desk with a gesture, she gazed out from the summit of Support's highest peak. Jagged snow-covered mountains stretched away merging with the misty horizon. Holoscreens surrounded and enveloped her, projecting whatever suited her pleasure—at the moment, the Silverthorne Mountains. Typically squat as someone born and raised in Support's higher than average gravity, she kept herself in good physical condition. Her dark brown wavy hair, which would have brushed her shoulders had she not kept it knotted in a bun, contrasted well with bright green eyes. She'd been told she had a kind face—an incongruity that had often worked to her advantage.

At least she wasn't huddled, freezing, exhausted and starving in a back alley that stunk of piss and puke waiting for a mark. She selected one of the pastries she'd ordered as a midmorning snack and savored the buttery confection. Yes, there were compensations.

A chime sounded—someone requesting admission to her office. With the chiming a holo flashed on, projecting the image of Khons standing outside her office door, shifting his weight from foot to foot and fiddling with his hands. This would be bad news. Fylan pursed her lips. "Come."

With a deep breath, Khons set his face and strode into the room, advancing across the deep living-fiber rug. "Tell me you didn't screw up," Fylan said before Khons could open his mouth.

"I didn't screw up," Khons said. "Dequan did."

Inwardly, Fylan sighed with dismay at the transparent blame shifting. She wished they'd just be honest, so she wouldn't have to waste time sorting out fault before punishing them. "What happened? After we uncovered what Aber did, I told you to pick him up and confiscate his discovery."

Khons held Fylan's gaze for a moment, then looked away. "It turns out Dequan sat on the information before he told me and I told you, so we had less time to act than we'd thought. I went after him as soon as you told me to, but he slipped away."

Muscles bunched in her jaw. *Idiots*, she thought. "How many times do we have to have this conversation, Khons? *Never* 'sit' on information—"

"But Dequan," Khons said, his hands out, pleading, "he's the one who—"

She cut him off with a gesture. "Never try to blame your subordinate." On her feet now, she rested her hands on the desk and leaned toward Khons, who stepped back from her cold glare. "And *never, ever* interrupt me," she hissed with suppressed anger. Khons cringed, swallowing a response, and held her eyes for a moment before ducking his head in

63

acknowledgement.

She straightened, folded her arms and fought her first impulse to kill him and be done with it. He'd performed reasonably well in the past. She'd give him another chance. "Now, tell me. How will you fix your mistake?"

Eager to give her good news, he raised his head again and met her glare. "See," he said, "I was going to tell you, even though Dequan—" she raised her eyebrows and tilted her head, thunder building on her face. "I mean, we screwed up the snatch and grab, we managed to plant a tracker on the ship." With a tentative smile, he continued, "so, we can pick him up any time we want." Pleased with himself, his smile broadened.

As Khons spoke, Fylan's glower relaxed, her irritation decreasing marginally. "At much greater expense than nabbing him while he was still here." Khons' face fell. "An expense you'll pay one way or another."

Fylan closed her eyes and massaged the bridge of her nose. This was a complication she didn't need. Yesterday, after Khons had reported Chandra's discovery and anticipating Khons bringing him in, she'd reported to her boss that Chandra had stumbled on what looked to be the locations of First Civ worlds, compiled by the First Stellar Civilization itself. It was a find of incalculable value, and she'd promised the boss Chandra and his information today. Now, she would have to explain her failure—with an excuse better than "my subordinates screwed up." A chill took her—the boss did not react well to disappointment.

"I think," Khons said eagerly, "we should wait until they've completed their trip, then swoop in and take everything they've collected when they try to sell it. And…and we should take his family hostage," he shrugged, "just in case."

Her eyes flew open. She shook her head and snapped, "Don't be an imbecile more than absolutely necessary, okay? We have to collect him as soon as possible. What if he discovers the tracker? How will we know when his trip has ended? And I've told you a thousand times, we can't operate on Del—

that society's too closed, we've never been able to penetrate it before, why would we be able to now?"

Khons' face fell and his shoulders hunched. "No," Fylan said forcefully, "we need to act now, and I need to do this myself." She felt herself calming. Yes, they could leave right away, take the new ship. But she had to come up with something to put the boss off, something that would not smack of failure. Calling up the boss' schedule, she grimaced. Kantic Burthen was still on Support. If she'd been off world, Fylan could have composed a drone message and by the time it reached Burthen, the crisis would have passed. But on world?

She'd made the mistake of mentioning Chandra and his discovery to Burthen yesterday in passing. Burthen had taken a keen interest. If she didn't report this latest screw up to Burthen right away and Burthen later found out... Well, the consequences would be unpleasant.

Fylan initiated the digital encryption routine. Burthen insisted on elaborate precautions, and the encryption she specified was the highest military grade available. At the apex of the Burthen industrial and financial empire, Kantic Burthen kept her and her interests' involvement in the Consortium a well-guarded secret.

Dark-skinned with a broad face and penetrating dark brown eyes, Burthen appeared in a holo projection hovering over Fylan's desk. Shocked at the speed with which Burthen had accepted the communication request, Fylan stammered. "Ah, Ms. Burthen...hello."

Muscles bunching in her cheeks, Burthen remained silent, waiting for Fylan to continue.

"You asked me to inform you of our progress with Aber Chandra."

Burthen raised her eyebrows. "You have him and the information?"

Devoutly hoping the sheen of sweat on her upper lip wasn't visible, Fylan said, "We missed him. He jumped before we nabbed him."

With a minute shake of her head and hardening eyes, Burthen said, "Disappointment is a rare experience for me, Domenica. I am not fond of the emotion—or of those who cause it."

After swallowing hard, Fylan added in haste, "But, before he and his crew jumped we landed a tracer on his ship." She fought the urge to lick her lips. "I'm on my way personally to track him down and pick him up. Only a few days more."

"I expect news of your success within the week." Burthen's image disappeared.

Mitsumi cleared his throat. "How far out did you say we were?" The screen showed a field of stars. Supposedly, they had arrived at their first destination. The system's sun showed only as a slightly brighter star at the center of the screen.

Koning flushed as blood crept up her cheeks. "Seventy-two light minutes."

"Which means," Mitsumi said, "without another jump we're two weeks away?"

"That's right," Koning mumbled.

A miss of that magnitude was not unheard of, but was also not the norm and well outside the least competent certified astrogator's range. A certified astrogator of any competence would have put them thirty light minutes away. Koning's claimed experience would appear to be quite overstated. Mitsumi swiveled toward Koning's station. Unable to keep impatience from his voice, Mitsumi said, "Please calculate a jump that will land us a tad closer to the planet."

Koning turned to her console, her shoulders hunched as if expecting a blow. "Done," Koning said a few moments later. "And transferred to the helm."

Mitsumi turned back to the main screen. "Mei?"

"Vector received and set," Ricci said.

"Execute," Mitsumi said. The screen blinked, and a planet

appeared. After a moment Mitsumi said, "Take us into a scanning orbit, Mei, and begin the scans."

"Analysis complete, Captain Mitsumi," Koning said a couple of hours later. "Those craters are within the five-thousand-year time horizon."

Blue-white, with large land masses green with plant life, the planet almost filled the screen. Obvious even from orbit, the telltale impact craters, snow-covered walls, sharp even after five thousand years, pocked the surface. Lakes or small seas glimmered in the craters.

"It's a living First Civ world," Ricci breathed. "Just like the other Federated Worlds when they were discovered."

Though Ricci's rising enthusiasm echoed his own, Mitsumi reined his feelings in hard. "Let's not get ahead of ourselves, Mei," Mitsumi said. "It's consistent with the discovered living First Civ worlds. We don't know if anyone's down there yet. Sentaa, any sign it's inhabited?"

"I'm not reading any signs of civilization," Koning said.

"But it's a First Civ world," Ricci said, her voice rising with excitement, "you can see the craters—we don't need the computer for that and look at all that green—it's alive. Those are the same characteristics the Federated Worlds had when they were discovered."

Ricci was right. After years of study, scholars had concluded that the people of the First Stellar Civilization had engaged in altering the biosphere of the planets they inhabited to accommodate human life. A word had even floated down through the Great Dark associated with that task—terraforming. Only on worlds where humans had sufficiently advanced the terraforming process had anyone survived the Horde's bombardment. Those were the Federated Worlds. So, here was a living First Civ world. From experience it should be inhabited.

"No signs of sentient life, Sentaa?" Mitsumi asked.

"None of the indications associated with the discovery of every Federated World. No traces of early industrial chemicals in the air, no anomalous patterns on the surface, nothing in space and certainly no EM."

"Yes," Mitsumi mused, "electromagnetic radiation *would* be odd, wouldn't it? But, the craters are the right age?"

"The computer puts them within the last five thousand standard years give or take a few hundred," Koning said.

"So," Mitsumi said, "the time frame matches, but every known living First Civ world has been populated."

"The Federated Worlds," Ricci said.

Mitsumi nodded slowly. "Aber," Mitsumi said, eyes still fixed on the screen, "where do we look?"

Chandra hesitated, rubbing his earring. "I'm not sure, Holtz. I told you I only had coordinates for the planet."

"Suggestions?" Mitsumi said.

"I'd try the poles," Ricci said.

"Why?" Koning challenged. "There's no cratering on the poles. All the other finds have been in or around the craters. I'd start with the largest craters. That's where the greatest population would have been and the highest concentration of tech." On the screen, the live view of the planet gave way to a snapshot from an earlier orbit. Two continents, one in the hemisphere the computer had arbitrarily designated as "northern" and one in the southern, dominated this half of the planet. Koning punched at her console. A red circle appeared, encompassing an enormous crater cluster on the northern continent. "There, that's where we should go. We shouldn't waste our time at the poles."

Koning was probably right, at least that would be the course conventional wisdom dictated. But something nagged at Mitsumi. Something about... "Is the crater count unusual?" Mitsumi asked.

"What does that have to do with anything?" Koning said. "We should stick to what's worked before."

"The sample size is small, Captain," Ricci said after a moment. "We only have the ten Federated Worlds and ten additional dead First Civ finds as a baseline. But the count on this planet is twice as great as the count on any of the other First Civ worlds including the Federated Worlds."

Mitsumi recalled the indecipherable writing marking this planet as different on the star chart.

"So they were more thorough here than with the other worlds," Koning said. "That still doesn't change the calculus. We're most likely to find what we're looking for there." Koning pointed at the red circle on the screen.

"This planet was important," Mitsumi said almost under his breath. "But there's something else..." Lifting a hand to tug on his knotted hair, Mitsumi stared hard at the screen trying to force the idea drifting through his mind to coalesce in his consciousness. "How old are they?" Mitsumi said suddenly.

"Holtz, we're wasting time here," Koning said. "I told you the computer says they're at least five thousand years old. We should be on the planet searching."

Mitsumi considered his astrogator. Koning glared at him from her post. Not wanting to yield to Koning's insistence, Mitsumi clutched the arms of his couch to avoid shrinking from Koning's glare. "No," Mitsumi said. "I want the individual craters' exact ages."

Koning frowned. "A few craters match the five-thousand-year age profile. That establishes this was a First Civ world."

Ricci poked at the panel in front of her. "That's odd," Ricci said. Mitsumi relaxed his grip on the couch.

Ricci continued tapping on the panel. The view on the screen changed back to a live picture of the planet. Numbers popped up overlaid on impact craters. "The oldest ones are five thousand standard years—those are the biggest ones. But the newest ones, the computer dates only from three thousand standard years."

Koning knitted her eyebrows. "That's not possible," she said. "On all the First Civ worlds the ages of the craters are the same—five thousand years. The computer's messed up."

Ricci shrugged. "Check yourself."

"They fought back," Mitsumi whispered, his face shining

69

with wonder. When the attack came, it didn't kill them off immediately as it had on the other worlds. These people had survived the destructive first wave and resisted. "Please double check, Sentaa, but I think you'll find the computer is correct. They might have been the last light in the Great Dark, and they fought the Horde for two thousand years."

"Fine, I'll check," Koning said turning to her console. "Even if it's true, how does that help us figure out where to look?"

"It might," Chandra said, his voice loud with excitement. All eyes turned to him. Chandra shrank under the scrutiny. "Think about it," he breathed. "The Great Dark descends with the impacts five thousand years ago timed to occur simultaneously across the known First Civ worlds. From what information we've been able to scrape together, the Horde used any means of radiated communication as targeting information."

"That last part's pure conjecture," Koning said, "even more than the Horde theory. No one's found any evidence to support the notion that a group of homicidal aliens swept down on the First Civ and destroyed it, nor that the mythical Horde used electromagnetic radiation sources for targeting."

"It is not a 'theory'," Ricci said, "that someone destroyed the First Stellar Civilization. Calling whoever they were the 'Horde' is a placeholder. No one knows who they were or their motivation." Koning glared at Ricci, but stayed silent. "If they used EM sources to establish targets, that would explain the EM taboo on all the Federated Worlds. Wherever humans survived that taboo survived with them."

"So," Mitsumi said, musing aloud, "they're isolated from other worlds and under attack. But they lasted longer than the other First Civ worlds. They fought back, but they must have heard world after world falling silent under similar attacks. After a while they had to realize they were losing, that the end was in sight and suspected they were the last to survive. If your doom is certain; your civilization is dying, what do you do?"

Even Koning was silent for a moment. The crew stared at the screen. Mitsumi imagined the end of everything he'd known. What was his first impulse?

"I'd try to leave something behind," Ricci said abruptly.

Chandra nodded. "To let others know I had lived."

"A cache," Mitsumi said.

"But where?" Ricci said.

"The Horde used rocks for weapons," Mitsumi said. "If the Horde had found the cache, they would have destroyed it."

"We're back to the poles," Chandra said.

"Where there are no craters," Ricci said brightly.

Koning shook her head in disgust. "Listen to yourselves. You've worked out this whole chain of reasoning linking baseless, wild assumptions. Holtz, we should stick with the tried and tested. We should start with the largest crater."

Mitsumi considered Koning, the euphoria of a new discovery fading. She might be right; it would be best to spend their time doing what had worked in the past. Chandra eyed him neutrally, absently fingering his earring, waiting on his decision. Koning tapped her fingers on the arm of her seat.

Intuition and intellect fought to control Mitsumi's decision. An urge to follow his intuition bubbled up and overwhelmed logic—they should search the poles. He cut his eyes toward Koning who returned his look with a challenge, promising resistance if he refused the traditional approach. Then he seemed to hear Kalal's voice from their last meeting. *"When you're in charge, be in charge,"* he'd said.

Mitsumi sat up straighter. "You may be right, Sentaa," Mitsumi said, "but this planet isn't like the others, and I think we should start at the poles."

Koning's face fell. "That's not the right decision, Holtz; we'll be wasting our time and resources. I had counted on a reasonable command when I—"

Mitsumi held up his hand to stop her. He looked to Ricci and Chandra for support, but they stared back at him impassively. "I've made my decision, Sentaa. Please ready the shuttle."

After Mitsumi's decision to search the polar regions, they'd circled the poles in the shuttle for several days trying to spot any sign of a hidden cache. Spiraling out from each pole using every probing device at their disposal, they'd found nothing —no cavities in the surface, no markers, no sign that the snow and ice covered anything but barren continents. Koning had been elated when Mitsumi had conceded failure and they had returned to the ship to prepare for a more traditional exploration of the largest crater.

"It's okay, Holtz," Koning said with a smug smile. "We haven't wasted too much time. At least we can now get back to real—"

"Captain," Ricci's voice over the intercom interrupted Koning in full gloat, "I think I may have found something."

Mitsumi waited for Ricci to continue. When she didn't, "What have you found, Mei?" Mitsumi said.

"Sorry, Captain, I was..." Ricci subsided into silence.

"Mei?" Mitsumi said with irritation.

"Ah," Ricci said, "got it. I'm on my way."

Koning frowned, but said nothing. In the pilot's chair, Quest had been silent through the entire conversation, seemingly paying no attention.

Ricci sailed through the hatch onto the bridge, arms flailing and out of control; she ricocheted off the opposing wall dissipating enough of her energy that when she banged into Mitsumi, it was more irritating than painful. Mitsumi grabbed Ricci's arm before she could float away and cause more damage.

"Sorry, Captain," Ricci said, her cheeks a bright red. "I was in a hurry and, uh..."

Koning, who had been watching this spectacle, shook her head in disgust and turned back to her instruments.

"What do you have for us, Mei?" Mitsumi said.

"I kept thinking that, if I were hiding something, I'd want to find it later or let someone else find it. And, if we assume that the First Civers weren't gods and we know they're not, their technology is beyond us, but not so far that we can't imagine the principles on which they work. So, the means of identification they chose should be within our ability to—"

"The point, please, Mei," Mitsumi said allowing his annoyance to show.

Ricci blinked, pulled out her assistant and tapped to link it to the bridge view screen. The screen changed from a view of the planet to a close-up of the northern ice cap. Superimposed on the view were two bright red lines intersecting at right angles over a spot on the ice.

Koning turned to the screen. Mitsumi squinted at the lines. "What do those represent?"

"The intersection is the spot of the cache," Ricci said triumph in her voice.

Koning snorted. "There's no way you can know that."

"How did you generate the data?" Mitsumi asked, hoping that Ricci had a rational explanation to support her claim.

"I searched for fluctuations in the level of background radiation and found a small, but consistent decrease along these lines."

Koning turned back to her instruments. "That means nothing."

"Then," Ricci continued, "I searched for gravitational anomalies and found the gravitational field declined along the same lines."

"That's not even possible," Koning said without turning around, "it must be an instrument malfunction."

"And," Ricci added, a note of triumph in her voice, "I examined the area for heat signatures and found a slight, but measureable increase in ambient heat once again on the lines."

Koning's shoulders slumped in defeat. Mitsumi stared at the screen. Ricci tapped on her assistant and the view of the icecap expanded. The lines intersected on an outcrop of rock free of snow and ice. A smile spread across his face. He rubbed his hands together. "I'm convinced, how about you, Sentaa?"

"I'll prep the shuttle—again," Koning said with resignation.

"Nice work, Mei," Mitsumi said. Ricci beamed.

Thundering from orbit, balanced on the energy from fusing hydrogen, Quest refined his calculations for a solid landing spot. They were heading for a high plateau on the central mountain chain at the northern pole. Their sensors had shown rock with only seven meters of ice. Mitsumi switched the view on his assistant to represent their actual-versus-plotted course and noted with satisfaction scant separation between the two. Quest's performance had been solid—surprising, given how poor his recommendations had been.

Clouds of superheated steam billowed from the ice until the shuttle rested on the underlying rock. Quest shut off the engines. "We're down," Quest said.

Mitsumi and the others unstrapped. Mitsumi, Quest, Koning, and Chandra donned their atmosphere suits. These were not meant to operate in a vacuum, but to protect the wearer from extreme heat and cold, and were another example of First Civ wizardry. Although scientists had duplicated the material using yet another magic tech, no one understood how the material maintained a constant comfortable temperature regardless of the ambient environment. The best guess was it was a molecular sieve passing more or less energetic molecules, depending on the surroundings.

Ricci had remained topside with Mantor. "To practice with the controls," she'd said.

It took well over an hour to make their way to where Ricci had identified the intersection of the mysterious lines.

"You should be there now," Ricci said over the com.

They stood on the ice in front of a shear rock face. Mitsumi poured over the rock, inspecting it for any sign of an entrance. Chandra stood beside him, also peering intently at the rock. He reached a hand up as if to touch his earring, but glanced around embarrassed when his hand struck the helmet. Koning walked up to the rock face and traced a gloved hand along it. "This is a waste," she said.

"Mei?" Mitsumi said, "Any help?"

Chandra placed his hand flat against the rock and caressed it. Quest stared straight ahead without expression.

"Nothing, Captain," Ricci said. "I'm sorry. It should be right there. The lines intersect on the rock at eye level within a meter of where you're standing."

Chandra lifted his assistant and passed it in front of the rock face, staring at the little screen. Readouts fluctuated as he canvassed the wall. Chandra moved to his right and repeated the process.

Mitsumi reached out and ran his gloved hand on the rock. He didn't know what he expected to find, but the face was rough and irregular like any other rock. Absent a more productive idea, he pressed on the rock at different points. An unrevealed pressure point might gain them access.

A few meters off to the right, Chandra completed his survey, lowered his assistant and stared at the unyielding stone as if his last friend had just died. After five minutes of this, Chandra snarled in rage and smashed the rock with the side of his fist.

"Open up!" he shouted. "You've got to be there!"

Mitsumi stared at Chandra in astonishment. With a gesture, Koning caught Mitsumi's eye, pointed to her ear and flashed two fingers. She wanted to chat in private on the second channel. Mitsumi tapped his communicator, changing channels.

"What's gotten into *him*?" Koning asked. "Why's he so upset? It's like his life depends on finding something here."

His chest heaving, Chandra stood rigid, glaring at the

stone face as if trying to bore holes with his eyes. This demonstration *was* out of character, at least for the person he'd lived with these last few weeks. But how well did he know Chandra, really? He seemed more upset than disappointed greed could account for. "I don't know, Sentaa. I've only known him a week longer than you have."

Koning shrugged, and they switched their communicators back to the main channel.

"It's right in front of you," Quest said, pointing to the wall.

Chandra stopped and shot a look at Quest. "Where?" he said, hurrying back to stand next to Mitsumi and Quest. His rage had evaporated as rapidly as it had appeared. "Show me," Chandra pleaded.

Quest shrugged, took a step toward the wall and pointed to an almost imperceptible discoloration of the rock. Chandra strode up to Quest and nudged him aside, lifting his assistant. After inspecting the readouts, Chandra shook his head. "Nothing," he said, turning to Quest and making the word an accusation.

"Magnify it," Quest said.

"But the readouts...there's nothing behind the rock."

Bored, as if it mattered not to him whether Chandra followed his suggestion, Quest shrugged. Mitsumi couldn't understand Chandra's reluctance. It could be he didn't want to raise hope, only to have it dashed again. Mitsumi inclined his head toward the rock. Chandra fiddled with his assistant switching it to magnify, then turned back to the rock. Mitsumi stepped up, peering over Chandra's shoulder at the assistant's screen. Just above the spot Quest had pointed out, the grain of the rock in a small circle the size of the pad of Mitsumi's thumb was subtly different from its surroundings.

Focused on his assistant, Chandra reached out and poked the circle on the rock with his finger. Nothing. Chandra tried again, this time pressing hard on the spot and maintaining the pressure for a minute. "That's not it," Chandra said in frustration.

"Perhaps we need to shine a light on it, or heat it or... something," Mitsumi said. Chandra glared at Mitsumi.

"Brilliant," Chandra spat. "Why don't you show us how it's done?"

Without comment, Quest removed the glove from his right hand and pressed his exposed finger against the rock face on the discoloration. A loud click reverberated as a section of the rock two meters high and one meter wide popped out from the face and, with a grinding sound, moved to Mitsumi's left. The section of rock continued moving a meter and a half and came to a halt. Bright light spilled from the opening.

Chandra gasped and his face lit with glee.

Koning's mouth gaped open in astonishment replaced by elation as she rubbed her hands together in anticipation.

"Hey, what did you do?" Ricci asked from orbit. "I can scan into the mountain."

Mitsumi's heart leaped to his throat. This was the motherlode. It must be. His mind reeled at the thought of the priceless treasures that must be there in such a well-hidden and still-operating cache. He swallowed hard. "We've found something," Mitsumi said, astonished at the level of his understatement. "What do you see?"

"An extensive set of tunnels leading to caverns," Ricci said after a moment.

Chandra moved to the opening, but Mitsumi grabbed his shoulder, holding him back. "Hold on, Aber. Let's take a minute and make a plan."

Yes, they should bring order to their exploration, but part of him also wanted to savor the moment before they plunged ahead. Their discovery was unprecedented and guaranteed they'd be rich beyond the limits of even his active and extensive imagination.

"What are we waiting for?" Koning said, pacing in front of the opening.

"Well," Mitsumi said, "aside from the value of whatever

we find inside, I know some of the institutes will pay a handsome price for complete scans of the cache before we disturb anything. This site may contain more information on the First Stellar Civilization than anyone's been able to scrape together since the Great Dark fell."

Chandra and Koning grumbled a bit at the delay, but the prospect of more credits brought them around. Between Chandra's assistant and Ricci's scans from orbit, a map of the cache built up on their assistants. One main tunnel penetrated a half klick into the mountain. Every thirty meters along this main corridor, tunnels branched off at ninety degrees on the left and right. These side tunnels traveled another half klick and ended in expanded spaces. Their instruments couldn't resolve the contents of those spaces, but, in his mind, they contained the treasures Mitsumi expected would allow him to launch his expedition to find the Artifact's planet and repay Jonta and Corban.

"Okay, are we clear?" Mitsumi said.

"I'm with Quest," Koning said, looking none too happy.

"And, we're together," Chandra said addressing Mitsumi.

"Right, and we record at all times and if we lose contact with the other group, we proceed to the main corridor and meet there or at the entrance if we don't find each other. For the moment, we don't touch anything. We're recording only. Once we've catalogued everything, we can choose the most valuable items to bring back with us."

Mitsumi surveyed the little group. Koning slouched, looking bored at the lecture; Chandra shifted from one foot to the other, his eyes fixed on the opening, leaning forward as if preparing to start a race. Quest stood still, staring at Mitsumi without emotion. They didn't look like a group of people about to change the worlds forever.

"Let's go then."

CHAPTER 6

As if Mitsumi's voice was a starting pistol, Chandra sprang through the opening. Mitsumi allowed the others to enter ahead of him and was the last one through the door.

Past the opening, the ceiling vaulted above them a good three meters over a large space leading to the main corridor continuing into the mountain. Between them and the main corridor a pedestal stood with a box on top. Light flowed from no visible source. Bright and even, it eliminated any shadows. Chandra, Koning, and Quest had advanced to form a rough semicircle in front of the pedestal and the mysterious box. Mitsumi approached the pedestal, stopping next to Chandra who was taking readings with his assistant.

"Well, that's impressive," Koning said, sarcasm tinging her voice. "Hallelujah, we're rich."

Chandra lowered his assistant and glared at Koning. "It's an intact functioning First Civ device," Chandra said, his voice rising in anger. "Who knows what wonders it holds!"

"How do you know?" Quest asked without emotion.

Chandra shifted his glare to Quest. "How do I know what?" Chandra snapped.

"How do you know it's functioning?" Quest said.

The anger clouding Chandra's face faded into confusion. "Well, it's...it's from the First Stellar Civilization."

Koning snorted. Chandra shot her an angry look then turned back to Quest. Quest held Chandra's gaze, his eyebrows raised. With a shrug, he turned away, examining the walls of the room.

"It works," Chandra said. "But even if it doesn't, the mechanism itself is worth a fortune."

"If it's more than just an empty container," Koning said with a smirk.

Anger flashed over Chandra's face again, and he opened his mouth to respond.

Mitsumi held up his hands in a placating gesture. "We should see what else we can find before we fight over an object we know nothing about." Koning, still smirking, inclined her head, swiveled on her heel, and sauntered past the pedestal into the corridor. Quest followed without comment.

Mitsumi chucked Chandra's shoulder. "C'mon, Aber, let's see what other wonders we can find."

Chandra narrowed his eyes as if inspecting Mitsumi for any signs of mockery. After a moment his face relaxed into anticipation, glee lighting his eyes. "Oh, this will be good." Chandra hurried toward the corridor.

Four hours later, Mitsumi and Chandra trudged from the last branch tunnel into the main corridor. Chandra leaned against a wall and slid down resting his crossed arms on his knees and lowered his head. Mitsumi eyed the small man from Del with sympathy. Disappointment was clearly a stranger to him, whereas for Mitsumi the emotion had become an intimate companion. Mitsumi only wished it had seen fit to postpone its return a little longer.

He squatted next to Chandra and squeezed his shoulder giving him a gentle shake. "The box may yield something, Aber. And we have those other worlds yet to visit and the rest of this one to explore."

Chandra raised his head and nodded, accepting the attempt at consolation. After staring at the wall across the corridor for a moment, Chandra groaned and lifted himself to his feet. "Yeah," he said with a worn smile, "you're right. No reason to be pessimistic. We've just started."

"Let's hope he's right," Koning said, emerging from the branch tunnel across from where Mitsumi stood followed by Quest. "Cause this place is a bust."

"Lights," Quest said, indicating the walls of the corridor from which the uniform light shone. "Power source. And the mechanism that allowed our entry. Keyed to our DNA."

"Meh," Koning said, turning and marching away down the corridor back toward the entrance. "Just trinkets. They might pay for the voyage, but it sure ain't the Sundered buster Holtz promised."

Quest followed Koning at a more leisurely pace. Chandra sighed and walked ahead.

"I never promised you anything," Mitsumi said, "you came with wide eyes knowing what you were in for. Besides, I thought you figured this voyage was only good for free space and consumables." Ahead in the corridor, Koning lifted her hand in a gesture that had become universal among the Federated Worlds urging him to perform anatomically impossible operations on himself.

Mitsumi trudged after Chandra. "Besides," he muttered, "we have the box."

"That's right," Chandra said, enthusiasm in his voice, "I forgot. The box! We have the box!"

"Uh, guys," Ricci said from orbit over the com. "You, um... uh also have company."

"What, the Fire?" "What?" "...Company?" their overlapping voices scrambled together.

"Quiet!" Mitsumi shouted. The babble ceased. "What do you mean company?" Mitsumi said.

"Well," Ricci said drawing out the word, "it looks like... another ship is in orbit around the planet and a shuttle from that ship has sort of landed close to your location."

Koning and Chandra stumbled over each other with accusations. "You're only telling us this now?" "Weren't you keeping watch?"

"And," Ricci added, raising her voice to be heard over

the others, "two people from the shuttle are meters from the entrance."

Ricci hadn't even completed the sentence when Chandra bolted ahead, moving fast for his stature. Koning ran after him. "This better not cost us our find, Mei," Koning said.

Quest and Mitsumi exchanged glances. Quest shrugged and jogged off along the corridor. Mitsumi followed. It was easy to blame Ricci—her assignment had been to remain behind as a lookout, but no one expected any visitors in an uncharted system. The odds against someone ending up here by chance were literally astronomical.

From the corridor, Mitsumi emerged into the vaulted entry room and came to a halt. A man and a woman in environment suits stood just inside the entrance. They held weapons pointed at Koning and Chandra. The man shifted his weapon toward Quest and Mitsumi, the message obvious: Stay where you are. The woman gestured with her weapon at Chandra who stood holding the box from the pedestal with his body turned away from the woman as if trying to protect it.

"No!" Chandra shouted shaking his head. "I told you. It's ours."

With her free hand, the woman fiddled with something on the side of her helmet.

"She can't hear you," Mitsumi said. "We've been operating—"

"On an unusual frequency," the woman completed Mitsumi's sentence. "But that's got it." She tapped her helmet again and spoke then tapped her helmet again. "You there, Dequan?"

The man, Dequan apparently, fiddled with his helmet. "Yeah, Domenica, uh, Ms. Fylan," he said.

Mitsumi longed to disappear. He hadn't signed up for a confrontation with armed hostiles. He flicked his eyes to the right and left. Koning, Chandra, and Quest shot him an expectant look. Of course. Mitsumi had served in the navy—they expected him to handle situations like this. But service in the navy for Mitsumi had meant detailed study of warship strategies and tactics at which he had excelled. It did *not* involve hand-to-hand combat or anything beyond basic weapons training. That's what Marines were for.

Mitsumi swallowed hard. "What's going on here?" he said trying, without complete success, to keep the tremor from his voice.

The woman ignored Mitsumi. "Aber," she said. "Have you been keeping secrets?"

"You can't have it!" Chandra shouted turning away from the woman.

The woman raised her weapon. Mitsumi took a step forward. "Now wait—"

The woman shifted her weapon to Mitsumi. "This has nothing to do with you lot. So, why don't you let us take Aber here, whatever he's holding, and be on our way? After we stop at your ship and collect the paper with the coordinates of the other worlds, we'll let you go. How's that sound?"

Right now it sounded inviting. They would still have a copy of the other worlds' coordinates, and it was looking as if Chandra had not been forthright.

"Holtz," Chandra said after the silence had stretched and become uncomfortable. "You can't let them do this, Holtz."

As he eyed Chandra, Mitsumi pondered what loyalty he owed the man. Chandra had advanced money for this expedition so they wouldn't be here without his help. But without Chandra, they wouldn't have people pointing weapons at them. "I'm thinking," Mitsumi said, but understood the woman's offer was too good to be true. Once they collected the coordinates, Mitsumi and his crew were dead.

"I'm not going with you," Chandra said, "and neither is this box."

"Suit yourself," the woman said and shifted her weapon back to Chandra.

Quest flicked his hands toward the woman and leaped

toward the man, clearing the pedestal by a good meter. The woman pulled the trigger on her weapon just as whatever Quest had thrown hit her wrist and her helmet. Tiny crystal iron flechettes from her weapon flashed into the outside of Chandra's left shoulder and the wall behind him. Her helmet exploded. The man tried to bring his weapon around on Quest, but Quest kicked the man's wrist while still in midair, before slamming into his neck a second later. With a snap the man's head lolled at an impossible angle and he collapsed.

Chandra lay on the ground, blood pouring from his shredded shoulder, whimpering but still trying to cover the box with his body. Mitsumi and Koning stood motionless. Quest yanked the weapon from the man's hand, then strode over to the woman and relieved her of her weapon. He looked at Mitsumi without expression. "Perhaps we should leave?" he said.

Mitsumi shook his head trying to clear it. At least now he understood what Quest got up to in the hours he spent in the exercise space each day.

"I don't know what's going on down there," Ricci said, "but if it's possible, make your way back to the ship—right now."

Mitsumi surveyed the destruction in the room trying to clear his mind.

"What's going on?" Mitsumi asked.

"That ship, the one with the shuttle your friends came from? It's heading toward us and it's armed."

Ricci checked the instruments again. It was unfair that the others blamed her for not picking up on the other ship. It had been orbiting on the opposite side of the planet. The only hint she'd had of someone else with them came when she noticed the other shuttle on the surface. She gnawed at her lower lip. The intruder was closing faster now.

After the confrontation on the planet, the other ship had altered its course for an intercept. Ricci had responded trying to put as much distance as she could between *Are We There Yet?* and the other ship, but she had to remain in a position to pick up Mitsumi and the others once they reached the shuttle and lifted. And the other ship had more powerful engines. Another ten minutes and *Are We There Yet?* would be within range of its beam weapons. Her scans had picked up missiles as well and they were close enough to deploy those, but hadn't, which Mitsumi and the rest had agreed meant they intended to disable their ship, not destroy it—not a comforting thought at the moment. She'd attempted to contact the other ship, but they weren't talking.

"We're five minutes from the shuttle," Mitsumi said. "It'll take us ten more minutes to lift to you once we reach the shuttle. You need to keep *Are We There Yet?* out of range of their weapons until then. Can you do that?"

A tear detached itself from the corner of her eye and floated away. This was not what she had anticipated when she snuck away on her great adventure. She was looking for fun, not danger. She almost wished she were back home. At home, she'd be waking to a sumptuous breakfast in bed delivered by her chambermaid, then dressing in the latest fashion, preparing for another day of studying the intricacies of parliamentary procedure and maneuvering. She blotted up tears with the sleeve of her shirt and gritted her teeth. "I'll try, Captain," she said with more conviction than she felt. She was out of ideas, and the enemy ship would still be in weapons range before the shuttle arrived.

"Atta girl. We're almost there."

Ricci couldn't see how that was any great news. Before the shuttle reached *Are We There Yet?* the intruder would disable their engines, and they'd be at the mercy of the crew whose mates they'd just killed. If only they could jump to the other side of the planet, but they were too far down the well for a jump. The HE drive functioned by warping space-time and ejecting everything within the warp to a different reality where the normal rules didn't apply. But early on, a few unfortunate souls discovered that unless the drive formed its warp in a region of space-time with a certain flatness, the HE drive tended to collapse into a singularity which was not good for anyone in the vicinity, but was especially troublesome for the ship and its crew.

Ricci stared at the screen showing the advancing enemy ship. She could see no escape. She switched the view to the planet below. Within minutes the enemy ship would be in range and beamed energy, unobstructed by anything like the swirling clouds on the planet below, would burn through their engines. Ricci bolted upright and hit the acceleration alarm. Reverberating in the ship's corridors and compartments, the blaring klaxon would wake the dead because, if you didn't hear it and prepare, that's what you'd be. Ricci smacked the control panel to open a channel to the shuttle and shouted, "Captain, don't lift yet." She triggered a com with engineering and gave Mantor an additional warning. "Viram, prepare for heavy acceleration."

Ricci performed a rough calculation in her head and engaged the fusion drive. The huge g forces she'd unleashed smashed her into her acceleration couch, immobilizing her.

"Mei, what are you doing?" Mitsumi asked.

"Coming to you, Captain."

Mitsumi was silent for a long moment. "Are you up to this? We could lose the ship."

Ricci struggled for breath against the weight pressing on her chest, trying to push back the blackness edging in at the corners of her sight and stay conscious. Brutal acceleration pulled her lips away from her teeth in a rictus grin. "We will... lose the ship...if I don't." Ricci gasped at the effort of speaking. *Are We There Yet?* wasn't designed for descent to a planet's surface and atmospheric flight was an iffy proposition, but its fusion engines should be adequate to keep it in the air long enough to attempt the dangerous maneuver she had in mind.

Unable to move her head, she was helpless as a monitor flared red. The other vessel had fired its beam weapons, but at that distance they wouldn't penetrate right away. At least it hadn't launched torpedoes. Eventually, the weight lifted. The savage burn had killed their orbital velocity; they were falling into the atmosphere, but at the leisurely pace gravity dictated.

Ricci stretched her limbs, aching from the punishment. Clouds grew larger, slowly at first, then with increasing speed until they rushed at her, their peaks and valleys looking like the mountainous terrain of her home planet. She had to remind herself that they were only clouds and still flinched as the ship passed through them. She engaged the fusion engines again, slowing their fall until they hovered just below the clouds.

"Are you done now?" Mantor asked. "Cause I need to see what you broke down here."

"Sorry, Viram, but it was that, or let your engines fry."

"Oh, well, nice job then."

"We see you, Mei," Mitsumi said. "We're lifting and will be at your location in ten minutes. In the meantime, figure out how to get us on board."

"Oh, I've got that covered, Captain."

Mitsumi checked the calculations again. It should work. The shuttle couldn't dock with its engines running; it could only dock in freefall, typically while in orbit as the ship and shuttle fell together around a planet. Their unexpected visitor spoiled those plans. In a synchronous orbit over their position, the enemy ship hovered like a raptor ready to stoop on the *Are We There Yet?* as soon as it ran for vacuum.

Falling together through an atmosphere was in theory the same as falling together in orbit. In practice two differences made the exercise a touch more complicated. An atmosphere had turbulence which could bump either craft at a crucial moment and send one or the other spinning out of control. Then there was the ground itself which imposed a hard deadline on their docking attempt.

They hung alongside *Are We There Yet?* eighteen klicks above the surface. *Are We There Yet?*'s docking bay appeared on the shuttle's view screen. Quest and Ricci had linked a coordinated engine cut off through the ships' computers. Mitsumi watched the count tick to zero. They plunged toward the ground and Mitsumi floated up against his chair restraints. Normally, the zig didn't affect him, but this was different; in his mind the ground rushed to meet them. His heart beat faster.

The docking bay moved out of sight as *Are We There Yet?* fell faster.

"Correct, Mei," Quest said over the com.

"Yeah, I see that, Tai," Ricci said. *Are We There Yet?* halted its downward drift. The docking bay crept back into view and crawled upward out of alignment.

"Overcorrection," Quest said.

"I'm on it, Tai," Ricci said, testy at the advice.

Quest sat without emotion staring at the view screen. Mitsumi rubbed his forehead and tried to work saliva into his suddenly dry mouth. Was Ricci up to the job? His eyes flicked to the counter reporting time to impact with the surface—six minutes gone, five minutes left.

Are We There Yet? stabilized, sank downward and halted dead on the shuttle. Quest eased the shuttle forward toward the bay. Fifteen meters, ten meters, five, three. An eddy or gust of wind caught the shuttle and slammed its port side into the bay. Somehow Quest stabilized the shuttle and centered it again when an updraft smashed the top of the shuttle against the bay's entrance.

Later Mitsumi reviewed the record of their docking. In slow motion Quest fired a microburst from a vertical thruster and in the microsecond of alignment triggered the rear thruster plunging them into the bay and killed their forward momentum with another micro burst. In real time they rebounded from the top edge of the bay and darted in. It was a virtuoso performance, something the highest qualified navy pilots would botch nine times out of ten.

Weight returned as Ricci slowed then stopped their descent. Mitsumi checked their position—they had a good five hundred meters to spare.

CHAPTER 7

Koning let out a long sigh and slumped in her seat. "I thought we were dead."

"Me too." Chandra pulled a cloth from his pocket, wiped his sweaty forehead, gave a weak smile, unbuckled his restraints, climbed out of his seat, and stumbled in a near collapse.

Quest unbuckled, rose from his seat, and strode to the shuttle's airlock. Mitsumi followed him, arriving when the airlock hissed open.

On the bridge, Ricci turned in the pilot's couch, greeting them with a smile. "Welcome back," Ricci said.

Without a word, Quest advanced to the first pilot's couch and motioned with his head for Ricci to leave. Ricci's smile faltered. She glanced at Mitsumi.

"Thanks, Mei," Mitsumi said. "You did a nice job."

Ricci lowered her head and taking her time, unbuckled her restraints. She rose. "But now it's time for the real pilot to take over, right?"

Quest frowned, as if puzzling out what Ricci had said. "Your performance was adequate, but I am the better pilot."

Mitsumi understood Ricci's frustration; her performance had been stellar, but escaping this planet intact would be hard. He needed, they all needed, their best pilot at the helm and, after what he'd just seen, that was Quest. Ricci swept her hand toward the seat, inviting Quest to take his place. She lifted her chin and marched toward the exit.

"Please stay, Mei," Mitsumi said. "We'll need all the help we can to survive this."

Ricci stopped. At that moment Koning appeared in the entrance and paused in front of Ricci.

"I have to admit, Mei," Koning said, "I had you down as a pretty ornament, only good for meeting regs. I didn't think you had it in you." Koning brushed past Ricci and took her place on the bridge. Ricci surveyed the bridge, then after a moment nodded her head then moved to take her position in the second pilot's couch beside Quest.

Mitsumi punched up engineering. "Viram, please come to the bridge." After Mantor didn't respond for several seconds, Mitsumi repeated his request. Eventually, Mitsumi heard a scraping sound and Mantor responded.

"Uh, sure, Captain," Mantor said.

Mitsumi shook his head. "Now, please, Viram."

"Oh, you meant now as in *right* now."

Mitsumi waited.

"Okay, I'm on my way."

Chandra appeared, clutching the box from the surface to his chest with his good arm as if he were afraid someone would appear and try to yank it away. He should have been in the auto-doc, patches of blood showed through the temporary bandage they'd applied from the shuttle's first aid kit, and Chandra's face had a disturbing gray cast to it.

Mantor wandered in, walking a little gingerly.

Mitsumi surveyed the crew. "Okay, everyone. We have a hostile sitting above us. From what we learned on the ground, they want the box we picked up and Aber's coordinates. So, while I'm certain they'd destroy us if they could lay their hands on those items, until they can, they need to keep us intact. That means no missiles, only beam weapons. Sentaa, what are those weapons?"

"From what we can tell, they have a terawatt coherent-light weapon with an effective range of sixteen thousand klicks in vacuum and by effective I mean at that range they could disable our jump capability within thirty seconds. Much beyond that range, it would take several minutes to impair our jump ability."

"Tai, what is their position?" Mitsumi asked.

"They are in a synchronous orbit thirty-eight thousand klicks above the surface."

"What about their engines? What acceleration can they make?"

No one spoke for a moment. "While you were on the surface and they came after us," Ricci said into the silence, "they were making ten standard gravities."

"Tai, can we outrun them?" Mitsumi asked.

Quest bent over his station, bringing up a schematic of the planet with a red dot representing their ship hanging in the atmosphere above the planet and a green one representing the hostile in orbit. The red dot moved away from the planet, chased by the green dot until a green line lanced out, intercepting the red dot which flashed and disappeared. Mitsumi raised his eyebrows. "Very evocative, Tai."

The exercise repeated itself with the red dot escaping at different angles and from different points on the planet. In the end, it was always the same—the red dot vanished before reaching jump distance. The iterations sped up. "That's enough, Tai," Mitsumi said. "We take your point." Clouds drifted by once more on the screen. No one spoke.

"They might not kill us," Koning said into the silence, "if we give them what they want."

Chandra clutched the box tighter to his chest and shook his head. "Not a chance," he said.

"Don't be stupid, Aber," Koning said, her voice rising in anger. "It's our only chance to survive. I don't care what you think. My life's on the line."

"No," Chandra said. "We can't. I won't let you. We have to get back with our find."

Mitsumi sighed inwardly. It hurt to watch dreams turn to ash before your eyes, but, "Aber," Mitsumi said in a calming tone, "you've seen the calculations—we've no other choice."

"I can get us out of here." Everyone on the bridge turned to Mantor who stood at the entrance, rubbing his eyes and yawning. His gaze rested a moment on Koning, who returned his look with hooded eyes and a rock hard face. "What?" he said. "I can."

"Explain, please," Mitsumi said, although he was certain the explanation would be nonsense. It wasn't in Mantor's power to alter physical laws. Not sharing Mitsumi's skepticism, Chandra glowed with hope.

"We need to jump before they can use their weapon to disable our jump drive, right?" Mantor scratched idly at the side of his head. Ricci looked expectant as if she thought Mantor had solved their problem. Mitsumi gestured for him to continue.

"So," Mantor shrugged, "we jump from here. They'll never have the chance to approach within sixteen thousand klicks of us." He smiled at the crew.

With that, Mantor lost his audience. Koning turned away in disgust, and Ricci with a sad smile looked to the view screen. Even Chandra's face fell. *And no wonder*, Mitsumi thought, *that was no solution*. If they jumped from this deep in the gravity well their chance of ending up as a black hole was greater than their chance of escape. Mantor must understand that.

After a moment, the crew's skeptical reaction penetrated Mantor's self-congratulation. With a concerned look he said, "Are you worried we're too close to the planet?" Koning gave him a withering glare.

Mantor shook his head. "That's not a problem," he said. "The warp and space-time interaction is only a matter of computation," Mantor said. "In theory there's never been an inherent problem with jumping from a gravity well—it's just that the steep curvature played fire with the calculations which have only ever been approximations anyway, which is why conventionally you need to be—"

"Are you telling us you've solved the curvature problem?"

Mitsumi said.

"Well, yeah," Mantor said, "that's what I'm trying to tell you."

Chandra looked up hope creeping back to his face.

"But it's only theoretical, right?" Mitsumi said. "You've never tried it?"

"No," Mantor said stifling another yawn as the crew looked on with a mixture of skepticism and curiosity. "Not on a ship, but with remote devices set up with HE drives." His face brightened. "But the success rate is now at a hundred percent."

"Now?" Mitsumi said.

"Sure," Mantor said. "I ran a hundred tests with various degrees of success. But the last two were golden."

"Captain," Koning said, "you can't be thinking of taking the word of a Rapt addict and risking our lives because this drug-addled, so-called engineer hallucinated accomplishing something no one else has done. I won't stand for it."

Mitsumi wondered how Koning had gained access to Mantor's personnel files. Only he and Chandra should have known about Mantor's past.

"We should jump now," Chandra said.

Ricci shook her head. "I agree with Sentaa. I don't know what she means calling him a Rapt addict, but I do not want to risk my life on the off-chance Viram has made a fundamental breakthrough in advanced physics. No offense, Viram." Ricci nodded at Mantor with sympathy. Mantor responded with a wry smile.

"We should jump," Quest said. Everyone looked to Quest, waiting for him to provide reasoning for his position. He met the eyes of each in turn without further comment.

Mitsumi eyed Mantor. His demeanor on this voyage had been relaxed, to be charitable, except when it came to the engines and the jump drive. To Mitsumi's knowledge, Mantor's drug problems were behind him, and Koning's accusation was mere scurrilous calumny. But Ricci had a point. How likely was it that Viram Mantor, a young obscure engineer, had stumbled into such a momentous insight? On the other hand, Hansor Engon's original discovery of the jump drive seemed just as unlikely—an invention that even the First Stellar Civilization for all its technological sophistication couldn't replicate. And the pirates meant to kill them once they retrieved the box and the coordinates, he was certain of that.

"Set up the jump, Viram," Mitsumi said.

Mantor's face lit up. "You've got it." Mantor hurried toward engineering.

"You can't do that, Holtz," Koning said, with ill veiled menace. She rose from her station and stood before Mitsumi, arms slightly bent and fists clenched. "I don't care what the others say," she cocked a thumb over her shoulder at Quest, "but I won't let you risk *my* life on the word of a druggie loser."

Without a sound, Quest left his seat and stood behind Koning. Without taking his eyes off of Koning, Mitsumi shook his head almost imperceptibly. "How do you know about his past, and why do you keep bringing it up?"

Koning's lips lifted in a smirk. "You're so clueless. It's not his past. I've seen him curled on his bunk in the trance. And *you* want to bet *my* life on that? Not happening."

Mitsumi turned to the rest of the crew in confusion.

"Perhaps," Ricci said. "At times I have tried to speak to him and received no response. Whether that was a drug, or he's a heavy sleeper...." She shrugged.

Koning smiled in triumph.

"Captain," Mantor's voice came over the com. "I've made the calculations and reconfigured the drive. It's all set on your order."

Koning crossed her arms; her smile faded into a look of defiance. She might be right. Maybe the risk was too great and he shouldn't trust Mantor's boast. But he had decided to trust Mantor. Mantor had assured Mitsumi he was clean, that he'd left the drug behind. Besides, Koning and Ricci underestimated their chances of survival at the hands of the pirates. On patrols, he'd seen too often the bloody aftermath of encounters where pirates promised safety, if only passengers and crew would cooperate. Once the pirates had what they wanted, he and his crew were doomed.

Shoulders squared, Mitsumi pushed aside his doubts and fixed his eyes on Koning. "Mr. Koning, Mr. Ricci, I have made my decision. Death at the hands of the pirates is certain while Mr. Mantor's path offers us a chance of escape. If you disagree, I will relieve you of duty, accept your resignation and, if we survive the jump, drop you at the nearest Federation world."

Koning raised her chin and searched Mitsumi's face. Mitsumi didn't flinch. Koning looked away and sighed, her body visibly relaxing. "That won't be necessary, Captain," she said.

Mitsumi looked over his shoulder at Ricci. She held his eyes for a moment, then nodded. "It's your ship, Captain, and I'm part of your crew."

Mitsumi faced the view screen. Quest had resumed his position at the helm. "Mr. Koning, calculate two jumps with random arrival coordinates and input for our pilot." Koning opened her mouth to comment. Mitsumi glanced in her direction. She closed her mouth without saying a word.

Koning turned to her console. "Vector transmitted," Koning said moments later.

Quest tapped the console before him. "Vector received and set."

Mitsumi took a deep breath. "Mr. Quest, execute."

CHAPTER 8

Featureless gray replaced tangled clouds on the view screen for several seconds followed by scattered stars. The cycle repeated. Mitsumi let his breath out, hoping he'd done so without a noise.

"Congratulations, Viram," Mitsumi said. "I believe we've just made—"

"They're back," Quest said, interrupting Mitsumi, "sixteen thousand klicks to port, engines firing to close."

Koning turned to her station and tapped at her console. "They're beaming us, targeting the jump drive. Thirty seconds to burn through."

"How is that possible?" Ricci said. "They were too close to the planet for a jump, and how could they have followed us through two jumps?"

Mitsumi sympathized with Ricci's confusion. Apparently, Mantor was not the Federation's only brilliant engineer. As to the pirates' ability to locate them, Mitsumi had been afraid of that possibility.

"Tai—" Mitsumi began then stopped as a uniform gray replaced the stars for a second. The stars reappeared followed a second later by the gray again. The pattern continued. Quest had set up a series of random jumps. Quest swiveled in his seat. Mitsumi inclined his head. "That's what I had in mind."

"Captain," Ricci said, "what's going on?"

"Yeah, what are we doing?" Koning stared at the alternating real and unreal space on the view screen, confusion clouding her face. *Ah*, Mitsumi thought. *That explains a lot*. Koning's lack of skill was not incompetence, just inexperience.

"Tai?" Mitsumi said.

"They're matching us."

Mitsumi nodded. "Sentaa, please check their weapons status."

Koning hesitated, then turned to her console. "They're jumping with their weapons hot and hitting us every other jump, but their distance varies. I estimate they'll burn through our hull in five minutes." She turned to Mitsumi. "Captain, how —"

"Viram," Mitsumi said, ignoring Koning for the moment, "are you following this?"

"Yeah, I'm looking, but there's no signal."

"They're landing closer, Captain," Koning said. "Burn through now in sixty seconds."

Mitsumi felt heat and smelled smoke rising from engineering. He told himself it was his imagination. "Viram?"

"Where could it be?" Viram muttered. "It must be piggybacking on..."

"Thirty seconds," Koning said.

"Any time now, Mr. Mantor," Mitsumi said.

"Fifteen seconds," Koning said, almost in tears.

"Got you!" Mantor said. "Now, if I can just..."

"Burn through," Koning whispered as the stars shifted three times more and stayed steady.

"Tai?" Mitsumi said.

"All clear," Quest said.

"No sign of them." Koning shook her head and giggled, on the edge of hysteria.

"Status, Viram," Mitsumi said.

"So," Mantor said, "I found it and neutralized it, Captain, but the drive will need work."

"Will someone please tell me what's going on?" Ricci said.

Chandra had been keeping secrets, the pirate woman had said, and those secrets had endangered them all. Mitsumi glared at Chandra who sat with his good arm around the box, protecting it from threats, eyes shifting from face to face, his own countenance set in stubborn defiance.

"Viram, please join us in the mess for a conference. Aber has something he wants to tell us."

Pain. There was nothing but pain. *And life*, she thought. Pain meant she was still alive. Now, the pain differentiated —separating into its individual throbbing components. That there on the side of her head was from a blow. At the end of her arm? Oh, her wrist must be broken. And the rest of her? That was a searing heat. No. Cold. Fylan's eyes flew open as the scene came back to her and she tried to sit up—big mistake. The world swam around her and she fought down the contents of her stomach. After the world stabilized, she surveyed the room. Dequan lay motionless, his neck broken. She shivered uncontrollably. She couldn't have been here too long since she wasn't frozen although her hands and feet were numb. Her suit had continued to operate but with a broken helmet most of the heat poured out into the frigid air. It had been enough to keep her alive—just. But she had to get to the shuttle.

She struggled to her feet, waited until the room stopped revolving then staggered toward the entrance. Fortunately, they had touched down close to the entrance, and Chandra and his gang hadn't trashed the shuttle on their way out. Amateurs. She tottered toward the shuttle, but a meter short of the ramp her strength gave out and she fell to her knees. A sound brought her head up, and she sobbed with relief as the air lock door slid open. The last erg of power in her suit had triggered remote actuation. Without it she would have been dead; she couldn't have opened it manually.

Careful to keep weight off her broken wrist, she inched

her way up the ramp and slumped into the air lock. After sensing her presence in the air lock, the outer door ground to a close. The inner door cycled and blessed warmth poured over her face. After a pause to savor that warmth, she peered around the air lock's edge locating the shuttle's basic auto doc. It wouldn't heal every injury, but it would make a start and keep her alive. She activated her enviro suit's emergency release and crawled toward the doc leaving the suit behind. At the doc which, it now occurred to her, bore an uncanny resemblance to a coffin, she raised a leg and tumbled inside. *Made it!* she thought and darkness took her.

Something was wrong. Something was missing. Gummy, her eyes wouldn't open at first and her movement was restricted. When her eyelids unstuck, she inspected the featureless curved panel inches from her face. Ah! The doc. And the pain was missing. Well, good news for a change. To her right, the countdown showed twenty seconds until the doc completed its cycle. With a gentle ding, the panel overhead slid back. She sat up with none of the dizziness that marked her previous return to consciousness and took stock. Although the pain was gone, her wrist was in a cast and her hands and feet bandaged. Right—limited treatments, not complete healing. After assuring herself that she was okay, memories returned and with them a smoldering anger. That worm Chandra had escaped with the help of his crew—a crew to whom she had offered uncharacteristic charity. And this was how they repaid her? Fine, if they wanted to be in the crosshairs with Chandra, they'd pay the price.

"Ship," she said, "contact *Give Me An Excuse*."

"That vessel is out of contact range."

"What?" Fylan said, slamming the doc's casing with a bandaged hand and yelping in pain. "Where is it?"

"Unknown," the shuttle responded. "The vessel jumped out system one hour and thirty-seven point six seconds ago."

They must have chased after...oh, crap. She lifted her hand and just kept herself from striking the doc again. That's what she got for bringing Khons along and leaving him in charge on the ship instead of killing him. Livid, she said, "Message to *Give Me An Excuse*: 'Khons, contact me on the shuttle as soon as you return. Fylan out.' Send in continuous loop."

Half an hour later, a half hour in which Fylan's dudgeon rose into a rage as she contemplated the magnitude of Khons' cock up, a voice crackled in Fylan's ear. "Boss, this...uh, is Khons," Khons' voice shook. "It's great to hear from you. I'm so glad you're, uh, still alive."

"Really," Fylan said, her voice hovering just above absolute zero.

Khons gulped. "Yeah, boss. I mean when you didn't respond after Chandra's group lifted from the planet, we thought they'd wasted you."

Her fury having compressed itself into a gelid, adamantine lump, Fylan whispered between clenched teeth. "I'm sure you did, Khons. I'm lifting now. Meet me in the shuttle bay. We'll continue this conversation in person." She severed the connection. "Shuttle, engage auto pilot and rendezvous with *Give Me An Excuse*."

An hour later, the shuttle floated into the bay and settled to the deck as the ship accelerated to a safer jump point. It was possible to jump from a gravity well, but the maneuver still carried more risk than jumping from flat space. After a few minutes, the shuttle's outer air lock door opened on the ship's shuttle bay. At the foot of the access ramp, Khons was there to greet her, along with the two security personnel she'd arranged to accompany him. Down the ramp, gliding in a magnetically suspended chair—she'd need a cycle in the ship's full auto doc before walking wouldn't be excruciating from the frostbite's residual effects—she came to a halt before Khons. He stood stiff, eyes hollow with dread. Fylan stared up at Khons, allowing him a good look at her hard, cold, rage. He licked his lips and attempted a smile that died. "Wel-welcome back, chi-chief." Khons stammered.

Fylan bared her teeth. "Khons, walk with me." Turning her chair, she maneuvered toward a personnel air lock set beside the main shuttle bay access door. Khons hesitated, then glancing at the two hard-faced security men flanking him, licked his lips and followed beside Fylan's chair.

"Remind me what your orders were, Khons," she said, her voice conversational as if she *did* need the reminder.

"I, uh, I was to keep watch, assist your mission, and try to keep them from jumping out system." Stepping in front of her chair and bringing her to a halt, Khons bent forward, actual tears shining in his eyes. She wondered if he thought this display would change the outcome of their little chat. "No one thought you would fail." Khons cringed and shook his head. "I mean that they would overpower you. When they took off, I thought, 'no way the chief would let that happen if she was still alive.' It's true, that's what I thought. Then we couldn't contact you. And I knew, I knew, you must be dead. They killed you." Eyes wide and shimmering, he pleaded, "So, when they jumped from the planet—and who expected that? No one. We're the only ones who can jump from a gravity well. Right?" He licked his lips. "I had to chase them and punish them for what they did to you. Well, and get Chandra and his information back, but…" Under her glare, his voice wound down.

She forged ahead in her chair forcing him to backpedal. "So," she said, "when they escaped from me, instead of recalling the shuttle and descending again to see if I was injured and in need of help, you know, *assisting with my mission*, you chased after Chandra's ship—"

"I didn't want him to get away!" Khons yelled. "If I hadn't chased him—"

"There was—" Fylan shouted then, closing her eyes and wresting back control, continued in a lower voice humming with tightly controlled fury. "There was a tracker on his ship. We could always find him. But no, you had to chase him, alert the crew to the tracker's existence and allow them to dismantle it." She brought her chair to a halt before the air lock and turned to face Khons. "I got that part right, didn't I, Khons?"

His face crumbling in misery, Khons said, "I was sure they'd never find the tracker in time."

"To summarize then," she ticked the points on her fingers, "you abandoned me when I was seriously injured almost causing my death, and you lost our tracker so we have no idea where they've gone, and if they change their ship registration, we may never find them." Head cocked, she regarded him with glittering eyes as her anger fed anticipation. "Did I miss anything?"

Falling to his knees in front of her, Khons lowered his head, his body shaking with sobs. She was pretty sure the tears were real now. "Please," he begged, raising his eyes to hers. "I know ... I screwed up, but I tried ... Don't do this. I've been loyal. I've worked hard. Give me another chance."

She nodded at her security men. They stepped up beside Khons and dragged him to his feet. Fylan gritted her teeth against the coming pain and forced herself upright; agony stabbed her injured feet. With an inward smile and rubbing virtual hands together in anticipation, she pressed the actuator. The air lock door cycled open. After a brief ineffectual struggle, Khons sagged in the security men's grip and they threw him into the air lock. Fylan closed the inside door and punched up the intercom to hear his last words.

Crumpled in a heap, Khons looked up at Fylan through the airlock window and made one last plea, his voice tinny over the small speaker above the door. "One more chance, please. It won't happen again. I promise it won't."

"Oh, Khons, you've watched too many holos. You know what I have to say now, don't you?" Without cycling the air from the lock, Fylan punched the actuator opening the outer door. Explosive decompression flung his soon to be lifeless body away from the ship. "I know it won't," she said.

Anger loosed its grip as she felt the cold, hard lump dissipate inside her. With a tight, cruel smile she realized she'd been right the other day—nothing satisfied like the hands-on personal touch. Dismissed, the security men returned to their duties, and she collapsed back into her chair. Medical personnel approached across the shuttle bay deck. Despite her need for attention, she had instructed them to wait while she completed her business with Khons. Now, they accompanied her to the full doc on board. A day in the doc would see her healed and back to Support.

In the medical bay, they steered her toward an empty auto-doc with its lid open. She did her best to screen from her mind the task she faced after her return—reporting to Kantic Burthen what a complete mess her subordinates had made of everything. She was pretty certain her knowledge and usefulness would shield her from any unpleasant consequences of this screw up. But Burthen had been intensely interested in Chandra's list of First Civ worlds and was not known for "understanding" failure. Burthen wouldn't know about the item Chandra and his crew had stolen from her on this planet. She'd leave that item out of her report—no sense in making her failure seem worse than it was.

After climbing into the doc, she watched the lid lower and heard the lock's distinctive click. As consciousness faded, she shivered and wondered if the sensation was anything like what Khons had experienced out among the stars.

"Our attackers," Mitsumi said, "were thorough." He surveyed his assembled crew who sat at the mess table. Chandra, his good arm still around the box in front of him on the table, looked away. Mitsumi had ordered acceleration at a standard gravity; he had found in his experience that acceleration bred into their blood and bones for uncounted eons calmed nerves, and they would need calm for the upcoming discussion.

"Most of you know that it's possible to track a jump if you're in the vicinity of a jumping ship, and you've trained a hyperspace flux monitor on the ship at the instant of its jump. But to use that method, you have to be present at the jump and it takes time, not a lot of time, but over thirty seconds, to perform the calculations and follow."

"Ah," Ricci said nodding slowly, "so, that's why when we jumped away at first you ordered a second jump right after the first one."

"Just so," Mitsumi said. "But what is less well known is that two years ago, Burthen Space Technologies developed a hyperspace tracker. Placed on a ship, oh, like ours for example, it keeps the ship's jump window open for a matter of weeks. With a jump detector it's possible to follow right on an escaping ship's thrusters."

"One of those was on our ship?" Koning asked.

"Viram found it just in time," Mitsumi said. "So, Viram saved our hides twice in the last hour. Nice work, Viram."

Slumped in a chair and staring at the ceiling, Mantor raised his hand in acknowledgment.

"Why would someone put a tracker on our ship?" Ricci said.

"They wanted to follow us?" Mantor said, his eyes still fixed on the ceiling.

"If you can't contribute, Viram, just shut up," Koning snapped, having rediscovered her persona. Mantor shrugged, unperturbed by Koning's anger.

"We're one of dozens of ships launching on prospecting missions," Ricci said. "Does someone pick random prospectors and attack them if they make a find? I've never heard of that. Pirates attack when they know they have a score."

"They knew we'd find something," Quest said then fell silent. All eyes turned to him. "They launched their shuttle to the surface before we managed access to the site."

"How could they have known?" Ricci said.

"Aber," Mitsumi said. "That's your cue."

Chandra shifted in his seat. His eyes met the others'. He lowered his head. "I...I don't know what you're talking about."

"Aber here," Mitsumi said, "recovered the coordinates for our exploration from First Civ paper which turns out to be quantum memory."

Ricci looked confused. Quest perked up and looked curiously at Chandra. Mantor had closed his eyes, his face slack; he didn't stir.

"You mean one of those broken sheets of stuff found on First Civ worlds?" Koning said. "I thought no one had ever figured out what they were. That quantum memory stuff was just a wild guess."

"It seems not, Sentaa," Mitsumi said. "I saw him access it and have reason to believe it's authentic." In his mind, Mitsumi saw again the Artifact lying on the alien plinth embossed with the same symbol from Chandra's video. "But Aber never told me how he obtained that piece of paper."

Chandra cringed away from Mitsumi and shook his head, his arm still protectively around the box. Anger simmering, Mitsumi continued. "I do remember him saying it was worth both of our lives if anyone found out about the memory. At the time, I chalked it up to raging paranoia. Then, when we were on station preparing to leave, something spooked him into wanting to advance our departure. You were being hunted, weren't you? Where did you find that quantum memory?"

Chandra looked like he wanted to sink into the deck and disappear.

"Those people on the planet knew you," Koning said, her voice rising with anger.

"Yeah," Ricci agreed sounding puzzled, "that woman, she said something about keeping secrets from us."

Chandra scanned the crew's faces and shrank back in his seat. "I'm not keeping any secrets." He pulled the box closer to him, hugging it to his chest. "I don't know who those people were. They must have discovered who we were when they put the tracking device on the ship. They're trying get us to fight among ourselves."

"Well, they've succeeded," Koning said. "Captain, I

don't believe a word he said. We have a First Civ device, the coordinates of the cache where we found it, and the coordinates of other worlds to explore. I say we put Aber here out the airlock and be on our way."

Chandra's eyes widened in shock. He searched the crews' faces. Koning was angry, Ricci contemplative, as if considering a purchase in response to a sales pitch. Quest nodded his head thoughtfully. "You...you can't be serious!" Chandra screeched, his voice rising a few octaves. "That's murder. You'd kill me in cold blood?"

"Oh, believe me, Aber," Koning said in a low voice humming with menace. "My blood's anything but cold right now."

Muscles bunching as he clamped his jaw, Mitsumi considered Chandra. "Viram," Mitsumi said, without taking his eyes from Chandra. "Could you reconfigure Aber's stateroom so he can't leave?" Mitsumi doubted that any of them really meant Chandra any harm, except Koning perhaps, but he wanted to make sure everyone was aware of his position. He was livid at the thought that Chandra had duped him into risking his life and the lives of his crew and wasn't coming clean, but he wasn't about to take Chandra's life in retaliation.

Mantor stared at Chandra for a moment longer then resumed his position gazing at the ceiling. He nodded. "Yeah, I can do that."

Mitsumi rose from his seat gestured for Chandra to give him the box. Chandra held on to it for a few moments, but eventually released it to Mitsumi. Mitsumi placed the box on the table then sat on the table's edge facing Chandra.

"Aber, I won't let them space you"—Chandra let out a deep breath—"provided you come clean." Chandra's face fell. "Come clean and I'll lock you up. When we return, you can work out your differences with whoever it is who doesn't know you and doesn't want your skin."

Chandra gulped. "If not?" he said. Mitsumi shrugged and

indicated Koning behind him with a nod of his head.

Tears formed at the corners of Chandra's eyes and spilled on his cheeks. "I was sure no one would be hurt," he said. "You have to believe me." Chandra lapsed into silence filled with ship sounds—the drive rumbled, air sighed through ducts, water rustled through pipes, motors and actuators grumbled.

Chandra reached up and smeared the tears from his cheeks. "Pari, that's what we named her." He raised his head. "No, I should start from the beginning. I was introduced to Lani when I was in my fifth year of advanced study just prior to my graduation in physics. We had been raised both of us to honor the traditions, so when I say 'introduced' I mean our parents presented us to each other as a future family. The introduction was to allow a period of acclimation before the wedding.

"But, that didn't matter to Lani or me. When we met... I know it's rare, but we fit. I thought she was exquisite, kind, generous. She thought, at least, said she thought I was—"

"Let's just jump to the find shall we?" Koning said, then dripping with sarcasm added, "You're married and you and your wife love each other." With a hand to her chest, she mocked him. "I'm touched, truly. Get to the part where you tell us why thieves and killers are hunting us."

Mantor yawned and nodded. Ricci studied her fingernails.

Mitsumi cleared his throat. "Sooner rather than later would be good, Aber." He didn't want to alienate Chandra more than necessary, but they needed answers.

"We had two children." Koning opened her mouth to object. Chandra lifted his hand forestalling her comment and continued with a determined tone before she could speak. "Two boys just two years apart and after our second, our doctor told us we wouldn't have anymore. We both had wanted a large family and not only to fulfill our repopulation duty. We both loved...love, children.

"So, when Pari was born four years later, we were thrilled.

Pari brought joy and light to us, like a miniature sun in our midst. She was perfect. She walked early, talked early, was so smart. The things that came out of her mouth astonished us. She scored off the charts in everything." Chandra stopped, his mouth upturned in a half smile, his eyes unfocused looking far away. Mantor snuffled in his sleep. Koning drummed her fingers on the table and cleared her throat.

"Last year, a year ago today in fact, just after Pari's tenth birthday, she was diagnosed with Karstov's."

Koning stopped drumming her fingers. That was a one in ten million diagnosis; only a thousand out of the federated worlds' twenty-five billion suffered from Karstov's syndrome at any one time. And suffer was the right word to describe Karstov's.

"She'd had issues before," Chandra said, "that's why we took her to the healers in the first place—generalized pain, difficulty swallowing, degrading coordination. We never expected..." Chandra hung his head. "The pain ramped up within days of her diagnosis. And nothing helped because Karstov's alters the chemistry of the nerve functions, including pain pathways, so standard pain blockers don't work. Without pain blockers the disease's full effect is transmitted to and processed in the brain."

Mitsumi had seen one late stage Karstov's patient writhing in agony, gasping that he was on fire in a never-ending conflagration. If they didn't kill themselves, Karstov's patients died within a few years from cardiac arrest, their hearts unable to cope with never-ending torture.

"Within a few months, she stopped attending school and spoke only a few halting words." Chandra raised his head and surveyed the group.

"Brill," Quest announced into the silence. Everyone looked at him. Chandra nodded.

"Yes, Brill. A week after Pari stopped attending school, a medical institute on Brill announced it had by pure chance developed a cure for Karstov's. Not ameliorating symptoms, not masking pain, but a cure."

"And?" Koning said.

"And it was expensive," Chandra said. "It wasn't the fault of the medical institute, they volunteered to perform the curing procedure without charge for anyone who could make their way to Brill, but the process requires rare elements not available on Brill."

"How expensive?" Ricci asked quietly.

Chandra's head drooped and he shrugged with resignation. "Does it matter? It was more than I or my family, or my extended family and our friends could afford in a lifetime."

"How expensive?" Ricci asked again.

Chandra shook his head. "A million credits." Silence descended on the group. Sundered's finds had so far netted him a little over a million credits. Chandra *was* betting on a find greater than Sundered's from this voyage.

Koning cleared her throat. "I uh, hate to do this but, how does your daughter's suffering factor into our predicament?"

Chandra's face fell in sorrow. When he spoke again it was with evident reluctance. "I graduated with middling grades from a common school on a backward planet. We had two children at the time and jobs were scarce." By this time, he was pleading for understanding. "What choice did I have?" He stopped again as if unable to force the words from his mouth. Quest came to his aid.

"You joined the Consortium," Quest said.

Chandra nodded. Koning groaned in dismay and slammed the table in front of her waking Mantor.

Mitsumi felt as if someone had slapped him hard in the face. Everything fell into place. "The quantum memory," Mitsumi said. "It belonged to...the Consortium?"

Chandra hung his head in acknowledgment.

"What's going on?" Mantor said, sleep heavy in his voice. "Do we know what happened?"

"You were a technology evaluator," Quest said.

Ricci looked at Quest in puzzlement. Chandra nodded.

"When the Consortium recovers items from First Civ worlds either by expeditions it sponsors or by ... other means," Mitsumi said in a voice heavy with fatigue, "it doesn't rely only on the market to determine the value of what they have. Instead it employs scientists like Aber to evaluate the finds' technological implications and worth." Mitsumi stood up from the table and sat in a chair facing the group.

"You stole from the Consortium?" Koning said her face contorted in fear and anger, any sympathy for Pari's plight a distant memory. "And they found you and followed you and now they're after us too?" She turned to Mitsumi. "Tell me again why we didn't give up Aber on the planet?"

"We didn't know," Quest said.

"Exactly," Koning growled. "That little worm held back vital information. If you don't want to space him, we should contact the Consortium, beg for mercy and offer up Aber and the device for our lives."

"But didn't you kill two of their crew?" Ricci said. "Won't they want revenge for that?"

"That might complicate the negotiations," Koning admitted. "Let's kill him and give them the body."

"No," Mantor said, stifling a yawn and stretching, "they'll want to torture him themselves—better to give him up alive." The rest of the group turned to Mantor at this unexpected comment. He shrugged. "It's what I'd want to do."

"I didn't steal the quantum memory," Chandra said. All eyes focused on him again. "Before my work, everyone saw what I now know is a quantum memory store as paper— useless pieces of First Civ detritus. They're not rare; you can pick one up on the market for a decicredit."

That was true. Mitsumi owned a couple of those pieces before he had to sell everything.

"So," Chandra said, "the Consortium allowed us to buy those pieces at a market price if we wanted. I bought the paper, the quantum memory, from the Consortium. I have the sales documents to prove it."

If Chandra owned the quantum memory, then the information on it was his, and he was the legitimate owner of their find. But something Chandra said at their first meeting bothered Mitsumi. "But you didn't buy it until after you'd figured out it was a memory device you could read, and after you discovered the information that 'memory device' held."

"So?" Chandra said defiance in his voice. "I made the discovery. I'm not obligated to tell them everything."

"A discovery," Mitsumi said, "you made using Consortium equipment while in the Consortium's employ. And wouldn't your employers have thought twice about selling you that 'paper' if you hadn't concealed your discovery from them?" He wasn't an advocate by any means, but even he understood that Chandra's ownership claim was tenuous.

His face set in a determined scowl, Chandra refused to look at the rest of the crew.

"What was on this memory device?" Mantor asked.

Mitsumi shrugged. "Coordinates for a dozen undiscovered First Civ worlds."

"And proof that the First Civ used the Underground," Chandra said.

Mantor perked up. "The Underground? I always thought it was a myth."

"Yeah," Ricci added, "a legend, like Terra—mystical planet of humanity's origin."

"No," Chandra said, "it's real."

"Right," Koning scoffed. "Let's go find one of the 'stations' then and hop on over to all the lost First Civ planets." With a mocking glare at Chandra, she raised her voice and opened her arms wide, "C'mon. What's the delay? Untold riches await."

Chandra glowered at Koning, but remained silent.

"Oh, right," Koning said, snapping her fingers. "The ancient alien transport system went poof with the First Civ's fall—disappeared without a trace."

"What was the proof?" Mantor said still intrigued.

With a sullen shake of his head, Chandra refused to answer.

"It was a video," Mitsumi said trying to bring an end to this meander so they could return to the subject at hand, "one that any decent vid specialist could render." Koning looked smug. *Except for the symbol*, he thought. *The same symbol on the plinth and on the planet in the sim when he'd picked up the Artifact.*

Ricci shook her head in bewilderment. "So, back to Aber's coordinates, if you have a legal claim to them, why is the Consortium after you?"

The others turned toward her, puzzled at her confusion. "Money," they said at once.

"The Consortium," Mitsumi said, "doesn't concern itself much with legality when money is in the equation. If they can steal our find or capture Aber before we sell it, they can dispose of the only rival claimant and keep the proceeds."

"So, what do we do?" Ricci asked.

"The way I see it, we have several options," Mitsumi said. "We can negotiate with the Consortium; see if we can pry any money from them for the box and for Aber." The look of despair on Chandra's face drove Mitsumi to add, "Or just for the box with Aber's relinquishment of any claim. We can continue our exploration and experiment with the box then sell whatever we find both in the box and in our explorations, split the money and go our way. Or we can just sell the box now. Anyone see another option?" Mitsumi surveyed his crew. No one spoke. He didn't prefer one option to another. Negotiations with the Consortium or selling the box wouldn't yield the credits necessary to fund his expedition, much less repay Corban and Jonta. But it would move him closer to his goal. Further exploration held out the possibility of a greater find, but might also be a time waster. "No? Then I propose we take a vote. Anyone in favor of the first option, negotiating with the Consortium?" No one spoke up.

"Okay," Mitsumi said, "we want to sell the box either now

or later. Who's in favor of selling it now?" Again, no one spoke. "Koning, calculate a course to the next world on our list. Tai, when you have the course, you may jump at your discretion. Aber," Aber swayed where he sat, Mitsumi had forgotten Chandra's injury, "put yourself in the auto doc. If we're letting you live, you might as well be healthy. You are dismissed."

"Uh, not quite, Captain," Mantor said. "I have to repair the jump drive."

"Oh," Mitsumi said, chagrined at having forgotten that vital detail. "At your discretion when Mantor has repaired the drive. Which will be?"

"Four hours ought to do it, Captain."

CHAPTER 9

The screens at the pilot's station glowed bright in the bridge's subdued lighting. The soft illumination reflected the artificial Federation standard night. Quest sat stiffly upright at his station, his head inclined to provide a view of the readouts. On the main screen, the next planet on their list floated, rotating with serene majesty beneath their orbiting ship. They'd identified it as a First Civ planet, but wouldn't start exploration until the next day.

The rest of the crew had retired to their staterooms, exhausted after the last eventful twenty-four hours, leaving Quest on duty. Ricci was his relief. Ship background noise was the only sound on the bridge as Ricci floated soundlessly through the hatch. At least she thought she had been soundless. As soon as she entered the bridge area, Quest unbuckled his restraints and floated away from the chair.

"How do you *do* that?" Ricci said with exasperation.

Quest rotated until he faced Ricci, then grabbed the back of the pilot's chair. He shrugged. "What?"

"I'm sure I didn't make a sound when I came on the bridge."

"Air currents," Quest said.

Ricci huffed. "You know, Tai, our conversations would be easier if you'd answer with more than one or two cryptic words. What do you mean air currents?"

Quest frowned in concentration. "When you entered the room, your presence altered the air circulation pattern on the bridge. I felt that."

Ricci smiled, pleased that for once she'd teased out a longer response; that was approaching the longest string of words she'd heard from him since they began their voyage. Maybe he was softening. She didn't know why, but she found the enigmatic chief pilot fascinating. She didn't have access to the personnel files and his reticence bordered on complete isolation, so she'd been working on prying more information out of him without success. "That wasn't hard, was it?" Ricci said. Quest looked puzzled.

Ricci drifted toward the pilot's chair. "Saying that many words at once," Ricci said. She grabbed the other side of the pilot's chair and floated upright, towering over the squat chief pilot. "I've never known anyone as observant as you. You know what's going on around you every second, don't you?"

Quest looked away and shrugged again. "I try."

Ricci sighed. "So do I, but it doesn't seem to do much good. Situational awareness, that's one reason you're a better pilot than I am."

With obvious effort, Quest allowed kindness to leak into his expression. "You're getting better."

"True," Ricci said, "but I still have a long way to go to be at your level."

"It just takes effort," Quest said, "and time."

This was new. Encouraged by his openness, she decided to dig a little deeper. "So, you're from Support right?" Quest raised his eyebrows in an unspoken question. Ricci chuckled. "I'm not entirely oblivious. Support is the highest gravity Federated World, so given your stature and your strength…"

Understanding replaced the question on his face. "Yes." Quest nodded. "I was raised on Support."

"So, what was that like? I never made it to the planet, but from what I've heard, the governing system is lax—almost nonexistent—you can pretty much do anything you want to. It sounds wonderful, but what was it like growing up there?"

Quest's eyes became hooded; he steeled himself as if

against a threat. Ricci instinctively swept the bridge looking for danger, but nothing was amiss.

"Hard," Quest said. "It was hard."

"What does that mean? Did something happen to you?"

Quest shook his head once and, with a flick of his powerful wrist, launched himself through the access hatch and off the bridge without another word. Ricci sighed, but her mouth quirked up in a half smile. That was progress at least. She strapped herself in. *Now*, she thought, *to make as much progress with my piloting skills by the end of the shift.*

Mantor locked his stateroom door, glanced at the storage lockers with his personal stuff, and licked his lips, his eyes riveted on them. He wrenched his gaze away, nudged himself from the door and drifted toward his work station. He'd completed the jump drive repairs and overseen the jump to their next destination without incident, now he needed shut eye, but he should write up what he'd accomplished with the in-atmosphere jump while it was fresh in his mind. That might also reduce the pull from the storage lockers so he could sleep.

When Mantor was fifteen, his enthusiasm for physics and math had thrilled his parents. They'd been less than pleased when he became associated with the Free Range Society. The FRS, inspired by the libertarian climate on Support, claimed emancipation from Wild's straightjacket legal system and imported from Support the latest fads and fashions. One of those had been Rapt.

Rapt combined an artificial dopamine with a particular sedative. The artificial dopamine stimulated receptors in the brain's pleasure center with none of the learning or memory side effects accompanying stimulated dopamine release. And because it was artificial it didn't interact with other neurotransmitters nor did its effects diminish with use.

Friends from the FRS had urged him to try it. They

claimed the drug offered the best of both worlds. He could party with the FRS, yet still continue to operate on a high intellectual level for his advanced courses in power engineering and HE drive physics.

His FRS buddies had explained that, unlike other drugs, Rapt produced no physical changes in the body related to addiction. Whatever compulsion a Rapt user experienced was purely psychological. Once Mantor had confirmed it with his own research, he was intrigued. The literature had warned that the Rapt experience was so powerful most users became instant addicts. He'd scoffed at that. No drug was sufficient to snare him with mere psychological effects. His will was more powerful than that. So, he'd given it a shot.

The sedative portion of the drug closed off other senses that might otherwise distract from the chemical ecstasy sluicing around the pleasure receptors. Think of sex, a good meal, laughter at a great joke, relaxing in the shade of a sparkling summer day, crossing the finish line first, but add to that reaching the summit after a hard climb, acing a test after weeks of study, winning the prize for best novel, best performance or best composition, all indistinguishable from the real thing.

Bundle them together, multiply by a hundred, and place it on your nightstand. The slightest disappointment, the smallest setback washed away in a tide of triumph and joy.

Mantor was hooked.

He assuaged his feelings of guilt by keeping his Rapt use always under tight control. Dosage didn't alter the nature of the trance—small or large produced the same euphoria—only the length of the trance. Mantor had never been a Needler, one of those who relied on intravenous fluid delivery systems to avoid dehydration in order to trance for days. He timed his doses with great care, ensuring he was always available when needed.

The regulators in charge of registering starship crews had come down hard on Rapt users after an engineer on the *"Oh Fire, What Now?"* was in trance when the oxygen regeneration system shut down and the crew couldn't revive their enraptured engineer until asphyxiation had almost taken them. Now mandatory testing was required on all starship crews. It wasn't fair to those like Mantor who always used "responsibly," but there it was.

Demonstrated Rapt use became cause for the user's immediate termination from a crew and banishment from service on any crew for two years. While banned, the individual had to present herself for monthly tests. After the new regulations, all starship crew were tested.

Mantor had figured out how to circumvent the testing with creative sleight of hand involving bodily fluids.

His former crew had never caught him in trance and he'd passed the regulators' tests, but they suspected him regardless and had dismissed him from his post and spread a rumor he was a Rapt addict. The baseless whisper campaign (well, the underlying accusation was true, but they didn't know that) had been enough to keep him off starships until this gig.

Strapping himself into his work station, Mantor tried to order his thoughts, only to have his lockers pull them apart as if they enclosed a thought magnet. He closed his eyes in concentration until he found himself unbuckling and drifting toward the locker. Without recalling the next steps, his mind cleared just as he finished loading the hypospray. Three hours —that was a safe bet. He was supposed to be asleep in his quarters after all. He forced his hand away from his neck and tried to open it and release the hypospray. *Who am I kidding*, he thought? He'd already decided. The hypospray was cool on his neck as he triggered the injection allowing bliss to sweep through him and pull him into the trance.

A view from the ship's internal cameras on the screen in front of her, Koning watched Mantor enter his quarters. The door slid shut behind him. Mouth turned down in a scowl, she shook her head and turned off the monitor. She was right. He couldn't be trusted no matter what the captain thought. She didn't know how he'd pulled that trick when he engineered the jump from the well. No matter that the others thought he was a brilliant engineer; they were wrong. He must have stumbled on that solution somewhere else and claimed it as his own. That was the only possible answer.

No one could play around with Rapt unaffected. She had spent years in a trash-strewn hovel trying to scrape something together to feed herself and her screaming little brother while her parents sprawled in a pool of urine on the floor, their gaunt, skeletal faces distorted in an obscene pleasure rictus. A soft chime brought her back to the present and alerted her that the training program she'd initiated had finished loading.

Restless, she hadn't been able to sleep, so she'd strapped into the chair in her room, cued up a training program, and worked the problems. She'd told herself that her blown jump calculations were no big deal, but the words rang hollow. Her performance so far was abysmal. And continued issues would invite unwanted questions.

Muscles bunched tight in her neck; she fought off a growing headache by losing herself in the training program. With each successful run, the pain in her head receded and her shoulders loosened. Time suspended and, when she next glanced at the display's chrono, she found more than an hour had passed. Cheeks puffing as she released a deep breath, she unbuckled from the seat and prepared for sleep. But away from the training runs' hypnotic routine, her muscles stiffened again as thoughts of being discovered crowded her mind.

She wouldn't let that happen. Her next runs in the real would be perfect—they had to be. Everything depended on it. Enveloped in sleep netting above her bed, she cut the lights— and floated with her eyes wide. *They were wrong. You're strong. You're capable. Look at what you've accomplished*, and repeating this mantra she eventually drifted off.

The box sat strapped in place on the table. Wires trailed from various sensors attached to the cube at different points. "You should have told me, Aber," Mitsumi said. Fresh out of the auto-doc, which had stitched up his shoulder and pumped him full of pain killers and antimicrobials, Chandra floated before a console where the wires from the box terminated. He stared at the console playing idly with his earring, ignoring Mitsumi.

"We could have been so much better prepared if we'd known what we were likely to face."

Chandra reached out and tapped the console, squinting at whatever results he'd come up with.

"You could've trusted *me* at least."

Chandra made further adjustments on the console. "Really?" he said staring at the console. "You're saying you would have gone with me knowing the Consortium might come after us, steal everything we found, and kill us in the process?"

Put that way, Mitsumi had to admit that, even with the tantalizing connection between the quantum memory fragment's depiction of the underground, the Artifact and his vision, he would not have joined Chandra.

"I didn't think so," Chandra said in response to Mitsumi's silence. Chandra tapped out instructions on the console. "Go get some sleep, Captain Mitsumi. You'll be busy the next few days exploring the planet."

Mitsumi contemplated Chandra for a moment, then left him to his work. Back in his quarters, Mitsumi prepared for sleep, but floated in darkness, his eyes wide open.

CHAPTER 10

Mitsumi headed to the bridge early the next "morning" before shift change. "Good morning—" An enormous yawn interrupted his greeting. He hoped the muzziness would go away after a few hours. "Mei."

Ricci turned in the pilot's chair. "Morning, Captain."

On the view screen, a planet rotated beneath the ship. The computer's assessment from the night before glowed on the bottom of the screen: "GV938572631:P3G-Positive for recent strikes."

"All quiet, I assume?"

"Everything's nominal." Ricci turned to face the main screen again.

Mitsumi strapped himself in to the command couch and perused his readouts to confirm Ricci's assessment.

"I was thinking, Captain."

"Hmmm," Mitsumi said, distracted by his status review.

"We should name the planets we explore."

"Uh huh," Mitsumi said, his eyes fixed still on a readout showing a minor glitch in the hydroponics water filtration system.

"We should call the first planet we visited Mitsumi."

"What?" The mention of his name brought his attention back to the bridge. He reviewed the conversation in his mind. "Sure, okay. We can take turns, but we're going to run out of crew members."

"I'm okay with that," Koning said drifting on to the

bridge. "But I vote we leave Aber out of the rotation."

"I guess I'm agnostic on that point," Mitsumi said, "but he *is* the reason we have any planets to name."

"He's the reason we almost died and have thieves and cutthroats waiting for us when we get back to civilization," Koning said, heat building in her voice.

"Morning, Tai," Ricci said as Quest appeared from the access hatch. "We've decided to name the planets we visit. We should name the first planet 'Mitsumi'. What do you think?"

"That's acceptable," Quest said.

"So, when are we going to explore 'Koning'" Koning said, with a smirk nodding at the planet on the screen.

Ricci looked at Mitsumi, clearly wondering whether Koning's appropriation would meet with any resistance. "As soon as the shuttle's ready and we have a place to start. Sentaa, you have ideas about how we should explore these planets? Please put together a search pattern for us."

Koning's face registered disappointment and mild distaste before she turned away. Mitsumi activated the com. "Viram, is the shuttle ready for launch?" Silence. "Viram?"

"Uh, here, Captain," Mantor said after a pause, his voice scratchy and slurred.

With a disgusted look, Koning shook her head. Mitsumi ignored her. Koning may have slept long and well last night, but he understood how Viram felt. "Is the shuttle ready for launch?" Mitsumi said.

Another pause. "Yeah, so I just need a few minutes, say ten, to make sure the injectors are still in alignment on the fusion drive then you're good."

"Sentaa, will you have a pattern for us by then?"

"I'm finishing up right now," Koning said.

"Okay, Tai, you'll pilot, Sentaa will come with us. Mei, this should be routine. Please set monitoring alarms and catch some shuteye."

Ricci looked like she was about to object, but her mouth caught open in a yawn and she nodded in acknowledgement.

"There's plenty of time. You'll have your turn," Mitsumi said.

"Aber?" Quest said.

Mitsumi looked around, addressing his response to Quest and the others on the bridge. "Mr. Chandra has decided his time and attention are best directed to examining the box we recovered. He will not be joining us on the surface in the near future."

A few weeks later, the crew minus Chandra gathered in the mess. They were under acceleration to a comfortable jump distance. On the table, the haul from "Koning," the latest planet they'd visited, lay spread out—five objects alongside a bag of "paper"—what they now recognized were quantum memory foils. The Consortium hadn't appeared, but the crew had been on edge the entire visit. Everyone would breathe a little easier once they had jumped away.

"Is that good?" Ricci said gesturing at the objects. "I mean, is that a typical haul from a First Civ world?"

"Sure," Koning said. "That's what you can usually expect. The value depends on whether we can figure out what the devices in that pile do, or if we can recover useful data from the memory foil."

Ricci nodded.

"And you know this how?" Quest said.

Koning glowered at Quest. "I've been on plenty of expeditions to First Civ worlds."

"How many is plenty?" Quest said.

"That's enough," Mitsumi said before Koning could respond. Quest had a point, but pursuing it would do nothing. "From what I have read of the expeditions, Sentaa is correct. We have only a two-week window for exploration on each planet. We mustn't expect to come close to replicating our find on…Mitsumi on any of the other planets."

"Does that mean we need to involve Aber?" Ricci asked.

Koning's face clouded. Quest narrowed his eyes. Pointing at the devices on the table, Ricci said, "We have to figure out if anything in that lot is valuable. That was Aber's job for the Consortium, wasn't it?"

Mantor's head jerked up from the table. "How much do we trust Aber?" Mitsumi thought he'd been asleep. "Suppose one of these things is worth a fortune, would he tell us?"

Koning nodded in agreement. Even Quest appeared to think Mantor had a point. Mitsumi thought they were being unfair. Over the past two weeks Mitsumi had concluded that in Chandra's mind withholding information had been the only way to assemble this voyage, but Chandra's avoiding contact with the others hadn't helped his case.

"I don't see we have much choice," Mitsumi said. "I know that's not the greatest answer, but we should allow him to make a preliminary assessment because he's the most qualified. We'll just have to make sure he doesn't come to any 'independent' arrangements when we return to the Federated Worlds."

Koning appeared skeptical, but Ricci and Mantor seemed mollified.

"I'll deliver these to Chandra for assessment. Sentaa, please calculate our next jump, we'll be in position in an hour and a half, then we'll jump to...Ricci?" Color rose in Ricci's cheeks, her lips quirked up in a half smile and she ducked her head.

"Congratulations, Mei," Koning said rising to her feet, "you're immortal."

On the bridge, Koning rechecked the calculations she'd been working on for more than a week. She shot the vector information to the pilot's station. Quest reviewed the results and based on her numbers, set up the jump. She produced the direction, speed, and length of the jump; the pilot initiated the rotation into jump space along the required direction and maintained the calculated speed for the dictated time. Quest had shown his piloting mastery in their first jump—he had hit the vector she had provided to perfection. Her vector calculation, however, had been abysmal.

"Vector received and set," Quest said.

"At your discretion, Tai," Mitsumi said.

On the screen, gray jump space replaced stars. The time in jump space depended on the length of the jump. This one would last several hours. *Three hours, twenty-seven minutes and thirteen point five seven seconds*, Koning thought to herself. She unbuckled and floated away from her couch. With an affected nonchalance she didn't feel, she launched herself toward the entrance hatch.

"I'm getting something to eat," she said.

She wasn't hungry, but waiting for the results of her efforts was unbearable. She didn't know why training runs differed so from the real thing. In the courses she'd taken, her instructors had emphasized the gap between simulated training runs and real-world experience and hence the need for serving as a trainee before attempting certification runs. But the only trainees being hired were those who had graduated from a handful of expensive schools, a fact no one had mentioned when they were taking her credits for the remote course she had purchased.

She'd thought their concerns overblown, her opinion bolstered by having dropped fifteen hundred credits on a course that might be worthless. She was uniformly perfect on her simulated training runs, so she'd had no qualms purchasing a certification on the black market. But her first two attempts (three if you counted the disastrous miscalculations on the Nova run) in the real world had missed badly. By the end of this voyage, she'd be competent, she was sure of it. Mitsumi and the others might be irritated at her having embroidered the truth a touch, but it wasn't any worse than what the others were hiding—Mantor with his "secret"

Rapt addiction, or Mei Ricci who was obviously hiding her own past. Ricci claimed to be from Neopa, but Ricci had avoided any conversation concerning their supposedly shared home planet. And Quest, who knew what pathologies lay hidden under that kilometer-thick crust of cold indifference?

As she floated into the mess, Koning pulled herself to a dead stop at the sight of Mantor strapped at the table slurping away at something out of a pouch, concentrating on his assistant lying on the table. Koning turned to leave, hoping she had made no noise.

"Hey, Sentaa," Mantor said. "Come join me."

She turned back to Mantor. "Hi, Viram." Koning considered making an excuse and leaving, but she couldn't afford to sever all ties with any member of the crew when they could be cramped together for a year. "Sure." Koning grabbed a snack stick and a juice bulb and strapped in across from Mantor.

"So," Mantor said with a smile, eyes sparkling with excitement, "what do you think of our little trip so far? Pretty thrilling, huh?"

"I didn't think I was signing on to risk my life. It makes me wish I'd turned it down, taken another offer."

Mantor looked at her quizzically and shook his head. "I don't think you could have landed another berth."

"Why would you say that?" Koning said, wondering where this was going. "There's lots of opportunity out there for a Certified Astrogator Communications Specialist."

"Sure," Mantor shrugged and returned his attention to his assistant, "but your certificate's a black market fake."

Koning froze in the middle of chewing on her snack stick. How did he know that? Pasting a smile on her face, she laughed —a high wild sound that screamed nervousness even to her.

"Right." She pulled out her assistant. "The captain saw it. I'll show it to you."

Mantor shook his head at the sight of Koning punching up something on her assistant. "Hey, it's okay. I'm sure the captain knows and is good with it, otherwise you wouldn't still be here."

Koning stopped tapping and stared at Mantor. He returned her look with a relaxed smile. "What makes you think…?" Koning's voice trailed off. She couldn't bring herself to complete the sentence. Mantor understood though.

"No one with a valid certificate misses jump vectors by *that* much. I mean," Mantor chuckled, "over seventy light minutes?" He returned his attention to his assistant.

Koning closed her eyes in mortification. Mantor knew. The captain knew. They'd known from the first. "Who else knows?" Koning said, her voice quavering.

"Everyone," Mantor said with a flip of his hand, his head still lowered. "Well." Mantor lifted his head. "Maybe not Mei, she seems pretty oblivious at times."

Koning's thoughts were in turmoil. With a mumbled excuse, Koning left the mess and headed to her quarters. Locked in her quarters, Koning floated in the room's center, her eyes closed against voices from the past. Eight years she'd been gone, eight years she'd fought the messages hammered into her brain, sought therapists, struggled to prove herself and still the lessons of her childhood echoed. *You're a stupid, worthless, piece of dung, good for nothing but eating our food.*

Determined to fight back the haunting scorn, Koning tried the therapists' exercises and reviewed her accomplishments: I passed the Astrogator pre reqs. I passed the Astrogator course. I've mastered the Astrogator testing. *You couldn't get a certificate,* the voices countered. *You blew your first three calculations so bad everyone knew you were a fake. They laughed at you.*

Teeth clenched, Koning repeated her mantra of accomplishments forcing the voices into retreat.

With fizzing nerves, Koning waited until just before they were to exit the jump. With thirty seconds left, she drifted onto the bridge and strapped herself in at her station, avoiding Mitsumi's gaze. She would have stayed away, but she had to be there to calculate another jump in the event her performance was substandard—again.

The countdown to transition flashed to zero. She glanced at the screen and her heart sank. The target was more star than sun. Turning back to her station, she calculated their distance from the star—sixty-five light minutes. Her cheeks burned, and she felt the voices hovering on the edge of her consciousness. As she calculated a nearer approach jump, her hands shook too much for her to continue. With a deep breath, she forced the tremors away. After she resumed calculating the jump, she waited for a comment from Mitsumi or Quest. In silence, she finished her calculation. "Vector calculated and transferred to the helm," she said.

"Vector received and plotted," Quest said.

"Execute," Mitsumi said.

Mitsumi requested access, without receiving a response. He tried again with the same result. After an unsuccessful third attempt, he used his override codes and opened the door to Chandra's quarters. At the sound of the door opening, Chandra looked up sharply. He had strapped himself into a chair at a table, the First Civ box secured on the table before him with various devices attached to it. "By all means, Captain, please come in," Chandra said.

"We need to talk."

"So I gathered—a need which apparently trumps any desire on my part."

Mitsumi advanced into the cabin; the door slid shut behind him. "We've arrived at Ricci."

"I'm aware of that." Chandra returned his attention to a device attached to the box.

"Have you examined the materials we recovered on Koning?"

Chandra sighed in exasperation. "I have had them less

than a day. As you can see, I'm otherwise occupied at the moment." Chandra continued to peer at the device, tapping the occasional note into his assistant.

"You should come back," Mitsumi said.

"What does that mean? I haven't gone anywhere."

"Back, out of your cabin, with everyone else. Be part of the crew again."

Chandra tapped at his assistant a moment more. He turned and examined Mitsumi. "That would be the crew who wanted to kill me? The one that locked me in my cabin and threatened to keep me there for the rest of the voyage—that crew?"

Mitsumi held Chandra's eyes for a few seconds then looked away.

"We may have...overreacted," Mitsumi said. "But in our place, what would you have done? We thought we had embarked on a voyage of discovery with the possibility of becoming rich along the way. At most we would lose only a few months of our lives, not die. We would never have agreed had we known what was at stake."

Chandra had returned his attention to the box, toying with his earring, while Mitsumi spoke.

"I persuaded the crew to let you leave your quarters. You know that wasn't easy. Why do you stay?"

Chandra continued, examining the box for what seemed a half hour, but was only a minute.

"I suppose I feel responsible," Chandra said with a sigh. "I had convinced myself not only that my claim was legitimate, but that the Consortium would recognize it and allow me to leave without retribution. That was the part of me that thought the money to cure Pari was more important than my life. At another, deeply buried, level, I was aware of what I was risking. But again, the risk to me was meaningless as long as it led to a chance to cure Pari. You and the crew were a means to reach my goal. If I thought of the consequences my actions might have for you, it was only whether those consequences would stop me from succeeding. I admit my self-interest overrode my judgment and put you and the rest of the crew in danger."

Mitsumi nodded as Chandra spoke, waiting for the apology. When none came, Mitsumi sighed, but his expectations were undoubtedly too high. At least he was willing to acknowledge fault. And to be honest with himself, if his son or his sister Saeko were in screaming agony descending to an excruciating death and a possible cure appeared, well, he'd move stars for the cure no matter who it hurt. "But what about your wife and other children? Is what happens to you unimportant to them?"

Chandra turned again and fixed his eyes on Mitsumi. "Why do you want me to reconnect with the crew?"

"If you stay in here, detached and uncommunicative, you'll become an abstraction. It's much easier to be harsh to an abstraction than with a real living, breathing human being. Right now the crew hopes you'll come up with something to enhance the box's value or identify something in our finds that improves our bargaining position when we sell them. That hope outweighs their desire to see you punished. If you become less real to them it changes the balance, and you may lose your life and your chance to help Pari."

Chandra nodded, accepting Mitsumi's analysis. "Okay, I can see that, but why do you care what becomes of me? I put you in the same peril as the rest of the crew."

And that, Mitsumi thought, was a good question. One for which he didn't have a great answer. He pictured Cala and Riga's disdain at their last meeting, and their vows to ruin his professional life. He saw again the disappointment when he'd informed Jonta and Corban of his failure and their condescending pity when he vowed to repay them. And stretching back to his childhood, jeers and taunting from most of his friends over his aspiration to roam the galaxy echoed down the years. "Let's just say I have reasons to sympathize with an underdog."

Koning adjusted the temperature control on her environmental suit. With exertion from climbing the hill and the rising sun, sweat overwhelmed her suit's capacity and trickled down her face, stinging into the corner of her eye. Rapid blinking was no substitute for taking off her helmet and smearing the irritation away, but discomfort trumped death, so she kept blinking. It was just another day in paradise. She swiveled looking back the way she had come, noted Ricci's progress, then turned to survey the horizon. From here the crater rims marched off into a series of mountains descending in height. Typical of First Civ worlds without human survivors, the only visible multicellular life were small plants. Here, they reminded Koning of a small Neopan shrub, only even tinier, with orange "leaves" that looked like corkscrews. She supposed animals might be around somewhere, but so far none had appeared.

Under the titanic forces unleashed when the Horde flung iron asteroids at the planet at a few percent of light speed, the impacts had broken up and ejected great chunks of the planet's crust. They dotted the mountainsides. With scant water in the biosphere, only the thin keening wind weathered surface features, so the ejecta were rough, jagged intrusions on the slopes. It was a miracle that anything recognizable as a ruin had survived.

They had put down near the crest of one of the larger impact craters and had split up from there to investigate what appeared to be ruins. Mitsumi and Chandra had descended farther into the crater toward one set; she and Ricci had headed to the other just beyond the crest.

Ricci struggled the remaining few yards to the crest and stood beside Koning, breathing hard. Ricci's inability to keep up nagged at Koning. Supposedly, both of them being from Neopa were unused to the planet's higher gravity, but Ricci had a much harder time adapting than Koning did, further cementing her conclusion that Neopa was not Ricci's home planet.

Koning tapped Ricci's arm and signaled to her to switch from the general broadcast band to another channel. Ricci frowned, but made the switch. Heavy breathing sounded in Koning's ears.

"Pretty hard climb, huh?" Koning said.

Ricci nodded.

"Reminds me a little of climbing up to the Norat plateau. Does it to you?"

Ricci's breathing had subsided somewhat. She shrugged. "Yeah, I guess it does a bit."

"Yeah, you've got that last push up the switchbacks in that nearly vertical wall."

"Mmmhmm."

"And then that little snack shack at the top of the climb. I've never tasted better Petrocals in my entire life. How about you?"

Ricci shrugged again, shifted her feet and gazed out toward the horizon.

"C'mon," Koning said. "You're telling me you didn't buy a treat up there? After that hike?"

"I...I don't remember. That whole experience is fuzzy."

Koning narrowed her eyes in skepticism. That hike, required of every Neopan child to visit the founding settlement, the point from which human life spread over the planet after the bombardment bringing down the Great Dark, embedded itself in each Neopan child's memory. The difficult hike, followed by the visit to the Neopan ark, the caves where humanity's ragged remnant huddled in the immediate aftermath of the asteroid bombardment, made a huge impression.

"Well, that's understandable, we were only twelve at the time." Ricci nodded. "Unless you were from the Olan district. I'm pretty sure their practice was to hike in the fifth form when they were ten." Koning gazed at Ricci, who continued studying the horizon avoiding eye contact. "Where did you say you were from again?"

"I grew up on the southern continent."

"That's right, in the Linton district. You know, I had a cousin from down there. He used to rave over the snow sports in the mountains."

"We should be on our way, Sentaa." Ricci moved toward the route off the ridge they had identified from orbit.

"Did you ever do one of the winter slides? My cousin said they were amazing."

"I never had the chance to. I was busy with school and later with work. Besides, the idea never attracted me much."

"Well, how could it? Linton has no mountains and no snow sports." She scooted in front of Ricci and pointed at her. "You're not from Neopa, are you?"

Without responding, Ricci pushed past Koning. They continued hiking off the ridge, navigating between boulders. After a few minutes, Ricci spoke. "I chose Neopa because of its low gravity and scant population. Neopa could explain my height and the odds of running into anyone from there were small. It's just my luck you showed up."

After a moment's thought, Koning declared, "Ton," not making it a question.

"Not difficult to figure out is it? The lowest gravity among the Federated Worlds. Yeah, I'm from Ton and had an Adapter shave a few centimeters from my height."

"Why the subterfuge? What are you running from?"

"Will you help me keep my secret?"

Koning shrugged, though the gesture was invisible to Ricci. "How will I know that until you've told me what it is?"

"It's nothing to anyone but me…and my family." Ricci paused. "And my planet."

"No delusions of grandeur there," Koning muttered.

They arrived at the ruins. Buildings, a few collapsed by falling ejecta from the strike that had formed the crater, others by the strike's seismic upheaval, were laid out in a pattern along what might have been streets. Nothing in the immediate vicinity appeared capable of housing valuable tech. Ricci gestured toward a structure a few hundred yards away that wasn't completely flat. "Maybe over there?"

Koning grunted assent as Ricci moved off in that direction.

"So," Koning said, "your story?"

"You know Ton is different from the other Federated Worlds?"

"You mean the whole matriarchal thing?"

"Yeah, that. Our ruling class is exclusively female. I was born into a family that controls a large commercial empire. My real family name isn't Ricci—it's Burthen."

Koning gave a low whistle impressed despite herself. "As in Burthen Electronics?"

"And Burthen Genetics, Burthen Engine Systems, etcetera. That Burthen."

Koning ran through her interactions with Ricci. Koning had always imagined a person from such wealth and privilege would stand out like a rescue beacon, her condescension toward and disdain for the little people broadcasting her prosperous background to the world. She had seen none of that in Ricci.

"You're a Burthen, heir to one of the largest commercial industrial empires in the Federated worlds, but here you are..."

"A second-rate pilot on a ramshackle starship risking my life to hunt First Civ treasure. Crazy, right?"

"Crazy isn't extreme enough. In fact, I am at a loss for words to express how insane that sounds."

Ricci sighed. "I know. That's why I had to change my name, my appearance, and disappear. From when I was a little girl, I wanted adventure. I wanted the stars, not the way I traveled with my family, but exploring, finding new worlds, hunting treasure. That life—that's the life I wanted. But for a Burthen that life is out of bounds. As members of the family, we are expected to assume the roles we are assigned for the good of the family. The family circumscribes our freedom in exchange for almost unlimited wealth and power.

"Done," Koning said. "On behalf of little people everywhere I say—give me that deal. Because we're poor our 'freedom of action,' as you call it, is pretty damned small, and I can't believe yours was all that limited."

"Sure," Ricci said. "I understand. Like I said, I'm crazy, right? I was the designated politician. So my education, my friends, my social life were designed to achieve that end. After graduation, Mother apprenticed me to one of the most powerful politicians on the planet. I gave that up because the desire for wealth and power forges chains. If you're not interested in either, the field is open; you can do anything and have sufficient to live."

Ricci's attitude was typical of the wealthy. Koning's own experience in a household where material things, food for example, were in short supply, led her to extreme skepticism at opinions such as Ricci's. "Whatever, I'd sure like the chance to try out your theory. I don't suppose you could steer some of that wealth my way for a little test? Just in the interest of science you understand."

Ricci chuckled. "Not even if you were serious."

"Oh, I'm serious."

"Besides," Ricci continued, ignoring Koning's comment, "as you might have noticed, I'm not a good fit for the life my family had in store for me. I'm too..." She waved her hands back and forth.

"Normal?" Koning said. "Not sufficiently arrogant, condescending, and entitled?" The reason Koning hadn't been able to guess at Ricci's background were the same reasons Koning even now couldn't picture Ricci exercising power over others.

Ricci sighed. "That about covers it." She kicked at a rock that went skittering down the slope in front of them. "So over three years, I siphoned off a few credits of that fabulous wealth, bought another identity, surreptitiously studied to be a pilot, purchased a certification in my new name, and pffft," she expanded her hands in magician's gesture showing they held nothing, "disappeared."

With a shake of her head, Koning marveled at Ricci's idiocy. Everything Koning had ever dreamed of, everything she'd scraped and sacrificed for Ricci had a million times over at her whim and she left it. "Stupid," Koning said. Ricci nodded. "Imbecilic, moronic, doltish, brainless—"

Ricci slapped a hand on Koning's helmet. "I take your point, Sentaa. You think my actions were inadvisable."

Koning barked a laugh. "That's one word for it, but I was trying to find a more fitting word. Nothing seemed quite strong enough."

They walked in silence for a moment. "Anyway, I booked a ticket off planet under my new name and headed for Support. I took enough credits to keep me alive until I found a posting. My funds had run out when I saw Mitsumi's notice."

"And even after being chased, shot at, and almost dying because an arrogant engineer thinks he can do no wrong, you've never considered going back?"

Ricci stopped and turned toward Koning hands outstretched, pleading. "Sentaa, you can't tell the others. Please promise me you won't. My family has no idea where I am and they mustn't find out. I won't go back to that life. Promise me you won't tell."

Puzzled, Koning looked toward the hazy horizon. She didn't understand. What was so awful about doing something not quite to your liking in exchange for the riches Burthens controlled? That was Koning's universe except the price was more than distasteful and the reward a pittance. She turned back to Ricci who stood body tense, face contorted with worry waiting for Koning's response. "I don't get it. Sure, what they want you to do may be uncomfortable, and you can't live your dream, but, fire, Mei, welcome to the human race."

Ricci took a step toward her, closed her eyes for a

moment, swallowed hard, then opened her eyes again. Each word pronounced with emphasis, she said, "Please promise me you won't tell."

Ricci's obvious desperation made no sense. "So, tell them yourself. Won't they leave you alone if you renounce any claim on them and insist on going your own way? What're they going to do, kidnap you and force you to be a politician against your will?"

Eyes wide with fear, Ricci clutched Koning's arms and stared at her. Ricci's rapid breathing sounded clearly over the com. "You don't know... They have...devices, techniques, ways you've never heard of. Please, promise me you won't tell anyone."

With effort, Koning wrenched first one arm then the other from Ricci's grasp and stepped back. Now she thought about it, Koning vaguely recalled something on the news-nets about a missing person, an important person. Was there a reward attached? If the Burthens wanted Ricci back, the reward could be substantial. Koning rubbed her arms. Ricci's grip had been painful even through her environmental suit. She considered Ricci. Desperation still burned in her eyes. Hands clenched into fists, she'd taken a step toward Koning.

"Fine," Koning said. "I promise."

The site turned out to be worthless, as did the others they visited during their two weeks exploring Planet Ricci. Koning had been paired with a quiet, tentative Ricci on several exploratory trips. Neither of them brought up their conversation again, and Koning wondered if it had happened at all.

Back on board *Are We There Yet?*, Koning sat in her quarters with her assistant and called up her cache of news-net stories. She told herself at the time it was idle curiosity.

Stories concerning the missing Burthen heiress always

mentioned the sizeable reward for information on her whereabouts. Koning's attention reverted again and again to the reward. This trip so far was a bust. She'd known a big find was improbable, but still... Now, staring from her screen was a way to make the trip pay handsomely. With that money, she could buy a place on Fit and only take the jobs she wanted. Maybe find someone to settle down with. And reunite the rich girl with her family and her opulent life. Whatever Ricci feared must be in her imagination. *Yeah*, she thought, *this is best for everyone*. She found the message drone menu and started composing.

Ricci stared at the uniform gray of jump space lost in its unreal depths and unaware of Quest's entrance onto the bridge. She started when he cleared his throat.

Quest floated next to the pilot's chair. "Didn't mean to startle you," he said.

"No, no. Tai, I was just thinking."

Quest nodded. "First time nerves, pretty common."

"Yeah." Ricci gave a tentative smile. "I guess that's it." Captain Mitsumi had allowed her to pilot this jump, and she *did* worry over her performance, even though she performed well in simulations and unlike astrogation, piloting simulations predicted real life performance well.

Ricci unbuckled and floated away from the pilot's couch. This was a long jump and her shift ended before the jump did. She and Quest were alone on the bridge for now. Captain Mitsumi and Koning would show up right before the jump ended. Chandra might also appear. He'd been trying of late to integrate with the crew.

Quest dragged himself into the pilot's couch and strapped in before the console. Rather than leaving the bridge right away, Ricci fidgeted with her hands, not understanding her discomfort. She should rest, but was sure that in her quarters she'd only stare at the walls.

On her way off the bridge, she stopped at astrogation peering unseeing at the unfamiliar readouts.

Quest gave Ricci a sidelong glance and returned his attention to the main screen.

"I wasn't born on Support," Quest said without preamble.

Ricci's head came up, and she turned to Quest. "What?" Ricci hadn't expected Quest to speak.

Without shifting his eyes from the pilot's readouts, Quest continued. "I wasn't born on Support. You asked where I was from and I told you I was raised on Support, but I wasn't born there."

Ricci now recalled the conversation. It had been over a month ago. On a few occasions at shift change, Ricci had attempted to explore the subject without success and after a while had stopped trying.

"Where were you born?"

Quest sat eyes fixed on the main screen's featureless gray until Ricci had decided he wouldn't answer.

"I don't know."

Ricci frowned. That made no sense. "Your parents didn't tell you?"

Another long pause. "I don't know who my parents are."

Eyebrows raised, Ricci moved toward the screen to see his face. "But every Federated World has open adoption record laws."

"I wasn't adopted."

"Who raised you then?"

"I was a wild child."

Ricci pushed off and stopped herself between Quest and the screen, trying to catch Quest's eye. Quest didn't meet her gaze. She'd heard the name before, but she associated the memory with crazy rumors and outrageous conspiracy theories. "But they don't exist. They're just stories."

"I have no recollection of parents or siblings. My earliest memory is begging on the street. I must have been about three years old."

"In the stories I heard, the children were taken from their parents."

Quest nodded acknowledgement. "I saw it done, later, when I was older."

"Who took them and why? If you wanted them alive, you'd have to take care of them and if you wanted them dead, you could kill them rather than take them."

"Support has almost no government."

"So I've heard."

"But there is a faction that believes even what exists is too much." Quest fell silent again.

Ricci considered that for a moment trying and failing to work out what it had to do with Quest's upbringing. "I don't see —"

"Forty years ago, that faction embarked on a project to form a society with no rules. Their first attempts failed because it turns out that a 'society' requires a principle around which it is organized, even if that principle is that there are no principles. But they didn't see it that way. In their minds, the failure stemmed from participants' contamination by exposure to conventional thought. The only way around that obstacle was to stock the society with blank slates."

"Children," Ricci said beginning to understand.

"The blankest slates," Quest agreed. "But the conventional route for producing children was too slow, so the founders took what they needed from across the Federated Worlds. I was part of that experiment."

Quest's description intrigued Ricci. How would that have been—raised with no constraints, free to be who and what you wanted to be? "No rules, no expectations, that sounds wonderful," Ricci said wistfully.

Quest flicked his eyes at her and pursed his lips. "I just told you I was begging in the streets at three years old. You think that was wonderful?"

Ricci's cheeks burned; she hadn't been thinking. "Well,

not the begging part, of course, but the rest…" Ricci shrugged. She couldn't imagine how magnificent the freedom Quest hinted at would be. "It couldn't have been too bad. You're here, an excellent pilot on a thrilling voyage of discovery."

"Like everyone else, you only hear what you want to. You have not the slightest concept of the price I've paid."

He was right of course. She didn't know. She knew only that in contrast to her own, his life was appealing. "What was the price?"

But Quest only shook his head. Ricci waited in silence for Quest to answer. When it became clear the conversation was over, Ricci moved past Quest patting him on his shoulder. "Good night, Tai," she said. "I'm glad you escaped and made it here with us."

Alone now, staring at jump space, Tai examined the memories his conversation with Ricci had stirred up. It always struck him as odd that an organization bent on constructing a society without rules would have as one of its rules the inability to leave that society. But among the wild children it had been enforced with lethal enthusiasm.

Ricci had shown interest in his upbringing, so he'd tried to open up, but beyond outlining the basics, he'd found he couldn't. Even after fifteen years the memories were too painful. When you were a child, not having rules meant you were at the adults' mercy because the truth was that the strong indulged their desires and the weak suffered. He'd been fortunate for a few years—one of the stronger women protected him, the sole price being she took everything he had gathered through begging or odd jobs. Until another wild child killed her.

Then, different groups passed him around, traded him like any other commodity and, like a commodity, anyone stronger than he used him to satisfy whatever whim passed through his or her head. Forced to obey the most powerful —beaten if he refused, tagged with a subcutaneous tracker and threatened with a painful death if he deserted, Quest submitted to the will of the mighty and vowed to be on top.

One day he stumbled into a part-time gig for a small manufacturer. The head of the concern took an interest in him. At first his employer had wanted to give him an instruction suite and access to basic education courses. Quest had persuaded him with an outlandish story he'd made up to let him access the courses from his workplace because, if he'd shown up at the nest—what the wild children called their "home"—with an instruction suite, a stronger child or a group of them would only have confiscated it.

Quest devoured every course he could find and moved up in his employer's business. Because of his increased compensation, he became more valuable in the collective. A particularly brutal clique acquired him. They looked askance at Quest's increasing knowledge and skills, but coveted the extra income. Among the subjects Quest studied were various arts of self-defense. He began training and improving his body.

Although he didn't know his age or birthday, he guessed he was sixteen years old when it happened. He wasn't ready. His desire to become the most powerful had shifted over the last few years to a craving just to be left alone, to be rid of the mess that had been his life to that point. Bit by bit he'd planned and assembled resources for his escape. Tai Quest was his new identity. Barthic, his wild child name, would disappear.

When the time came, he had access to a ground vehicle but only a few credits stashed away and no solid scheme for ridding himself of his tracker—he wasn't even positive where it had been implanted. A temporary measure he'd developed would in theory block the tracker signal. It was still untested though—any gap in his location information would have given his game away.

On that day, he returned to the nest in the evening. It had grown dark while he stayed at work to complete a course,

143

and windblown trash whisked through pools of light from the occasional street lamp. In the humid breeze the smell of rotting food, old vomit, and fresh urine told him he had almost arrived. As he approached the blind alley that led to the nest's entrance, an eerie silence drew his attention from the evening's lessons to the present. Night or day, shrieks of delight, screams of pain, raucous play, and even louder music from the nest echoed in the alley. At the alley's mouth, he peered along its length. Nothing appeared in the dim reflected light from the street. In the windows set high on the side of the abandoned building where they made their nest, Quest glimpsed four heads ducking below the window. At the closer end of the alley two shadowed doorways concealed anyone who might be standing in them.

Spurred on by the silence and the dark, he walked past the entrance to the alley.

"Hey, Barthic." It was Holbart, one of his clique's oldest members, who had been sniffing around asking questions about Barthic's preparations to leave. Brutal and obsessed more than most with keeping the wild children together, Holbart had been the rumored force behind the disappearance of wild children suspected of preparing to desert the group. "We need to talk."

"Talk" he was pretty sure was not high on Holbart's agenda. Something he had done must have given away his plans. It was too soon. He wasn't ready, but he had no choice. In a flash, he thrust a hand into his pocket, activated the jammer, and sprinted down the street juking right and left. Flechette launchers hummed and dust exploded from the buildings on either side of the street. Foot planted hard, he cut down another alley and burst through a door he had previously marked as never being locked.

Behind the door, a hallway led to a set of stairs. He slammed the door shut and jammed several wedges of metal he had squirreled away just for this purpose between the door and the frame and raced to the stairs, then up to the roof.

On the roof, he followed a path he'd scouted earlier back to the manufacturing facility where he worked and let himself in to the now empty building. With killers hot on his trail, what had been vague plans for removing the tracker now came into focus. As he stood in the darkened facility breathing hard from his narrow escape, his mouth lifted in a smile. He was almost free. Not fully prepared, but prepared enough, his new life was only minutes away. Now if only the next step went as smoothly as the first.

Quest pulled out his assistant and called up a light. Shadows from the factory's equipment loomed high on the walls darting as he hustled across the factory floor, approaching the quality scanner. This device used penetrating radiation to detect flaws in products. It was not made for human use and, in fact, one task he had set himself for the near future was investigating the effect the device would have on a living human. A concern he could no longer afford. He had to find the tracker and remove it. Fortunately, he had convinced his employer to let him use the scanner and become familiar with its operation.

As he switched on the device, Quest extinguished the light from his assistant. He set the scanner to take a series of exposures at ten-second intervals while he placed various parts of his body in front of the scanner, doing his best to track the order in which he proceeded. Even at its widest setting, the scanning window was narrow. With the results up on the screen, he reviewed them, breathing deeply to calm his building nerves. Not having the chance to try out the scanner on living tissue, he didn't know how to decide if he found what he was looking for. After a few minutes, he was pretty sure the clear images were bones, but couldn't identify the shadows. In his mind, his pursuers, guns in hand, sprinted toward the building. Time was ticking down. Finished with the last image, he slammed his fist on the scanner in frustration. Nothing he'd seen looked like the tracker. He had assumed it would be easy to spot.

Turning from the scanner, he paced the floor shaking his hands, almost hyperventilating. As agitated as he was, he might have missed the tracker, even it had been right in his face. He had to calm down. In mid stride, he stopped, closed his eyes, and pulled up in his mind's eye a beautiful younger woman. His parents were unknown to him, but over the years he'd formed this picture from people he'd met and decided it was his mother. In his imagination, she still missed him, still searched for him and would never stop. After a moment, his heart slowed and his mind cleared. Once again, starting with the first scan, he reviewed them all again, forcing himself to be more methodical. As he approached the last few scans for the second time without having seen any likely candidates, his hands trembled. Eyes closed, he once again retrieved the calming picture.

From across the factory floor the sound of someone trying the door floated from the darkness. Three deep breaths. When he opened his eyes, a small thin capsule stared at him from the last scan. Where was that scan from? His right shoulder. So where was that capsule? Off in the darkness, wood splintered. Quest slapped the scanner's power button. Three hand-held lights advanced into the building's interior. Quest ducked behind the now dark scanner and peered around one of its edges. From the lights, indistinct voices spoke. Words were undiscernible, but one light waved to Quest's right, to his left, then straight at him. When the discussion concluded, the lights split up.

The light advancing toward him veered to Quest's left. The manufacturing facility wasn't large enough to hide in for long. His hunters would stumble on him...unless he could get above them. Overhead, a series of walkways crisscrossed the space, but the intruders were focused on the ground. Quest crept to his right, away from the advancing light, and headed toward a ladder leading to the overhead walks. At the ladder, Quest eased his way up to the walkway as the closest light rounded the corner of the scanner and shone where he had been moments before.

"You got anything?" Holbart's voice from the farthest corner of the space echoed in the intermittent darkness.

"Nothing here," another voice from the other end of the facility responded. The light by the scanner passed over the device examining the control panel. The man focused his light on the panel and leaned closer. With his free hand, he activated the scanner.

Careful to stay to the center of the walkway, avoiding areas that were loose on the edges, Quest inched his way along the walk.

"He was here," the man inspecting the scanner control panel said. Quest was three quarters of the way to the door and freedom.

"Within the last ten minutes," the man at the scanner said. "So, where are you, little Barthic?" The man waved his light around. It passed the ladder and swung up following the ladder to the walk.

Sneaking no longer an option, Quest sprinted along the walkway reaching the end as the light raced toward him. It caught him as he grabbed the ladder to the floor.

"There!" the man by the scanner said. With a crack, flechettes streaked through the air where Quest had been a moment before he leaped from the overhead walkway. He plunged out of control to the ground landing off center. Pain bloomed from his ankle and forced a groan from his lips, but he threw himself to his left behind a hydraulic metal press as three lights converged on him. Three more almost simultaneous cracks echoed in the facility.

Light spilled around the press, illuminating a rounded metal object on the press bed placed off center. Quest huddled against the press, his head by the activation button. The lights remained still.

"He's all yours, Atcan," Holbart said from behind him. A hand light from the doorway dazzled Quest. As he reached up to shield his eyes, Quest felt the activation control. In his mind, he pictured the round metal object offset on the press bed and activated the press. With a growl, it rumbled to life.

"Shoot him already, Atcan," Holbart said.

Atcan's flechette gun appeared in the light. "Sorry, kid," Atcan said.

Quest rolled to his right; the force of the press spat the metal object toward Atcan where it ricocheted off some pipes; Atcan fired but flinched, sending his shot wide. Quest vaulted to his feet and fled the building while Atcan waved his light in great arcs attempting to find his attacker.

Out the door, running along the street, Quest slowed as the fire from his injured ankle burned through the adrenaline from his near-death experience. He turned right and hobbled down an empty side street. He had stashed away an escape vehicle in a storage unit down a cross street. At any second he anticipated shouts of recognition from his pursuers. Quest ignored his twisted ankle and walked faster.

At the cross street, he turned right again. Not long now. He clawed the key to the storage unit from his pocket at the moment he arrived before the door. But in his shaking right hand the key scratched along the lock's surface. With both hands, he controlled his tremors and slipped the key into the lock. He yanked the door open, lurched inside and slammed the door shut.

Excited shouts came from the street as his pursuers questioned the few passersby. He limped to the vehicle and slumped into the front seat.

"Barthic, code 56cv2, identify," he said and held his breath. He hadn't checked the vehicle's status in over a year. He'd intended to do that within the month.

A light flashed on the dash. "Identity accepted," a young female voice issued from the dash. "Welcome Mr. Barthic. What is your destination today?"

He released his breath. "Dark Zone—random route avoiding main thoroughfares."

In another stroke of luck for him, the vehicle's entrance

to the storage unit was on the opposite side of the storage unit from the door he'd come through. The unit's door slid open, and the vehicle eased out onto the street.

Prone across the front seat, Quest fought his breathing under control. What was next? Still shaking in reaction to his narrow escape, he probed the area around and under his right shoulder for the tracking capsule. There. On the edge of his pectoral muscle. Was that it? He continued exploring the area without finding another candidate. His plans had been advanced enough that he'd hidden a knife and medical supplies in the vehicle. As he activated the vehicle's privacy settings, the windows tinted—from outside they would appear as silvered mirrors.

From a storage compartment, he yanked out the medical supplies, tore open the anesthetic pack, rubbed it on the area where he would cut, and waited for the anesthetic to take effect. A soft beep sounded. Thinking he'd imagined the sound, he ignored it. The beep sounded again. Afraid of what he'd find, Quest withdrew the interference device he'd cobbled together. The beep sounded again. It was a low power warning. Twenty minutes. The device would stop working and the tracker would broadcast his location in twenty minutes.

He fingered the skin where he would cut—and felt the touch. The anesthetic should have kicked in by now. It must be a bad batch. Maybe it just needed more time to work? He had no clue how much of the twenty minutes were left.

To this day, he had no memory of cutting himself and probing until he located and removed the device. He remembered only blood and screaming pain and holding a slippery capsule. At his command the window lowered, and he threw the capsule outside. With a grimace, he shoved aside the pain and checked the view from the outside cameras. An oncoming vehicle passed him and turned to follow. His eyes flicked to the interference generator. The power light was dead. The driver must have caught his capsule's signal before he had thrown it away. As the car surged after him, he called for manual control.

He whipped the car into a screeching left turn in front of an oncoming car that clipped his vehicle's right rear. Quest struggled for control, fighting to keep the vehicle on the road, looking up just before he rear-ended a car. Yanking his car into oncoming traffic, he squeezed between an approaching vehicle and the one he was passing. Foot jammed on the accelerator, he rocketed forward.

As he screamed around slower traffic, threading through oncoming cars, he weaved his way into the Dark Zone —here the inhabitants routinely discovered and destroyed surveillance equipment. After losing his tail, he pulled over to the side of a road and shook. In the future, he vowed, he'd be better prepared.

A sharp beep from the control panel pulled him back to the present. Six hours until the end of the jump.

Stars appeared on the view screen replacing jump-space gray. Koning sat with her eyes fixed on the readouts in front of her. Ricci floated behind Koning, watching. They both had an interest in the accuracy of this jump though based on Ricci's previous performance Mitsumi was more confident in her abilities. "Distance?" he said.

"Twenty-nine light minutes," Koning said with a broad smile of satisfaction. Ricci patted Koning's shoulder in congratulations.

Mitsumi nodded in Koning's direction. "Well done, Sentaa, Mei," Mitsumi said pleasantly. "An approach jump please, Sentaa. Tai, when we're in range, burn us into orbit around planet Quest."

CHAPTER 11

Several hours later, the computer's report appeared on the screen: "GV398509213:P2G-Positive for recent strikes." Mitsumi called his engineer. "Viram, is the shuttle prepped for launch?"

After a few moments of silence, Mitsumi thought, *I really need to talk to him.* He had dismissed Ricci and Koning's allegations, but each time Mantor was late or unprepared or unresponsive, Ricci and Koning's accusations gained more credibility and Mitsumi's suspicions sharpened. "Mr. Mantor?" Mitsumi said, impatience edging into his voice.

"Uh, I'm right here, Captain."

Mitsumi waited for Mantor to complete his response. "The shuttle?" he said prompting Mantor.

"Oh, right, the uh... It's uh, well...Yep all prepped and ready to go, Cap."

Quest stared straight ahead at the planet on the screen. Ricci attempted, without success, to stifle a smile.

His lips a flat white line, Mitsumi was not amused. He hated the thought that Mantor might have lied to him, but the time had come. When he was next alone with Mantor, he would confront him. "Mei, I'd like you to pilot. You're not on duty for another hour, but would you mind?"

Ricci smiled and nodded with enthusiasm. "Of course."

"Viram and Sentaa, you'll come with us. Tai, that leaves you here on monitor duty with Aber, though I expect another quiet stay." After they had lost their tail from Planet Mitsumi, there'd been no sign of pursuit from the Consortium.

"Yes, Captain," Quest said. Chandra nodded agreement.

The planet they called Quest was typical of discovered First Civ worlds without survivors—it was dead. Not wholly dead but, lacking sufficient oxygen and carbon dioxide, its biosphere consisted only of rudimentary multicellular organisms. Scholars had speculated ad nauseam regarding possible life forms arising on worlds without carbon or oxygen available in the atmosphere or dissolved in liquid water—but no one had yet discovered such life forms. On the Federated Worlds, inhabitants of the first stellar civilization had transformed the planets into habitats capable of sustaining carbon-based life. Outside the Federated Worlds, every First Civ planet exhibited signs of beginning that transformation, but the Horde's attack ushering in the Great Dark had interrupted the changes before they could become self sustaining. Planet Mitsumi, a living First Civ world without inhabitants was the only known counter example.

This world was not—it was dead, dead, dead, Koning thought as she adjusted her atmosphere mask and surveyed the dry landscape of various shades of brown stretching out before her. Patches of purple and pink interrupted the browns here and there, the only life capable of survival. She stood at the top of a slight rise, one ripple from the colossal impact that had formed the mountain range in front of her. Turning her back to the mountain range, Koning walked downhill following Ricci. Their target was mounds of debris two klicks distant that scans had identified as one-time buildings.

Ricci stopped and turned back to Koning. "C'mon, Sentaa, keep up."

"Yeah, yeah, you've got an advantage with those long Tonian legs on you." Even from a distance Koning could see Ricci start in surprise and glance around looking for someone who might have overheard.

"Hey, we're on a private channel, remember?" Koning said. "Your secret's still safe."

Ricci relaxed. "Right. Thanks, by the way for not saying anything to the crew. It means everything to me. You can't know how much."

Koning walked up to Ricci and stopped in front of her. "I still don't understand what the big deal is. What's the worst that could happen? Your family would force you into a life of extravagant luxury, compelled to have your every whim satisfied in an instant?"

Ricci turned away and stalked toward the ruins. Koning hurried to catch up.

"You don't know what you're saying," Ricci said after a few paces. "The compulsion and force my family would exert is beyond your imagination."

"I don't know. My imagination's pretty good."

In silence they approached the ruins, halting at the outskirts. Collapsed buildings lined cleared areas—streets or walkways, no one had yet discovered how the First Civers had transported themselves from place to place.

"Have you heard of personality disruptors?" Ricci said.

It took Koning a moment to recover the thread of their conversation. "Sure." Koning shrugged. "Every couple of years someone claims to have invented a process to 'fine tune' your personality, turn you from quiet to gregarious, flamboyant to conventional"—she shot Ricci a pointed look—"eliminate paranoia. But it's nonsense. Believe me if it existed, I'd try out a few new personalities myself, split a few off, so I could amuse myself."

"From what I've observed, the process is excruciating and not to be undertaken lightly."

"Oh, no, Mei, this isn't a story about secret trillionaire tech kept from the public and used only for nefarious trillionaire purposes is it? Because I'm not as gullible as I look."

"When I was twelve, my mother sat me down and explained my life's path. Where I would go to school, what I would become. It was all laid out. Even at twelve, I resisted the thought I was bound for a particular life. I don't remember

153

what I said, but it was enough to disturb my mother. A few days after that conversation, we had another one." Ricci walked a few steps into the ruins, pausing at a pile of rubble. She bent over to examine the ruins. A sudden breeze kicked up dust swirling in the air.

"I have an uncle, my mother's brother, Melor. As long as I had known him, he had been the perfect Burthen male—docile, compliant, deferential. My mother told me a story about Melor I hadn't heard before. He had been... unconventional, she said. Brash and assertive, he had wanted to overturn Ton society and change the established order. His relationship with the most powerful family on the planet gave him the perfect platform.

"I couldn't believe what she was saying. The Melor I knew was different. She showed me recordings. I saw him giving thundering speeches, giving media interviews, mingling with people. They let him go for a while, she told me, just to see if he'd come to his senses on his own. When he didn't, they disrupted his personality, calmed him, altered him to an accepting, passive, good boy."

"So, he grew up," Koning said. "He decided he'd rather live in opulence than cause trouble. People can change."

"No, Sentaa, you don't understand." Ricci stood. "My mother showed me the procedure. While he was under sedation, but still awake and helpless, women in white coats strapped him to a table and fitted a helmet on his head. My mother was there by the table. She spoke to him, told him that this was the only way, and it was for his own good, the good of the family and the planet. She gave a signal to someone off screen.

"Melor screamed." Ricci stopped and looked off to the horizon. "No, that's too weak. The word 'scream' doesn't come close to the sound he made. I've heard someone scream in pain, shriek in agony. That sound, the sound that exploded from his throat was nothing I'd ever heard before, and nothing I want to hear again. It was as if part of him was being pulled from his body through his throat, across his vocal chords."

Koning walked to Ricci's side. "C'mon, Mei," Koning murmured. "That must have been a fake." Ricci shook her head. "And besides, your mom would never let anything like that to happen to you. She was just trying to scare you into falling in line."

"Well, it worked," Ricci said, "the scaring part anyway. That moment set me on the path to where I am now. I pretended to go along, but in secret I constructed my new identity, studied piloting, and waited for my chance." Ricci smiled. "And it worked. Look at me," she stretched her arms out and turned a half circle, "piloting a starship, exploring worlds, becoming part of a crew." Ricci laid her arm across Koning's shoulder with a squeeze. "A crew that watches out for each other."

In irritation, Koning shrugged out of Ricci's hug and stalked off along the cleared path deeper into the ruins. Why did Ricci have to be so pleasant and grateful? A few steps beyond where Ricci stood, Koning halted, turned and yelled at her. "You're delusional," Koning said. "I still say you'd be happier cocooned in obscene wealth." Koning marched off into the ruins. *And that's true*, Koning thought. *Who wouldn't want that?* Ricci's fantasy "personality disruptor" tech was only a way to justify her ridiculous claim that piloting a ramshackle starship searching for First Civ tech crumbs was better than living in pampered luxury. Farther into the ruins, it became easier to discern where buildings had stood. The shock-wave had blown some away. Others seem to have crumbled in what must have been massive tectonic shifts. Enormous pieces of the crust had flattened still others.

A metallic glint drew Koning's eye. Off to her left, in the remains of a large structure, something had reflected the sunlight. Or, had it been a reflection? She stared at the place from which she thought the flash had come. There, in a gap between one of the boulders that had destroyed the structure and a partially standing wall—a glimmer of light there and gone. Not reflecting the sun then, the light had flashed from deep in shadow.

Koning picked her way into the ruin, testing the ground in front of her before putting her weight on it. She didn't want to crash through a weakened floor into a basement. She arrived at the gap from which the light had come. The gigantic boulder, at least five meters high, had smashed through the roof and both floors of the two-story building. Still proceeding with care, Koning tiptoed around the boulder to her right. Nothing remained of the building between the "street" and the boulder, but beyond where the boulder lay, the building was intact.

With a step back to her left, she faced the gap again. Koning glanced over her shoulder at the way she had come —there was no sign of Ricci. She should tell Ricci what she had found and get her help, but Ricci annoyed her at the moment. The light blinked again. It was a reflection after all— a reflection off of a piece of metal set into the wall. The light source was farther back around the curve of the boulder. The gap between the boulder and the wall looked just large enough for her to crawl through. Koning hesitated. But she didn't want to talk to Ricci at the moment, and the boulder and wall had been in this position for five thousand years give or take. Nothing would change just because she was crawling around.

She sank to her hands and knees and inched into the gap.

Holding onto a handle with his right hand, Mitsumi lowered himself into the underground room and increased the weight on his left foot resting on a tilted surface. His foot shot out from under him. The sudden increase in weight on his right hand broke his grip and, flailing for a hand hold, he slid down the tilted surface thudding to the ground and knocking the air from his lungs. He gasped for breath, smarting from his fall. Laughter echoed in the room.

"Sorry, Cap'n," Mantor said, without sounding the least apologetic.

Mitsumi raised himself from the floor and dusted himself off. "That's okay, Viram. I'm glad I amuse you. I wouldn't want you bored."

Mantor, ignoring or not recognizing Mitsumi's mordant observation, waved his handheld light around the room revealing glimpses of a few empty tables, scattered chairs, and piles of rubble from the half-demolished ceiling. "There's nothing worthwhile here. But, it looks like there may be a hall that way." Mantor advanced toward what could be a collapsed doorway. "I'll go see."

"Viram." Mantor turned back to Mitsumi, shining his handheld light in his eyes. Mitsumi closed his eyes against the light and turned his head. He pointed to his communicator and gave the sign for a channel change and held up four fingers— the private channel he wanted to use. The light held steady and Mitsumi wondered whether Mantor had understood. Mitsumi adjusted his own communicator. After a moment the light left Mitsumi's face. Mantor's voice sounded in his ears.

"What's up, Cap'n?"

"Viram, you lied to me." Mitsumi hadn't meant to be so blunt. In his mind he had intended to approach the subject obliquely, with understanding.

"What?" Viram chuckled.

"Back on Five High Station when I interviewed you, you told me you were clean." Mantor stood in silence, his face shadowed by the indirect light from their handhelds.

He drew his shoulders back and jabbed a finger at Mitsumi. "I *am* clean."

"No, you're not." Mitsumi tried but failed to keep anger from his voice. "You arrive late for meetings, respond sluggishly to requests, and are always on the edge of sleep. Sentaa says she's seen you using. That's Rapt, and it has to stop."

"I never lied to you. The engines run, don't they? I saved

everyone's lives from the Consortium, didn't I?"

Mitsumi bit back his first response and shook his head. This was not going the way he'd planned. Mitsumi held out his hand in a placating gesture. "Look, Viram—"

"No, Captain." Mantor spat the word and shined his handheld in Mitsumi's eyes. Mitsumi flinched away again from the light. "I've done everything you've asked, and I'm a fantastic engineer, better than you deserve. You can't insult me like that. I'm clean."

Mantor touched his communicator, turned away from Mitsumi, and wormed his way through the collapsed doorway.

"Yep, another brilliant interaction with the crew," Mitsumi muttered. He switched his communicator to the common channel. Mantor appeared again in the broken doorway as Ricci's voice sounded in his ears.

"—respond. This is Mei, Captain Mitsumi, please respond. Again, Sentaa—"

Mitsumi interrupted Ricci. "What is it, Mei?"

"Captain, where've you been? I've been trying to raise you for the last ten minutes, but you wouldn't answer and I didn't know if something—"

Mitsumi raised a hand, forgetting for a moment that Ricci was on the com. He needed to stop her rambling. "Mei," Mitsumi interposed, "what's going on?"

Rapid breathing echoed in Mitsumi's ears. "It's Sentaa… she's…just come now. We've got to help her."

Mitsumi and Mantor followed Ricci's com beacon; Sentaa's beacon wasn't broadcasting. Ricci wouldn't or couldn't provide more information on Koning's condition. She only hurried them along. As he approached a set of ruins, Mitsumi saw Ricci pacing back and forth in the middle of a long strip of cleared ground.

As Mitsumi and Mantor walked up to Ricci, Ricci wordlessly gestured them to follow her. As they wended their way through a debris field, Mitsumi and Mantor trailed Ricci toward a large boulder resting in a collapsed building next to a crumbling wall.

"I didn't know where she had gone," Ricci said, standing before the gap between the wall and the boulder. "She dropped off the com system and her beacon disappeared. I thought I'd seen her walk off this way, so I tried that and..." Ricci's voice trailed off. She pointed to the gap.

Mitsumi gazed at where she had pointed. A light flashed. "What's in there, Mei?"

"I don't know what she did. She must have tripped something and now she's in there spinning and frozen or dead. I couldn't find any controls and you've got to help her, Captain, Viram. You have to help her."

Ricci wasn't making any sense, but clearly something Not Good lurked in that artificial cave. Mitsumi turned to Mantor now standing at his side.

"I'm not going in there," Mantor said, his face unyielding stone.

Ricci stood mute pointing at the gap. Mitsumi supposed he didn't have a choice. Mantor wouldn't obey an order at the moment and whatever was in that dark crevice had frightened Ricci into incoherence. Mitsumi approached the gap, strapped his handheld light to his forehead, lowered himself to his hands and knees and crawled forward.

CHAPTER 12

A meter in, before rounding the boulder, the light from Mitsumi's handheld glinted off a metal strip running up the wall. *That must be what's reflecting the light from beyond the boulder*, Mitsumi thought. He cleared the boulder and halted. A meter in front of him the narrow passage he was in opened into a cavity. Before him, Koning floated a meter off the floor. Her arms were ramrod straight to her side, her legs stiff and straight. She rotated slowly, frozen in that posture. When her face came into view, her eyes were wide with fear, her mouth gaped open as if suspended in the act of screaming in terror.

Mitsumi glanced at his com unit. Koning's beacon didn't register. After crawling out from under the curve of the boulder, Mitsumi stood and advanced with caution toward Koning's slowly spinning form. He had approached within half a meter when he bumped into something solid that threw him back. Nothing he saw separated him from Koning. Mitsumi extended a hand until it encountered the transparent barrier. His hand bounced off. Curious, Mitsumi tapped the barrier with his fist. His hand flew off the barrier as if it had been pushed. Somehow, the barrier turned the energy from his hand back onto itself. *So, projectile weapons are out*, Mitsumi thought blanching at the image of flechettes reflected at the shooter with all their original energy. Turning to his left, Mitsumi walked toward the visible wall, trailing a hand against the transparent one. The transparent wall ended at the strip of metal.

The metal strip ran up the wall to the ceiling then diagonally across the ceiling to the far wall. A strip of metal on the floor paralleled that on the ceiling. A light flashed on the far wall. It came from a box on the wall set next to the metal strip. Mitsumi turned his attention back to the space in which Koning floated. A wide chest-high podium stood a meter beyond Koning's rotating form. Suspended above the podium a thin metallic sheet that looked to be twenty centimeters wide and thirty long faced to Mitsumi's right and below the sheet a thicker plaque floated. From his vantage point he couldn't see whether the sheet or the plaque contained writing.

Mitsumi activated his com. "Mei, Viram, would you join me in here please? Aber, Tai are you monitoring us?"

Mitsumi explained what he had found to the crew as Mantor appeared a few moments later, followed by a visibly reluctant Ricci.

"Scientists have dreamed of fields that could obstruct physical penetration," Mantor said with wonder as he moved his hands over the barrier, "but no one's ever been able to make one work. And gravity nullification or whatever it is," Mantor nodded toward Koning, "and could that be a stasis field she's in? Captain, if we can transport this tech or even just sell its coordinates, we're set for life."

"I agree with Viram," Chandra said. "This is bigger than Sundered's find. We'll be rich beyond our wildest dreams."

"What about Sentaa?" Ricci said. "We can't leave her there. We have to save her."

Mitsumi had drifted over to the far wall and was examining the box from which light shone at thirty second intervals. The box was black without surface markings. Mitsumi touched its front. It sprang to life. Squares containing unfamiliar characters covered the box. "This looks like a control device," Mitsumi said turning back to the others. "Can we turn off the field somehow?"

161

Mantor lifted to *Are We There Yet?* and brought Chandra back with his specialized equipment. While Chandra started tracing connections and testing the device's properties, Ricci put herself in charge of exploring the characters Mitsumi had discovered on the black box. Ricci tried pressing the characters with varying degrees of force, selecting single characters then random combinations. Nothing she did affected Koning's condition. Eventually, she set up a mechanism to press buttons in different combinations, attempting to crack the code with brute force. That it would take several hundred years to try every possible combination didn't slacken her enthusiasm. Instead it left her free to offer Chandra and Mantor helpful suggestions.

"Have you tried varying current on the lines from the box?" Hovering next to Chandra who was kneeling on the ground, Ricci peered over his shoulder at the equipment he had set up. Shoulders hunched, Chandra continued with his work. "How about cutting the lines? That might shut everything down." With a heavy sigh, Chandra straightened up and turned toward Ricci. "Mei," he said struggling to maintain an even tone, "I've tried everything you suggested and everything you suggested yesterday and the day before that. Please go bother Viram for a while."

They worked on the problem for a week. Mitsumi hadn't expected any progress. He'd hoped that the time spent would allow Ricci to come to grips with the idea that they wouldn't be able to recover Koning.

"I can't make anything out of it," Chandra said, gesturing toward the control box. They had installed portable lights in the space. Koning's rotating shadow crept along the back wall of the room. "I can detect what I'm pretty sure are control circuits in the unit. I can trace connections from the unit to the strips which I'm also convinced are field emitters. And the power seems to run through the unit to the emitters as well. But I can't access any of the control circuits. I can't even guess at the origin of the fields. Do the emitters generate them or only amplify and configure what the unit sends them? I have no idea."

Mitsumi, Mantor, and Ricci had gathered in the room to hear Chandra's conclusions.

"So, we can't rip it out and take it with us?" Mantor asked.

"No, I can't risk attempting to dismantle it," Chandra said. "We have to leave it intact and sell the location. That'll decrease our take." Chandra shrugged. "But we'll still be fabulously rich."

Mantor had remained uncharacteristically attentive during this exchange. "I say let's be on our way then," Mantor said.

Ricci stared at the ground, her shoulders slumped, and she shook her head. Mitsumi sympathized; he wasn't keen on leaving a crew member behind. But Koning was alive or dead. From everything they had gathered her condition would not change in either case. "Mei—" Mitsumi began.

"We can't leave her," Ricci said through clenched teeth, dabbing at the corner of her eye.

Chandra huffed in frustration and looked like he wanted to speak. Mitsumi quieted him with a gesture. "We've been over this before, if she's still alive, she'll live until a more competent evaluation team arrives." Mitsumi ignored Chandra's frown. "If she's not..." Mitsumi shrugged at that alternative's hopelessness.

"*You've* been over it before and have convinced yourselves, but we can't know what will happen. Sentaa could be dying by centimeters right now. The only way to be certain of what's happened to her and what will happen is to remove her. You know that." Ricci turned from Mitsumi and glared at Mantor and Chandra. Mantor met her gaze for a moment then averted his eyes. Chandra fixed his eyes on a point over her shoulder, his mouth compressed into a tight line. "But the money's too good to pass up, right, Viram? Is this your million credits, Aber?"

Chandra met Ricci's eyes with defiance and said, "With our other finds so far, I'm convinced it is. Don't try to guilt me into throwing away Pari's life on the off chance it'll help a bumbling astrogator who brought trouble down on her head by wandering off on her own and who, by the way, never gave a second thought about you or any of us. If she were in our position, do you seriously think she'd hesitate one nanosecond?"

Ricci shook her head slowly. "You don't know her," she said. "On the surface she may be abrasive, but underneath she's —"

"Caustic?" Mantor said.

"Cantankerous?" Chandra offered.

"Cutting?" Mitsumi said with a grin allowing the moment to overcome his judgment.

Ricci's face crumpled as if trying to hold back tears. Instead she burst into laughter. "Cranky," Ricci gasped between bouts of guffaws.

Chandra smiled. "She's quite the curmudgeon," he said.

Ricci's laughter subsided. "You're right," Ricci said, her mouth turned up in a subdued grin. "She's all of that. But once you establish you're willing to trade life, even the possibility of life, for money, there's nothing you won't exchange for money. And no matter how important or desirable that exchange appears, and you'll just have to trust me on this one, the money's not worth it."

Ricci shrugged. "Sure, you may say to yourselves you're not doing it for the money because there's no harm in leaving Sentaa. As the captain said, if she's alive now, she won't die before help arrives. But are you more willing to believe that because if she dies before her rescue, well, her death reduces the split?"

Mantor's eyes flicked to Koning. Her face with its expression of abject terror rotated into view. Mantor licked his lips. He looked at Ricci, then his eyes narrowed and he glanced back to Koning, studying her with obvious intensity.

"And perhaps that guarantees enough money to save Pari and live in comfort?"

Chandra's face hardened, but he kept his peace. Mitsumi didn't feel as if money had clouded his judgment as Ricci suggested, but perhaps that was the idea: money's lure was so pervasive and insidious that it was impossible to know with certainty if your judgment had been affected. And it had definitely occurred to him that the take from selling this location would fund his search for the Artifact's planet and ease that constant pressure behind his eyes.

"Let's assume for a moment you're right about Sentaa," Mitsumi said, "and she's dying—what can we do? We've tried every means at our disposal to free her. Nothing's worked. What more can we do?"

Chandra nodded in agreement. Mantor, fiddling with his assistant, appeared not to be paying attention.

Ricci's face hardened, and she glared at the crew before fixing her eyes on Mitsumi. "We haven't tried everything, Captain." Stabbing a finger at him, she continued. "Money has already blinded you."

Puzzlement flashed onto Mitsumi's face. He didn't understand what she was saying. Chandra too was perplexed. Off to the side, Mantor was studying his assistant, working on something.

In disgust, Ricci tossed up her hands and said, "We can destroy the device."

Mitsumi's instinctive reaction matched the look of horror on Chandra's face. But a moment later it occurred to him—they *could* destroy the device. Why hadn't he thought of that? Was Ricci right, had the lure of wealth so bedazzled him he couldn't see the obvious?

"That's preposterous," Chandra sputtered. "And before you say it, it's not just the money. This technology will benefit billions of people. It will—"

"She's alive," Mantor said, interrupting Chandra. All eyes fixed on Mantor. He pointed at Koning with his assistant. "She's alive, and she wants our help."

CHAPTER 13

Pulling at his hair, Mantor gathered his thoughts and swallowed hard. "During, uh, Mei's little speech," Mantor said, with a nod toward Ricci, "after she told us what creeps we were, I studied Sentaa's face. It looked like her lips had shifted while we were talking." He licked his lips and shuddered as he replayed in his mind the scenario that had forced him into action. "What if she was alive, her body not in absolute stasis, just slowed down, but her mind unaffected?"

The crew shifted, uncomfortable at the picture Mantor had painted. But Chandra scoffed, "That's not possible."

After holding up his assistant's screen to the crew's view, he activated his program. On Mantor's assistant's tiny screen Koning's mouth moved forming two words. "Help me."

In the stunned silence. as Koning's mute plea looped over and over, Mantor explained. "I pulled up the recordings we made, separated out every one showing Koning's face, and sped up the playback compressing a week's worth of observations into five seconds." Mantor surveyed the crew, his expression sober. "We have to save her," he said, "no matter what it costs."

Mitsumi nodded. "You were right, Mei."

Ricci beamed with relief. Head down, shoulders slumped in disappointment, Chandra nodded once. "We'll have to destroy it. We can only be sure of shutting it down if we reduce it to useless slag."

With sympathy, Mantor returned his look and agreed.

167

"Yeah, that's the only way." He shared Chandra's reluctance. Not because of the money, or not just because of the money, but also because he would never be able to delve into the technology and wrest its secrets.

His last attempt rebuffed, Chandra straightened his shoulders and held his head up. "We'll need Chemtex."

Mantor placed a couple cubic centimeters of Chemtex, their most powerful explosive, on all sides of the box even on the underside which he reached by tunneling into the rock on which it rested. A standard day after they had made their decision, Mitsumi and Ricci stood behind Mantor in the room with Koning. Chandra had absented himself, muttering that he couldn't stand to see such incredible tech destroyed. Ricci was looking at Koning as Mantor triggered the explosives. The sharp bang was more subdued than Mantor had expected. Koning collapsed to the floor screaming. "Help me!"

Ricci rushed to her side and after a few moments calmed a severely traumatized Koning. At the sound of the explosion, Chandra hurried back into the chamber and examined the ruined device on the wall. After his inspection, Chandra joined the others. "Nothing salvageable's left," he said, staring straight at Ricci, bitterness plain in his voice.

Teeth chattering and muscles convulsing, Koning sat on the ground, arms wrapped around her knees drawn up to her chest, her head lowered. Ricci sat beside her with her arm around Koning's shoulders. After a while, Koning raised her head and spoke. "It was horrible." She stared ahead, hollow eyed, lost in the memory of her experience. Eventually, she shook her head coming back to the present.

"Thank you," Koning said, shifting her gaze from Mitsumi to Mantor and resting on Chandra. "I would never have escaped if you hadn't blown up the device. I know it must have been hard destroying something so valuable."

Chandra held Koning's eyes for a heartbeat, then dropped his head and ran his hand through his hair. "Yes, well it was a collective decision."

"Still, it was harder for you than for the others," Koning said, a note of bitter irony in her voice.

Chandra lifted his eyes sharply and met Koning's. He stiffened. "Yes, it was," Chandra said quietly, then turned and left in a hurry without another word.

Mitsumi squatted beside Koning, studying her face. "What happened, Sentaa?"

Her face vacant, staring blankly after Chandra, Koning didn't appear to have heard Mitsumi's question. Visibly shaking off her thoughts, she responded. "I...I followed the box's reflection into this room." She cut her eyes toward Ricci then looked ahead again. "I know I shouldn't have gone in alone, but Mei and I...I saw the inscriptions on the metal sheet." Koning nodded in the direction of the sheet that remained suspended above the podium.

Eyes closed, she took a deep ragged breath. "I reached out to touch the sheet." She stopped and opened her eyes. Her mouth tightened and her eyes clouded with pain. "And...and next thing I knew was terror." She shuddered and her breath quickened. After a moment, her breath slowed and her shaking subsided. "Well, I was caught up off the ground floating with my arms pinned to my side and my legs stiff, but that was nothing compared to..." Closing her eyes again she visibly fought against the memory. "Nothing, nothing I've ever felt compared to that horror. I was doomed to die in the most excruciating pain.

"Waiting for that painful death was almost worse than the experience itself would have been, I think. Not that I'm eager to find out." She shook as she visibly tried to suppress the memory. "Anyway, I was aware the whole time—I could still think. I could see and hear."

Mitsumi's face colored, "So you heard our, uh, deliberations?"

Koning nodded and leaned her head against Ricci's shoulder. "Thank you, Mei, for sticking up for me. If you had left..." Koning's voice faded out, and something of the look of horror she'd had while floating in the suspension crossed her face.

"You would have been awake for years, unable to move," Ricci said, giving Mitsumi and Mantor a penetrating look, "while you wasted away."

"It could have been a full stasis field," Mantor said, defensiveness plain in his voice. "She could have lived."

Ricci shook her head. "You found out she was alive, Viram, because you saw her move—the suspension wasn't complete."

Koning took in the others. "But I'm alive and here thanks to you all."

Mitsumi stood and reached a hand to help Koning up. Koning took his hand and, with a muted groan, stood. "Let's get you back to the ship and in the auto doc."

Mantor indicated the sheet. "We should take a look at this, Captain."

Koning flinched away as Mantor spoke. "Don't touch it, Viram," Koning said.

"C'mon, Sentaa," Ricci said. "Let's get you to the ship." Ricci cupped Koning's elbow with a hand and led her toward the exit.

At the exit, Koning glanced behind her at Mantor eyeing the sheet. With wide eyes she held out a quaking hand toward the sheet. "Be careful, Viram," she said before she ducked and crawled out of the room.

Mantor moved in front of the sheet. Cautious, Mitsumi remained behind the metal strips, eyes riveted on Mantor and the sheet. Covered with engraved characters, it looked metallic but was as thin as a piece of paper. At its top was a stylized depiction of a spiral galaxy as seen from above the plane of the ecliptic looking down at the center. A point at the center of the disk glowed brighter than the rest of the representation. From this center point faint rays emanated spreading throughout the disk. Below the sheet, a separate plaque also contained characters Mantor didn't recognize but seemed familiar somehow in contrast with the others which were entirely foreign.

Mantor could just discern an impossibly thin rod rising from the podium. The sheet was affixed to this rod. He reached out to touch the sheet.

"Should we just take recordings?" Mitsumi said, causing Mantor to pause.

Mantor shook his head. "We destroyed whatever held Sentaa captive. This looks like a display, and I bet what Sentaa stumbled on was an anti-theft device. Whatever this was, someone must have thought it valuable." Steeling himself, because despite what he'd said, part of his mind was raising an alarm, Mantor ran his hand along the surface of the sheet. It was smooth to the point of being slick. With his assistant, Mantor recorded it from every angle. As he moved to the rear, Mitsumi stepped onto the podium and in front of the sheet. He stiffened visibly and stared. After a minute he shook his head then reached out with both hands and, taking the sheet by the edges, lifted it up.

"Captain?" Mantor said, wondering what had happened to just taking recordings.

"We need to take this," Mitsumi said.

CHAPTER 14

Back in the portable habitat they'd erected as a base camp for exploring Planet Quest, Mitsumi sat on his bunk holding the Artifact and stared at the metal sheet he had removed from the site of Koning's debacle. When he had stepped in front of the sheet and seen the inscriptions, he'd been shocked to find the galactic symbol from the plinth and other symbols resembling what he had seen in his vision. Then the writing glowed as the Artifact hanging around his neck had warmed and, for an eye blink, he'd been back, standing before the rock face, lifting the Artifact toward the glowing receptacle. The "vision" had disappeared leaving behind only a growing compulsion to find the Artifact's planet. Once back to the shelter, he'd consulted the drawings he had made of the symbols in his vision. He had been right—some of them looked identical.

The sheet and the Artifact were connected somehow, and they were both intertwined with a star in an extragalactic globular cluster around which orbited a planet with a rock wall where the diamond rectangle fitted into a shining receptacle. The symbol of the galaxy seen from above linked them and, if Chandra was right, the fabled Underground.

But at the moment none of that was obvious since Mitsumi couldn't coax either of the items into repeating their fantastic demonstrations. Once again, he moved the Artifact toward the sheet until the two touched. Nothing. He placed the Artifact on top of the sheet. Nothing. He brought to mind his memory of the vision. Nothing. As a last resort, embarrassed even though he was alone, he tried thinking at the sheet first and then at the Artifact—asking questions, requesting a sign that what he'd seen had not been an illusion. Nothing.

He tried to convince himself that what he had experienced had been a fantasy, but he couldn't manage it. If that were true, it would mean something had compromised his mental health, and that possibility was just too disturbing. He picked up the Artifact, pulled the lanyard he'd fixed to it back over his head and let it rest against his chest. The strange metallic sheet, he stuffed into his carryall. Perhaps on the ship they'd be able to discover something useful about it.

Within the week they finished surveying Quest and returned to the ship, finding nothing else as Koning recovered from her ordeal. They had made no headway in deciphering the sheet, or in analyzing its composition. The plaque also remained untranslatable, although Chandra had identified its composition. Mitsumi, Koning, and Ricci were floating in the mess discussing what planet they should survey next when Chandra appeared at the entrance.

"Ah, Captain Mitsumi," Chandra said. "I wonder if I might have a word."

Mitsumi nodded. "Go ahead, Aber."

Chandra glanced at Koning and Ricci and licked his lips, hesitating.

"Go ahead, Aber, we've no secrets," Mitsumi said.

Chandra looked as if he were engaging in an internal debate. He came to a conclusion and pushed into the room. "I've unlocked the box we found on, uh, Mitsumi."

Mitsumi frowned in puzzlement and looked at Koning and Ricci for help. Ricci grinned back at him. Koning shook her head.

"Your planet, Captain." Koning smirked. "The first one we explored."

"Oh, right," Mitsumi said. He should never have agreed to that request. "So what do you mean, you've 'unlocked' it?"

"I've opened it," Chandra said then added, "not literally, you understand. It's a memory store; I've found my way in."

In Chandra's quarters, as Mitsumi had remembered, the box sat strapped in place on the table, wires trailing from it connected to a console. A screen above the console glowed with characters. Mitsumi, Koning, and Ricci gathered in front of the screen. Chandra floated in the background. Mitsumi peered at the screen, the characters tickling something in the back of his mind.

"Why do those look familiar?" Mitsumi asked.

"The plaque," Ricci and Koning said at once, Ricci giggling at the coincidence.

"That's right," Chandra said. "I ran a comparison. Some of them are the same characters as the plaque we picked up from Quest. I'd say the writing systems are related."

"What does it say?" Ricci asked, indicating the screen.

"I don't know," Chandra said. "We know of only two First Civ writing systems. They differ completely from each other and the fragments we have aren't enough to allow anyone to interpret them. This," Chandra nodded at the screen, "represents a third First Civ writing system. I checked and the characters differ from the other two known examples. But I think there's enough here that, with time and effort, we might unravel parts of the data store." His head swiveled from Ricci to Mitsumi. "A lot of time and stupendous effort."

"Even though you can't read the writing, do you have any idea what we're looking at?" Mitsumi asked.

"It's a menu," Chandra said. He shouldered his way between Ricci and Koning and manipulated something on the console that moved the indicator on the screen and highlighted one set of characters. The characters on the screen disappeared, replaced by a second set. Chandra highlighted a third set; the screen changed again. If the first screen had been a menu, Chandra was now accessing sub menus. Chandra continued burrowing into more and more sublevels.

After five minutes of this, Ricci spoke with awe. "How

many levels are there?"

"Three hundred fifty-six," Chandra said, "on this one path. I've followed other paths where I've descended ten thousand levels before giving up."

Mitsumi studied the box with wonder. "Ten thousand levels," he said. "How much data is in there?"

Chandra shrugged. "I can't tell you. But based on the examination I've performed so far, I estimate it to be at least several orders of magnitude more data than all the information stored in the Federated Worlds combined."

Koning gave a low whistle. Mitsumi had read estimates of the combined Federated Worlds' data stores. They came in around 3.2 times 10^{40} binary bits. And this small box carried at least thousands of times as much?

"What's in it?" Ricci asked. "What happens when you come to the end of the sub menus?"

A schematic drawing of a rectangular object with rounded edges appeared on the screen below a paragraph of characters. Groups of similar writing surrounded the drawing. From each group a thin line extended to part of the drawing. Chandra highlighted one of the groups. Another schematic flashed up beneath another paragraph of the unknown script. Other groups surrounded this drawing connected with thin lines.

"Most of what I've found so far has been similar to this," Chandra said.

Ricci pointed at the screen in wonder. "Could those be...?"

"Detailed drawings and schematics of a First Civilization device?" Chandra said. "Yes, I believe so."

Koning laughed out loud and covered her mouth with her hand. She turned to Ricci next to her, put her arm around her shoulder and squeezed. "We're rich!" Koning said with astonishment.

Ricci answered with a sad smile, "Yes, we are."

Chandra grinned in return. He gazed at the box on the table. "You have no idea. I've found hundreds of these schematics," Chandra said. "I think this device may be a data ark."

Mitsumi considered the box. After the Horde's bombardments had destroyed all functioning tech and ninety-nine percent of the human race, survivors had scrabbled in the dirt for two thousand years, clinging to life by a worn, fraying thread. The origin of the term "Great Dark" to describe that period following the bombardments was unknown, but its universal adoption testified to the name's accuracy.

When humanity's ragged tag-ends had crawled back to their worlds' surfaces as the Great Dark began, they brought with them two traditions common across the Federated Worlds—the EM taboo and the ark myth. In the legends of the events leading up to the Great Dark, their ancestors had named the places of refuge where they had burrowed into the ground to hide from the Gods' wrath, Arks. Etymologists had searched in vain for the origin of the word's association with a haven and had concluded that its beginning lay in the First Stellar Civilization's ashes.

"You think," Mitsumi said, "this data ark contains, what, vital information from the First Civ?"

"I think," Chandra continued, his eyes still fixed on the box, "this data ark holds information on every aspect of the First Stellar Civilization including every piece of technology they had developed."

Mitsumi studied the box. If that was true, Aber was right —they didn't know the box's value or how disruptive it could be. Mitsumi turned to Chandra. "Aber, do the memory stores give enough detail to manufacture any of these devices?"

"I don't know yet, Holtz," Chandra said with irritation. "I've only scratched the surface of what's on here. Another forty layers below this one, we run into what might be mathematical notation, although the symbols are unfamiliar. But let someone else worry about that. We sell this; we get rich.

Pari has her life back. Sentaa"—Chandra shot a scathing look at Koning—"can redecorate her cave. We're all happy."

"I'm good with that," Koning said with a smile, ignoring Chandra's dig.

The door signal to Chandra's room sounded. "Come," Chandra said. Mantor floated in.

"Hey, Viram," Ricci said. "Come join us."

Mantor circled around the back of the screen, avoiding Mitsumi and coming to rest beside Ricci. "What's going on?" Mantor said.

"Aber," Koning said, "discovered the box we found on Planet Mitsumi is an enormous First Civ tech data ark. Now we're rich, apparently."

Mantor leaned toward the screen and squinted. "The fourth level something something shell will something something and result in something." He straightened. "Huh, that's great."

All eyes had turned to Mantor as he read from the screen. They continued staring at him as he glanced around. "What?" Mantor said.

"Did you just read what was on the screen or are you playing with us?" Koning said.

Mantor, confusion plain on his face, eyed Koning, then took in the others. Chandra stared at him, hope lighting his face. Ricci studied him with narrowed eyes, her skepticism plain. "You can't read that?" Mantor asked.

"No," Mitsumi said flatly, "we can't. And Aber just finished telling us it was an unknown First Civ language. So, you can understand our thinking your claim is just a bit... dubious."

Mantor held Mitsumi's eyes for a moment then surveyed the others. He shrugged. "I don't know about any dead First Civ language, Cap'n, all I know is that on Wild where I grew up there's a religious sect, the Priests of the Holy Text. They worship their ancestors and claim to be guardians of a sacred book with the wisdom of the ancients. The sect's priests teach members the language of the sacred book." Mantor waved his hand at the screen. "Of course, it's been several hundred years since anyone has seen the Sacred Book so most people think the whole thing's a hoax." Mantor considered the screen again. "But maybe it's not."

Mitsumi studied Mantor. This could still be a joke or a Rapt fantasy from his former life so often repeated it seemed real to him.

Koning was having none of it. "You're not funny, Viram," Koning said. "Couldn't you have come up with something more amusing like, I don't know, you're a time traveler from the past with secret knowledge, or maybe you've had a vision?"

"Shut up, Sentaa," Mantor said with unusual heat. "I don't care if you don't believe me, but I can read that language, or at least part of it."

"Oh right, because you were one of the priests."

"Sentaa, that's enough," Mitsumi said. "Don't listen to her, Viram. Tell us more about this language."

Mantor shook his head once. "I'll be with my engines." Mantor pushed through the group and left the cabin.

"Sentaa, you need to apologize," Mitsumi said.

"No, I don't," Koning said. "He was just making stuff up. Besides what do we care if he knows a few words of the language? Like Aber said, it doesn't matter to us. We can sell it as is, wash our hands and finish this."

Aber nodded along with Koning, on board with the idea, keen to lay hold on the funds to save his daughter. Ricci looked thoughtful. At the thought that their voyage may be on the verge of a fantastically successful conclusion, Mitsumi's heart lifted. Finally something was going right. If Chandra was even close to accurate, that box would launch his search, pay back Corban and Jonta, and let him thumb his nose at his exes.

"We should talk this over," Ricci said.

"This what?" Koning said, shaking her head in disgust. "Missing out on a sure thing on the word of a brain-fried pleasure junkie? You want to work out what's in the Ark and what, make it ourselves?"

Ricci huffed in frustration. "I'm not proposing we start a business together. I want us to weigh our options."

Koning eyed Ricci, then glanced at Chandra and Mitsumi. "Okay, I'll tell you what, here's your 'option.' Pay me my share of the proceeds from our voyage, including the value of the Ark, and I'll be on my way."

Chandra nodded. "I understand the impulse, Mei, but I only have time to sell the device and save my daughter—nothing more."

As much as Mitsumi wanted to push through Ricci's resistance, he couldn't bring himself to simply roll over her suggestion. "We should at least discuss what Mei has in mind," Mitsumi said. "We're only two months into what we'd planned on being a year-long voyage, Aber, you still have time." He turned to Koning. "That's true for you too, Sentaa."

Koning regarded Ricci then lowered her eyes and licked her lips. "Well…."

"Every day I delay," Chandra said, "Pari lives in horrible pain. How can you extend that punishment?" Chandra studied their faces, evidently not liking what he saw there. With a sigh, Chandra said, "I don't suppose it could hurt to discuss the matter."

They adjourned to the mess. Mitsumi coaxed Mantor from engineering; Quest joined them from the bridge. After filling Quest in on the true nature of the Ark and on Mantor's surprising knowledge, Mitsumi addressed his crew. "I propose, with Aber and Sentaa's backing, to jump to Support and sell the Ark." He paused to gauge Mantor and Quest's reaction, but both remained neutral. He lifted a hand indicating Ricci. "Mei has a different suggestion."

Ricci looked at Quest and Mantor. "Viram can read at least some of what's in the Ark. I think we need to know more about what Viram knows. We can't decide on a course of action until we know what our choices are."

Koning opened her mouth to speak, but Ricci touched her

shoulder. Koning closed her mouth.

"So, Viram," Mitsumi said. "How extensive is your knowledge of this language?"

Mantor, looking sullen, surveyed the members of the crew then addressed Mitsumi. "It's not huge. I only studied with the Priests for two years."

"Aber brought with him a few pages from the Ark. Would you look those over and tell us how much you understand?"

Chandra handed his assistant to Mantor. Mantor focused on the screen and pursed his lips. He touched the assistant and moved his finger up.

"I can get about twenty percent of what I'm reading. Enough to know it's a device that cuts material and it uses... well, I can't tell what it uses even as a basic description. The technical discussion is way beyond my capability." He passed the assistant back to Chandra. "I can see it is handheld and will cut any substance."

"From your brief examination," Ricci said, "do you think you could reproduce this device?"

"No," Mantor shot back, shaking his head. "I told you any of the technical stuff is way beyond me. When I studied the language, I was reading stories, not blueprints."

"The priests taught you?" Ricci asked. Mantor nodded.

"How much of this language did they understand?" Ricci asked. "Do you know if they'd be able to understand this?"

"I'm not certain," Mantor said, then squinted his eyes in thought. "But there's one person who knows the language even better than the priests. He's a professor on Zong named..." Mantor put his hand to his forehead. "Oh, I can't remember now, but he's made a career of studying the Holy Text. No one else will touch it because they think it's made up garbage, but this guy...I don't know if he thinks it's real, but he at least pretends it is. If anyone can make sense of this right away, he's the one."

"But you don't know whether he could," Koning said.

"Nope."

"I think we've heard enough," Chandra said. "You aren't seriously saying we should travel back to Zong on the off chance this...professor, we don't even know his name—"

"Aten," Mantor said, snapping his fingers. "Lentar Aten, that's his name."

Chandra waved a hand at Mantor, "On the off chance this Aten fellow can interpret the information on the data store well enough to allow us to produce tech from the Ark and that we then attempt to manufacture it ourselves?" Chandra glared at Mitsumi. "The idea's insane. I repeat—which is all I do lately it seems—we've found what we sought. It's time to pack up the expedition, cash in our prize and be off."

"I understand your frustration, Aber," Ricci said.

Chandra slammed the table in front of him forgetting they were in the zig, the momentum carrying him toward the ceiling.

"Do you have children?" Chandra asked Ricci as he continued to float around the room. "You can't fathom the agony of watching your child suffer when you hold in your hands the way to stop the pain, but others prevent you from using it. Frustration isn't even close." Chandra bumped against the ceiling as he finished speaking and drifted on the rebound back toward the table.

Ricci bowed her head, staring at the floor.

"You're right," Ricci said after a moment. "But I still think we should at least try with this professor Aten, if only to give us a better idea of what's in the Ark to improve our bargaining position. We won't know what the device is worth unless we know what's on it."

Koning flicked her eyes at Ricci, then addressed the rest of the crew. "I don't think we need to discover everything on the Ark to make the best bargain. There are lots of ways of doing this. We could negotiate a contingent deal where we get an upfront payment and a percentage of the profits from the sale of tech resulting from the Ark. There's no reason to mess around with trying to understand what's on it."

No one spoke for a moment. Quest interrupted the silence. "I vote to visit the professor." The others turned to Quest, waiting for him to expand on this declaration. Quest caught the eyes of each in turn. Evidently deciding that they expected something more of him, Quest added with a shrug, "I believe with Mei that maximizing our knowledge of the Ark maximizes our return."

All eyes turned to Mantor who returned their look without emotion. "I'm with Aber and Sentaa. We shouldn't waste time trying to figure out what's on the Ark; we should just sell it. Sure, we might make more money if we identified in detail what we had or if we developed the tech piecemeal and sold it, but how much more do we need? What we know right now will set us up for life."

"Mei and Tai are right," Mitsumi said. "If we know the specifics of what we have, it might mean an exponential increase in price. That's the benefit side. On the cost side, we have a delay of a few weeks at most. We want to be at Support to sell our find, but the detour to Zong would only add two weeks tops to our schedule. It might not work, but the upside of a vast increase in price for our find outweighs a two-week delay."

Mitsumi turned to Koning. "Sentaa, you suggested a very creative approach, and it's one we could use if the upside doesn't materialize. But actual knowledge of the Ark's contents would boost the return even higher than the approach you suggest, and it doesn't suffer from the drawback of having to wait while someone we can't control tries to implement the tech."

During this speech, Chandra became more and more agitated until he couldn't restrain himself. He scowled at Mitsumi, Ricci, and Quest. "You all would condemn Pari to two-weeks' additional torture, just for a few extra credits? Have you never seen anyone in the grip of Karstov's? Here," Chandra punched at his assistant, "let me show you what you're doing." Chandra had set his assistant on display mode.

A holo video appeared above the table. A young girl, Pari presumably, writhed in a bed. Straps bound her hands and feet, tubes and wires extended from various parts of her body to locations out of the image. A small, clear piece of plastic held her mouth open and a web of wide strips immobilized her head.

Chandra flinched from the video, then caught himself and slowly turned his head to confront the horror displayed. "Pain from Karstov's is so severe," Chandra said through clenched teeth, "patients lose control of their bodies. Muscles contract without the patient's volition." Sweat sheened Chandra's forehead, but he continued without pause to describe the scene. "The restraints prevent Pari from injuring herself. Without the block in her mouth she would bite off her tongue."

Her arms and legs moved constantly, jerking against the restraints. Her body bounced on the bed. Against the backdrop of ship sounds, Mitsumi heard her body thudding on the bed, the hand and foot restraints snapping and a continuous, muffled, gargled scream. Mitsumi and the crew stared at the tortured girl.

Mitsumi swallowed hard and his hands went clammy. "That's enough, Aber," Mitsumi said after a moment, turning his head and striving to block the sounds of agony.

"Is it?" Chandra demanded.

"Yes, Aber, it is." Mitsumi couldn't hold out against the sounds and images. As long as Pari's true torment remained hidden, he could pretend a two-week delay was meaningless. The reality displayed before him left no such refuge. Chandra extinguished the hologram. But one detail remained. "Aber, what's your plan?"

Chandra returned Mitsumi's gaze with a puzzled look. "My plan? You mean other than sell the Ark and make everyone rich?"

"The Consortium, Aber. You remember, your former employers who tried to steal the Ark and kidnap you to torture

183

for amusement?"

Chandra shrugged and licked his lips, looking uncomfortable. "They don't know about the Ark."

"They know you found something on, Mit—that planet and they know you were with us. If we or you show up now with the Ark, don't you think they'll be interested in talking to you about it?"

"We," Chandra's eyes darted to the rest of the crew, "uh, we'll sell it anonymously. Give out sample data to interested parties and channel the purchase price to blind accounts."

Mitsumi wasn't convinced that would solve the problem, but Koning nodded in agreement along with everyone except Quest. With an inward sigh, Mitsumi gave the order. "Sentaa, calculate a course to Support. The best market for the Ark is there I think. Anyone disagree?"

No one responded. "Tai," Mitsumi said, "it's your shift, right?" Quest regarded Mitsumi without a response. Mitsumi had learned to interpret this as assent; Quest would only respond if he disagreed with the assertion. "Jump us as soon as Sentaa has provided the calculation. How far out are we, Sentaa?"

Koning closed her eyes, moving her lips in silence. "Forty-eight hours." Koning opened her eyes. "Give or take."

Mitsumi surveyed the crew who remained floating in front of him. For all their expressed desire to sell the Ark, collect their riches, and move on, they weren't jumping to the task.

"You're dismissed," Mitsumi said. "I'll be in my quarters until the next shift change."

CHAPTER 15

Koning's calculations put them a mere thirty light minutes from Support. She smiled and clenched her fist at the result. Captain Mitsumi acknowledged her improvement. "Well done, Sentaa." Ricci was glad for Koning. After this voyage she should be able to land another Astrogator spot with ease.

Weight ramped up as Quest engaged the in-system drive. Ricci studied the controls and readouts suggesting a slight alteration to the drive profile. Quest nodded in agreement and tweaked the setting. Ricci beamed with pleasure.

"Sentaa," Mitsumi said, "prepare to transmit the encrypted summary package and request for offer for our finds to the twenty-three prospects we have identified."

Koning turned to her work station and opened the directory with the files. "Ready, Captain."

"Let's get this party started. Transmit the messages."

Koning turned back to the console and entered the transmit command.

The first step in setting up a bidding process was inviting prospective purchasers to inspect the object on which they would bid. To that end, their initial transmissions included an offer to travel to their ship and examine the merchandise. In theory, the encrypted communications with potential purchasers would prevent the Consortium from discovering their return to civilization and the treasure they brought with them. They could arrange a rendezvous with interested purchasers well outside Support's traffic control zone and hide their presence in the system. Sure, based on their broadcast, everyone, including the Consortium, would know a ship had jumped into the system, but not which ship. This was a common enough maneuver for returning prospectors that it would be difficult for the Consortium to investigate every such occurrence. That was the theory. At the moment, as she and the rest of the crew watched the approaching ship carrying the first of the likely bidders, the theory wasn't giving Ricci warm fuzzies.

"What kind of weapons?" Ricci said, cutting off Mitsumi who had opened his mouth to pose the same question—the one on everyone's mind at the moment. The crew had gathered in the bridge to witness the first of their meetings with a potential purchaser.

"It looks like they have a magnetic store of anti-protons and a mechanism for expelling them at close to the speed of light," Koning said.

With a tremor in her hands she tried to quell, Ricci turned from Koning. It wasn't possible. The magnified image of the ship they were meeting loomed large in the screen. For all outward appearances it was a late model passenger yacht, but in Ricci's mind it pulsed with menace.

"Why would they send an armed ship?" Mitsumi wondered aloud.

"And armed with a weapon I've never heard of," Koning said.

"I'm familiar with it," Mitsumi said. "It is, or was, a military weapon. I hadn't heard of it being deployed in civilian craft, but I suppose it was inevitable."

"Hensatic Armaments," Quest said.

"Tai?" Mitsumi said, after Quest failed to explain himself.

"The manufacturer of the A-Beam weapon," Quest said. "Hensatic Armaments, a division of Burthen Space Industries."

Koning caught her lower lip between her teeth and shot a look at Ricci. Ricci, eyes riveted on the screen and the ship, was unable to turn away from the sight. A Burthen ship here. Did that mean someone had tracked her down?

"Thanks for that, Tai," Mitsumi said. "Sentaa, send them our bona fides."

Ricci went cold. She rotated to Mitsumi with a look of horror. "We're not telling them who we are, are we?"

Mitsumi frowned. "No, Mei, we're just giving them the code that identifies us as the ship who contacted them with information regarding the Ark." Ricci stared at Mitsumi and tried to force her heart rate to slow. "Is that okay with you, Mei?"

Ricci nodded and turned back to the screen. There was no need to worry. The people on the other ship didn't know who they were dealing with. And in any event, nothing she had done connected her former self with this ship. It was pure coincidence the other ship had an advanced Burthen weapons system. The family had released the system to the public earlier than planned, that's all.

"They acknowledge, Captain, and are prepared to board for the inspection."

On the screen a small vessel detached from the larger one and moved away toward *Are We There Yet?* "Okay, Aber," Mitsumi said. "Let's get this over with. Tai, you're with us." Tai turned to Mitsumi, a question on his face. "I'm confident the interaction will be peaceful, but not certain. You're my insurance."

Ricci hadn't had a problem with visitors to the ship until this vessel showed up. But now she very much wanted to avoid any chance of interaction with what might be a Burthen crew who might also be on the lookout for a missing and wanted Burthen heiress. Substantially having altered her appearance should prevent casual identification, but she didn't want to take even that small chance. "I'll be in my cabin," Ricci said, moving to unstrap from her couch.

Mitsumi with a quizzical look held up his hand. "No, Mei, I need you on the bridge. Until our visitors leave, we have to be able to move at a moment's notice if something goes awry—not that it will."

Ricci's eyes swept the bridge as if searching for an escape. She was cornered. "But we won't be able to leave as long as they're on board, so I'll just—"

"Stay on the bridge, Mei," Mitsumi said. "That is an order, not an invitation for discussion."

Ricci stared at Mitsumi, her face a mixture of fear and defiance. She turned her head and nodded. If she forced the issue much further, it would raise uncomfortable questions. Mitsumi and Quest pushed off leaving Ricci, Koning, and Mantor on the bridge watching as the shuttle from the other ship approached and docked.

Ricci noted the airlock cycling as the visitors boarded. The minutes inched by, Ricci dreading the prospect of Mitsumi deciding in a last minute fit of hospitality to offer a tour of their ship. Ricci fixed her eyes on the airlock indicator as if trying to force its use by power of mind. At last, the inner airlock door opened then closed, the outer door following a moment later. Their visitors had left. In gravity Ricci would have slumped. In the zig her arms floated away from her sides. She worked her jaw, trying to unknot the muscles she'd used to clamp her teeth.

As she marched along the walkway daring anyone to obstruct her passage, Fylan's determination hardened into an iron resolution. A month since Chandra and his crew had slipped through her grasp and there hadn't been a sign of them. Chandra's crews' identities were still a mystery. She hadn't had a good look at any of them on the planet, and her injuries had clouded what memory she had. And Khons hadn't watched Chandra's ship before its departure, so they had no record of who was on board. She took grim satisfaction at having discovered yet another reason for having thrown Khons out an airlock.

At one level their failure to appear was understandable since they had no doubt planned a lengthy voyage searching however many planets Chandra had on his database. But they had found something on that first planet, and despite the feelers she'd sent out by message drone to the Federated Worlds, she'd received no word that their ship had turned up with anything to sell. Maybe they were operating under false registration. Maybe the item had been worthless. Maybe both.

Kantic Burthen was still intensely interested in Chandra's list and had ordered her to use all the Consortium's resources in finding him. Fylan hadn't needed that order; she had already brought those resources to bear on the problem. She had a personal score to settle with Chandra and his crew. They had nearly killed her—no one escaped punishment for that. She'd find them somehow.

At headquarters in the business district of Support's principal city, one of her implants transmitted an encrypted access code, and the door slid open. With a deep scowl and invisible lips, Fylan projected her foul mood like a flashing radiation warning, and people stayed well clear of her as she strode through the lobby. Once in her office, she settled into the chair behind her desk and waited while her assistant acted as an interface with the much more powerful processor sitting unobtrusively in a corner and connecting her to the Consortium's central hub. The connection made, a holographic dashboard appeared before her and she fixed her eyes on priority communications.

Still nothing on Chandra.

More disappointment to stifle. She moved on to her list of the crises de jour. One of her idiot subordinates on Garden had killed the head of the family that was their principal Rapt manufacturer in a duel over a man. She swore under her breath reading that. Love triangles caused more havoc than most wars. Now she had to repair relations with the family. A contract prospector out of Neopa had bolted and set up his own organization that she was just now finding out was stronger than the Consortium on that planet. And to round the morning off, her brain dead organizational head on Newome had massacred three prospectors and their crews. "To send a message" he'd said in his defense. Although his heart was in the right place, he'd tried to shoot the men in broad daylight at the spaceport which turned into a running battle before the task was accomplished. For that lack of subtlety Newome's constabulary, one of the few she didn't have in her pocket, was all over her operation there like prospectors on First Civ tech.

She picked the Rapt problem first and began the task of putting together a peace offering she could afford. An hour into this effort a notice popped up. One of her subordinates had asked to communicate with her, the subject—Chandra. Expectations rising despite her attempts to keep a lid on them, she accepted the request. Omari's head emerged from the dashboard.

Despite her attempt at restraint, her eyes sparkled with anticipation. "Do you have Chandra for me, Omari?"

Omari's eyes widened in surprise. He shook his head in negation and looked like he wanted to disappear. "N-no, boss." He swallowed hard. "You said you wanted us to report anything, the smallest thing even, that might have the slightest connection to Chandra." He spoke as if the speed with which he delivered this qualification might insulate him from a backlash.

Her eyes dulled and her spirits sank. This would be another Andack chase. She'd had enough of those in the last month. She should be used to them by now. With a sigh and doing her best to keep disappointment from her voice, her subordinates reacted badly when she displayed disappointment, she said, "Tell me what you've got."

Omari's face brightened, and he nodded. "Like I say it might be nothing, but I've picked up rumors of prospectors who claim to have a data store with designs of spectacular First Civ tech."

Fingers drumming on her desk, she felt her lips compress. She expected a modicum of common sense from her people. Thousands of prospectors had made similar claims. "Omari," she drew out his name making it into a threat.

Omari licked his lips then continued speaking faster. "But this group, they're trying to remain anonymous. They aren't letting anyone know who they are."

Her fingers stilled, and she perked up. Anonymity was rare but not unheard of among prospectors. Most wanted the world to know what they had found. "And you think this might be Chandra's group."

Somewhat alarmed, Omari shook his head. "I'm not saying that, boss. You wanted to know unusual activity involving prospecting."

That wasn't quite what her orders had been, but she'd let it slide for the moment. "Where are these prospectors now?"

Omari frowned. "We don't know—somewhere in the system. I only know about them from sources with one of the tech companies that received a request for bid. Whoever is behind it, their security is pretty good. All I have is what I told you."

Fylan nodded. That was also normal for prospectors who wanted to remain anonymous. Omari had been fortunate to gather as much information as he did.

"What concern is your source with and who are the other bidders?" With that information, she could target the bidders.

"My contact is with Consolidated Tech, but they aren't bidding and my source couldn't identify any other bidders."

With that idea spaced, only one option remained.

"It's not much," Omari said, "but what if we broadcast that we claim this data store for ourselves and put out the word we'll be inspecting exchanges?"

Oh, that was tempting. Her organization wasn't large or well connected enough to make good on the inspection threat, but the Consortium's unsavory reputation would inject enough fear into the system to disrupt whatever exchange this prospector might arrange. Unfortunately, it would also disrupt every planned exchange, not just the one she wanted to target. That would cause a lot of heat. It was an anti-matter planet buster. She'd use it, but only in response to solid information. "No, we won't do that—yet. Keep digging. See if you can come up with something solid."

His face relaxing with relief, Omari nodded. "Will do, boss."

She terminated the connection. Omari's face faded back into her dashboard. Her face grim, she stared unseeing at the tasks mounting in front of her. In her imagination Chandra's crew writhed in pain under her hands—the personal touch.

Only fifteen of the twenty-eight contacts showed any interest in the Ark. Chandra expressed surprise at that, but Mitsumi thought fifteen showed exceptionally high response. "Look at it from their point of view, Aber," Mitsumi said after they wrapped up their last demonstration of the Ark. The airlock door had just closed on the Altamira Tech Group. Mitsumi pushed off to head to the bridge. Chandra followed.

"When they return, most prospectors don't understate what they've found. Prospectors think wild claims will attract interest and money when the opposite is true; the grander the claims, the less interest they generate. I worried that potential buyers might see our description even as modest as it was as too extravagant."

This explanation mollified Chandra, but it did nothing to reduce his impatience. "Everyone who's interested has seen the Ark," Chandra said, "so now the bidding's open. When can we expect it to start? We need to move this along."

"Aber, Altamira's delegation hasn't even made it back to their ship yet, and the others have only had days to evaluate what they've seen and prepare a bid." Mitsumi emerged onto the bridge, Chandra right on his heels. "You can't expect them to—"

"The first bid's in," Koning said, cutting Mitsumi off.

Chandra rubbed his hands in delight. "You were saying, Holtz?"

"Let's see, Sentaa," Mitsumi said.

A list of bidders replaced the image of the retreating shuttle on the view screen. There beside Altamira Tech was the first bid: two hundred and fifty-thousand credits.

Chandra's glee at the bidding having started turned to indignity. "That's outrageous," Chandra said. "It's worth a hundred times that, easy."

Mitsumi chuckled. "You've never done much negotiating, have you?"

Chandra bristled at the suggestion he lacked experience in business affairs. "I've been involved in lots of transactions, Holtz."

Mitsumi spread his hands. "Relax, Aber. That wasn't an attack. This is just throat clearing. We'll see the real action toward the end of the auction window. With that opening bid, you won't be disappointed."

Two hours later at the auction's close, the Elstone Combine's winning bid was eight and a half million credits and despite Mitsumi's prediction, Chandra was dissatisfied. "But the Ark's worth at least two hundred times that, just based on the skimming we've been able to do."

Mitsumi smiled to himself at Chandra's having doubled the Ark's estimated worth in two hours. Among the crew assembled on the bridge to watch the bidding, no one else appeared to share Chandra's feelings.

"Aber, I don't like recriminations," Ricci said, "so please don't take this the wrong way when I point out that we expected this precise outcome. Your share is enough to cure your daughter and never work again. Wasn't that what you wanted?"

Chandra glared at Ricci for a moment, then his countenance softened. "You're right. I can accomplish what I set out to do. But it galls me," Chandra said, regaining his outrage, "to think of those bandits paying a pittance and making off with something so valuable."

"Another rule of negotiation," Mitsumi said. "Don't second guess yourself at what might have been. We made our decision—it worked out; you've accomplished your goal. Let the rest go."

CHAPTER 16

The Elstone Combine insisted the exchange take place on Support. Mitsumi had resisted, but Elstone wouldn't budge. It was on planet or the deal was off. This presented issues everyone had wanted to avoid. They could make planet either by using their own shuttle from orbit or docking at a station and using the station's shuttle. Security concerns eliminated the latter option. No one wanted to carry eight and a half million credits worth of First Civ tech through a station and board a shuttle. But dropping into orbit meant providing identifying information to traffic control and that meant exposing themselves to the Consortium.

A transponder embedded in the ship's hull provided identification information. Except for a power connection, the transponder was isolated from every ship's system and was designed to be unalterable. A planetary system database retained ownership data; the data changed with each new owner, but the ship's identification was static. Or at least that was the intent.

Twelve hours before the exchange, the crew had gathered in the mess to discuss alternatives.

"We could risk it," Koning said. "We weren't broadcasting our identity around Mitsumi when the pirates found us. They don't know our ship's ID."

"But they know Aber," Ricci said. "And they planted a tracker aboard the ship. Isn't the ship registered to him?"

Chandra perked up at that. "But registration information

195

is confidential. They can't access it."

Mitsumi shook his head and dismissed Chandra's comment. "This is the Consortium, remember? I don't think we can count on their observing legal niceties. We have to assume they have tentacles everywhere."

"Send the shuttle?" Mantor said. "What if we hung out outside traffic control space and had the shuttle just drop on in? The shuttle doesn't have an ID transponder."

"Because," Mitsumi said with exaggerated patience, "traffic control watches shuttles descending from orbiting spacecraft. It would spot our shuttle and, without knowing where it came from paste all kinds of warning signs and alerts over it—something sure to catch the Consortium's attention."

Mantor gave Mitsumi a sour look, but remained silent. They looked at each other at a loss for ideas.

"I can do it," Quest said without preamble.

"You can do what?" Koning asked.

"I can spoof the ID transponder," Quest said without emotion.

"That's great, Tai," Ricci said with a broad smile. "Problem solved."

Mitsumi was not as sanguine, nor as trusting as Ricci seemed to be. "Tai, how do you propose to spoof the ID transponder?"

Quest shrugged. "I have a device that, placed inside and outside the hull at the transponder's location, absorbs the radiation and emits in its stead a signal of our own design with ID information we dictate. I can turn us into another ship."

"See," Ricci said, "problem solved."

Of all of his crew, Quest had proved himself to be the most trustworthy and reliable, but Mitsumi had a hard time convincing himself Quest could perform as claimed. Besides, there were other issues. "Okay, Tai, let's suppose for a moment you can perform this magic. What ID are we going to send? Because if we send the wrong one, it'll raise as many alarms as using the shuttle without one."

Quest surveyed the skeptical crew for a few moments. "I have a list of phantom ships registered to various aliases. We use one of those and no one knows who we are."

Mitsumi raised his eyebrows in surprise. It appeared that Quest *had* thought of everything.

A few hours later, the starship *Understated Subtlety* transmitted its ID to Support orbital traffic control and was assigned an orbit without appearing to raise any concerns. Mitsumi wasn't thrilled when everyone but Ricci and Mantor wanted to be part of the exchange, but Chandra's insistence on being present particularly annoyed him.

"I don't want you on the planet, Aber," Mitsumi said. The crew had gathered again in the mess to plan strategy for the exchange. Mitsumi glanced at the others for help before focusing again on Chandra. "The Consortium must have identified us. After it placed the tracker in our HE drive, they undoubtedly watched who showed up to crew the ship."

"Which is why," Chandra said with some heat, "we have ident kits to defeat facial recognition systems like almost everyone else on Support. Besides, we don't know the Consortium is looking for us here, and in what universe can they know of a private transaction between us and Elstone, anyway? We engaged a third party to make the actual delivery, so even if they targeted the exchange they wouldn't be able to tie us to it."

Mitsumi tried changing tactics. "Why do you want to be there then? We'll be monitoring the transaction remotely which you can do just as well from the ship as on the surface."

Chandra shook his head, refusing to yield. "I need to make sure it's a smooth exchange."

"Which," Mitsumi said, "you're not equipped to ensure, even if you were close enough to attempt an intervention." With the precautions they had taken, the odds were small that anything would interfere, but Chandra's presence would needlessly raise those odds. "Look, Aber, Sentaa wants to travel with us as well, and I won't allow that."

Koning started in surprise. "Since when?"

"Since now," Mitsumi said. "Every extra person on planet makes the exchange more dangerous."

Koning shot back. "So why do you and Tai need to be there? You're just 'extra people' aren't you?"

Mitsumi closed his eyes and took a deep breath, releasing it slowly. He did not need this fight right now. He opened his eyes and tilted his head in Quest's direction. "Someone has to pilot the shuttle. Tai has demonstrated a unique ability to handle emergencies and I'm in charge."

Koning opened her mouth to offer a rebuttal, but Chandra jumped in.

"No, Holtz, *I'm* in charge." Chandra glowered at Mitsumi. "Remember? *I* put up the money for the ship and supplies. *I* provided the coordinates for our find. *I* figured out what we had and told you what it was worth."

Mitsumi bristled at Chandra's selective memory. "*You're* the one who betrayed us and almost killed us all. *You're* the reason we have to take these precautions in the first place, and *you're* lucky to be alive after the stunt you pulled. Or don't you remember that the rest of the crew was ready to flash freeze you in space?" Mitsumi swept his eyes over the others. He had everyone's attention, but he wasn't sure he had their support.

To Mitsumi's surprise, Quest was the first one to voice an opinion.

"Captain, I believe the additional risk to be miniscule. He wants to go. I think you should let him."

Koning looked thoughtful. "I was as mad at Aber as anyone. Fire, I led the charge to airlock him. But without him we wouldn't be where we are, and he does have more to lose than any of us. I say let him go even if I have to stay behind because of it."

Mitsumi saw how this would end. If he'd lost Koning he'd lost everyone. "Mei?" Mitsumi said.

Ricci glanced at Chandra, then fixed her eyes on Mitsumi. "I'm with Sentaa—he should be there if he wants to."

Mantor shrugged. "Sure."

"Fine," Mitsumi said. "Aber comes, but you know what I think. It's a bad idea."

"C'mon, Holtz," Chandra said in a conciliatory tone, a broad smile on his face. "It'll be okay, you'll see. Four more hours and we're rich."

CHAPTER 17

The descent was uneventful. As the shuttle settled onto its assigned pad, Mitsumi called for passage to the planetary transportation hub. Quest prepared to lock up the shuttle with thumb and eye biometric scanners. What government existed on Support was notoriously lax in securing property from theft. If the authorities discovered the theft and caught you, they would prosecute, but expending resources on prevention was not high on the government's priority list.

Chandra struggled out of his couch—Support's high gravity, a lead weight on his limbs. This would not be a pleasant stay, short though it would be. He had taken "Muscle Boost$_{en}$, a guaranteed boost to your hi g prime or your money back!", but either the extra muscle took a moment to kick in, or he was getting his money back. Mitsumi and Quest didn't seem to feel the effect.

"Okay, are we ready?" Chandra said, eager to be off. Now that the prospect of concluding this chapter in his and his family's life was close, the slightest delay was intolerable. Mitsumi gave him a cool look.

"Patience, Aber," Mitsumi said. "If the shuttle disappears while we're gone, that would ruin your whole day."

Chandra resisted the urge to snap back a scathing retort. He could afford to be generous now on the cusp of ending the nightmare that had started a year and a half ago with Pari's diagnosis. Quest completed his security procedure. Chandra rose from his chair and stood in front of the airlock ready to leave.

"Aber," Mitsumi said. Chandra turned. Mitsumi held out a facial identification suppression suite. "Don't forget this." On Support, people routinely used suppression suites to avoid the ubiquitous watchers. Mitsumi had had a hard time convincing Chandra to spring for them, but he was glad he had.

Chandra accepted the small box from Mitsumi and opened it. Inside was a cloth mask that fit over his face with straps around his head and a smaller box with a red button. "I've never used one of these before," Chandra said, examining the mask and straps. Mitsumi and Quest were fitting their masks to their faces. His work for the Consortium had been on Support Five High Station; he'd never taken a trip planetside.

"You just put on the mask like we're doing," Mitsumi said, "and trigger the suite with the actuator." He held up a small box identical to the one in Chandra's kit and pressed the button. "The active molecular machines in the mask infuse into your face. They are pre-programmed to use atoms from your bones and blood to reshape your face."

"Yes," Chandra snapped, "I'm familiar with the concept. I just didn't know how to begin." Chandra pulled the mask over his face and stared at the button for a moment. The process was harmless. People used them every day, but faced with the prospect of trillions of nanometer scale machines pulling atoms from his bones and placing them elsewhere, his skin crawled.

"Couldn't we wear the masks and do without all the reshaping?" Chandra asked, wishing that the answer was yes.

"Scans penetrate the cloth," Quest said.

Chandra eyed the box and the button. With a deep breath, he pushed the button. Light pinpricks erupted over his face, although he was certain that was his over-active imagination since the machines were a thousand times smaller than the pores of his skin through which they traveled.

"How long does this take?" Chandra said, resisting the

urge to scratch what was rapidly becoming an intolerable itch on his face. At that moment a chime sounded from the box Mitsumi held.

"About that long," Mitsumi said. He removed the mask and replaced it and the actuator device in the box. Although Chandra had expected a change in Mitsumi's countenance, the reality was startling. Mitsumi produced a pair of lenses and slipped them on his eyes. He gave a pair to Quest and to Chandra. The lenses would mask biomarkers associated with their eyes.

"While on the surface, we should assume someone is monitoring our communications and provide as little information as possible. Elstone Combine knows us only as representatives of a prospector, so don't refer to anything that might identify us."

Chandra's actuator beeped. He took off the mask, replacing it and the actuator in the box.

Chandra held up his assistant and enabled the mirror function to see the result. His face had been re-sculpted. Nano machines had narrowed his nose, lengthened his jaw and raised his cheekbones making them more prominent. They had deepened his eye sockets and moved them a centimeter wider apart. As with Mitsumi and Quest, the result was unrecognizable on cursory inspection.

"If you're finished admiring yourself," Mitsumi said, "we should leave."

Chandra lowered his assistant and gestured toward the airlock, then gave in to his imaginary itch and scratched his face. Chandra picked up the Ark which was in a container Mantor had manufactured. Quest carried the equipment Chandra had used to access the ark.

At the top of the ramp just outside the airlock Chandra hesitated. Clouds lowered overhead, and a brisk chill breeze redolent with growing things and rain's damp scent swirled around the shuttle. A few drops spattered on Chandra's face. Chandra savored the clean scent of life in air that hadn't been filtered, recirculated, and sterilized in a futile effort to remove the persistent smells of six people trapped in a sealed can weeks on end.

They had put down at the principal spaceport in Alcante, the largest urban area on Support. An automated ground vehicle appeared. Programmed to take them to the Planetary Transport Hub, the car would complete the journey in fifteen minutes and twenty-three seconds according to the display inside. As they wound through shuttles and other larger vessels, Mitsumi spoke.

"I have the coordinates of our meeting. At the Hub we'll engage a private urban car to take us to our destination. We are arriving a little over an hour early. I want to circulate around the area, make sure no one has followed us, and no one's waiting for us."

Their vehicle pulled into a line of identical cars in front of a large building. They left their vehicle and joined a flood of people from every Federated World heading toward the Hub's entrance. Chandra spied a few tall Neopans and even taller Tonians—identifiable not only from their height but from their carbon fiber exoskeletons. No amount of muscle enhancement would permit inhabitants of those planets from wandering on the surface without mechanical aid. Only a few squat forms of people from Support returning home were mixed in with the crowd. As they approached the entrance, the throng became more compact. Despite the breeze that continued to blow, the air became more pungent; diets from across the Federation varied as did the resulting metabolites. Chandra wrinkled his nose. After a brief respite in clean air, the strange scents reminded him of *Are We There Yet?*'s aromatic atmosphere from the first few weeks of their voyage until he had become accustomed to the smells and they faded into the background.

Once inside the Hub, the arrivals were jammed even closer together in a low-ceilinged screening corridor. Shuffling down the passage, the scent and noise from close packed humanity each trying to be heard above the din almost overwhelmed his senses. The government on Support had no immigration or arrival checks to speak of. It did, however, frown on the use of weapons above a particular destructive threshold. The hall through which they passed spotted any mechanical, chemical, energetic, or biological weapon capable of killing twenty people or more in one activation.

Once through the corridor and into the building, the crowd thinned, expanding into an enormous vaulted arrival hall. Chandra and Mitsumi fell in behind Quest. Mitsumi had left transportation arrangements up to Quest who was native to Support. Up ahead, a line of colorfully dressed individuals spread out in front of the arrivals. These were salesmen, and they broadcast their offerings for anyone with an assistant and a pair of flash glasses to see.

Chandra pulled his assistant and flash glasses out of a pocket and connected. The line of people in front of him exploded into a mass of color and animation. Each of the gaudily dressed individuals offered a service or product which, in keeping with Support's open culture, included satisfying every imaginable desire or whim. Much of what was on offer had never even occurred to him. Some things appeared downright impossible.

About half the arriving crowd stopped to investigate or procure the displayed delights while the rest proceeded straight toward transportation services. Past the line of salesmen, Quest led them off to the right only to stop before a blank wall. Chandra glanced over his shoulder at the crowds flowing toward ground transportation.

Quest tapped on his assistant and a door popped out of the wall. Quest pulled it open and gestured Mitsumi and Chandra through. Chandra stopped opposite Quest before following Mitsumi through.

Doubt seized Chandra. "How did you do that?"

Quest lifted his eyebrows.

Frustrated, Chandra asked again. "The door, how did you

manage that?"

Quest shrugged and remained silent.

"Aber," Mitsumi said. "Let's get going."

Chandra held up a hand, forestalling Mitsumi. "No, I demand to know what's going on here. Where are you taking us?" Chandra had raised his voice. A few arrivals stopped and looked their way.

"Aber, don't be silly," Mitsumi whispered, with a worried look over Chandra's shoulder and gesturing him to come along. "He saved your life, remember?"

"He saved my life *before* I unlocked the Ark's secrets and *before* we knew how valuable it was. And I want an explanation. Why are you taking us this way?"

In response to Chandra's shouting, a few arrivals drifted in their direction. Chandra understood he had no choice but to trust Quest and Mitsumi, but concern with being this close to his goal and somehow failing overrode reason.

"Aber!" Mitsumi hissed. "Aber, we need to go, now."

Chandra glared at Quest who returned his look without expression. Mitsumi grabbed Chandra's arm. Chandra wrenched it free. "Well, Tai?"

"I've had occasion to travel to Support and make my way on the planet without being observed. I set up this access to a private secure mode of planetary transport to ensure I could do so. Since it worked well in the past, I thought to take advantage of it now. Your outburst has potentially compromised that plan."

From Chandra's right a half-dozen people were making their way toward them. What choice did he have now? Chandra licked his lips, nodded once and followed Mitsumi through the door. Quest closed the door behind them. Lights flickered on at the door's closing.

Quest strode ahead past Chandra and Mitsumi down a wide hallway. Mitsumi marched after him without a backward glance.

After a ten-minute twisting and turning hike through

the bowels of the Hub they arrived at another door. Quest again manipulated his assistant, the door popped open, and they emerged onto a busy street. When a vehicle pulled up, Quest gestured them inside. Chandra climbed in the back seat while Mitsumi and Quest took the front.

Mitsumi twisted in his seat, confronting Chandra. "What was that back there, Aber?" Mitsumi fumed. "I agreed to let you come with us on the exchange only because you wouldn't cause trouble or call attention to ourselves. Then, first thing you make a scene? Do you want to screw up this deal?"

Chandra had been asking himself the same question. Confused by his own doubt, Chandra extended a hand toward Quest. "It's just he always seems to have the perfect answer, the perfect solution almost as if," Chandra hesitated, knowing where he was going with this sounded absurd. "As if he's planned the entire expedition," Chandra finished his voice trailing off.

Mitsumi snorted. "Are you listening to yourself? Because you sound crazy."

Chandra remained silent. It was absurd, but surely someone else could see how strange Quest's flawless performance was.

"I prepare," Quest said.

"What do you mean, Tai?" Mitsumi said.

"I've been on a number of crews and prospecting voyages. Over the years, I've noted common problems and have prepared for those eventualities. It seems I've anticipated several of our difficulties, not because they are particular to us, but for the opposite reason."

"There you go, Aber," Mitsumi said. "No hidden motive required."

Chandra grudgingly accepted his answer with a nod. Prospectors want to hide for any number of reasons, and who knows what Tai's life on Support had been like.

Dismissing Chandra's concerns, Mitsumi asked, "Tai, you have the coordinates for meeting our proxy, don't you?" Quest nodded assent. "All right, take us there in a roundabout route. I want to make sure we're not followed and no one's putting together a greeting party for us."

Quest pulled his assistant out and plugged it into the vehicle. A gap in the traffic appeared for their benefit, and Chandra sank into his seat as the silent vehicle shot away from the curb. After a few moments as they sped silently along what appeared to be a main thoroughfare, Chandra was glued to the window. Support was unlike Chandra's home planet Del in several ways. Del had been one of the last planets discovered and incorporated into the Federation and to this day remained somewhat backward.

Though its inhabitants had worked hard to catch up to the other Federated Worlds, Del was a backwater. Partly that was down to the prevailing religion which had maintained as one of its taboos a prohibition against seeking any knowledge from nature. Del's creation myths bore similarities to those of the other Federated Worlds, but Del's early inhabitants had taken a somewhat different lesson from the sky gods' attacks. That lesson was that the sky gods had punished Del's inhabitants for seeking to uncover the sky gods' secrets.

By the time Chandra was born, the old religion had faded from prominence in Del society, but Chandra's parents had followed the old ways and raised him accordingly. It was only after his parents had formed his family, selecting his wife from among the children of friends, that Chandra had rebelled and enrolled in a local school that emphasized science and scientific and technical knowledge. But even with exposure to other Federated Worlds and, despite increasing variations from the old ways, Del's society remained remarkably homogeneous.

Support was a different matter altogether. From earliest times, its culture had advanced the notion of individual liberty and non-conformity. Support had historically enjoyed limited governments.

Chandra stared in fascination at the results as their

vehicle passed in the midst. No two buildings were the same. Here was an unadorned multi-story oblong next to a squat structure with twisting spires, followed by another with pitched roofs partially obscuring the spherical building beside it. The people walking along the side of the street dressed in varied, contrasting fashions—skintight outfits, long flowing robes, helmets and hats—and had altered their appearance in bizarre ways: piercings and rings and tattoos, fully and partially shaved heads. The variety made Chandra dizzy. How could you evaluate someone by their appearance in such a welter of individual expression? You wouldn't have any idea upon meeting someone what to expect.

Their vehicle glided to a stop at an intersection, awaiting its turn to proceed. As Chandra gawked at the passing parade and idly fingered his earring, a man walked around the corner staring at his assistant. He stopped opposite Chandra and raised his head. Chandra froze. It was Kelton, his supervisor at the Consortium. They had interacted every day, multiple times a day. Their eyes locked. Sweat prickled Chandra's forehead. *He can't recognize me.* Yet, Kelton's eyes narrowed, studying him, and he lifted his assistant. Chandra looked away, willing the vehicle to move. They accelerated through the intersection.

He shouldn't, but curiosity overwhelmed his common sense. Chandra looked back as they pulled away. It was a mistake. Kelton had his assistant up, pointing at their vehicle. The backward glance offered Kelton one last direct view of his face. Chandra whipped his head around. Kelton absolutely did not know who he was. The ident kit had reconfigured his face and even disguised his eyes. He reached up absently and rubbed his earring.

They continued circling the area. After ten minutes, Chandra concluded that it had been his imagination; Kelton hadn't tumbled to anything.

A solid red bar flashed across Chipta's face in the middle of his report on the latest prospector "accident" he had arranged. Without a word of explanation, Fylan terminated her communication with Chipta. The emergency override meant either someone had located Chandra or her life was in danger. Either way it demanded her immediate attention above everything else. Kelton's face, covered with a huge, triumphant smile, emerged from the background.

"I've got him," he said, his grin widening even more.

At last! But tamping her excitement—she didn't want to overreact—she said, "Where? And how did you identify him?"

"Noallig Prospect with two of his crew. It was his diamond stud. I saw someone suspicious fondling the same kind of diamond stud Chandra has."

She deflated—diamond studs were common as dirt.

Upon seeing her reaction, Kelton shook his head beaming still. "No. This guy was rubbing at his stud just like Chandra used to do all the time. So, I captured an image and ran the diamond through a comparison with an image on file. It's the same—same flaws, same cut with identical planes. It's him all right. I have someone following them right now."

An answering smile appeared on her face, though anyone looking would have described it more as a snarl. Anticipation glowing, she imagined her hands around his throat. "Pick them up."

"Captain," Quest said, "I think we've picked up a tail."

"Not possible," Mitsumi said.

"They're being careful, but someone is definitely following us."

Chandra's cheeks burned. It must have been Kelton. *He recognized me*, Chandra thought. He toyed with his earring. But that was inconceivable. His face and eyes were out of the question; his clothes were nondescript and, in any event, were nothing he had worn before in their interactions. He had no other identifying characteristic.

"Who could it be?" Mitsumi said. "And why would they want to follow us?"

In desperation, Chandra assured himself that their mysterious pursuer had nothing to do with Kelton because nothing could have given away Chandra's identity. Chandra became aware he was rubbing his diamond stud, a gift from Pari on his birthday five years ago. He jerked his hand from his ear in horror. His wife had since commented on his habit of rubbing that diamond when he was thinking or under stress. If Kelton remembered that gesture.... An image of Kelton pointing his assistant leapt to mind. He went cold. They could analyze the stone.

"I don't know—" Quest began.

Chandra sobbed and buried his face in his hands. He had been so close.

Quest and Mitsumi turned toward Chandra. "Aber," Mitsumi said with an undertone of menace. "Do you have something to add here?"

Chandra couldn't bring himself to speak. For a moment he remained with his face covered, unable to confront his action's consequences. He lifted his head. "It's the Consortium."

Mitsumi cursed, then contemplated Chandra in silence. After a full minute he asked, "What did you do, Aber?"

Chandra explained that he'd seen Kelton. He described his habit and Kelton's look of suspicion. "I'm sorry, Holtz." Chandra said. "I should have listened to you and not come to the planet. It's just, I...What are we going to do?" In panic, Chandra struggled for breath. He had to make that rendezvous; he had to save Pari.

Mitsumi turned from Chandra. "What are they doing, Tai?"

Tai shrugged. "Just watching us." He stiffened. "Check that, they're moving to intercept us."

Chandra shuddered. They had to escape. It was Pari's life if they didn't. But just under the surface of his concern for Pari, his imagination ran a little film starring him and Domenica and featuring gleaming, sharp torture implements. He gulped. Pari's life came first, but his followed right after. He pounded on the back of Quest's seat. "We have to lose them and make the exchange."

"Can you lose them, Tai?" Mitsumi asked, ignoring Chandra's outburst.

"Yes."

"And still make our exchange?"

"Probably."

Chandra was horrified. "What probably? We have to be at the exchange. We have to complete the deal."

Mitsumi turned to Chandra. "We'll do our best, Aber. Instead of issuing decrees why don't you contemplate how much easier this would be if you'd listened to me and stayed away?"

Chandra leaned back in his seat and closed his eyes. He was so close, and Holtz was right—it was his fault. His stomach churned at the thought that he had put the meeting in jeopardy by insisting on being present and by questioning Quest's motives. If he hadn't protested and slowed them down Kelton never would have seen him.

"Okay, Tai, it's your show. What did you have in mind?"

Quest reached out and touched a red circle on the console in front of him. The console morphed into a cluster of gauges and readouts. A stick popped up next to Quest's right hand and pedals emerged from the floorboard at his feet. Restraints appeared by Quest, Mitsumi, and Chandra.

"I have activated the seat restraints," Quest said. "I would strongly suggest you use them."

Despite an outwardly calm appearance, Quest's heart pounded

as he recalled the last time he'd been on Support manually controlling a ground vehicle. Remembering his route and hoping there'd been no major changes he lowered the gear ratio, whipped the vehicle one hundred and eighty degrees and slid between two vehicles in what had been the lanes for oncoming traffic.

"Are you crazy?" Chandra screamed. "You'll kill us all!" Chandra closed his eyes and cringed, bracing for a crash. Quest yanked the vehicle to the left back across into oncoming traffic avoiding a truck and jolting across a strip of low shrubs, tearing up the plants. They plunged down a grassy embankment and slammed into another street. With a screech of rending metal the vehicle's left front bumper gave way, but the wheels bit the road surface and they shot off dragging a shrub behind them. Still rocketing down the street, the traffic signal at the next intersection changed from advance to stop, but Quest engaged the side scanners and timed the approaching vehicles to shoot a gap. They just made it, but lost the shrub. Quest stood on the brakes and hauled the steering to the right, juddering the car around a corner and narrowly missing a pedestrian who saluted them with an obscene gesture. Now he was in familiar territory. He gripped the steering to still adrenaline fueled tremors, slowed and turned right down a street lined with grimy industrial warehouses and manufacturing plants. He checked the rear scanner. "We've lost them," Quest said.

"Are you sure?" Pale and trembling, Chandra raised himself from the back seat where he had huddled during their escape.

With a deep breath to calm his hammering heart, Quest checked the scanners once more. "Yes," he said.

Chandra ran a sleeve across his forehead. "Can we make it in time?"

"Yes."

"I'm impressed, Tai," Mitsumi said. "Where'd you learn to drive?"

Quest remained silent, certain the ache in his right shoulder was a phantom pain.

CHAPTER 18

Teeth grinding in frustration, Fylan glared at Kelton. He'd pay for his screw up, but that was for later. Now, she had to fix his mistake. "You're certain they didn't arrive from any of the Support high stations?"

Kelton's eyes shifted away, then focused again on Fylan. "Yes," he said.

Fingers drumming on her desk, Fylan decided to take his word. If he was wrong, he was a dead man. "Okay, cover the spaceports—seal them tight. They have only one way off planet. I don't want them to use it." Chandra and his friends had evaded capture, so someone in their group was familiar with Support. He'd know the only place to hide would be... "Get people in the Dark Zone scanning for their vehicle. We know what it looks like?"

Kelton looked like he wanted to protest, but after this fiasco he deserved to have everything he did questioned. "Yes, we have multiple images. We'll find it."

What else? Well, they weren't getting away without rejoining their ship. If they managed to find a way off planet, someone should be in orbit to intercept them. "I'm lifting in the *Excuse*. I'll monitor the situation from orbit and chase them down if they make it off planet."

Kelton nodded. "Okay, boss." He reached forward to disconnect.

"Oh, and Kelton." Kelton looked at her, waiting for her command. "Spread the word. The Consortium claims an interest in the stolen technology and will inspect every transfer." She smiled inside. *You and your crew won't get paid today, Chandra,* she thought. *Unless I find you—then I'll pay you in full with plenty of interest.*

They met their contact on the city outskirts by an abandoned factory. Quest steered them toward the only other vehicle in sight. Their plan to arrive early had been shot when they'd had to escape the Consortium. They rolled to a halt a good distance away.

"That must be him," Chandra said to Mitsumi. "You should go."

Yep, this was it. Although the payment was not as generous as it might have been, it would still fund his expedition. His thoughts flashed to the sheet they'd recovered and the Artifact. Once he finished with Chandra's nonsense, he could concentrate on that mystery. Mitsumi nodded and instructed the door to open.

The low overcast from earlier had broken up allowing glimpses of Support's pale blue sky in between puffy, scudding clouds. Weeds poked through cracks, bending and swaying in the steady breeze in the paved surface around the factory. Mitsumi shivered and drew his light jacket closer to him. They had agreed that he would make the exchange—Quest would watch for trouble, and Chandra would remain hidden in the car. Mitsumi removed the Ark and the access equipment and approached the other vehicle.

A woman stepped out, gesturing for him to stop. Puzzled, Mitsumi came to a halt and rested the Ark and access equipment on the ground, waiting for the woman. She approached within a meter and stopped. He surveyed the surrounding area again for any signs of a trap or double cross, not that he thought it likely, the woman represented a highly recommended and bonded intermediary service.

"You're the sellers?" the woman said, combing a strand of wind-blown hair from her face with her hand.

"We are," Mitsumi said. "Is there a problem?"

"I would have contacted you if I'd found out sooner, but..." She shrugged. "The deal's off. We won't make the exchange."

Mitsumi's eyes widened, and he looked around wondering if he'd been wrong, and this was a trap. "What? Why not? Your organization agreed to. We paid you."

Apparently sensing trouble and unable to control himself despite recent events, Chandra emerged from the car and trotted over to Mitsumi. "What's going on?" he said.

Mitsumi glared at Chandra and held up his hand motioning him to silence. Chandra's meddling was the last thing he needed right now. Turning to the woman, Mitsumi said, "We have a contract. You're in breach and not completing our transaction will lower your perfect rating."

The woman shook her head. "No, we're invoking the unforeseen contingency cancellation clause. You'll get your fee back minus the agreed upon cancellation charge."

"You can't do this!" Chandra shouted. "We have a contract. You have to perform."

Mitsumi whirled on Chandra and through clenched teeth said, "Get back in the car before I have you picked up and carried there."

Chandra glowered at Mitsumi and the woman, but after a moment turned and trudged back to the car.

From every outward appearance, the exchange was routine. What would have made them change their mind? "What's the unforeseen contingency?"

"A short time ago the Consortium circulated information that it had a claim on certain First Civ technology and that it knew of all scheduled tech transfers. They said they'd be inspecting each exchange to find the claimed item." The woman tapped on her assistant. A hologram of the ark hovered above the device. "Look familiar?" The woman closed the hologram. "We're not willing to proceed under these circumstances."

Mitsumi's thoughts whirled. He had to be able to change her mind somehow. "The Consortium doesn't know about every exchange. Don't you think they're just bluffing to halt any exchanges?"

"It might be a bluff, but we can't know that and, since our contract allows us to invoke the unforeseen contingency clause at our sole and unfettered discretion, we don't have to try. It was a pleasure doing business with you." Turning on her heel, the woman marched away.

Disappointment clouded Mitsumi's mind, followed quickly by a growing anxiety. With the Consortium looking for them, how would they leave the planet? The lure of promised power and pressure from the Artifact that had faded into the background reasserted itself. He had to find a way off Support. The Ark was his best chance to fund his expedition and Support was a dead end now.

Chandra met him halfway back to the car. "What happened? Why did you let her go?"

Chandra looked past Mitsumi to the woman entering her vehicle. "Hey, you!" Chandra yelled his voice squeaking. "You can't leave. We had a deal!" Chandra tried to follow, but Mitsumi grabbed his shoulders and held him back. The woman sped off. Chandra wrenched himself free from Mitsumi's grip, roundly cursing Mitsumi. "What's wrong with you, Holtz?" he spat the words. "Why didn't you do something?"

Mitsumi ignored the outburst and moved toward their car—Mitsumi had had enough of Chandra for the moment. Chandra stood forlorn, gazing after the receding vehicle taking away their intermediary and their fortune. The wind whipped his hair across his face. Sunlight and shadow from the passing clouds illuminated and obscured him. He reached a hand toward the earring in his right ear, caught himself mid gesture and lowered his hand.

"After spotting Chandra on planet," Mitsumi said, "the

Consortium assumed he was here for a transfer and put out word they were looking for the Ark. They claimed to be monitoring every potential transfer."

Quest snorted and shook his head. "Yeah," Mitsumi said, "I don't believe it either, but it spooked our intermediaries."

"We could go ourselves," Quest said.

"Sure, except the Consortium has already identified Aber, and no doubt has pictures of us now too, not to mention a line on our vehicle." Mitsumi sighed. "No, we need to get back to the ship and review our options."

Quest eyed Mitsumi and nodded his head at Chandra, "What about him?" he said.

"Can't we leave him?" Mitsumi said. "We'd be sitting pretty right now if only he'd done what I told him to. Who's to say he won't screw up any of our other plans?"

Quest nodded in agreement, moved around the front of the vehicle and got in. He looked at Mitsumi, waiting for him to enter. Much as he wanted to at that moment, Mitsumi found he couldn't actually leave Chandra behind. Without him, they wouldn't have the Ark. "Aber," Mitsumi said, raising his voice over the wind. Chandra didn't respond. "Aber," Mitsumi said with more force. Chandra turned toward Mitsumi. "Get in the car; let's figure out what to do."

Chandra hesitated. *Seriously?* Mitsumi thought. *What does he think his options are? If we leave, he has no way off planet. The Consortium will find him in a heartbeat, and that's the end of everything he cares for.* Chandra turned away. Mitsumi walked to Chandra and stood beside him, gazing into the distance after the long departed intermediary.

"Look, Aber. This isn't the end. We'll figure something out. You can't stay here. The Consortium will find you. They'll torture you before they kill you. Then where will your family be? Where will Pari be?"

Chandra shook his head. "It was my fault, wasn't it? Without me here, the exchange would have been completed and everything would have been fine. I ruined it all."

"No argument here, Aber."

Chandra's shoulders slumped as he drew into himself. "So, maybe I should give up. None of my plans have worked. Perhaps my family would be better off..."

"Perhaps," Mitsumi said, not in the mood to coddle.

With narrowed eyes, Chandra shot a venomous look at Mitsumi, who continued staring in the distance.

"But I think you're overreacting. We're free and we have the Ark. As long as those two things are true, we still have a chance. But, as you've amply demonstrated, I can't order you around. You need to suit yourself."

Mitsumi turned and paced toward the car without looking back. They had no more time to waste—either Chandra would come along or not. The Consortium would be trying to locate them. They needed to be off planet—now. Mitsumi reached the car and glanced back. Chandra trudged toward them.

CHAPTER 19

"You can't get back to the shuttle," Ricci said again. Quest had directed their car to a sector of the city devoid of the otherwise ubiquitous video monitors —what Quest had called the Dark Zone. Private interests were keen on observing activity on the public streets, but in the Dark Zone the inhabitants regularly identified and destroyed any attempt at street surveillance.

"Oh, let 'em try, Mei," Koning said over the com. "More for us if they're caught."

"We have the Ark, Sentaa," Mitsumi said.

"Right," Koning said. "Like she said, you can't reach the shuttle. Even with the windows obscured, they must have enough on your car to spot you."

"Tai has that covered." Quest inclined his head. "We're on our way to switch vehicles."

"But that still leaves the approach to the shuttle—the Consortium will be watching," Ricci said.

"Mei, if they didn't understand that the first million times you said it," Koning said, "why would they get it now?"

Mitsumi stared out of the car window. A brilliant red and gold sunset beamed between buildings flashing by in the dusk. They had been hashing the same points for half an hour. Mitsumi worried that the Consortium might decipher their conversation, despite Quest's assurances that the encryption he'd installed on the *Yet* and on his assistant was impenetrable.

"Again," Mitsumi said, "Tai has the approach to the

220

shuttle under control with his contacts—"

"Who leak like a Tonian frigate. No offense, Mei," Koning said.

"So," Mitsumi said, "your solution is to retrieve the shuttle and send it to a different city? How is that any better? You think the Consortium won't extend its watch to every spaceport?"

"We've arrived," Quest said.

Their car pulled out of traffic and stopped behind another vehicle. It was a commercial model, emblazoned on the sides and rear with the images of naked or scantily clad women and men in provocative poses—advertisements for a popular local pleasure service. Chandra ogled; Mitsumi shot a look at Quest. "That's our next vehicle?" Mitsumi said. "I thought we agreed on a low profile."

Quest shrugged. "Stay or go, it's up to you."

Mitsumi, Quest, and Chandra left the car and piled into the other vehicle. Once on their way again, Mitsumi resumed arguing with Ricci and Koning. "We have to trust Tai's contacts. We have no other way out."

"Arrrgh," Koning said, "you're impossible. You can't—"

"We could jump," Quest said interrupting.

"Jump?" Mitsumi said, incredulous.

"The *Yet*," Quest said, "could jump to the surface, pick us up, and jump off. Viram's solved the gravity well problem."

The suggestion's improbability silenced everyone. For a full minute, no one spoke. "Well," Mitsumi said eventually, drawing out the word, "no one would expect it; *that's* for sure. But, one," Mitsumi held up a finger, "it would require a jump solution with a precision I'm not certain we can achieve. No offense, Sentaa." Koning didn't respond. Mitsumi held up a second finger. "And two, there's the explosion to consider."

"Explosion?" Ricci said.

"No one's ever done that maneuver before," Chandra said, picking up on Mitsumi's thought. "So, we're just guessing, but if you materialize a million cubic meters of starship in the atmosphere, you'll displace the same amount of air. That's what an explosive does to create a shock wave—displace air. I'm not sure how severe the shock would be, but I'm guessing you wouldn't want to be closer than twenty klicks, and it would destroy any structures in the vicinity."

"We could cross the Alticanel Mountains to the high desert," Quest said. "Two hours from here."

"Okay," Mitsumi said, "perhaps, but that still leaves the problem of—"

"I could do it," Koning said.

"Sentaa," Mitsumi said, "this is no time for your ego. Not to put too fine a point on it, but your performance has been marginal at best."

"I'm better, Captain, a lot better," Koning said. "You have to give me that."

"Sure, but a lot better compared to your starting point still doesn't make me glow with confidence when a mistake would destroy a planet."

"What do you mean?" Ricci said.

"A million cubic meters of displaced air is one thing, but if you appeared in the center of the planet," Chandra said. "That's a big boom. Lots of earthquakes and volcanoes. It might even crack open the crust."

"You know the accuracy of a jump increases with the inverse of the jump distance," Koning said. "Besides, I can control how close I want to come to the jump point and on which side of that point I'll err. There is no chance I'll put us in the ground."

Quest cleared his throat. "We need to decide," he said. "We know the options and risks. Every minute brings the Consortium closer."

"Tai, take us to the shuttle," Mitsumi said.

"That's your decision?" Koning said.

"Yes, Sentaa, it is," Mitsumi sighed, bracing for the backlash. To his surprise, none was forthcoming—Koning remained silent, although to Mitsumi the silence had a definite sulkiness to it. *Let her mope*, Mitsumi thought.

"I'll ping my contacts to prepare for us," Quest said, tapping away on his assistant.

"Okay," Ricci said. "Let us know when you've arrived at the shuttle. *Are We There Yet?* out."

Full dark had fallen on the city and, with the coming of night, this sector thrummed with activity. Buildings sported colorful flashing signs promising participation in or observation of any imaginable human experience, though the vast majority centered on sex and violence, combined with a wide variety of drugs and intoxicants. Servicers of any imaginable age and body type offered to satisfy your every whim. And there Mitsumi saw a sign showing a looped image of men dying at another's hand—strangled, beaten, knifed, shot. Below the holo what appeared to be dripping blood traced out the establishment's name: ThrillKill. And below that the slogan: "Death as close and personal as you want it to be."

Mitsumi recalled from previous postings that on Support it was legal to murder someone who wanted to commit suicide. Both parties, the argument went, came away happy— well, one was happy, the other was off to wherever he thought life's end would take him. But his beneficiaries were happy— they received the price of the contract.

Mitsumi surveyed the scene, wondering how it would be to worry only about a night's pleasure.

He closed his eyes against the flashing glare and leaned back against the seat. Maybe he should have opted for Quest's suggestion. No, it was too dangerous. This way gave them their best chance.

"We have a problem," Quest said.

Of course we do, Mitsumi thought. He waited a beat for Quest to offer an explanation.

"What is it, Tai?" Mitsumi said when Quest didn't provide one.

"My contacts report increased activity around the spaceport."

That sounded ominous, but they had expected that eventuality. Mitsumi thought they had it covered. "And?"

"Someone is interested in people leaving the planet."

"Right, we knew the Consortium would be looking for us. Your contacts were to prevent those interested people from finding us."

"They won't now."

Mitsumi waited again for Quest to fill in the blanks. When he failed to, Mitsumi prompted him, though this exercise was becoming tiresome. "Because?"

"The Consortium has announced anyone they catch helping us will incur the Consortium's wrath."

That was unexpected. The Consortium had escalated more than any of them had expected which meant Koning and Ricci had been right. He knew the answer to the next question, but he had to ask, anyway. "If we switched spaceports?"

"Won't work. They've covered all the ports."

Although he had expected the response, Mitsumi was disappointed. He wasn't sure whether he was more annoyed at having to trust Koning and Ricci or at having to admit they had been right. Imagining Koning's smug satisfaction at hearing the news, Mitsumi thought it was the latter. "Okay, we've no choice now. It's time for Plan B. Raise *Are We There Yet?* again.

Triumph rang in Koning's voice. She *knew* she'd been right. This was her chance to prove herself. "The first possible landing site is here," Koning highlighted a point on the map at her station, which was mirrored on the crew's networked assistants. "This flat spot two klicks from the mouth of Etkon Canyon. There's nothing around for kilometers. Mei has started the shuttle recovery," Ricci nodded acknowledgement. "I'll calculate the jump and shoot you the coordinates. Then we'll have Viram alter the HE drive. As soon as we're ready, we'll jump and meet you."

"We're on our way out of the city, Sentaa. In an hour and forty-five minutes, we'll be in the area you described."

"Okay, see you there," Koning said. "Hey, Captain, don't worry, we'll do this." Koning waited for Mitsumi's acknowledgement. After a moment when none was forthcoming, she said, "*Are We There Yet?* out." She guessed she could see Mitsumi's point; her performance had been less than outstanding. But she had this. She immersed herself in the jump program. Forty-five minutes later, she surfaced, having run the calculations five times until she was certain of the result. She transferred her result to the pilot's station and to Mitsumi's assistant.

"Did you see the jump coordinates, Mei?" Koning said. "Where are we on the shuttle?"

"I saw. The shuttle's ten minutes out," Ricci said.

Koning unbuckled from her station and floated to look over Ricci's shoulder. Everything was in order, but something nagged at her, she was forgetting something.

"So, we're ready to jump?" Koning said.

Ricci frowned. "Not until Viram's reconfigured the HE drive."

Koning snapped her fingers. Right, that was what was missing. "Hey, Viram," Koning said over the com. "We've got a little job for you." Mantor didn't respond—not unusual for him. Koning waited a moment and tried again. "Viram, please respond, we need you to reconfigure the HE drive for a jump down the well."

Ricci met Koning's eyes, her lower lip between her teeth concern on her face.

"I'll go," Koning said. She launched herself off the bridge and made her way to engineering, hoping the lack of response was a com fault. He wasn't in engineering. With increasing dread and anger, Koning shot down the ship's corridors to Mantor's cabin. Without success, Koning tried to gain entry. She pounded on the door. "Viram, open the door. We need you to configure a jump." No response.

225

Koning boiled with frustration. This was her moment to be the hero, show her stuff, earn everyone's adulation, and Mantor was going to screw it up. "Mei," Koning yelled into her communicator, "I can't raise Viram. He's not in engineering or anywhere else on the ship and his cabin door is locked. He must be in there. We need to do an override."

"I don't have those codes, Sentaa, and I don't know where to find them. Only Captain Mitsumi does."

"Well, raise him then." Koning was shouting now. "Without Viram we can't make the jump."

"I know that, Sentaa," Ricci muttered. Koning fumed, waiting to connect with Mitsumi. A moment later, Captain Mitsumi was on the com. Koning explained the situation and Mitsumi gave her the codes. Koning punched them in and burst into Mantor's cabin. Slack-jawed and unresponsive, Mantor floated above his bunk restrained by the sleep netting. Koning shook him. "Viram, wake up!" Koning glanced around the cabin for an explanation, although she was certain he was in a Rapt trance. There! The hypo spray floated in a corner turning lazily end over end. Anger boiled up. How dare this useless piece of flesh indulge his addiction now when she needed him? Koning found herself slapping Mantor's face again and again until Ricci caught her arm, spinning Ricci in the reaction.

"Sentaa, Mei? What's happening?" Mitsumi said.

Ricci stopped her spinning and appearing perplexed, fixed her eyes on Koning.

"Viram's in the trance," Koning spat the last word.

"How long?" Mitsumi said. "What was the dosage?"

"How should I know?" Koning shouted.

"The hypo spray memory should tell you."

Koning grabbed the hypo spray and fiddled with it until a dosage appeared. "This reads forty cc's," Koning said. "What does that mean?" Mitsumi remained silent. "Captain?"

"It means a three-hour trance give or take. When was it administered?"

Koning called up the display. "An hour ago. He'll be under another two hours. We don't have that kind of time."

"There's no choice, Sentaa. We'll have to wait."

"I'm not sure waiting is an option, Captain," Quest said joining the conversation.

"Explain, Tai," Koning said, preempting the usual dance of pausing until they had to prod Quest for an explanation.

"I think we're being followed," Quest said.

"Why do you think that?" Mitsumi asked.

"Traffic through the mountains to the high desert is sparse at this time of night. I tried to leave the city without passing through a monitored zone, but was unsuccessful. I watched the zone after we passed. A vehicle tracked our route through the zone and onto the Alticanel mountain highway. They don't appear to be trying to catch us up now, but if we have to wait for *Are We There Yet?*, they will see us and prevent us from boarding when the ship arrives."

"See us how?" Mitsumi asked. "We'll be invisible with only starlight."

"Infrared," Koning said, surprised Mitsumi didn't catch that. "In the cold night desert, you'll stand out like a beacon."

"So, that's it then," Ricci said, her voice heavy with resignation. "We have no way out. We're done."

Koning shot a frustrated look at Ricci and muted the connection. "That's your trouble rich girl. You've never had to think outside your tiny box, never had to fight for anything in your life." Ricci drew back stung by the accusation. *Except for me*, Koning thought. *She fought for me.* Koning's face softened with sympathy. "We're a long way from done, Mei. We'll come up with something." Koning unmuted the connection. "How are they following you, Tai?" Koning asked. "Do you think they planted a tracker on you?"

"They didn't," Tai said.

If it had been anyone but Quest, Koning would have questioned that conclusion. Koning recalled the images she'd seen of their route. "Right, once you're out of the city on the

227

highway there's no place to go except the next town out in the desert, so they're just following you because your departure looked curious." Koning thought through the implications if that were true. "What if you pulled off the road somewhere in the mountains and hid?" Koning asked. "If they're just following a hunch, they might head out of the canyon into the desert knowing there's nowhere you can go and that they can catch up with you at their leisure."

"Might work," Mitsumi said. "Let them zip on past us, then follow well behind them into the desert once they've passed our rendezvous point."

Koning glared at Mantor floating slack-jawed in his bunk. None of this would be a problem if Mantor hadn't been so reckless and selfish. Of course, on the plus side of his ledger, they wouldn't be here now if he hadn't solved a fundamental problem of HE drive physics.

Ricci left Koning to babysit Mantor while she returned to the bridge. Minutes crawled by. Fifteen minutes before leaving the mountains for the desert, Mitsumi reported finding a suitable place to pull off where a series of boulders would hide their heat signature. On the screen in Mantor's cabin, Koning watched as the following vehicle passed Mitsumi and Quest's hiding place, Quest's strategically placed assistant capturing the scene. After allowing the vehicle a good fifteen minutes head start, Quest reported retrieving his assistant, pulling their van onto the highway and preparing to proceed to the desert to await Mantor's revival and *Are We There Yet?*'s jump.

"We found the car." Kelton said. In synchronous orbit over Alcante on the *Excuse's* bridge, Fylan steeled herself—from Kelton's pained expression, she didn't expect good news. "It was empty and no sign of them in the vicinity."

Fylan squelched a rush of irritation. This just showed their desperation. They were trapped. "Oh," he added as an afterthought, "one of our men is tailing a vehicle into the Alticanel Mountains."

With a frown, she shook her head, annoyed. "Why would he do that? We need all our men in the Dark Zone."

Worry creased his forehead. "Uh, he said the vehicle looked like one belonging to a local business. He thought it was weird it was headed into the mountains. And they left a vehicle behind. Maybe they switched."

She opened her mouth to yell at Kelton and tell him to call off the tail. Kelton held up a hand and glanced off to his right. Fylan raised her eyebrows at the interruption. This had better be good.

"He just reported that the vehicle he was following tried to lose him by pulling off to the side of the road and letting him by."

Maybe, Fylan thought. There were lots of reasons someone would not want to be followed in the mountains in the dark. But why head into the mountains? That road didn't lead to a spaceport. On that road there was nothing on the other side of the mountains but desert—a vast expanse of nothing and no one. They needed to find a way off planet why would they go to the middle of nowhere? She straightened and smacked her acceleration couch's arm. Because you're desperate and you can jump in a gravity well.

"It's them," she said. "Tell your guy to stop them at any cost."

"Immediately," Kelton said and cut the connection.

They were planning an unprecedented maneuver. If they made it to the desert and evaded Kelton's man, there was only one way to stop them.

"That's trouble," Mitsumi said over the com.

Koning who had been leaving Mantor's quarters pulled up short. "What's trouble?" Koning asked. Silence. "What's trouble, Captain?" Koning said louder.

"Yeah, they turned around," Mitsumi said.

Koning slammed her hand against the bulkhead and shouted, "Captain, tell me what's going on!" She couldn't help if he wouldn't let her know what was happening.

"Sorry, after we were back on the highway a vehicle came at us from the other direction. I wasn't sure till it passed us, but it looks like the same one that was following us. Now it's turned around and is following us again. We can't wait at the rendezvous point. They'll be on us."

Koning wracked her brain, but couldn't dig up another suggestion. "Maybe they won't approach you if you stop at the rendezvous point. Then, once we jump you can make it to the ship before they intercept you."

"No, they're accelerating now to catch us and gaining. It's thirty minutes to the rendezvous point; we need you on the ground." Mitsumi fell silent then mumbled, "I didn't think it would come to this."

"Captain?"

"Sentaa, I need you to go to my quarters as fast as you can, I'll tell you how to access them. We have to use the Clear."

Sentaa rocketed along the corridors, absorbing energy with her legs at corners and launching herself as she changed directions. Mitsumi explained as she went.

"After interviewing Viram, I worried that he may not have been off the Rapt. I bought Clear just in case...well, just in case of a situation like this. Clear yanks a Rapt user from a trance in an instant."

"So, why did you wait until now?" Koning asked. "Why not use it the moment I found the dung heap in his cabin?"

"Clear pulls a Rapt user from the drug's effects in an instant," Mitsumi repeated as if that explained everything.

"Great," Koning said. "I can't wait to reintroduce him to reality."

"You may not have the chance, Sentaa," Mitsumi said. "Sixty-five percent of the time, the shock from being pulled back to the real world from Rapt's ecstatic experience and the abrupt return of normal sensory input induces psychosis."

Koning gulped, her enthusiasm for the procedure a tad diminished but, slamming into a bulkhead for her final turn, Koning clenched her jaw against the flash of empathy. Mantor deserved whatever happened to him. In fact, if he made it through whole, she might just grind him to pulp anyway.

Koning shot toward the captain's cabin, grabbing a handhold at the last second and twisting to absorb her kinetic energy with her legs. She punched in Mitsumi's code, entered the cabin and grabbed the tube Mitsumi had identified. Clear in hand, Koning flew back to Mantor's quarters. By Quest's calculation they had twenty minutes to rouse Mantor, make the changes to the HE drive, and jump to the surface.

In the air beside Mantor, Koning felt a pang of guilt. She could be sentencing Mantor to a lifetime of hell. *Like he condemned Mitsumi, Quest, and Chandra to death*, she thought. Lips compressed into a determined white line, she slapped the hypo spray to Mantor's neck and actuated the injection.

Mantor's eyes flew open, his face contorted in agony. He flung his head around and a tremor ran through his body followed by an endless scream from the depths of his bowels, tearing through his throat. *That's it*, Koning thought, *I've ruined his life*.

As he thrashed about, Mantor entangled himself in the sleep netting. Eventually, his screaming died away. When he stopped moving, he was facing Koning. Eyes snapping open, Mantor held her gaze. His eyes flitted to the hypo spray and back to Koning's face.

"Clear?" Mantor asked.

Koning nodded.

Mantor turned away from Koning and extracted himself from his sleep net. "Did you know the possible side effects of using Clear on someone in a Rapt trance?" Mantor said in a hoarse whisper. "Or did you care?" Mantor unwound the netting from his left foot and swiveled to Koning. Eyes bulging from his flushed face, his voice choked on his rage. "Did you *want* to hurt me, drive me insane?" Mantor yelled, his voice rising in tone, "or are you stupid—blundering forward with any random plan that pops into your head, no matter the damage?"

"Viram," Mitsumi yelled, his voice coming from Koning's assistant. "She did it on *my* order."

Anger draining from his face, Mantor fixed his eyes on Koning's assistant.

"*I* told her to use the Clear because we need our engineer *now*. Our lives are in danger, and we need a clean engineer not a tranced out Rapt junkie. I thought that's what I was getting when I hired you; you promised me that's what I had."

Mantor lowered his head, shriveling in the glare of Mitsumi's accusation. "Cap'n...I didn't mean to...It was only for a couple of hours..."

"Later, Viram. Right now, you need to configure the HE drive for a jump to the surface. You have fifteen minutes."

CHAPTER 20

Quest coaxed every last erg from the vehicle's engine. He had reactivated the manual controls to override the built-in safety limiters, yet the trailing car inched ever closer. At least they hadn't started—The distinctive whine of flechettes deflecting off the vehicle interrupted his thought.

"We're armored?" Mitsumi said with a note of incredulity in his voice.

Quest nodded once. His adventures after escaping the Wild Children had taught him the value of hardened ceramic plate, and he made sure that any vehicle at his disposal was so equipped. Mitsumi shifted his gaze in Quest's direction.

"I'm beginning to understand Aber's thinking," Mitsumi said.

Quest gave Mitsumi a sidelong glance. The prospect of "opening up" about his past to his crewmates didn't thrill him. He'd made an attempt with Ricci, but couldn't bring himself to finish what he started.

"You want me to stop?"

"Nope," Mitsumi said, holding up his hands in a placating gesture. "Just attempting a little humor."

They rounded the first bend losing sight of the vehicle behind them. The map showed them to be eight klicks from the mouth of the canyon, nine and a half from the rendezvous point. *Are We There Yet?* hadn't made the jump—they were still waiting on Mantor to reconfigure the HE drive. Quest frowned at the thought. He didn't want to be too close to the ship when

233

it exploded into the atmosphere.

After a series of curves, they screamed around a sharp turn and the road straightened out. Quest's eyes darted to the rear view as the pursuers appeared. They were gaining.

A world-ending thunderclap hammered their ears and impact resistant polymer sprayed the cabin as the vehicle's windows detonated inward. A giant fist shoved the vehicle to the left side of the road and pressed them brutally into their safety harnesses. Quest yanked the steering mechanism to the right. Tires juddered as Quest tried to stay on the road. The brutal force reversed again. After wrestling with the steering, Quest straightened the vehicle out. Wind streamed in from the hole where the windshield had been. The car's armor had held up against their pursuers' weapons, so that must have been—

"We're here," Koning's chipper voice came from Quest's assistant.

"We noticed," Mitsumi muttered.

"I came in high. I ballparked the effect our shock-wave might have and tried to minimize it. How'd I do?"

Mitsumi shot a look at Quest, then glanced back at Chandra who was curled up in a ball on the floor. "We're alive."

"That's good to hear," Koning said sounding pleased.

Quest checked the rear view. The pursuers were still on the road but not as close as they had been.

"Yeah," Koning said, with barely restrained pride, "I figured that, with the geometry of the canyon you were in and the strength of the supersonic shock-wave we would generate, we needed to come in high and offset to the west from our landing point. I nailed the jump, by the way. Just in case you were wondering."

They left the straightaway, shooting into a curve. Quest saw the boulder just in time to wrench the car around it. Rocks and boulders littered the road ahead. Quest weaved them around the obstacles.

"That's great, Sentaa," Mitsumi said, sounding as if it was anything but. "When will you be on the ground?"

"Twelve minutes."

With the boulder field behind them, Quest accelerated.

Mitsumi focused on his assistant. "That's when we arrive," he said. "We'll need help."

Mitsumi described their situation. "I have an idea," Ricci said and explained what she had in mind.

"That should work," Mitsumi said glancing at Quest.

Quest nodded. "I agree, Mei. Good thinking."

Ten minutes later, Quest, Mitsumi, and Chandra swung out of a curve onto the final straight run from the canyon. Moments later, their pursuers rounded the same curve. The whine of flechettes deflected by the vehicle's chassis sounded again. Quest felt a tug on his shoulder followed by sharp pain.

"Get down!" Quest shouted. Mitsumi and Chandra collapsed to the floor. With the windows gone, flechettes streamed through the cabin. Quest tried to engage the auto drive and follow everyone else to the floor, but the explosion had damaged the function. He ducked his head as much as possible to still see the road and steered with his left hand.

They shot out of Etkon Canyon onto a high desert plateau, pursuers hot on their tail. Quest's eyes flicked between the rear view and the road ahead. *Any time now would be good, Mei*, Quest thought.

A searing white flame in the rear view forced his eyes forward. He sat up straight and brought the vehicle to a halt then reversed course. *Are We There Yet?* straddled the road. A short ways beyond it, the car that had been chasing them was a steaming puddle on the road.

"Remind me never to piss you off, Mei," Koning said over the com as they stared at the solidifying mass of plasteel, ceramic, and humans.

"Where I come from," Ricci added from the bridge "there's an ancient saying tracing back to our very earliest history, maybe from before the Great Dark: 'a drive is a weapon with destructive power proportional to its efficiency.'" With a shrug in her voice she continued, "When Captain Mitsumi explained your predicament, I remembered that aphorism and it occurred to me—hey, that's our fusion drive. I wonder what would happen if I hovered over the car chasing you?"

"Efficient," Quest said. Mitsumi wondered whether he referred to their drive or Ricci's actions.

On the way to the ship, Mitsumi insisted that Chandra and Quest, carrying the Ark and the interpreter, precede him up the loading ramp. Aboard *Are We There Yet?*, Quest relieved Chandra of the Ark and stowed it away with the interpreter. They made their way to the bridge. Quest approached the pilot's couch beside Ricci and sank onto it. Ricci smiled in greeting, then stared with horror at Quest's shoulder. Quest followed her stare and his face blanched white.

Mitsumi appeared on the bridge. "Sentaa?" he said.

"Three random jump vectors, two short, one long calculated and transferred to the helm," Koning said.

"Vectors received and plotted," Ricci said.

"Viram?" Mitsumi said.

"I've configured the HE drive for a jump at 3,000 meters," Mantor said, responding without a pause.

"Mei," Mitsumi said, "let's leave."

"Captain," Koning said with a frown, "I'm receiving a request for communication. It's from a ship in orbit." Her eyes cut toward Chandra. "They want to talk to Aber."

Ricci engaged the fusion drive, vaulting them into the air.

Mitsumi caught his breath. Only the Consortium knew Chandra was on Support. He could ignore them, but since the Consortium wasn't giving up, it might be best to find out about his pursuers. "Accept," he said, "but transmit audio only and only on my command."

A woman appeared on half the main screen. She was familiar, but Mitsumi couldn't place her.

"Domenica Fylan," Chandra breathed. "I thought we'd

killed her."

Ah, the woman who had ambushed them at the cache on Planet Mitsumi.

"Aber, I know you're there, even if I can't see you. I also know what you're trying to do. I won't let you." She narrowed her eyes and her smile twisted into loathing. "Your ass is mine. I'll kill the rest of your crew, but you won't be that lucky."

Mantor had reconfigured the HE drive to enable a jump at a set altitude. Ricci fixed her eyes on the altitude indicator and reached to initiate the jump. Under the glare of Fylan's open hatred, Mitsumi was glad they were out of here. Another vessel appeared four klicks away.

"Mei, don't jump," Mantor screamed.

A violet beam stabbed out from the other ship.

Fylan's smile returned. "See, we're full of surprises aren't we?"

At a rough guess, they had less than a minute before the beam penetrated their hull.

"Oh," Fylan said with mock concern, "I think we ruined your jump window. And I bet I'll destroy your drive before you recalculate."

Ricci turned to Mitsumi in confusion. "Why can't we jump?" Mitsumi said.

"Hold on," Quest said.

All eyes turned to Quest. "Shock wave," Quest said, strapping into his couch.

The ship jerked hard. Ricci and Koning had strapped into their couches, but Mitsumi hadn't taken the time. He was standing beside Ricci's couch when the wave hit, throwing him off his feet and slamming him to the deck.

"You thought you were so clever," Fylan continued, "faking your registration and returning to Support in disguise. Trying to sell my find, the artifact you stole from me. It must be worth a bundle if you're willing to risk your life for the sale."

"They're targeting our HE drive," Koning said, "but the atmosphere is attenuating the energy."

Mitsumi pushed himself to a sitting position. "We need to jump, Mei," he said.

"Mei, don't," Mantor said again over the communicator. "We can't. That ship jumping in messed with my calculations. I have to redo them."

"What effect is their beam having?" Mitsumi asked.

Koning tapped at her console. "We've got thirty seconds before it penetrates."

On half the screen, Fylan turned her head listening to a report they couldn't hear. Turning back to face the camera she said, "I'm getting close, aren't I?" She leaned toward the camera, her face a mask of determined, implacable malice. "But know this—if somehow you escape today, I will never rest. To my dying breath, I will hunt you and your crew. And I swear to the gods, I'll bathe my hands in your blood."

Mitsumi flinched at the raw hatred flowing from the screen. "Viram?" Mitsumi said, "I'd rather not have another last second heroic."

"Jump," Mantor said.

CHAPTER 21

On the view screen stars flickered twice, replaced by uniform jump space gray. A minute later, the stars reappeared. Mitsumi waited for another ship to pop out of jump. They could have followed the first jump, but the other two should have lost them.

Just to be sure though, Mitsumi said, "Sentaa, any sign of pursuit?"

"No, Captain, we're all by our lonesome out here."

Ricci and Quest unbuckled from their couches and turned to face Mitsumi. Chandra hovered in his peripheral vision. A small globule of blood floated away from Quest's shoulder. "Nice job, Tai, Mei, Sentaa," Mitsumi said, pointedly ignoring Chandra and Mantor. "We'd be dead or good as without your courage and ingenuity. Tai, you should be in the auto-doc. Everyone else, rest up for a few hours. We won't need anyone on the bridge while we're here in the middle of nowhere. We'll convene at 16:40 to discuss where to next."

"I'm sure I speak for everyone here, captain," Koning said, "when I say you're welcome, and when I say that you, Tai, and Aber should return your appearance to normal right now, because you're freaking me and Mei out."

Mitsumi put a hand to his face. He'd forgotten the change to his appearance. He'd become so used to Chandra and Quest's altered faces, the change had slipped his mind.

Quest pushed off through the access to the rest of the ship. Ricci and Koning followed close behind. Chandra remained on the bridge fidgeting with his hands, eyes downcast.

"Holtz," Chandra said, without looking up, "I wanted to tell you again how sorry I am for muddling things up on Support. I'm sorry I didn't listen. And thank you for not giving up on me down there. I..." Chandra lifted his head and locked eyes with Mitsumi. "It won't happen again. The part about not listening to you, I mean, not the part about your not giving up on me. I hope that does happen again."

Mitsumi considered Chandra. Now that the immediate threat was behind them and his anger had cooled, Mitsumi felt pity for the man—Chandra would blame himself for every extra moment Pari suffered.

"That's okay, Aber. Let's put our faces right and figure out what to do next."

Chandra nodded and headed toward the shuttle to retrieve his facial reconfiguration kit. After returning to his normal appearance, Mitsumi moved with dread to his next task. Chandra had been the easy part. His sin had been too much anxiety for his daughter and zeal to ensure their venture's successful completion. Mitsumi understood that—it was something he'd been familiar with in the past. What he didn't understand and found more troubling was deliberate deception.

Mitsumi found Mantor in engineering, floating in the middle of the compartment facing the entrance. He looked like he'd been waiting for Mitsumi's visit, but as soon as Mitsumi entered, he maneuvered to a console and tapped away.

Mitsumi paused, attempting to control the anger that had built as he had made his way here. The increasing emotion surprised him. He hadn't decided how he would approach Mantor, but he was pretty sure a screaming rage was not the correct one. When Mitsumi hadn't spoken after two minutes, the silence apparently was too much for Mantor. He turned from his console and pretended to see Mitsumi for the first time.

"Ah, Captain," Mantor said. "The, um, HE drive is ready. I, uh, reconfigured it for flat space."

Mitsumi had almost reached the point when he could speak without shouting, but hearing Mantor's voice rekindled Mitsumi's ire. Mitsumi remained silent, not trusting himself to speak.

"That was quite a shock wasn't it, when that other ship jumped to the planet? I mean, who would have thought they were so desperate to nab us that they would try the same crazy stunt we pulled?" Mantor's voice trailed off, his eyes swept the engineering compartment as if searching for an exit.

"I'm disappointed, Viram." Mitsumi shook his head at the level of the understatement. "No," he said, his voice dropping to a whisper, "disappointment is much too weak." Mitsumi cocked his head and narrowed his eyes. "Angry's better, but still not there." Mitsumi's voice rose of its own accord.

Mitsumi's jaw clenched, his hands squeezed into fists and his eyes bulged as he gave himself to burning—white hot, fury cleansing him of rational thought. "Try volcanic rage, you stinking, lying junkie." Mitsumi was yelling now. A part of his mind attempted to reassert control, but the part that wanted to ride the storm kicked it to the curb and shot it in the head.

"You come on this ship, on *my* ship, claiming to be clean, swearing up and down you're off the drug, that I can trust you, that nothing was going on behind my back and it was a lie. You'd have let me, Tai, and Chandra die, just so you could pleasure yourself. I should do everyone a favor and kill you right now." Mantor had retreated into the farthest corner of the compartment. Mitsumi followed him there. He lifted his arms, ready to grasp Mantor by the neck as if he wanted to carry out his threat with his bare hands.

Shaking, his rational mind returned from the dead and fought for control. Mantor, hands raised as if to fend Mitsumi off, cowered away from the captain. What was he doing? He lowered his arms.

"I...I'm sorry, Captain, really I am. I didn't mean any

241

harm. I tried to limit my use to times when no one needed me. It never occurred to me you'd need me when you did."

Mitsumi backed away, allowing Mantor to float from the corner. With the return of control, Holtz's cheeks burned with shame at his outburst. Mantor's eyes shifted beyond Mitsumi who closed his eyes, unwilling to look behind him, suspecting what he'd see. "It's over now, everyone. Go back to your quarters and rest."

Indistinct murmured voices drifted into the compartment and faded out. How was this going to look to the rest of the crew? He'd have to deal with that later; right now he had to decide what to do with Mantor. Mitsumi opened his eyes and blew out a breath. He *was* a great engineer.

"Do you want to keep your engineer's license?" Mitsumi said.

Mantor's eyes widened in panic, as if Mitsumi had just threatened to kill his favorite pet.

"Do you want to remain with this ship and crew?"

Mantor nodded. "Yeah, I like it here and all of you."

"These are the conditions." Mitsumi ticked them off on his hand. "I won't report you and will allow you to stay if one, you'll tell me where you've stashed your Rapt so I can destroy it. Two, you allow me to inspect your quarters and destroy the Rapt you have hidden away there, and by inspect your quarters I mean tear them down to the hull and rip open your belongings. Three, Sentaa will test you for Rapt usage each day at random times she selects. If I find any Rapt when I inspect your quarters you haven't disclosed, I'll confine you to quarters until we can reach a planet to drop you off. If you're positive on any of the tests, I'll confine you to quarters until we can reach a planet to drop you off—no warnings, no slack. In either of those cases, you'll forfeit your proceeds from the voyage."

Mantor hung his head and mumbled, "That sounds fair."

"I don't care what you think. That's what we're doing. You betrayed my trust, Viram. I'm not sure if you can ever regain it, but under my terms we can work together. You're on a short leash, Viram, if you tug on it, you're done."

Mantor lifted his face and locked eyes with Mitsumi. "I'll do what you say, Captain, and I'll earn that trust back."

Mitsumi held his gaze for a moment, then turned without comment and launched himself from the compartment. He wondered if he would ever trust Mantor again.

They gathered in the commons at 16:40. To prepare for their discussions, Mitsumi had ordered Quest to fire up the fusion drive to increase everyone's comfort. Mantor had been the first to arrive. He sat in a corner away from the main table half in shadow. The others wandered in and took seats around the table, occasionally looking curiously at Mantor off by himself. When Koning entered, her glare projected animosity by the megajoule.

Chandra, the last to arrive, took a seat at the table. Mitsumi remained standing. He swept his eyes over his crew and cleared his throat. "I'm sorry you had to see what happened in engineering. I lost control and I shouldn't have."

Koning turned from glaring at Mantor. "You have nothing to apologize for except maybe for not believing me when I told you there was a problem. So, where are we dropping him off?"

"We're not," Mitsumi responded and explained the terms on which Mantor would still be part of the crew. Koning was not pleased.

"You'll keep him even after he almost killed you? Because you think these 'conditions' will make him change?" Koning shook her head. "Believe me, Captain, junkies are all the same; you can't rehabilitate them and you can't trust them. It doesn't matter what you do. He'll find a way around your restrictions; no matter how long he stays clean, it won't last and when he reverts to type, it will be at the worst possible moment." Koning turned her glare on Mantor once more. "We should cut him loose or space him." She turned to Mitsumi again, "Your choice."

Mitsumi considered the force of Koning's hatred. "I've made my decision, Sentaa. And need I remind you that Viram was the one who discovered you were pleading for help in that stasis field on Quest? Without his genius at developing the gravity well jump, we'd be dead twice over."

Koning's face soured at that and she lowered her head.

"Okay," Mitsumi said, turning from Koning to face the others. "Let's move on to more important topics. The Consortium is on to us and now knows what we have. We can't sell the Ark."

"What makes you say that?" Chandra said. "We were unable to sell the Ark on Support to the Elstone Combine. That doesn't mean we can't sell it on any other Federated World."

"The Consortium knows you were on Support trying to sell the Ark," Quest said. "It also announced it was aware of every scheduled sale of First Civ tech."

"That was a bluff," Chandra said, waving away Quest's concern. "It couldn't have that information."

"But if it did," Ricci said, "that would mean it had channels into the major First Civ tech buyers which means it has reviewed our sales pitch and knows what the Ark is and, unlike any of the buyers we contacted, it knows the Ark is genuine, because, well, they were there, weren't they?"

"And if they know how valuable it is," Koning said, "they'll be desperate to get it back—desperate enough to let every Federated World know their interest in anyone trying to sell it. If we try to sell it, we won't find a buyer, but the Consortium *will* find *us*."

"Pure speculation on your parts," Chandra said. "The Consortium was merely attempting to scare away potential buyers on the off chance the Ark had value. They can't know what it is or how valuable. They wouldn't go to the expense of spreading the word to all the Federated Worlds for a box of unknown value."

Mitsumi had to concede that the cost of sending dedicated messenger drones to all the Federated Worlds would be substantial, and the Consortium would be loath to bear the expense without good reason, but, "Who's willing to take that chance? Who wants to set up a sale without knowing whether the Consortium will show up instead of the buyer? Because intermediaries like we used on Support are scarce on other worlds—we'd have to be there in person."

"I'm out," Koning said. "I vote no on the sale thing. Even if I'm not the one on the planet, this time the Consortium will make sure to find the ship itself."

"Other opinions?" Mitsumi surveyed the others waiting for a response.

Ricci looked down at the table. "Sorry, Aber, I vote no as well—it's too much risk."

Chandra raised his eyebrows at Quest. "I didn't want to conduct the sale in the first place," Quest said.

Mantor didn't speak up. Mitsumi considered asking his opinion then changed his mind. He didn't care what Mantor thought. "Okay," Mitsumi said. "We won't sell the device. It's too risky. We'll visit Zong and call on the professor Viram told us about, what was his name, Viram?"

"Lentar Aten," Mantor said.

"Right," Mitsumi said. "Lentar Aten and see if he can help us with translating the Ark. The Consortium doesn't know about the Ark's language so it won't be expecting our visit. How long to Zong, Sentaa?"

Sentaa pulled out her assistant and poked at it for a minute. "Forty-eight hours give or take," she said.

"Okay, Sentaa, get the jump vectors to Mei. Mei, execute as soon as you get them."

CHAPTER 22

From six light-seconds out Zong, like every other Federated World, was a small blue-white marble. With the shape of the continents obscured, it could have been any of them.

"Nicely done, Sentaa, Mei," Mitsumi said.

Color rose in Koning's cheeks at the compliment. "Captain, Zong traffic control has pinged us," Koning said.

"Tai, what ship are we officially for the good people of Zong traffic control?"

"I have switched our identity to the '*What Have We Here?*'"

"Excellent," Mitsumi said. "Sentaa, request an orbit that will allow us to land the shuttle. I still want to avoid the extra scrutiny of their orbital docking platform. Mei, take us in when you've received permission."

Mantor had complied with Mitsumi's conditions and had disclosed three stashes of Rapt—one in the mess which Mitsumi would never have discovered. Mantor had tested clean and over time become more animated. Mitsumi punched up engineering. "Viram."

"Yes, Captain," Mantor said immediately.

"Have you contacted Professor Aten?"

"I...have," Mantor said with hesitation in his voice.

"And?" Mitsumi said. "Will he see us or not?"

"Oh, he'll see us. In fact, he seemed excited for the visit."

"Then what's the problem?"

"No problem. He just mentioned that this was the second contact he'd received concerning an obscure language."

Mitsumi's brow furrowed. Could the Consortium have discovered their interest in the language of the Holy Text?

"Okay, I'm sure it's nothing, but I'll take extra precautions just in case. When and where are we meeting?"

"Tomorrow in his office at local noon."

The descent to Jing, Zong's principal city, was uneventful. On the western edge of the largest continent in Zong's northern hemisphere, Jing was a seaport built on a large harbor resembling two overlapping circles. Access to the ocean was through an opening in the circles' western edge. As they descended from orbit, breaking through a deck of high clouds, Mitsumi admired the city's neatly laid out roads and plentiful open spaces flowing from the harbor over the surrounding hills. Not for the first time, Mitsumi wondered at how human habit persisted. Two asteroid strikes when the Great Dark descended had formed Jing's current harbor which meant that Zong's inhabitants had established a city or cities there before the bombardment.

Mitsumi had relinquished direction of the shuttle to spaceport traffic control which steered them to their assigned pad at the spaceport's edge. Once they settled onto the ground, Mitsumi opened the airlock and extended the ramp. A humid summer breeze wafted into the shuttle, carrying a sea tang mixed with the heavy scent of growing plants.

In stark contrast to their visit to Support, a small official delegation greeted Mitsumi and Mantor as they descended from the shuttle. A small, pudgy, dour-looking man appeared to be in charge of the group. "Transmit your identification," he said brusquely without preamble.

"We did that from orbit," Mantor protested. Hand held up to forestall further comments from Mantor, Mitsumi complied with the official's request. Mitsumi had explained at length the tight restrictions Zongers imposed on visitors and the convoluted nature of Zong's impenetrable bureaucracy, but the reality was always worse than any description. Mantor shrugged, pulled out his assistant, and complied.

In advance of their encounter with the Zong bureaucracy, Mitsumi with Quest's help had compiled alternate identities for himself and Mantor. They were now Aptor Ruttle and Hallten Newell, two acolytes of the Priests of the Holy Text who were traveling from Wild to meet with Professor Aten regarding new insights into the language of the Holy Book. Quest had assured him that the identities would withstand the level of scrutiny they'd encounter on Zong and they'd not run into problems when initially providing the false identities, so this recheck should be a formality. Nevertheless, Mitsumi held his breath.

The lead official scrutinized his assistant at length. After a time much longer than that required to review their information and just as Mitsumi was considering a Plan B, the man lowered his assistant.

"The purpose on our planet is to visit a 'Mr. Lentar Aten,' is that correct?"

Mitsumi resisted the urge to let out a deep breath. "It is."

"You have an appointment with Mr. Aten?"

"We do."

"Transmit the details of your schedule and planned route."

Mitsumi input commands on his assistant. Again, the man studied the information at length, pursing his lips in distaste at what he saw. With a deep sigh of disappointment, the man looked up from his assistant. "I see all is in order. Today is 13 Qi. Are you aware of Zong's importation laws for this date?"

Mantor gaped. "They have different rules for different dates?"

With a silent curse for inattentive engineers—Mitsumi

had explained the whole system to him on the way down—he ignored Mantor and said, "We are."

"You have nothing to declare. You are not transporting any contravened material?"

"How could we know?" Mantor muttered.

This time Mitsumi did glare at Mantor, praying the Zongian hadn't heard him. "We are not."

The man's mouth puckered again as if he'd bitten something sour. He tilted his head at the shuttle, and his entourage scrambled up the access ramp. "You are aware of the penalties if we catch you violating the importation laws?"

Mitsumi nodded. The man regarded them with skepticism for a moment, then joined his companions in the shuttle.

Mantor relaxed visibly as the lead official disappeared and ran a hand through his hair. "You warned us that the Zongians controlled access to their planet, but isn't this overkill?"

"Haven't you ever visited Zong before on any of your trips?"

Mantor shrugged. "Well, yeah, but I was an engineer so not required on planet and besides, it provided me downtime to, uh, you know..."

"Go into a Rapt trance," Mitsumi said, unwilling to let Mantor off the hook.

"Yeah." Mantor lowered his eyes. "That."

Mitsumi glanced toward the edge of the spaceport. A couple of hundred meters away the landing pad's concrete gave way to a few trees intermixed between low shrubs and bushes that climbed a hill, beyond which lay the harbor. Trees at the crest of the hill swayed in a wind that, to where Mitsumi stood, faded to a pleasant breeze.

"How long will this take?" Mantor said, nodding in the shuttle's direction.

"Depends on how much of a hassle they want to give us," Mitsumi said. "I don't think they expect to find contraband—

no one in their right mind tries to smuggle anything past the Jing port border authority, but if they want to make an obscure point about how serious and thorough they are, they'll make us wait two or three hours."

A few minutes later, the lead inspector appeared in the airlock and descended. The rest of his crew followed him. "We have completed our initial inspection," the man said. "I have transmitted your provisional landing permission."

Mitsumi glanced at his assistant. The screen showed receipt of permission.

"You understand that this permission is temporary and subject to revocation at any time for any reason at Port Border Authority's absolute discretion?"

"Yes," Mitsumi said.

The man extended his assistant to Mitsumi. "Imprint acceptance," the man said.

Mitsumi placed his thumb on the screen hoping the false fingerprint was as good as Quest's promise. The man examined his assistant, nodded once, then turned and marched to the vehicle he and his group had arrived in.

"Okay," Mitsumi said. "Let's go see professor Aten. We don't want to be late."

"What are you talking about?" Mantor said. "It's only 10:00 local. Our appointment's not until noon."

"And?" Mitsumi said.

"And, it's only a few klicks from here."

The corners of Mitsumi's mouth quirked up. "Like I said, let's go. We want to be on time."

Two hours later Mitsumi and Mantor walked into the building housing Lentar Aten's office. "How do these people do anything?" Mantor said. "I've never heard of so much bureaucratic garbage in my life. I mean, three different sets of permissions from three separate departments each wanting to know distinct information, just to hire someone to bring us a few klicks. We could have walked faster."

"Well, maybe," Mitsumi said. "A pedestrian passport

is simpler. Haven't you ever heard the expression 'fighting through Zong paper'?"

"Sure, but I didn't think anything could be that bad."

Aten's office was on the third floor. Mitsumi called for a lift. On the third floor, they exited the lift and looked in vain for a receptionist. A hallway, gray and dingy from the half functioning lighting units, extended in both directions from the lift. A sign on the wall opposite the lift directed them to Professor Aten's office.

Mitsumi stood before the door and gestured for Mantor to announce their presence. Mantor searched in vain for a button or pad then looked at Mitsumi in confusion. Mitsumi mimed striking the door with his fist. He understood Mantor's confusion. Until his first visit to Zong, Mitsumi had never encountered a door without a way to inform the occupants behind the door that someone waited outside.

Mantor shrugged, lifted his hand and struck the door with his palm. And kept striking the door in this way until someone on the other side started shouting and yanked the door open.

"I'm here, I'm here already. Once would have sufficed, twice was excessive, three times was annoying, but you are beyond reason."

A tall gaunt man stood before them. Though stooped with age, he still sported a head of thick, bright red hair and lively green eyes that at the moment displayed annoyance. But it was his nose that commanded attention. A curved beak, his nose exploded from his face all out of proportion to his other features.

After he'd recovered from shock, Mantor remembered why there were there. "Professor Lentar Aten?" Mantor said.

The professor nodded once and glared back.

"Uh, I'm, uh," Mantor hesitated. C'mon Viram, Mitsumi thought, we practiced and practiced this you can't have forgotten already. Mantor looked to Mitsumi for help then his eyes lit. "Aptor Ruttle," Mantor finally said. "And this is Hallten

Newell."

The professor continued to glare at Mantor.

Mantor shot a sideways glance at Mitsumi for support, then continued. "We have an appointment?" Still no acknowledgement from the professor. "We wanted to discuss the Priests of the Holy Text and the language of the Holy Book?"

At the mention of the Holy Book, Aten's face cleared, and he grinned. "Oh, that's right," he said, lifting the palm of his hand to his forehead. "How could I forget?" Aten turned from the door and wandered back into the depths of his office. "Well, I know how I could have forgotten. I didn't put it in my planner. Now why didn't I do that?"

Mantor stared after the professor, uncertain whether to stay where he was or walk in.

"Well, do you want to talk to me or not?" Aten said moving into his office.

Mantor still hesitated until Mitsumi gestured him into the expansive room. Light streamed in from floor-to-ceiling windows that occupied one entire wall, illuminating a large desk which dominated the space. Aten gestured for them to have a seat in two comfortable looking couches placed next to a low table in front of the windows. Bookcases covered every other wall except for a few cupboards and kitchen appliances.

The office was the polar opposite of the picture in Mitsumi's mind of the stereotypical absent-minded professor. He had expected a warren of narrow pathways between piles of unsorted books and papers. But the books were shelved and nothing cluttered any of the flat surfaces. Even the desk was immaculate.

Aten's office building sat on the crown of a hill overlooking the bay surrounding Jing. Jing spread out before Mitsumi as he walked toward the seating area. The high clouds through which Mitsumi had descended had passed. The bay sparkled in sunshine, its pale blue waters a pleasing contrast to a strip of dark green foliage that extended from the water's edge a few hundred yards before giving way to the outskirts of the city.

Mitsumi and Mantor settled into a couch facing the windows. Aten sat before them perched on the edge of an overstuffed chair.

"So," Aten said rubbing his hands together, "tell me what you have. Your message said: 'We believe we've stumbled across a cache of material written in the language of the Holy Book of the Priests of the Holy Text, and we want to speak with you regarding possible translations.' How mysterious, what could you mean?"

Mitsumi was not certain, but thought that might have been word for word the text of their message. Had Aten gone to the trouble of memorizing it? As if in answer to his thought, Aten pointed to his head and said, "Selective eidetic memory."

Mitsumi wrinkled his forehead. "How can a photographic memory be selective?"

"Easy," Aten responded with a wave of his hand. "I select what I want to forget and dispose of it which leads to an extensive recursion of forgetting what I forgot, but I get there in the end. So, what have you found?"

Mitsumi hoped Mantor would remember the script and stick to it. Mantor shifted in his seat and cleared his throat. "I'm from Wild and growing up there I studied for several years with the Priests. I left them eventually and became a starship engineer—"

Aten shook his head and snapped his fingers. "The material, the Holy Text, what did you find?"

"I joined a prospecting crew," Mantor continued ignoring Aten's outburst. "At one of our sites we found written material, I recognized a few words as part of the language of the Holy Text, but—"

Aten snapped his fingers again. "Show me."

Confused, Mantor looked to Mitsumi for assistance, not wanting to go off script without permission. Mitsumi nodded. If Aten wasn't interested in background, all the better. Mantor pulled out his assistant. They had searched the Ark for a section that to the best of Mantor's knowledge was not too technical and had agreed to use it to test Aten's ability to translate what they gave him. At the sight of Mantor's assistant, Aten rose and hurried to the desk.

"If this is truly new material, I'll be able to test out my theory and prove those skeptics wrong. Won't *that* surprise Loran," Aten chuckled. He retrieved his assistant from the desk and strode over to stand in front of Mantor. "Okay," Aten said. "Let me have it."

Mantor tapped at his assistant transmitting the selected text to Aten. Aten studied his assistant. His mouth lifted into a smile. "This *is* new." He turned on his heel and rushed back to the desk, throwing himself into the chair behind it.

Mitsumi and Mantor exchanged puzzled looks, then rose and made their way to the desk. Aten had pulled out a mesh headset from somewhere in the desk. He slapped it on his head, then reached out and tapped the air in front of him. A holographic display from a larger computational unit appeared above the desk. Aten poked at his assistant. The material Mantor had transferred to Aten appeared above the desk.

Aten looked through the display at Mitsumi and Mantor. "What do you know of the language of the Holy Text?"

Mitsumi shrugged and turned to Mantor. "The Priests worship it as the language of the ancients," Mantor said. "Lots of them think it's the First Stellar Civilization's language."

"They're right," Aten said, typing away at the air in front of him. After a moment he sat back in his chair. "The First Stellar Civilization fell five thousand years ago, give or take, when the Horde appeared. At least that's what most people call the mysterious, never identified, interlopers. As their first and last acts, the Horde boosted asteroids, comets, sometimes small moons to relativistic speeds and obliterated humans' First Stellar Civilization. As far as we can tell, the attack happened across all the worlds of the First Stellar

Civilization at the same time. It appears from the record we've been able to reconstruct that the initial strike destroyed all cities, towns, hamlets, and crossroads. After the first wave of strikes, the Horde targeted isolated individuals, space habitats, mining colonies, and outposts. The Horde obliterated anyone who used electromagnetic communication. The catastrophe left only a few scattered remnants. Commerce and communication among the worlds ceased. Without the technologies it required for life, humanity scratched out a meager existence or died off."

"The Great Dark," Mitsumi said. Aten so far was repeating what had become well known after Hansor Engon's first discovery of another populated world.

"Just so," Aten said. "The Great Dark descended on humanity. On those worlds whose inhabitants hadn't completed the transition to a life sustaining biome, life disappeared. But on worlds where the change was complete or complete enough, a few people were able to survive the raging storms and darkness, in caves deep underground. Eventually, those people re-emerged and crawled back from near extinction."

"The Federated Worlds," Mantor said.

Aten nodded, raising a finger in the air. "I have postulated that, before the Great Dark, humanity spoke at least one common language. Individual groupings may have had their own internal languages, but the common tongue allowed everyone to communicate. If that is true, it may be possible to approximate that language."

"Really? How would you do it?" Mantor said.

Aten regarded Mantor with surprise. "No one taught you my theory of linguistic drift in your linguistics courses?"

In confusion, Mantor glanced at Mitsumi. Mitsumi shook his head; he did not understand what Aten was saying either.

"Linguistics?" Mantor said.

"Yes, linguistics. The study of language and its structures," Aten said.

Mitsumi and Mantor stared at Aten, incomprehension clear on their faces.

Aten bowed his head and held it in his hands. "I knew the schools had deteriorated, but I hadn't dreamed the rot was so extensive." He raised his head with a look Mitsumi recognized from his school years—it was lecture time. "Linguistic drift is the tendency of a language to mutate in predictable ways. Humans have an innate tendency to alter their communication patterns. I discovered that those alterations follow rules. I believe based on those rules and the different forms of language on the Federated Worlds, I can reverse engineer the First Civ's language."

"So you think you can read the material we brought?" Mitsumi asked.

"Over the last ten years I've developed a program to interpret the First Civ language. I have successfully tested my program on the Holy Book which proved my supposition that it was written in the First Civ language. Your text appears to be in the same language and so the translation program should work." Aten stabbed at a virtual button and the text above the desk changed into modern Federation Standard.

Mitsumi scanned the words. The text was part of a history of a planet called "Earth" which according to the text was the world on which humanity had originated, a belief long thought among scholars in the Federated Worlds to be a baseless myth. Never moving his eyes from the text, Aten lifted a finger. The text scrolled upward. After a minute the scrolling ceased.

Aten slapped the desk. "Yes!" he shouted. "I was right, and it had every word, did you see that?" Aten pointed at the words floating above his desk. "Every word. Is there more where this came from?" Aten asked, hunger in his voice. "Do you have an even larger sample?"

Mitsumi frowned. He hadn't thought meeting with Aten would yield a complete immediate translation. In fact, his expectations had been low. He had imagined they might come away with a rudimentary dictionary or at best a Holy Book translation they could use to decipher the Ark which would have been of minimal help given the vocabulary differences between the highly technical Ark and the decidedly non-technical Holy Book. But to see a program translate the Ark material wholesale stunned him. They had to have that program, but how to get it without giving away their secret?

"There might be more text from the site where we discovered this." Mitsumi nodded toward the hologram. Aten leaned forward in anticipation. "But we would need an incentive to return and dig around."

Aten leaned back in his chair and regarded Mitsumi with narrowed eyes and pursed lips. "You want money," Aten said. "I understand that. I have access to funds, but my resources aren't great. Surely, this additional material cannot be worth much to anyone other than me. I'm the only one who can translate it."

Mitsumi thought for a moment. He wanted to barter access to the program for something, but he wasn't sure money was enough leverage. Something Aten had said earlier suggested a more sensitive pressure point. "There must be other linguists with an interest in studying the First Civ language, even if at the moment they cannot translate it. This material might enable them to construct their own theory of language change over time, one this text would support."

Aten's eyes widened in horror. "You wouldn't," he said. "How much did Loran offer you?"

Mitsumi remained silent, but tried to project knowledgeable confidence.

"How much?" Aten said. "Ten thousand credits?" Mitsumi smirked. "More?" Aten said. "Fifteen thousand credits?" Mitsumi remained silent. "Twenty?" Aten said his voice rising in tone and volume.

Mitsumi made a placating gesture. "Now, Professor, we may be able to come to another arrangement."

Aten sprang from the chair, ripped the mesh from his

head and paced behind his desk. "I don't have twenty thousand credits. Maybe if I sold some of my collection of *Legends of Newome*, that might do it. But no, how can I—" He halted mid-stride and stared at Mitsumi. "Another arrangement? What do you have in mind?"

Mitsumi spread his hands. "We might be willing to make an in-kind exchange, say use of your translation program for additional material."

Aten returned to his chair and sank into it considering Mitsumi. "I might see my way clear to allow its use, but I wouldn't want to see any translations published without full attribution." Aten stopped, with a cagey look. "And royalty sharing."

Gotcha, Mitsumi thought. He considered Aten for a moment, then stood and turned to Mantor. "Aptor, I think we'd best be off." He turned back to Aten, who leaped to his feet in panic.

"Okay, no royalties," Aten said. "But I must have full attribution."

Mitsumi bowed his head pretending to consider Aten's condition. He lifted his gaze and regarded Aten. "I can do better than that, Professor. I guarantee we will not publish any translations."

Aten beamed at that and reached out his hand.

"But in return," Mitsumi said ignoring Aten's hand, "we must insist on the right to redact technical information from any text we deliver to you."

Aten's eyes lit with understanding. "You think you've discovered First Civ tech at this mysterious source." Aten waved away Mitsumi's concern. "That's not an issue. I have no interest in scientific or technical advances. Even if something slips through your scrutiny, your secrets are safe with me."

Mitsumi nodded. He should run this deal by the others, but saw no downside to sharing non-technical portions of the Ark with Aten—it certainly wouldn't cost them anything. What they were receiving in return was invaluable. "Have your legal program draw up the papers," Mitsumi said.

With a grin, Aten sank into the chair behind his desk, replaced his neural mesh and again typed on the air. After a minute of this he leaned back in his chair. "Send me your address," he said. Mitsumi pulled out his assistant and identified the connection to Aten's system. He paused. This was something he hadn't expected. He had no address for "Hallten Newell," but he did have a couple without identification. After selecting one of those, Mitsumi transmitted the information. In return, the documents detailing their transaction appeared on Mitsumi's screen. Mitsumi scrolled through the document occasionally stopping to object and negotiate terms. After half an hour of this, Mitsumi connected his authentication under the name Hallten Newell to the document; Aten did the same. Mitsumi squirmed with guilt for a moment at deceiving Aten—enforcing this agreement against Hallten Newell would be impossible, but he dismissed his qualms. Mitsumi would keep his side of the deal; Aten would never have to enforce it.

Aten then opened an access panel on the desk and removed a memory device. As he gave the device to Mitsumi, he said, "Here's the program. As we agreed, I'll send the authorization code when I receive your material."

Mitsumi took the memory device and nodded. "We should be able to send the material to you by tomorrow morning at the latest."

His eyes gleaming with avarice, Aten slapped his desk. "This will cement my reputation as the greatest linguist among the Federated Worlds," he said.

Mitsumi smiled at the professor's enthusiasm. As he and Mantor turned to leave, it occurred to him that if Aten was the greatest linguist in the Federated Worlds, he might have the expertise to shed light on the language of the metal sheet they'd removed from Planet Quest and perhaps on the associated plaque. "I have one more question about language, Professor," Mitsumi said.

Aten gestured for him to continue. "By all means, what else can I assist you with?"

Mitsumi called up an image of the metal sheet and plaque. They hung in the air above Mitsumi's assistant. "We stumbled across this in our travels. Have you seen anything like it before?"

Aten glanced in the image's direction then focused on it. He moved around his desk and approached, peering intently. "The plaque looks to be a variant First Civ language, but this..." He gestured at the sheet. "Where did you get this?" he asked.

Mitsumi flicked his eyes to Mantor, then back to Aten. "In our travels, like I said. Can you tell us anything about it?"

Aten leaned in closer studying the characters in the image. "Extraordinary," he said.

"Professor?" Mitsumi said after a long silence. "What can you tell us?"

"May I have a copy of this image?" Aten said.

Mitsumi closed the file. The image disappeared from above his assistant. "What do you know about those characters?"

Aten shook his head as if clearing it. "They're nothing human," Aten said. "But I've seen them before."

"Can you translate the characters?" Mitsumi said.

Aten shook his head again. "No, I can't. But I might work something out, if I had that image to compare with this one." Aten moved behind his desk again, replaced the mesh, and called up a hologram showing characters resembling the ones on the sheet. Mitsumi passed the image of the sheet to Aten who opened it up in a display next to the one hovering above his desk. As he studied the images, Aten's eyes flickered between them, his brow furrowed in concentration. "Definitely the same language," he muttered.

The resemblance was obvious; they both contained some of the same symbols he'd seen in his vision. Here was another possible lead to locate the Artifact's mysterious planet. "Where did you find your sample?" Mitsumi asked.

Aten continued peering at the two images. "Professor?" Mitsumi asked raising his voice.

Aten looked away from the images. "Someone brought it in last week with the same questions you posed. Did I recognize it? Could I translate it?" Aten shook his head. "Odd."

"The characters?" Mitsumi gestured at the floating images.

"No," Aten said, "the folks who brought them in. Struggled with Federation Standard—their syntax and vocabulary were fascinating. Spoke with an accent I'd never heard—unusual because I'm quite good at identifying accents. Dressed strangely. Smelled funny. Didn't say where they were from. Didn't say where they'd found their sample either."

Mitsumi shrugged. It had been worth a try. "I'd be interested in any progress you make toward deciphering that." Mitsumi nodded toward the images.

"I'll let you know if I can work anything out," Aten said. "I told the others I'd do the same, but you might meet them."

Mitsumi looked puzzled. "Meet who?"

"The ones who brought me the other sample. They wanted to know if anyone else had run across something similar. I told them I'd let them know if that happened. In fact, while we've been talking I sent them a message about you. So, they may be in touch."

Mitsumi's skin tingled at that. Those people might have information about Mitsumi's sheet or the translation. At the very least, if he knew where they found their sheet it might help him with his future search. "I'd like to talk to these people myself. How can I contact them?"

Aten shook his head. "I promised them confidentiality. They shared what they had with me on the condition that I not let anyone know who they are."

Frustrated, Mitsumi said, "I don't want to cause them any trouble, I just want to talk to them. If we combine what we know, we might help you with your translation."

"I'm sorry, but I can't go back on my word." He extended

a hand, gripping Mitsumi's upper arm. "Don't worry. I'm sure if they think it would be helpful to meet, they'll be in touch."

They said goodbye to Aten and left his office. Their meeting with Aten had occupied the better part of the afternoon, and Zong's star had sunk behind the same foliage blocking the view of the bay. Beng, a gas giant and the next planet closest to Zong's star, peeked its colored disk above the horizon opposite the setting star.

The breeze from earlier in the day had died. The leaves of the trees and bushes hung without stirring. Heat and humidity gathered them into a close embrace. Sweat ran down Mitsumi's side and prickled his upper lip. Eager to return to the ship and see how Aten's program performed, he dreaded the wait while legions of Zongian bureaucrats processed their various requests for transportation.

Mitsumi took out his assistant and started the process. The first permission form, from the planetary Bureau of Personal Activity, "Authorization to Expend Electrical Resources for Personal Transportation For 1-5 Individuals On Odd Numbered Week Days," appeared on the screen. He'd had to complete this same form for the ride out to visit the professor but, of course, they preserved none of the data from that earlier form. He knew from experience that if his assistant attempted to autofill the fields, the Bureau's computer would sense the attempt and not only reject the form, but lock the system for thirty minutes.

Mitsumi filled out the fields, submitted the form, and followed the same procedure for the planetary "Authorization to Enter Jing Spaceport For Engaging in Space Travel," the planetary "Consent to Expend Funds—Personal Ground Transportation," and the city of Jing's "Permission to Cross Zonal Boundaries" forms.

With the forms completed, Mitsumi looked around for a place to sit while they waited for the Zongian bureaucrats and spotted a bench a few yards from where they stood. Like everything else on Zong, a single agency controlled ground transportation. Once the agency had processed their forms and granted permission, it would dispatch a vehicle to take them to their destination. In Mitsumi's experience, that could be anywhere from an hour and a half to three hours.

"Let's go sit while we wait." Mitsumi gestured toward the bench.

"I don't think we'll have to wait," Mantor said.

Puzzled, Mitsumi turned in the direction of Mantor's gaze. A ground car had broken out of traffic and stopped opposite them. Mantor strode to the car, opened the front door, and slid inside. Mitsumi remained on the walk, suspicious of the efficiency. He'd taken leave on Zong more than once while serving in the navy. Zongers took a perverse pride in how difficult their layers of permissions, authorizations, approvals, consents, and licenses made even the most routine activity.

Until this moment, their experience matched Mitsumi's recollection. The speed with which their request had been granted bordered on unseemly. It was as if he'd seen a stately, elderly gentleman in formal attire ambling sedately down the street break into a sprint chasing a cat. Sure, it was possible, but it was out of the ordinary.

"Hey, Captain," Mantor yelled from inside the car. "What're you waiting for? Let's go."

Mitsumi surveyed the scene. Cars whisked along the street; a few Zongers walked past with their heads lowered eyes fixed on actual screens, others with their heads up but with eyes focused on virtual displays only minimally aware of the world around them. Nothing else seemed out of the ordinary.

Thankful that he'd registered to have many communications to orbit with the Office of Surface to Orbit Signaling, Mitsumi pulled out his assistant and contacted the ship. "Mei, we've completed our business here. We're on our way to the shuttle and should lift within the hour."

"Got it, Captain," Ricci responded. "Clean boost."

"Captain!" Mantor yelled again and urgently waved him

to enter the car. With a hand on the car's roof, Mitsumi glanced around once more then shrugged off his disquiet, slid into the car beside Mantor, and shut the door.

CHAPTER 23

What he wouldn't give for a dose right now. Without a doubt, the captain meant every threat he'd made, and Mantor was ashamed for having let down the crew on Support, but he'd been clean for two weeks and the pressure of withdrawal was building. He'd been told repeatedly that any withdrawal symptoms were purely mental without any physical basis. So, the craving eating him up was all in his head. But then, so was every physical sensation. In any case, the yawning seething abyss inside him felt as real as the seat he was sitting on.

When the captain had discovered his secret and offered him a way out, the second chance thrilled Mantor. But after a few days, his satisfaction thinned; the restrictions rankled. He was a great engineer, Mitsumi had said as much. His use was under control. Why should he be punished because the idiots bought trouble doing something he had opposed in the first place? Or had he? He didn't remember. Whatever. He was itching to collect his loot and blow these guys off. Maybe Aten's translation program was the key to a quick score and exit.

What was Mitsumi waiting for now? He yelled at Mitsumi again.

Mitsumi slid in beside him on the seat and shut the door. As the car pulled into the street, Mantor turned toward the window and watched buildings and people slide by. Jing's architecture came in two varieties: commercial and residential. Commercial buildings were great cubes of stone with tiny windows, their height varied, but nothing else did. Aten's office with its huge windows was clearly an exception. Residential buildings were smaller stone cubes with larger windows and balconies. The structures' bland sameness made it difficult to recognize their route. He hadn't been paying a whole lot of attention to their surroundings on the trip from the Spaceport but even so, after an hour he grew uneasy. They should have arrived by now.

Then, a gap opened between the buildings and he saw the bay off to the left. They turned toward it. "Captain," Mantor said. Mitsumi, who had been even more absorbed in his private thoughts than Mantor focused on the engineer. "I don't think we're on our way to the Spaceport." Mantor nodded at the body of water. "I'm pretty sure we didn't pass by the bay going to the professor's."

Mitsumi frowned as he took in their surroundings, obviously puzzled. He held up his assistant and tapped at it.

"I'm sure we didn't," Mitsumi said. He lifted his eyes from his assistant. "I can't get any information from the car." They had traveled into what appeared to be an industrial area—windowless buildings and heavy machinery lined the street. Traffic was sparse and pedestrians nonexistent. "That shouldn't be possible."

The car slowed in front of a building identical in size and shape with the other buildings along the street. Part of the building retracted upwards revealing a lightless cavity. They turned toward the entrance. Alarm replaced what had been mild curiosity. Mantor searched for a way of escaping the car. But Mantor pulled on every lever and pushed every button without success. Mitsumi followed his lead with similar results.

"Call the ship," Mantor said, his eyes wide, "and let them know what's happening. Maybe they can help us from their end."

"I've tried that, Viram. Whatever is blocking my assistant from communicating with the car is also blocking our connection to the ship."

The car moved forward toward the building interior's stygian darkness. Panic built in Mantor's mind. Someone had control of them and was abducting them. It must be the Consortium; torture and death awaited them. *How did they find us?* Mantor thought. They'd been careful not to disclose any of the original language of the Ark, so it shouldn't have been possible to trace them to Professor Aten.

"This car is seriously out of compliance with safety regulations," Mitsumi said, tugging on a handle protruding from the door.

Mantor's jaw dropped. "We're going to die a slow painful death, and you're worried about regulations? Open the door!"

"I can't! You're the engineer. Can't you rig something?"

Mantor shook his head in disbelief. "With what?"

Mitsumi stared at Mantor as the car eased into the building and the door descended behind them shutting them in the lightless interior.

"Try them again, Sentaa," Ricci said.

Koning, attempting to suppress annoyance, turned to Ricci. "We've tried them five times in the last ten minutes. If they're not responding, it's because they can't. We'll have to see what we can pry out of the authorities."

Ricci shifted her eyes to the planet on the main screen, fretting. Two hours ago, Captain Mitsumi said they were on their way and would be at the shuttle within an hour, but now they were out of contact.

In between attempts to reestablish communications, Koning waded through oceans of Zong paper trying to prod someone into looking for their missing crewmates.

"I've already completed Form 570 B—Persons Missing Less Than Twenty-Four Hours," Koning said on the com with gritted teeth, "twice. And Form 4502 F—Search After Loss of Communications, now you're telling me there's *another* form?" Koning stabbed at a button on her console to mute the conversation howling in frustration. "I swear when this is over, I'm taking a blaster and reducing the entire Office of Missing Offworlders—Mixed Crew Composition to charred bone." Koning closed her eyes, took a deep breath, held it for a moment, then let it hiss out in a long, controlled stream. She opened her eyes. Calmer, not calm—that was too much to ask —but calmer, Koning pushed the button on her console again and resumed her conversation.

A blinking light came on in front of Ricci. She peered at it trying to remember what the telltale indicated. The light went solid. Moments later the fusion drive ran its pre-ignition sequence. While trying to halt the process, Ricci wracked her brain for the malfunction's cause.

She couldn't stop the ignition. What was happening? It was as if a ghost was at the controls. Then it came to her. The telltale light showed the ship's neural interface in operation— the one she'd discussed with the captain on her first day. There *was* a ghost in the ship, and it was Captain Mitsumi.

"Acceleration!" Ricci said. Koning and Chandra looked at her sharply.

"Strap in, we're about to maneuver!" Ricci said.

"What are you doing, Mei?" Chandra shouted.

"Nothing," Ricci said through clenched teeth. Koning and Chandra pulled their restraints tight just as the fusion torch lit, pushing them deep into their couches.

Once inside the building, Mantor's worst fears had failed to materialize. They sat in darkness searching for a way out or for a way to talk to somebody, anybody. After an hour of this, lights flared. Blinking against the sudden brilliance, Mantor saw a woman and two men walking toward them dressed in identical loose-fitting shirts and pants. What were obviously weapons, though of an unfamiliar design, rode their hips attached to a belt around their waists. On their feet were black boots that appeared to be plastic. *Those must be uniforms*, Mantor thought, but no kind of uniform he'd ever seen before. He wondered if they really had fallen into the hands of the Consortium.

When the group was within meters of the car, the men stopped, as the woman strolled closer to the car. In a last ditch attempt to do *something*, Mantor pulled on what he had tentatively identified as the manual door release—but had so far not actually released anything. Much to his surprise the door popped open.

Mitsumi turned to Mantor. "Let me do the talking, Viram."

Mantor nodded. He was more than willing to let Mitsumi take the lead on this. Mitsumi and Mantor climbed out of the car. The woman and the men behind her stared at them in silence. After a moment of this, Mitsumi spoke up.

"You brought us here. Are you going to tell us what you want?"

"We crave the slab." At least that's what it sounded like. She spoke Federation Standard with such a heavy accent, Mantor strained to make out the words. She "craved the slab?" What was that? Mitsumi looked as puzzled as Mantor was.

"I don't understand," Mitsumi said. "Slab of what?"

The woman frowned and gestured with her hand. "The slab, the slab you fetched with the chirography on it." Mantor turned the words over in his mind. Her Federation Standard was so bizarre, it seemed unlikely they were associated with the Consortium. The woman, now frustrated, half-faced one of the men flanking her and engaged him in a brief conversation in an unfamiliar language. The woman turned back to Mitsumi.

"The slab you fetched from the globe."

Mitsumi continued to look mystified.

"You displayed it to Aten," the woman said.

Realization dawned on Mitsumi's face. "You mean the metal sheet we found with writing on it? Is that what you mean?"

The woman wiggled her chin in a figure-eight pattern. "Yes, the…shit with the writting. We crave it."

"Do you mean you want to buy the sheet from us?" Mitsumi lifted his hand and fingered something under his tunic. "It's not for sale."

The woman moved her head in the figure eight gesture again. "Yes, acquire. You to give us the shit we to give you benefit."

Mitsumi shook his head. "I already told you, but you didn't understand. The metal sheet with the alien writing on it is not for sale at any price. But from what I understand you have something similar. Maybe we could work together. You know, pool our information."

Mantor wondered where that had come from. If the price were high enough, they would sell it. They at least ought to explore what these people would pay. Mantor cleared his throat. "Uh, Captain?"

Mitsumi held up his hand forestalling Mantor's comment.

The woman's shoulders sagged with disappointment. "That is untoward. We are not partial to uniting information. We want the shit." She turned to Mantor. "Are you eager to peddle the shit for benefit?" She gestured to one of the men behind her. He reached into a pocket in his pants and withdrew a cylinder which he handed to the woman. The woman held it up. Mantor saw it clearly, but he didn't need to. He'd recognized the shape as soon as the man had pulled it from his pocket. It was Rapt. Dealers often packaged and sold the drug in containers just like that one. Only this one was larger than any other container he'd seen before. There must be enough to keep him in continuous trance for a year in her hand right now. At his normal usage rate, she held a ten year's supply.

Mantor's vision clouded and his breath quickened. His

cravings redoubled, overwhelming his mind with longing and desire. Almost of its own accord, his hand lifted toward the container and he took a step forward, then stopped with an effort of will he'd not thought himself capable of. He lowered his arm slowly.

"You perceive this vessel," the woman said with triumph. "It encloses something you suspire."

Mantor licked his lips. Mitsumi seemed to have lost interest in the proceedings. His eyes had glazed, and his brows knit in concentration. Mantor fixed his eyes on the container once more and nodded. He didn't know what 'suspire' meant, but he wanted that container even more than he wanted to breathe.

"If you concur with our system, you may to have the substance."

Fine, Mantor thought. *You want the sheet with the alien writing, you've got it. What do we care anyway? Why does the captain care? We have a copy of the writing, that's the only thing he needs. But how am I going to give the sheet to these people when the captain doesn't want to?* Mantor flicked his eyes toward the captain again, who didn't seem to be following their conversation at all. Just as Mantor was about to take a step forward, the captain's arm shot out and grabbed him. Face contorted in concentration, the captain shook his head in negation.

"This one," the woman inclined her head toward Mitsumi, "will to have a calamity and expire. After, you to give us the shit and we to give you the substance."

The woman's words pierced the desire clouding his mind. She meant killing the captain. As he turned the idea over in his head, he was surprised at his lack of concern for the prospect. Why should he care for the captain's life? Mitsumi had taken his one source of pleasure. With Mitsumi dead, he'd have all the Rapt he needed for years, and his share of the money from the Ark—a bigger share in fact with the captain gone. The canister in the woman's hand glowed with a soft golden light. Subtle, divine music only Mantor could hear flowed from it promising endless, effortless bliss.

What was Mitsumi's life compared to the canister's promise and the Ark's wealth? From the depths of his mind, a doubt nosed into the flow of euphoria. Did he want Mitsumi dead? Because even though Mitsumi had hurt him, the captain had acted in what he considered to be Mantor's best interest and, as uncomfortable as the idea was, the captain may have been right.

His eyes shifted to Mitsumi. The captain still appeared lost in his own thoughts, oblivious to the woman's threat. As Mantor watched, Mitsumi came to himself and turned to Mantor. Their eyes locked.

"I won't give up the sheet," Mitsumi said finally, bringing his focus back to Mantor. "What will you do?"

Mantor broke eye contact with the captain. He longed to give in to the woman's proposal. Everything he wanted in life was on the other side of his agreement. But he couldn't do it. That understanding surprised him. With the thought, the canister lost its luster, and the music faded. He lifted his head and faced the woman, squaring his shoulders.

He opened his mouth to speak, but nothing came out. It was as if his body rebelled at the mind's decision. Snatching control back, he forced his body to behave. "I won't do it." Mitsumi had returned to his trance, but a smile played on his lips.

With a sigh, the woman shook her head and the two men stepped forward beside her. She handed the canister to one of the men. "I bewail your verdict," she said. "Perchance your troop will to be more sane when they detect how your dearth of collaboration concluded."

The men drew their weapons and pointed them at Mantor and Mitsumi.

Mantor raised his hands in panic. "Wait, don't do anything yet. Let me try to talk sense into him."

The woman weaved her chin in the figure-eight pattern

Mantor had concluded meant assent wherever she was from. Mantor turned to Mitsumi who now looked as if he were solving a complex equation in his head. "Captain, we can't let them kill us over a piece of alien junk when any information of value will be in the scans."

Mitsumi didn't appear to have heard Mantor. Mantor shook his head in frustration. Out of the corner of his eye, he saw the woman incline her head and put a hand to her ear. She spoke rapidly in her unknown language, then straightened her head, eyes wide with surprise. A low rumble built rapidly to continuous rolling thunder emerging from the depths of the building. Mitsumi smiled and leaped behind their car, falling to the ground, beckoning Mantor to join him. Mantor, overwhelmed by the now ear-shattering roar, flung himself to the ground by Mitsumi as the far end of the building exploded inwards and a star flared into the gap.

"What did you do? Where are we headed?" Koning said.

What great questions, Ricci thought. *I wish I knew the answer.* The captain had overridden the ship's systems, so in point of fact Ricci had done nothing. On full override, the neural interface locked out manual controls. Ricci watched helplessly as the fusion drive completed a re-entry burn and attitude control thrusters altered their orientation.

"You're the astrogator, Sentaa," Chandra said. "Can't you tell us where we're headed?"

"The planet," Koning said, waving at the screen where Zong swelled rapidly. "That's as much as I've got right now. Somewhere in Jing, I think. And I have to tell you, Zong traffic control is none too happy either. They're threatening to vaporize us if we don't alter our course. I think we're only alive because someone didn't properly fill out form 156 B— Destroying Out of Control Spacecraft."

"It's the captain," Ricci said. "He's taken control with his

273

neural interface and there's nothing I can do."

"How's that possible?" Koning said. "We lost communication with the captain hours ago."

"The neural interface uses quantum entanglement. Nothing can block it."

Koning swore. "Isn't that peachy, so the captain just figured the shuttle wasn't fast enough and wouldn't now be a great time to break every one of Zong's million and two rules and regulations and kill us all in the process?"

Ricci didn't respond. She didn't know enough to come to the captain's defense, even if she felt inclined to do so which at the moment was debatable. Koning's rant was almost certainly an overstatement—the unauthorized landing in Jing wouldn't kill them all. She, Koning, Chandra, and Quest would survive; any casualties would be on the ground. But Zong's authorities would be apoplectic at their violating so many regulations and, while those authorities might not destroy the ship and its crew out of hand, she and the others would spend the rest of their lives locked in small rooms with barred windows and steel doors.

"We're almost down," Ricci said, nodding at the screen on which an industrial district close to the bay expanded. "We'll be able to question him then and wring his neck if necessary." The ship was dropping toward one of several identical buildings that looked like large warehouses. Ricci searched for an open area on which to land, but that didn't appear to be the captain's plan. The force of their drive blew the end off a building and melted parts. Even before they touched down, the access ramp deployed.

The star winked out; the thunder died. Mitsumi leaped to his feet, grabbed a fistful of Mantor's shirt and yanked him up. He pointed toward the ship's landing ramp, yelled something Mantor couldn't understand because someone had shoved a bunch of cotton in his ears, and pushed him in the ramp's direction. Mantor understood that and sprinted toward the ramp. The woman and her compatriots had disappeared, perhaps to find shelter when the ship touched down. Mantor had a fleeting glance of the shuttle barreling toward the ship and slamming into its bay. Mitsumi must have been controlling it too.

Mantor pelted up the ramp breathing hard, the captain right on his heels. Before they hit the outer door, the ramp began to rise. Through the airlock, Mantor felt the drive rumble to life. Acceleration pushed on his shoulders and buckled his knees. The captain grabbed him from behind and spun him around. He leaned toward Mantor. The captain's voice sounded from a great distance—cotton still firmly packed his ears.

"We need to jump, now!"

Right, at this moment they were outlaws and the most wanted people in the system. Even on Support, what they'd done would have violated half a dozen serious safety mandates and, on Zong, well, Mantor wondered if he could even count that high.

Mantor nodded, stumbled through the inner airlock door and made his way to engineering, occasionally leaning against a corridor wall as he lost his balance. In the engineering compartment, Mantor strapped himself into a couch before the jump drive console and called up the ship's speed and location. They were well into the stratosphere and would clear atmo within a few seconds. Their acceleration in the planet's well would complicate his calculation; he'd need to alter the parameters. With a few taps on the keyboard, the formulas appeared on the screen in front of him, but his vision blurred and darkened at the edges.

Mantor closed his eyes and forced a deep breath. Another. He opened his eyes. The symbols on the screen were sharp; the darkness had receded. "Viram," Mitsumi said over the communicator, his voice taut with tension. "We could really use those calculations. The Zongians have decided putting us on trial for our crimes is too much trouble. We're ninety seconds away from becoming a ball of gas."

Mantor didn't respond. Fingers flying over his virtual keyboard, he altered his program to compensate for their acceleration, configured the HE engine and shot the okay to Koning's station. Eyes fixed on the console without seeing it, he was aware of their successful jump only by his continued existence.

CHAPTER 24

The passing weeks had only whetted her thirst for vengeance. It burned, disturbing her sleep and disrupting her concentration. Eyes boring through her desk display, and ignoring the walls' screens surrounding her with scenes of an erupting volcano, in her mind's eye Fylan once again saw Chandra's ship disappear seconds before she managed to stop its flight. There on Support, she'd had them. An incoming communication drew her attention to the present. With an effort of will, she forced her clenched hand to relax and accepted Kelton's request. His head emerged from the holo display. "Well?" she growled.

He swallowed visibly and avoided her eyes. "We've completed the survey. Chandra and his crew were traveling in a ship registered as the *Understated Subtlety.* That ship doesn't show up on any Federated Planet database." Her mouth hardened. Although she'd expected the result—it would have been too easy if Chandra's ship had been broadcasting its true identity when he'd slipped away—the confirmation added a few degrees to her thirst's heat.

Under Domenica's glare, Kelton added in haste, "But we've made sure to advise everyone on the Federated Worlds— the Consortium claims an interest in that cube. Chandra won't be able to sell it. They'll have to show up, eventually."

Amid fountains of molten rock splashing around her, Fylan considered Kelton's comment. That would be true of any normal prospecting crew, but any normal prospecting crew would already be writhing in pain in her private vaults. While rubbing the tips of her fingers together, she ignored Kelton squirming. It wasn't unknown for a prospector to contract manufacture discovered tech—unusual, but not unheard of. They'd been unable to discover what the artifact Chandra's crew had stolen actually did. But what if *they* had uncovered its use?

Her hands flat on her desk, she fixed her eyes on Kelton. "Alert our assets on Charlotte." If their gambit was to contract manufacture, that's where they would go. "Tell them I want to know about any rumors a prospector is contract manufacturing."

His face relaxing with relief, Kelton said, "Immediately," and cut the transmission.

Eyes shifting to the cascading lava, she pictured Chandra's crew screaming for mercy before dissolving in the molten rock and smiled.

Chandra was in a funk and wouldn't be consoled. Mitsumi understood at some level, but his frustration at Chandra's inability to face reality and deal with its consequences forced its way past his sympathy and into his voice. "That's not possible, Aber, and you know it. How many times do you have to hear that?"

Chandra's face remained stony, his lips compressed into a flat line. "C'mon, Aber," Koning said. "Cheer up. Our first product will net us plenty to cure Po... Pi... uh, your daughter."

Mitsumi shook his head. Koning wasn't helping.

"Pari," Chandra yelled. Then in a lower voice said, "Her name is Pari."

An embarrassed silence enveloped the group. They'd been trying since their narrow escape from Zong to persuade Chandra to go along with Mitsumi's plan—a plan everyone had agreed to but Chandra. Mitsumi had ordered acceleration for this discussion. Seated around the table in the mess, the entire crew focused on Chandra who, with his arms tightly folded across his chest, glared back at them.

"Aber," Ricci sitting next to Chandra said, breaking the stillness. She reached out and gripped Chandra's shoulder, "we need your help. You're the best one to use Professor Aten's translation program and identify the tech that will make us the most money in the least amount of time. And we've agreed that the only way we can turn the Ark into money now is by identifying and selling off the tech piecemeal."

Chandra shrugged Ricci's hand from his shoulder and remained silent, his face set hard against her argument. Ricci turned to Mitsumi and shrugged.

"*I* never agreed," Chandra said. "You all decided that we couldn't sell the Ark and hared off to Zong with disastrous results—"

Irritated, Mitsumi resisted the temptation to raise his voice. Leaning forward, Mitsumi fixed his eyes on Chandra and spoke, letting his annoyance show. "We obtained a translation program that will let us figure out what's on the Ark, and what the most valuable tech is. That is no disaster."

Chandra unfolded his arms and stood facing Mitsumi. "You almost killed us, and now we're wanted throughout Federation space! There's no way we can sell off any of the Ark tech now."

Mitsumi scowled. Chandra's unreasonable resistance to the only logical course of action frustrated him.

"Then how can we sell the Ark itself?" Quest said in a mild voice. A look of concern crossed Chandra's face. "If you are correct and we are not in a position to sell any individual pieces of Ark tech, because the Consortium is after us and everyone knows who we are, why would your conclusion be any different if we were to sell the entire Ark?"

Chandra sat down and surveyed the others around the table. He appeared to be trying, without success, to summon a response.

Koning perked up at Quest's observation and sought to press the advantage. "In fact," Koning said, "it'll be easier to sell the tech by itself because its value will be obvious; we won't have to convince anyone. But if we sell the Ark, we'll have to convince potential buyers of its overall value which, as we saw, was not an easy proposition." Koning glanced at the others seeking their approval.

The others around the table nodded their agreement. Chandra's face remained stubborn.

"Besides," Ricci added, "The Consortium is looking for someone selling an alien memory device—if they even know what the Ark is—not a group of prospectors offering bits and pieces of tech they picked up on various worlds."

"And the authorities on Zong," Mantor added, "are looking for a vessel that doesn't exist, right, Tai?"

Quest nodded at that. "The *Without a Trace* has disappeared."

Chandra appeared unmoved, but he slouched in his chair and his shoulders slumped, signaling his fading resistance. It occurred to Mitsumi that if he provided Chandra a way to salvage his pride, he would go along. Chandra had put up too much of a fight to back down easily.

"Look, Aber," Mitsumi said, "you're much more familiar with the tech world than any of us." Mitsumi swept his hand encompassing the rest of the crew. "You're in a better position than we are to pick what'll provide the most boost for the credit and will be the easiest either to contract manufacture or sell the schematics and designs."

The crew nodded and murmured affirmations.

"We can't do this without you, Aber," Mitsumi said. "Won't you help us so we can free Pari right away?"

Chandra eyed Mitsumi, then swept his gaze around the table. Ricci perched on the edge of her chair looking as if she expected to hear good news. Quest returned Chandra's look without emotion. Mantor looked through Chandra; his attention focused elsewhere. Koning yawned and shook her head, trying to stay awake.

As he reached a decision, Chandra straightened up in his seat and pulled his shoulders back. "Our best bet will be to find that gravity control system used on Planet Quest to suspend Sentaa in midair. That tech would be invaluable across multiple fields. We just need to figure out how easy it'll be to produce."

Ricci smiled. "That's great, Aber," she said. "Can I help you with the search?"

Chandra shook his head. "No, I'll go it alone. If I need assistance, I'd think Viram would be in a better position to aid me."

Ricci shrugged off his rebuff. Mantor returned from wherever he'd been at the sound of his name, confusion on his face as he tried to track the thread of the conversation.

"How long will this take?" Koning asked.

"You have somewhere to be, Sentaa?" Quest said, uncharacteristically injecting himself into the conversation.

Quest's response must have taken Koning by surprise because she didn't snap back.

"I have no idea," Chandra said without heat. "But I'm more anxious than any of you to complete the process and get our money."

It was only a matter of weeks until Chandra announced success. With Mantor's help, he'd found the antigravity device, examined the schematics and instructions, tracked down the schematics and instructions for components unknown to Federation science, these last being themselves a significant source of potential revenue, and put together a plan for manufacturing the whole bundle. The debate now was whether to sell the plans or contract for the manufacture and sale of the device.

"Charlotte's our best bet for manufacturing if that's what we want to do," Mantor said.

They had gathered once more in the mess to discuss their options. Life on board had settled into a comfortable routine during the weeks Chandra and Mantor had performed their search. Mitsumi had kept a close eye on Mantor in the days following their adventures on Zong. Mantor had refused to trade Mitsumi's life for a supply of Rapt, but did he regret that decision? Would he dig up an undisclosed Rapt store and begin using again? But Mantor had thrown himself into helping Chandra chase down the threads in the Ark and come up with the manufacturing strategy. Mantor had only occasionally lapsed into a parsec stare as he fell into contemplating another reality.

Ricci and Koning had cultivated their budding friendship—voyaging on numerous immersive adventures and discussing at length matters of common interest which included, as Mitsumi had overheard on occasion, a somewhat odd fixation on the Burthen financial and industrial combine.

Quest remained aloof, but on occasion succumbed to Ricci's entreaties to take part in an immersive or to join a conversation.

Eventually, they were ready to approach someone to manufacture their device.

"Charlotte?" Koning said. "Isn't that an agricultural world?"

"That hasn't been true for a while, Sentaa," Ricci said. "Charlotte has developed the most sophisticated industrial base in the federation. Lots of companies, including the Burthen combine, have their goods manufactured on Charlotte."

"Then Charlotte it is," Koning shrugged. "If we want to contract for manufacture rather than sell the plans. If we contract manufacture, won't we have to worry about getting Idea Rights for the devices and components?"

"IR for First Civ tech are easy to come by," Mitsumi said. He'd investigated that issue exhaustively in preparing his presentation to Corban and Jonta for his failed expedition.

Chandra nodded waving away Koning's concern. "We file a Declaration of Discovery and the rights are presumptively ours unless someone can prove prior invention which in this case will be impossible. What we will have manufactured has no precedent except in wildly speculative fiction."

Quest eyed Chandra coolly. "You're in favor of contract manufacturing then?"

Mitsumi raised his eyebrows at that. He'd expected a knock-down fight at this meeting—Chandra resisting the manufacturing option until blood flowed.

But Chandra spoke with enthusiasm. "We've developed the specs and instructions to where we'll get our money just as quickly by doing the manufacture through a proxy. If we tried to sell the idea, even with the details we've developed, no purchaser would pay us until it built and tested the device, so we might as well do that ourselves and reap the greater reward."

"So," Koning said, "how much money are we talking about? If we have this device made and sell it ourselves, how much can we expect to get?"

Chandra grinned. "We've discussed that, and we think the market for an anti-grav device is huge. Every time we discuss it, we imagine new applications."

"How much?" Koning said.

"Think for a moment," Mantor said. "Anything involving transportation or lifting or movement of any kind will employ a version of this device."

"How much?" Koning said with more force.

Chandra licked his lips looking around the table at each crew member. "There's little precedent for this," he said. "None of the other discovered First Civ tech had nearly this universal impact."

"How much?" Koning yelled.

Mantor paused. His mouth lifted in a huge grin. "We think at least a billion credits."

CHAPTER 25

Blue and green with swirling white clouds—the image of Charlotte filled the view screen. While they boosted into the system from their jump point, which Koning had calculated at just under a light minute from the planet —a feat that earned her well deserved compliments from the crew—Mitsumi had negotiated with potential manufacturers and selected Alloran Combine as the most promising. After transferring the schematics to the combine, they had waited in orbit while the combine worked through the drawings and assembled a few prototypes. After completing the prototypes, Alloran representatives had invited Mitsumi to the planet for an inspection and to authorize producing the first units.

"I don't understand why we can't all go," Ricci said. "We've been over two months away from civilization, except for our brief stops at Support and Zong, and only you, Tai, and Aber made the trip down the well on either of those occasions." The crew had gravitated to the mess to celebrate the successful conclusion of their first attempt at producing a device from the Ark. As soon as the manufacturer had announced it had completed the prototypes, Ricci had campaigned to be among the surface party. Ricci's pleas had only intensified with Mitsumi's announcement he was thinking of taking Mantor with him and no one else.

"We can't all go, because I won't leave the ship without crew while we're on the surface." Mitsumi held up his hand, forestalling Ricci's predictable protest. "I know you think nothing can happen to the ship in orbit, but I'm not comfortable with the idea."

"Well," Chandra said shrugging, "*I'm* not going planet side. I've learned that lesson."

"So, the rest of us can go," Ricci said with a smile. "Thanks, Aber."

Mitsumi considered the crew floating in the bridge. Quest appeared interested in the prospect which was unusual. Koning, eyebrows knit in worry, seemed less sanguine.

"I'm not sure that's a good idea," Koning said.

Ricci shot Koning an annoyed look. "What're you saying, Sentaa? A few minutes ago the chance to breathe unprocessed air and wash off shipboard grime thrilled you."

Koning held Ricci's eyes for a moment, then shifted her gaze. She opened her mouth to speak, then closed it again. Finally she said, "I meant I'm not sure that's a good idea for *you.*"

"What're you talking about?" Ricci said, her voice rising with heat. "Why is it okay for you but not for me?"

Koning looked to Mitsumi and Quest seeking help for her position. Mitsumi wondered what Koning was on about. Koning lowered her eyes and mumbled, "Never mind."

Ricci's request was not unreasonable. Mitsumi's initial inclination to allow only Mantor with him on the planet had resulted partly from the fear that if he opened the option to everyone, he'd have to order someone to stay with the ship and engender resentment for that decision. But, with Chandra volunteering to stay behind, maybe it would be good for everyone to have a break from the ship on a planet with the comforts of home.

"Okay," Mitsumi said. "If Aber's willing to stay aboard," Mitsumi looked in Chandra's direction. Chandra nodded. "Then I don't see why the rest of us can't unwind on planet."

Quest's mouth quirked up in as close to a smile as Mitsumi had seen. Ricci beamed. If they'd been in gravity, she'd have bounced on her toes. Koning frowned and turned away, disturbed at the decision. "Tai will arrange our alternate IDs. It'll take two days at least to complete our negotiations, so pack accordingly," Mitsumi said. "I'll arrange for our accommodations in the same block. And make sure you pick up your facial ident kit."

When the call came, she was hunting, huddled in a blind high in the jungle's forest canopy on Support's largest continent overlooking a clearing. She'd been waiting most of a day for the promised gerophant, Support's largest gen-engineered game animal. Sweat dripping down her back and running into her eyes, she nearly missed the communication alert in the jungle's screeching cacophony. When she distinguished the tone, her pulse raced—she'd left instructions no one was to disturb her except with news of Chandra and his gang. She tapped acceptance. Kelton's voice sounded in her ear.

"Hey, boss."

"Give me good news, Kelton."

"It's not much," she heard the shrug in his voice, "but you wanted anything. We've picked up rumors on Charlotte that a prospector is having some spectacular tech built."

Fylan wiped sweat from her eyes and shook her head. "That's awfully vague. Who's the prospector? Who's the manufacturer? What's the tech?"

"Don't know, boss. I've told you everything we've been able to pick up."

Fylan hung her head. That *wasn't* much to go on, but it was something. She brought her head up as, with a trumpeting roar, a gerophant ripped through surrounding trees into the clearing. Its massive head rose to the blind's height, and she stared into its small, red eyes. Although it shouldn't have been able to spot her in the blind, with another roar exposing rows of razor teeth, it lowered its two pointed tusks and charged.

Heart pounding, nostrils flaring at the pungent

distinctive musky odor, she only hesitated a fraction of a second before bringing her beam weapon to bear. She'd only have one shot at the tossing head before it speared her or bit her in half. With a deep breath, she waited for the head to enter her sights.

Now.

The invisible beam flashed out, and the gerophant collapsed midsprint in a tumble of legs, its momentum carrying it crashing into the tree where Fylan perched.

Grinning with exhilaration and shaking with residual adrenaline, she pumped her fist—that was *much* better than she had expected. Maybe it was a sign that her other hunt was at an end too. "Kelton, prep the ship, we're leaving for Charlotte."

Ricci luxuriated in the water heated to within a breath of scalding. She felt it dissolving the gook that had precipitated atom by atom onto her skin from the sweat, grease, and grime floating in the ship's atmosphere. Even efficient, uncompromised ship's filters didn't completely clear that gummy mix from the air and shipboard mist showers never entirely removed it from her skin. Her romantic vision of life among the stars hadn't included such gritty details. Her leap into the real world had introduced her to many such minor annoyances from which her family's incalculable wealth had protected her. Regardless, she didn't regret her decision; she viewed those annoyances as badges of honor she wore proudly as emblems of her freedom.

As she toweled herself off after her bath, Ricci called up communication with Koning. "Sentaa, I'll be ready in five minutes."

"Fine," Koning replied curtly. Ricci wondered what had gotten into her friend. Ever since the decision to descend to the surface, Koning had been surly and uncommunicative. As she stepped from the bathroom, Ricci told the room window to depolarize. Captain Mitsumi had secured rooms on one of the higher floors of a guest house on the outskirts of Charlotte's principal city, Natan. Rows and rows of Orana orchards stretched to the horizon.

Charlotte's inhabitants had developed a thriving agricultural economy by the time the first HE driven ship from the newly formed Federation appeared in system. It was years after being introduced into space before Charlotte's inhabitants became interested in more industrial pursuits. By that time the agricultural tradition was so ingrained, they built their manufacturing and industrial base underground leaving the surface for more traditional uses.

Ricci dressed in a loose-fitting shirt and pants. The tight outfits most practical for extended periods in the zig grew tiresome after a while. She was glad to be free of them for a few days. She signaled Koning to let her know she was ready and on her way. With a scowl, she shook her head in irritation at Koning's failure to respond. Ricci marched down the hallway to Koning's accommodations and stood in front of the door, waiting for the system to recognize her and announce her presence. The door opened. On the edge of a bed, Koning sat staring at the floor, shoulders slumped in dejection. She did not look up as Ricci entered the room and the door slid shut.

What now? Ricci thought. *First she's prickly, now she looks like someone close to her died.* Koning's mood swings were something Ricci had become accustomed to, but this felt extreme even for her.

"Hey, Sentaa. What's going on? Aren't we off to explore the city?"

Koning shook her head, but otherwise didn't respond.

That was worrisome; this wasn't the Koning she knew. Her Koning would have snapped a scathing retort. Ricci examined her friend. Was that a tear at the corner of her eye? Yep, there it went down her cheek. Her eyes went wide and her muscles tensed—she had yet to see Koning cry. Alarmed, she moved into the room and sat next to Koning on the bed, their shoulders touching. Koning leaned away then inched sideways to avoid further contact.

Had she hurt her? *Something* was seriously wrong. "Okay," Ricci said, "so you don't want to go. That's fine. But please talk—let me know what's going on."

Koning hung her head and shook a negative.

"Sentaa," Ricci reached out a hand toward Koning's shoulder, but let it hover a few inches away not knowing if her touch would console or irritate. "Did I do something? Have I hurt you?"

Koning stared at the floor unresponsive, except to wipe a tear from her face with the back of her hand. Ricci lowered her hand to the bed behind Koning and regarded her in puzzled silence. It must have been something she'd done or said. How else to explain her reaction to Ricci's presence?

"Look, Sentaa," Ricci said with a sigh, facing forward and clasping her hands together. "Whatever it is I've done, I'm sorry. I can't bear it when I hurt someone. That's one thing Mother told me I had to fix to be a proper Burthen. I cared too much about the effect my behavior had on others. 'People care what Burthens think and feel' she told me 'not the other way around.'" She turned toward Koning again. "But I couldn't do it then and I can't do it now. Please forgive me."

At this, Koning sobbed. Without thinking, Ricci put her arm around Koning. Koning stiffened at her touch, then relaxed and allowed Ricci to pull her toward her side. Ricci waited for a response, anything to show her what she'd done to cause such pain. Koning sniffled, but didn't speak. After a minute, Koning drew back without breaking away from Ricci. With puffy red eyes and a red nose, Koning scrunched her face to keep more tears at bay.

"You didn't do anything, Mei." She drew a shaking hand across her eyes. "It was me. I..." Koning worked her mouth, trying but unable to complete her thought.

Ricci frowned. What had Koning done? She pulled

Koning into a hug. "No matter what you think you've done, Sentaa, I guarantee you it can't be as bad as you think it is." Koning shook with another round of sobs as the door to the guest room opened.

Ricci glanced at the door in irritation, but terror froze her into immobility.

"Hello, Folami," her mother said with a smile.

Fear was an iron band around her chest; she couldn't draw breath. In a panic, she released Koning and shot to her feet. Her eyes skittered around the room searching for any avenue of escape. Visions of her uncle writhing in agony filled her mind. Two large men wearing Burthen Security uniforms moved past her mother and flanked Ricci, each gripping one of her arms.

"You're surprised to see me," her mother said then cocked her head. "But not pleased I think."

At the sound of her mother's voice, Ricci's paralysis disappeared. After breaking the grips on her arm, she slid from between the men as her self-protection routines, implanted in her motor cortex via mRNA and reinforced with hours of practice, kicked in. She lashed out furiously at the men, raining blows on them aimed at nerve clusters and soft flesh. But the men countered each slashing, grabbing, kicking move.

"I hadn't forgotten your training, Folami," her mother said in a loud voice over the grunts and impacts from the battle raging in front of her. "They're more than a match for you, but I've instructed them not to hurt you, only to keep you from leaving."

Her mother's words barely penetrated her consciousness as she whipped through the routines at her disposal. Eventually though, she tired while the guards fought on without seeming to feel fatigue. In the end, Ricci's blows were sluggish and ineffective when she managed to land any. Then, her energy exhausted, Ricci slumped to the floor.

Panting, struggling for breath, fear, held at bay by her fight, gripped her once more. She couldn't go back. But piercing her fear one question echoed. "How?" she said. "How did you know?"

She'd been meticulous in constructing Mei Ricci. Nothing pointed to her true origins; she was sure of it. One of the security men stepped up to her and laid a device on her arm. She recognized a gene reader. Despite having altered her appearance, Ricci's reaction must have told her mother she was at the right place, but her mother was thorough. The machine flashed green and the security man nodded at her mother.

Her mother nodded back then turned to Koning. "Our thanks, Ms. Koning," her mother said. "I have posted payment to your account. It's been a pleasure doing business with you."

Ricci's eyes widened and her jaw went slack. "Sentaa?" Ricci said. How could Koning betray her? After she'd rescued Koning, they'd spent more and more time together comparing notes on their past lives. Koning had shared with Ricci horrific tales from her childhood and the agonizing self-doubt she tried to hide with caustic callousness, while Ricci had revealed her fear of her family and dreams of a different life. This had to be a mistake or a game her mother was playing. Ricci turned to Koning who continued to stare at the ground, tears running down her face. Ice flowed through Ricci, numbing her. It was true. She'd trusted her life to Koning, and Koning had traded it away. She turned from Koning. Kantic Burthen smiled, by all appearances the epitome of a loving mother.

"Come, Folami, your destiny awaits—one you will long to embrace after but a small moment of discomfort."

Ricci pushed herself to her feet, shaking off the guards' attempts to help her up. If she had to go, if her future was now fixed, she'd go under her own power with as much dignity as she could scrape together. Without a backward glance, Ricci paced toward her mother who moved aside allowing her to proceed first. A few steps down the hall, Ricci heard the door to Koning's room slide shut.

CHAPTER 26

"You're what?"

Seated across from Mitsumi at the conference table, Barde, the Alloran Combine's point man in the negotiations spread his hands. "It's out of our hands, Holwel. The Consortium has asserted a claim to any new First Civ tech manufactured for prospectors. And they've posted a bounty for the prospectors themselves."

Mitsumi shook his head, incredulous. "What makes you think we're prospectors?" He swept his hand out to include Mantor, sitting a few chairs away at the conference table.

"One, you're peddling First Civ tech," Barde ticked off the points. "Two, you don't represent any of the combines that buy First Civ tech. So, you're either prospectors or thieves. I'm giving you the benefit of the doubt."

Mitsumi closed his eyes, gritting his teeth with frustration. They had had this sealed. The prototypes were perfect. This meeting was a formality—inking the final approval to manufacture and split profits. How had the Consortium spoiled this? "But, so what? Isn't that our problem? The Consortium can't touch you if you're operating in good faith, and you've seen our Idea Rights claims—they're solid."

At this last statement, Barde looked askance at Mitsumi and said, "Assume that's true. The Consortium can tie us up in the courts while we test their claim." Mitsumi opened his mouth to protest, but Barde continued before he could speak.

"And extra legally, the Consortium has been known to exert more immediate physical pressure to achieve its goals. As you can imagine, Alloran's officers, not to mention its board members, would prefer not to accept that risk." Barde looked at Mitsumi and Mantor, his face drawn in sympathy. "I'm sorry, Holwel, I don't know how word of this deal leaked, but it has and as I said, it's out of my hands."

Mitsumi tried once more. "But the profit. Think of the hundreds of millions of credits you're giving up."

Barde rose from his seat and gathered the papers spread out before him. "I'm only the messenger, Holwel. But for what it's worth, I made the same point vociferously and repeatedly." He slid the neatly arranged papers into his case. "Unfortunately for you, they ignored my entreaties." He turned from the table and the door slid open for him. Turning back to the room he said, "You can keep the prototypes and this piece of advice. If it *is* you and your crew the Consortium is looking for, you might want to leave Charlotte's system sooner rather than later because eventually they *will* find you."

Mitsumi's skin tightened as he recalled Fylan's threat. Being at her mercy was not high on his to-do list. "Uh, Barde," Mitsumi said. "About that, how would you feel about wiping all records of our proposed transaction and our, uh, identities, from your systems? Not that the Consortium is searching for *us*, but to untrusting souls it might appear that way, and I like to avoid misunderstandings."

With a rueful smile, Barde nodded. "Already done. You are not alone in wishing to avoid...misunderstandings with the Consortium. You can see yourselves out." He marched through the door which slid shut behind him.

Stunned at this turn of events, Mitsumi stared at his hands. All his ideas had failed, and he had no more to replace them. The Consortium had stymied them at every turn. He would suggest just giving up and turning the Ark over to the Consortium, if it didn't mean a painful death for him and his crew.

"Uh," Mantor said, "that didn't go well did it?"

Without responding to Mantor, Mitsumi commed Quest, who was spending the day at the planetary library, and told him to return to the guest house where they were staying. He tried to raise Koning or Ricci, who had announced plans to sightsee, but neither of them responded.

Determined to track them down, Mitsumi decided to start with their rooms on the off-chance he would discover something useful.

There was no response at Ricci's room.

"When did she leave?" Mitsumi asked the room's subsentient AI.

"I can neither confirm nor deny that my human occupant has left," the program said. Mitsumi was sure he wasn't imagining the undertone of smugness and wondered how you programmed for that.

"But she didn't answer the summons," Mitsumi said. "She's not in her room."

"My human may be asleep or simply unwilling to respond to the summons either here or somewhere else."

Mitsumi huffed and pinched the bridge of his nose. The last thing he needed now was an AI cracking wise. "Or dead or dying," Mitsumi said.

"She is neither."

"Then you know where she is," Mitsumi said his voice rising in frustration.

"She is not dead or dying to my knowledge," the AI added belatedly.

Mitsumi pounded a fist on the door frame. "Read my ID. I'm the captain of her crew. I paid for this room."

"Acknowledged," the AI said, after a moment in a voice Mitsumi would have described as "grudging" in a human.

"My contract with this guest house gives me access to information on the occupant's location."

"Agreed," the AI said after a pause.

Finally, Mitsumi thought. "So when did—"

"Unless the occupant selects the highest privacy rating for the accommodation in which case the information is restricted."

With a growled curse on stubborn AI's, Mitsumi moved along the hall to Koning's room with little expectation of success. To his surprise, the door opened as soon as Mitsumi signaled his presence. The room was dark. Koning had opaqued the windows and turned off the lights. With a step into the room, Mitsumi called for lights as the door slid shut behind him. On the edge of the room's single bed, Koning sat, resting her head on her crossed arms. Something was going on —he'd never seen Koning in such a state, but irritation snuffed out the spark of sympathy. "Sentaa, why didn't you respond to my communications requests? We agreed to stay in touch. And now we have to get our butts off planet."

Koning remained still. Mitsumi's irritation flared. He stepped closer and squatted so that his head was on a level with hers. "Sentaa, I'm talking to you. Why didn't you respond? What's going on?"

Koning raised her head. Her eyes were red and puffy, her face wet with tears. His expression softened. Only an exceptional trauma would draw tears from Koning. Despite a rising anxiety about being discovered, Mitsumi stood and moved to sit beside her on the bed. He let silence fill the room before speaking again, this time with a softer tone. "I don't mean to intrude on your personal life, but if whatever happened affects the crew, I have to know what it is."

Koning bowed her head, burying her face into her folded arms once more, and mumbled something unintelligible.

He leaned closer to her. "What was that? I didn't hear you."

Koning raised her head. "I killed her," she whispered.

He sat up and leaned away from Koning. Koning was rough, but he hadn't thought her capable of killing someone. He'd come to believe her expressed desire to get rid of Chandra and Mantor had been bluster.

"Killed who?"

Without responding, Koning stared ahead. Mitsumi allowed her time, but after a moment asked again, "Killed who Sentaa? Who did you kill?"

"Mei, I killed Mei."

Then the story came out—who Ricci was, her flight from her family, and what Koning had done when she'd found out.

To Mitsumi, the story answered a lot of questions. In hindsight, it made sense of Ricci's incompetence and desire to learn and fit in.

"I couldn't believe someone would want to run from the wealth and power I've coveted my whole life," Koning said wiping more tears from her cheeks. "She must have exaggerated what her family would do to her if they found her. I figured she was going through a phase and would secretly be glad to see an end to the whole charade. So, when I saw the reward posted for information on the whereabouts of Folami Burthen, I decided we'd both benefit. I'd get the reward, and she'd reunite with her family and position and power, something I'd convinced myself she wanted to do, but pride kept her from doing. I thought she just couldn't bring herself to admit to her family she was wrong."

Koning shook her head again and pleaded for understanding.

"So I was doing both of us a favor when I sent the message drone to her family with Mei's information and a picture of her new face. I was helping her when I broke my promise to keep her secret."

Koning turned from Mitsumi and lowered her head again. "But that was before we became friends—before she saved my life." She raised her head and eyed Mitsumi. "I figured after we went to Zong and Support with Tai's magic hiding the ship and changing our identity on planet, Burthen wouldn't be able to find her—I guess I was wrong."

"So, why didn't you say something then?" Mitsumi asked. "If you changed your mind and realized what you'd done was wrong, why didn't you tell us and let us try to fix things?"

She sniffled and wiped more tears from her eyes. "I was so ashamed. I didn't want to admit what I'd done. Then I convinced myself that that her family wouldn't be able to find her with the scant information I'd sent and, even if they found Mei, her family couldn't be that bad. But when Mei's mother showed up, and I saw Mei's reaction..."

Memories of their time aboard ship floated up from the depths of Mitsumi's mind. Ricci almost blowing the ship open to space from its dock, almost killing them trying to maneuver into the shuttle bay. Ricci taking huge pleasure in her increasing skill, integrating into the crew, fiercely defending Koning and saving her life. If Koning was right, Ricci would never be the same after the procedure—her body wouldn't die, but who she was, the person she'd become, the crew member he liked, admired, and relied on would. That also was a form of death. Resolve hardened in his gut. He wouldn't let the Ricci he knew be destroyed. No matter what it took, no matter what it cost in terms of his plans, he would find Ricci and bring her back.

Koning lifted her head again and fixed her eyes on Mitsumi. "We have to get her back, Captain. We can't let her stay with them. They'll kill the old Mei and replace her with a money-driven, ambitious monster."

Nodding, Mitsumi said, "I agree. We will rescue her." Face set in determination, Mitsumi rose from the bed. At this, Koning rose as well and faced Mitsumi. Mitsumi took her by the shoulders. "We'll find her, Sentaa and bring her home."

Thirty minutes later, the crew had responded to Mitsumi's emergency recall broadcast and assembled in Mitsumi's room —Chandra joined them from orbit, his projection floating around the room even wafting through people in disregard of holographic etiquette. At a sharp word from Mitsumi, Chandra stopped in mid-wander inside Mantor. Flustered, Chandra pushed away and remained still. After filling in the crew on the Consortium frustrating their plans and searching for them in system and on Ricci's identity and Koning's perfidy, Mitsumi stated his position. "Sentaa and I are going to rescue Mei. Will you help us?"

Mantor looked at Koning with sorrow and disgust. "How close is the Consortium to finding us?"

Mitsumi shrugged. "I don't know, Viram. You heard Barde as well as I did—the Consortium is looking for 'prospectors,'" Mitsumi looked at Quest. "You find anything while snooping around the Consortium's electronic footprint?"

Quest nodded. "I did. They have been unsuccessful, but they have feelers out with the manufacturing combines. If Alloran gives us up…"

"Alloran took care of that," Mitsumi said. "They wiped their records."

"Then we're good, right?" Mantor said, begging for reassurance.

"I did run across something that might be of interest and might affect our plans." Quest had his assistant display what appeared to be a series of credit transfers and a convoluted organization chart.

Mitsumi stared at the display showing a handful of the Consortium's financial transactions. He shifted his attention to the org chart and followed its lines. Mitsumi gave a low whistle. At the top of the chart showing a convoluted connection to the Consortium was Burthen Industries. So, Kantic Burthen, Ricci's mother, and Domenica Fylan were connected. "Where did you find this?"

"The financial records were easy," Quest said modestly. "I just had to penetrate the banking structure on Charlotte. The chart was buried in a network the Consortium operates—*that* took effort."

Mantor nodded at the display. "Alloran scrubbed us from

its records so the Consortium won't find out about us from them, right?" Eyes on the others, he wrung his hands and continued. "But what about Mei's mom? She knows who we are. Won't she give us up?"

With a shake of his head, Quest said, "If she had, we wouldn't be sitting here."

Mitsumi agreed. "And even if they're inclined to compare notes, Domenica's looking for Aber. Unless Sentaa provided more information than she's told us," he raised his eyebrows and looked at Koning who shook her head vigorously, "Kantic Burthen is unlikely to know Aber is part of Mei's crew. So, we have some leeway. Back to the question, will you help us rescue Mei?"

Chin in hand Chandra was thoughtful, eyebrows brought together in concentration. He spoke first. "It was her mother?" Chandra asked, surveying the others for confirmation. "The one who Sentaa says took her away?"

Koning exploded to her feet burning with anger and righteous indignation, fueled, Mitsumi suspected, by guilt as much as anything else. "She fought them," Koning shouted at Chandra. "She fought those goons. They dragged her away." Koning turned to Quest and Mantor for support. "It's not like her mother politely requested her company."

Surprised at her ferocity, Chandra shrank away from Koning and raised his hands in defense. "It *was* her mother though, right?" Chandra sat straighter rebounding from Koning's outburst. "Her family wanted her back. Isn't it possible that her family knows what's best for her?"

Koning seethed and opened her mouth to interrupt Chandra. Mitsumi coughed, catching Koning's attention. "Let him talk, Sentaa," he said, "and anyone else who wants to speak." As the captain, he'd already announced what his ship and crew, whatever remained of it after this meeting, would do. This meeting was to determine who the remnants would be and the best chance of keeping any of the crew was to let everyone air their point of view. His decision might upset some—they might decide not to support it and leave. It was remarkable how little the prospect troubled him. Not that he wanted anyone to leave. Far from it he valued each crew member for his or her particular abilities. But his priorities had shifted. He would do the right thing as captain and, if members of his crew chose not to support that decision, perhaps a separation was necessary.

Chandra licked his lips then speaking hesitantly, as if the next word might trigger an explosion, continued. "I know it's a foreign idea to many of you, but for me the family is sacred." Eyes moving to the others, Chandra watched for a reaction. Mitsumi was noncommittal, Quest stone faced. Anger still burned in Koning. Determined to have his say, Chandra set his face and plowed ahead. "We all have relationships that help define who we are. For the most part, we choose those ties and surround ourselves with people who make us comfortable with who we are or think we are. Family is different. We don't choose. Family requires us to associate intimately with people who might make us uncomfortable, but who know us in our most unguarded moments and, most of the time, care for *us*, not for their own comfort and advantages."

Chandra fixed his eyes on each of the others. If his speech was having an effect, it didn't show in their faces. Mitsumi's mind turned to the two women with whom he'd tried to form the kind of family Chandra was describing. Neither Cala nor Riga had seemed to have any interest in him above their own comfort and desires. When more powerful men had expressed interest in them, off they'd gone with almost the same complaint each time—he was loving and loyal, but a bit of a ditherer—afraid of making a decision. Chandra's plea didn't move Mitsumi one angstrom.

"Could it be," Chandra continued, "that what Mei's family has in mind for her is best suited to Mei's strengths and talents? Best not only for Ricci, but for her family, its enterprise, and even the Federated Worlds? After all, the life Mei said she wanted was obscure. As a nameless pilot, she would never have the widespread influence she'll have as the political scion of a great family. Perhaps her family is right."

Mitsumi scanned the group. Koning's anger still bubbled hot below the surface. Something in Chandra's speech obviously resonated with Quest and Mantor. So far only Koning was in Mitsumi's corner. But rescuing Ricci was the right thing to do. He had to make them see that.

Mitsumi spoke, breaking the silence. "I appreciate your view of family, Chandra, but consider this. Mei knew from birth what her family expected of her. Through her childhood, adolescence and into adulthood, she understood the role her family had groomed her for. You argue that knowing her well, her family was better able than she was to decide what to do with her life. As you said, just being uncomfortable with a decision doesn't mean it's the wrong one."

Mitsumi paused, meeting the eyes of each of the crew. He hadn't spoken with any heat—to the contrary his words were cool and measured, but spoken with an intensity that carried more weight than any angry outburst.

"Over the years of being prepared for her role, Mei had ample opportunity to weigh her family's wishes against her heart's desires. She considered everything you've said—her family's ability to understand her character and her ability to exert a wider influence for good. With that, and even assuming their concern for her interests, she chose to follow her heart. That doesn't mean she was right, but it was her choice. Her family might have tried to persuade her, entice her, or bribe her even, back into the fold. Instead, they chose force. That is a step beyond the pale. It cannot, it must not, stand."

His face set hard, Mitsumi fixed his eyes on Chandra. Chandra held Mitsumi's gaze for a long moment, then glanced away backing down from the confrontation. Koning beamed, nodded and pumped a fist.

His head cocked, Quest eyed Mitsumi. Nodding once he said, "I agree."

Mantor's eyes narrowed in concentration, as if trying

to make sense of a puzzling readout from his engines. Then, his face relaxing into satisfaction, the puzzle resolved, Mantor nodded.

Koning beamed, pleased at their decision. With hooded eyes, Chandra remained noncommittal.

Okay, thought Mitsumi, *I still might lose Chandra, but I have everyone else.* "Aber," Mitsumi said, "do you have reservations?"

After considering the crew's reaction, Chandra spoke with a note of bitterness. "My reservations are meaningless. You are the only chance I have to save Pari. If you want to risk our lives and my daughter's life, I have no choice but to do my best to succeed and survive."

"Right, then," Mitsumi said, "we'll make our way back to the ship. We have to plan and we don't have much time. Aber, see if you can locate Mei and find out when her mother is planning this procedure. Sentaa will help out when we return."

Chandra nodded and his hologram winked out. The rest of the crew stared at each other without speaking. Now that they had decided to retrieve Ricci, everyone was wondering what they'd signed up for. Everyone but Koning. Eyes bright with excitement she was taut, ready to act. *And do what?* Mitsumi thought. He still only had the vaguest notion of what might in the fullness of time become a plan. He doubted she had the faintest clue. She just wanted to do something. For the rest, qualms flocked thickly around. Mantor gave voice to their thoughts.

"So," Mantor said into the silence, "I think it's great we decided to rescue Mei and all, but, uh, just so we're reading from the same schematic here, everyone knows Mei's mom runs one of the largest and richest enterprises in known space, right?" Anger flashed in Koning's eyes. "I mean, I said yes," Mantor said, raising his hands in a placating gesture to Koning. "But Burthen Industries has some pretty high tech stuff. She'll be well-guarded and hard to reach and, uh, well," Mantor turned to Mitsumi, "do we have like a *plan* or anything?"

Eyes on Mitsumi, Mantor, Koning, and Quest waited. *I wish I knew*, Mitsumi thought. The notion he'd had earlier was resolving into an idea which he expected to coalesce into a plan, but at the moment it was all rather nebulous. But they would come up with something—he was certain and this was no time to dither. With a smile and a nod, Mitsumi spoke. "Absolutely," he said. "And it's brilliant."

CHAPTER 27

A scant six months. She'd only been gone that long, but in that time she'd forgotten how different life is with unlimited resources. With the riches of her former life once again at her fingertips, all the delicacies of the Federated Worlds were but a suggestion away. Of the luxuries she'd foregone when she ventured into the real world and separated herself from complete satisfaction of her every wish, Antiquine was the one she missed the most. A lotion with mild psychotropic properties that relieved stress and stimulated cells to produce subdural collagen, Antiquine had been a reward after her most demanding outings and a celebration of pleasurable ones. Fashioned from a rare succulent that grew only in Garden's polar regions, a mere ten thousand bottles of Antiquine were made each year for the twenty-five billion inhabitants of the ten Federated Worlds.

After being ushered into this suite atop the tallest building on Charlotte, Ricci—she couldn't bear thinking of herself as a Burthen—had inspected the lavation room on the off-chance a bottle was there. When she came up empty, Ricci had sagged in disappointment—the lift would have been welcome, and her skin had suffered from months aboard the ship. But she would have to do without. A chime announced someone at her door.

A shiver of fear pumped her heart and prickled her upper lip with sweat. Had Mother advanced the timeline? Were they coming to take away her life already? Ricci considered not responding. *Sure*, she thought, *that'll work because mother can't come in without your permission.* When the chime didn't repeat and no one burst into the room, Ricci's fear receded—her life wasn't over just yet. Her curiosity aroused, Ricci went to the door.

"Open," she said aloud. The door whisked open to an empty hallway. Puzzled, Ricci poked her head into the hall. Empty in both directions. *That's odd.* About to order the door to close, Ricci glanced to the floor and gasped. A diamond bottle with distinctive curves sat in the hall. Reverently, Ricci sank down next to the bottle and caressed its surface, tracing the stylized entwined heart shapes that proclaimed its contents better than any label.

She stood, cradling the bottle. Turning from the door and ordering it closed, Ricci opened it, breathing in the singular aroma—vanilla, cinnamon, cloves, nutmeg swirled through her senses. The scent alone transported her to the best days of her life as a Burthen before she ran away—cloud riding on Fit, orbital diving into the grand caldera on Newome, plunging through the continental cataracts on Del, exploring the bioluminescent underwater caverns on Wild.

With narrowed eyes, Ricci examined the suite and noted the contrast. On the station above Support, scouring the hire lists to find a crew, she'd squeezed herself into the cheapest basic cube. When extruded, the bed had filled the space, the regenerator good for tasteless survival rations—all she could afford. Shipboard, her quarters had been a little larger, the menu a touch more varied, and the aroma of sweaty bodies mixed with the tang of sewage from the faulty recycling system had faded into the background—eventually.

As she rested the bottle of Antiquine on a side table of dark Garden rockwood inlaid with an intricate pattern of lighter Support candlewood, Ricci sank into the mist couch and plucked a spice apple from the diamond bowl on the side table.

Juice dribbled down her chin as she bit into the perfectly

ripe fruit and savored the sweet, spicy meat. Why had she wanted to run away from all this? Sure, there was pleasure and, more importantly, satisfaction in being on her own and making her own decisions. She still found the idea of playing politician repugnant. Was it any more distasteful, though, than layers of grime or fifty different flavors of algae and yeast?

Finished with the apple, Ricci tossed the core on the table and picked up the Antiquine. But, she thought, in her new life she'd had friends, close because of shared experiences and interests rather than money and power. *Like Koning?* a part of her asked. No, Ricci believed Koning regretted her decision.

Still.

Would it be so bad to accept the opulence, revel in the extravagance? Was the price of that comfort any greater than the price of the independence for which she'd fought and schemed? Eyes wide with anticipation, she tilted the bottle of Antiquine toward her palm, a tingle running up her arm, as if her skin too awaited the soothing, creamy, liquid silk.

A drop trembling at the bottle's lip, Ricci paused, staring at it. It wasn't coincidence. She'd thought of Antiquine, and a bottle appeared at her door.

Righting the bottle and replacing it on the table Ricci considered how it had appeared. She hadn't asked anyone for it. *I wondered if there were any in the suite*, she thought, *and I went looking for it where it might be.* Someone was watching her, someone or something that knew her well enough to know what it meant when she went snooping in the lavation.

Ricci surveyed the room, although she knew it would be useless—the cameras would be impossible to see with the naked eye. Heart pounding, Ricci breathed as if the room's oxygen had disappeared and, no matter how hard she tried, she couldn't satisfy her need for air. Around her the room seemed to shrink, closing in on her until she was immobile. It wouldn't be cameras only. Somewhere, invisible beams reached out and measured her heart rate, her breathing, the perspiration on her skin. Machines sampled her breath, inspecting her metabolites, weighing the chemistry of her emotions—and reacting—pushing, pulling, shaping her into the perfect Burthen.

She'd been naïve to imagine she wasn't being watched but, more than that, it was the idea that someone or something —probably an AI—knew her well enough to anticipate and fulfill her every desire. Which would have been okay if it wasn't a finely tuned process to manage her, to mold her into something else. The room pressed harder. With eyes closed, shutting out the room, Ricci focused on her breath, forcing her lungs to slow, fighting the illusion she lacked air. Gradually, she regained control. Breath and heart slowing, Ricci opened her eyes and saw the luxury for what it was, for what she'd described it to Koning as being—a trap. Anger at being trapped and forced and shaped her whole life seared her.

"No, Mother," she said aloud, her voice quivering with suppressed rage. "You can't manipulate me into being your puppet. If you want me, you'll have to force the change. And afterward, I'll be compliant, but I won't be the same. I won't be your daughter—I'll be your construct."

And I am *going to fight.* As she clung to that desperate determination, Ricci rose from the couch and stalked out onto the suite's balcony, pressing up against the railing, removing herself as far as possible from the insidious devices inside. Spread out below in the growing twilight, Charlotte's fields and orchards stretched into the horizon, vanishing in a haze. Amid her buzzing thoughts she ignored the view, her mind racing with plans of escape. One after the other, she considered and rejected the plans, her anger's heat dissipating as despair crept in. Each plot was more desperate than the last. When she inspected the outside tower walls for hand and footholds, reality smashed her illusions—escape was impossible. She passed a trembling hand through her hair, turned away from the darkening world, and stared with morbid fascination into the room. The apartment glowed with menace, a symbol of the destruction and pain awaiting her. Cold sweat broke on her upper lip, and muscles bunched on her forearms. Tears leaked down her cheeks as Ricci admitted she had no way out.

After wrenching her gaze from the apartment, she forced herself to turn away and lifted her head to the sky. The first bright sparks of stars were just visible and ghosting among them, the glowing reflection of ships in orbit. Eyes on the moving pinpoints, Ricci imagined that, if she stared hard enough, she could pick out *Are We There Yet*? They wouldn't complete their business for several days. She pictured them on the ship right now—Mantor obsessing over his engines, fighting Rapt's ravages, Quest floating motionless in his cabin absorbed in a search of Charlotte's database looking for any hint of his lost family. Chandra burrowing into the Ark's depths desperate to distract himself from his family's pain, Captain Mitsumi completing negotiations, worrying what the crew thought of him, and Koning. Her skin flushed with heat and her grip tightened as she pictured Koning and remembered her betrayal.

It was an impossible task identifying any one ship in the sky above and, after a time, she grew cold. With a shudder, Ricci steeled herself and stepped into the apartment trying to ignore the itch of a thousand sensors assessing, weighing, judging her every eye blink and breath.

CHAPTER 28

As Mitsumi pushed into the ship's mess in the face of Chandra and Koning screaming at each other, memories of his failed military career, the collapse of his two marriages, the failure of his first expedition, Kalal's advice, his humiliation at the hands of his wives and their new husbands, and his recent experiences onboard flashed in Mitsumi's mind and roiled together in a seething mass of frustration. They had no time for these antics. Koning and Chandra needed to locate Ricci and discover when and where the "procedure" was to be performed. Every second wasted decreased their chances of finding Ricci and saving her. Oblivious seemingly to this basic fact, Koning and Chandra faced each other across the mess table, both livid with anger, yelling over each other—neither paying any attention to what the other was saying, rage distorting their voices so much that Mitsumi couldn't understand a word.

He launched himself from a bulkhead and into Chandra, knocking his grip loose from the chair back he'd been holding and sending him drifting across the room. Before Chandra reached the opposite wall, Mitsumi grabbed a chair back, using his momentum to swing around to face Koning. He pulled himself close to Koning, whose shock at the interruption was quickly morphing into amusement and pointed at her. With as much menace as he was able to muster, he said, "Not another word, Koning, or you're cut off and on the planet."

Koning's nascent amusement turned to outrage. She

opened her mouth to protest. Mitsumi cocked his head at that, anger and frustration putting force behind his words. "Don't try me, Sentaa. Not. Another. Word."

Koning studied him, calculating the odds he'd carry through on his threat. Apparently not liking her chances, she snapped her mouth shut and returned his look with a sullen glare.

For a moment, Chandra gloated, obviously thinking Mitsumi had come down on his side of whatever argument he had with Koning. With a fierce scowl, Mitsumi disabused him of that fantasy. "Both of you look at me." With visible reluctance, both dragged their gaze to Mitsumi.

Their attention secured, Mitsumi took a few deep breaths, trying to control his own frustration and annoyance. When he felt he could speak without yelling, Mitsumi said, "I don't know what this is about."

Koning and Chandra each pointed at the other and said, "He—" "She—" Mitsumi cut them off with a savage gesture. "No," he shouted. "That was not an invitation to speak." Koning and Chandra both lapsed into angry silence.

"I don't care what it's about," Mitsumi said. "I care that we find Mei and find out when they'll perform this procedure on her. I thought you cared about that too. If you two can't do that without clawing each other's eyes out, I'll cut you both loose and do it myself." Warily eyeing each other with obvious distaste, Koning and Chandra looked like two people trying to decide between eating shit sandwiches with mustard or ketchup.

"You need to tell me now that you can work together and get this done." Mitsumi waited for their response with increasing impatience. Chandra broke the silence.

Tearing his eyes from Koning, he addressed Mitsumi. "I can work with her."

Mitsumi nodded once and turned his attention to Koning. Visibly wrestling to control her anger and disgust, Koning said between clenched teeth, "Fine."

Unwilling to let Koning off that easily and, understanding that the more she vocalized her commitment, the more likely Koning was to follow through, Mitsumi said, "Fine what, Sentaa?"

Reluctantly, Koning took a deep breath and let it out through puffed cheeks. "Fine. I'll work with Aber. We'll locate Mei and find the information we need."

With an inward sigh of relief, Mitsumi smiled. "Now that you two have kissed and made up, when can I expect an answer to our two burning questions?"

"We're close to finding her, Captain," Koning said.

"Yes," Chandra agreed. "We've narrowed it down to a building in Natan." Chandra licked his lips and continued. "A sniffer bot inserted into the building's environmental routines should allow us to locate her room."

"And expose our entire operation to the Burthen network," Koning said, her voice rising with gathering heat.

Chandra bristled before visibly collecting himself. "That *is* a possibility." Pleased at this admission, Koning smiled and raised her eyebrows, flaunting her vindication. Not wanting to concede too much, Chandra added in haste, "But a vanishingly small one."

Anger flared red spots on Koning's cheeks, she maintained her composure and remained silent. After a moment, her anger faded along with the spots on her cheeks. "You're right, it's not likely," Koning conceded. Then regaining her passion, Koning turned to Mitsumi and pleaded, "But the consequences are so horrendous, I don't see how we can take even a tiny chance."

Mitsumi didn't want to referee a dispute when he was unqualified to weigh the alternatives. But before he could speak, Chandra chimed in again.

"You're right, Sentaa," Chandra said. "It would be a catastrophe." Koning allowed pleasure at the concession to show on her face. Eyes going distant, after a moment he said, "Perhaps if we changed the node through which we introduced our probe..."

Head tilted as she considered the idea, Koning nodded. "One of the low-level basic maintenance ones, maybe?"

Mitsumi pushed away, leaving Chandra and Koning engrossed in an arcane discussion of Charlotte's communication architecture. *That turned out well*, Mitsumi thought. Pleased with the way he'd handled the dispute, Mitsumi wondered whether he was getting the hang of this command thing.

As he poked his head into engineering, Mitsumi heard the low hum of the replicator. Mantor hung over the control panel peering at the readouts. Since the confrontation on Zong, Mantor had kept to himself even more than usual while performing his duties without hesitation. Either he had no additional hidden stash, or he'd found a way to control his addiction because he'd been clean. Mitsumi hoped it was the latter. At the moment, he was adapting the prototypes from their recent failed transaction for the rescue attempt.

"Hey, Viram," Mitsumi said. "How's it coming?"

Eyes fixed on the readouts, Mantor ignored him or hadn't heard him. After nudging into the room, Mitsumi anchored himself next to Mantor and touched his shoulder. "How's it coming, Viram?"

Mantor shrugged off Mitsumi's hand and kept his eyes on the readouts. Muscles bunched in his jaw as he clenched it, trying to keep himself from snapping back at Mitsumi. Miffed at this lack of response, Mitsumi tossed aside his initial impression to say something placating. Instead, drawing on his recent experience, Mitsumi raised his voice and put force behind it. "Viram, I asked you how it was coming. I wasn't just being polite. I need to know if we're on track."

Still staring at the readouts, Mantor narrowed his eyes, pain and anger reflected in his face. "You have my reports," Mantor said, biting off each word.

Briefly considering leaving Mantor to himself, Mitsumi decided that he had to air whatever it was now. They couldn't afford any crew issues with the upcoming rescue attempt. "I can't afford to tiptoe around you. Everyone, including you, has to do their job, which among other things means you have to talk and tell me what I need to know."

Fear, pain and anger chased across Mantor's face, anger winning out.

"The devices will be ready within the hour, Captain," Mantor said, spitting out the last word. "If you need any help with the replicator, I'm sure you're more than capable of handling it."

Mantor bounced off a bulkhead and shot out of engineering heading toward his quarters. Flabbergasted, Mitsumi glanced at the replicator's readouts. Meaningless numbers and graphs flowed across screens surrounded by buttons with inscrutable designations and symbols. It was incomprehensible gibberish. Mitsumi stared along the corridor after Mantor. *Yep, that turned out well. I* am *getting the hang of this command thing.*

Outside Mantor's quarters a few minutes later, Mitsumi contemplated his options. Mantor wouldn't let Mitsumi into his quarters and wouldn't talk to him. They needed the engineer and couldn't afford to wait for him to emerge from his funk. The kick butt and take names approach that worked with Koning and Chandra had been a jump from a grav well with Mantor. Mantor required a softer approach, obviously—a fact he should have recognized and would have, if he was even within light years of the command thing.

Unsure of Mantor's reaction, for the second time this voyage, Mitsumi overrode a compartment's system. The door opened just as Mantor said, "Come."

In the center of the compartment, Mantor floated, his head hung like a disobedient child caught stealing. Bewildered at Mantor's reaction, Mitsumi eased his way into Mantor's quarters, not trusting what he saw, expecting Mantor to explode at any moment. Instead, Mantor peered at Mitsumi through half-closed eyes sheepish at his behavior.

"I'm sorry, Captain," Mantor said. "You were right to yell at me."

Mitsumi squirmed with discomfort. "It wasn't pleasant, Viram, but I'm reentering without power here. What's going on?"

Even more embarrassed than before, Mantor shook his head and looked away. Then, gathering his courage, Mantor looked Mitsumi in the eye. "I agreed to the operation to help Mei, but...having our deal fall through and deciding to stay instead of jumping away to turn the Ark into credits... It was almost as hard as..." Mantor's voice tailed off.

Mitsumi knew where this was going. He didn't understand exactly, but he understood that it was important for Mantor.

"As giving up the Rapt on Zong?"

Pained at the memory, Mantor broke eye contact with Mitsumi. "I figured once I made that choice, gave up the Rapt to...save your life, I was done with it. But when we figured out how much money our discovery was worth," Mantor shook his head and sighed deeply, "it all came back."

With a look of pure bliss, Mantor said, "If I had that money, everything would be perfect. Back to Rapt I'd go, fall into my personal singularity and bliss out the rest of my days without hurting anyone else." Mantor clenched his fists as if trying to contain something that escaped through his fingers, no matter how hard he gripped. "Then Sentaa rats out Mei who shouldn't have lied to us in the first place and..." The picture of frustration, Mantor let his arms fall to his sides.

That was rich. Mantor complaining about duplicity and betrayal given his recent history, but now may not be the best time to score rhetorical points. "Yet you agreed to rescue her."

With puffed cheeks, Mantor lowered his head obviously wondering once more at his decision. "I couldn't vote to leave her. But I'm furious at her and Sentaa for robbing me of my chance, and guilty as fire for being angry, which makes me even madder at them for making me feel guilty..."

Watching Mantor torture himself, Mitsumi wondered what the best course of action was. He needed Mantor back at his post creating what they required for the rescue. Mentally surrendering, Mitsumi jettisoned calculation for the moment and gave into his gut.

He gripped Mantor's shoulder. "Thank you, Viram, for voting with us to help Mei." Mantor raised his head and broke into a rueful grin.

"Yeah, I guess helping Mei's the most important thing right now, not how Viram Mantor feels about himself or others." Mantor broke eye contact and continued all business now. "We're on schedule, Captain," Mantor said. "The gadgets will be ready within the hour." Mantor pushed into the corridor, heading for engineering.

Gathered in the mess, Mitsumi, Quest and Mantor floated in front of a monitor displaying a building in Natan's central district while Chandra and Koning reported on what they found.

"At Sentaa's suggestion," Chandra nodded at Koning who beamed, pleased at the compliment, "we inserted an autonomous sniffer bot in the sewage maintenance module of the building where we suspected the family was holding Mei." Chandra paused, allowing Koning to pick up the thread.

"No one would think of looking for an intrusion there because an electronic barrier walls the system off from the rest of the building's computational array, except for once a week, when the maintenance module reports to the greater array that shit still flows downhill. Sounds perfect, right? We send our sniffer along with the reporting packets, but each of those reporting packets has an encrypted header hashed from a one-time pad—"

"Sentaa," Mitsumi interrupted her, not wanting to jump into that worm hole, "just tell us what you found."

Vexed at the interruption and irked that the full explanation of their brilliance was being cut short, Koning said, "I'll summarize then." Koning continued, "Thanks to Aber's dazzling display of coding, we inserted our sniffing routines—"

"Pithy, Sentaa," Mitsumi said interrupting again. "That's what a summary should be—short and to the point, here the point being—where is she and when is the procedure scheduled?"

With an eye roll, Koning said with sullenness in her voice, "She's in the top penthouse suite." On the monitor, the building expanded, the top floor outlined in red. "The procedure is scheduled for the morning, three days from now."

"Good work, Aber, Sentaa," Mitsumi said. "What have you found out about Mei's condition? Is she healthy? Able to walk out of the building—that sort of thing?"

Chandra took the cue and launched into an excited recitation. "Yes, as a matter of fact. Mei's quarters are saturated with surveillance. An AI monitors everything—her breath, her skin, her organs—even her excretions. Fortunately, Sentaa built into our sniffer the ability to discover and sample information from any monitoring system without being detected. It was ingenious. She—"

"Pith, Aber," Mitsumi said mildly. "Remember that word? Wrap it up, please."

Embarrassed by his excessive enthusiasm, Chandra glanced a silent apology at Koning for not being able to extol her coding prowess. "She's fine physically and can move freely in her apartment, but can't leave the suite."

Mitsumi nodded. That was not unexpected. He knew Ricci's mother had locked her up somewhere. He hadn't known whether her mother had also hobbled Ricci's movements within that space. "So," Mitsumi said, "how's she protected?"

Koning and Chandra exchanged an uncomfortable look. "We believe we've mapped every protective measure," Koning said.

Chiming in, Chandra said, "Well-armed humans and a subsentient AI guard the entrance to the building. The AI is connected only to the sensor inputs from the building's public spaces, the lobby and hallways and the like. It has a list of people with permission to access the building. A live human carrying a memory device updates the list several times a day. The AI controls armaments in the lobby and in the hallways—focused microwave emitters, megawatt coil guns shooting hyper velocity fragmenting flechettes, and for special occasions anti-matter mines."

Mitsumi raised his eyebrows in surprise at this last item. "Anti-matter mines?" he said. "I've never heard of those. Wouldn't that be just a bit excessive—blowing up the city to protect a building?"

His face shining with excitement, Chandra explained with enthusiasm. "No, no. You've got the scale wrong. They're shells of anti-carbon the size of dust particles with a pico-field generator at the center to keep normal atoms away. At the AI's signal, the field generators in a defined area shut down, normal atoms are no longer excluded and boom. The shells are only a few billion atoms, so the yield is low, say the explosive power of one of those poppers used at parties."

"No big deal then," Mitsumi said, wondering why you would go to the trouble of making something with such a limited effect. "I've had one of those pop in my hand. It smarted, but didn't burn me or break the skin even."

"You're breathing," Koning said. At Mitsumi's puzzled look, she continued. "In the lobby or the halls, you're breathing, inhaling the anti-matter 'dust' in concentrations of five hundred particles per liter and, at a typical resting respiration rate, you inhale half a liter of air with every breath, so every breath, at least two hundred and fifty nano-mines lodge in your alveoli. When they pop in there, your lungs cease to exist and so do you."

Mitsumi felt queasy imagining a thousand little explosions shredding his lungs. "They don't want uninvited guests, do they?" Mitsumi said.

Chandra shook his head in agreement and continued with his presentation. "The building's outside windows are force enhanced diamond nanocrystal—impenetrable by any means at our disposal."

Mitsumi considered the building on the display. "The roof?" he asked.

"Those railings you see here," Koning pointed to railings that ran along the edge of the roof on all sides, "contain active laser sensors with three-hundred-and-sixty-degree coverage. The sensors tie into the AI which can pump them to deliver petawatt defensive pulses."

"And the roof itself," Chandra said, "is composed of a meta-material. When a small switching current is applied, it morphs into a surface that binds with any electron shells in the neighborhood."

"Sticky," Mantor said.

"Yep," Koning agreed. "When every atom on the sole of your shoe or your foot binds to an atom on the roof, you're not going anywhere."

"The balcony?" Mitsumi asked, hoping for a little good news.

Koning shook her head. "Same set up as the roof. And we haven't even mentioned what you'd have to do if you made it through the lobby or into the building through other means. Everything's sealed tight with multiple layers of biometric and encoded locks." She looked at Mitsumi. "That's the lay of the land. So what's this brilliant plan you have for us?"

Mitsumi hung his head and massaged the bridge of his nose. He'd had in mind a plan, that plan wouldn't work with the defensive layout Chandra and Koning had just described. "Viram has cobbled together a harness and control unit for the prototype anti-grav units. My plan is to swoop in and pluck Mei from the building."

Koning's face fell in disappointment. "That was your plan? How were you going to avoid the security measures?"

That was a good question. He had not thought the security measures would be proof against a single flying individual because with current tech that was impossible, and who secures against the impossible? The Burthens apparently. But he had to come up with something. Every system had a weakness. After reviewing Chandra and Koning's presentation, Mitsumi thought aloud. "The building's AI controls these security features, right?" Chandra nodded. "So," Mitsumi continued, closing his eyes in concentration, "if we could take the AI offline for long enough, we have a chance?" Opening his eyes, he waited for Koning and Chandra's agreement.

"Yes," Koning said running a hand through her hair, "but the AI is isolated. There's no way to hack it."

"But, we don't need to hack it, right?" Mitsumi looked from Koning to Chandra. "We only need it not functioning." Something was there along that line of reasoning. Trying to coax the idea from his brain, he reached back and pulled on the knot of hair at the back of his head. "But not permanently because, if it was permanent, they might move Mei somewhere more secure. So, a reboot then?"

Koning and Chandra exchanged glances. Chandra nodded. "A reboot would give us a two minute and forty-five second window."

There was light at the end of this tunnel. Mitsumi nodded. "That should be enough time."

Koning rolled her eyes. "We can't force a reboot—we can't hack it, remember? Only Burthen security personnel can order a reboot. How can we make that happen?"

Mitsumi caught movement from the corner of his eye. Mantor had raised his hand like a child in school. "I might be able to help out with that," he said.

CHAPTER 29

"I'm going," Sentaa said glaring at the rest of the crew. This was her problem. She couldn't bear the thought of anyone else taking the risk.

"I understand your emotion," Quest said impassively. "But any dispassionate analysis demonstrates that the mission has a better chance of succeeding, and therefore Mei has a better chance to escape with her life, if I do the snatch and grab."

Thoughtful, Mitsumi nodded in Quest's direction. "Tai has a point." Koning shook her head, opening her mouth to object. Mitsumi continued before she had a chance. "He has skills none of the rest of us do, and has shown a remarkable ability to improvise in difficult situations. Sentaa, I'm sure you want the best chance of success for Mei."

Koning squirmed as she considered Mitsumi and Quest's arguments. Quest was stronger. He had better reflexes and had survived more dangerous situations than she could count. Purely based on abstract capabilities, they were right. But was that enough? "What if something comes up with Mei herself?" Koning asked. "I know Mei better than Tai does," her eyes swept the rest of the crew, "better than any of you."

Quest frowned and shook his head. "I don't see how that plays into this situation. Nothing we are doing depends on how Mei will react. Whoever goes needs to control the harness and act within the short gap we'll have while the defensive systems are down and," he said pinning Koning with his gaze, "be strong enough to hold Mei until arriving at a point where she can put on the spare harness."

She waved away the objection. "I can use a quick attach safety rig to help hold her—two seconds to attach max."

"Those two seconds could be—" Mitsumi began.

"Oh, please," Koning said with an irritated sigh. "If the tolerances are that close, we might as well give up now. No plan will succeed if two seconds one way or another makes a difference. And I can 'improvise' just as good as Tai." Koning scanned the crew, noting their skepticism. "Besides, Tai's wrong. It's crucial to anticipate Mei's reaction. If she hesitates for any reason, our window could close. We don't know what pressure she's been under, what psychological manipulation she's undergone. If someone has to persuade or reassure her for more than a few seconds, time will run out."

"I thought our time tolerances weren't that close," Chandra said archly.

Koning shot a venomous glance at Chandra; she didn't need wise cracking interference just now. "You know what I mean," she spat. "We have two seconds to spare, but we don't have thirty, and that's what it might take if Mei balks."

Mantor cleared his throat. "And you think she'll go willingly when the woman who betrayed her rides to her rescue? Don't you imagine your presence will make her hesitate?"

Koning felt sick. Her face tightened in pain, as Mantor's words landed like a gut punch.

"I'm sorry, Sentaa," Mantor said, sounding anything but apologetic, "but someone had to say it." Deflated, Koning had to admit it had been in the back of her mind too. She yearned to be the one to rescue Mei, to show her how much she regretted her actions—her betrayal. Koning lowered her head, and her shoulders rounded in defeat.

Mitsumi considered Koning, his brows knit in thought. "We'll tell her," he said after a pause. "We have to communicate with her in advance, anyway. We'll tell her Sentaa will be the one to retrieve her. And ask her if that's okay. If not, we'll send

321

someone else."

A weight lifted from Koning's shoulders. With a sigh, releasing a held breath, she looked at Mitsumi and nodded. "Thank you, Captain." In the other's faces, Koning saw Mitsumi's decision accepted with reluctance. *That's okay*, she thought. *I can live with that as long as I have the acceptance part.*

On the table, the remains of a picked-over meal cooled slowly. Ricci had stirred, cut, and crushed food on various dishes spread before her, but eaten little. From a cup, steam floated, curled and twisted by unfelt currents, thinning by minute degrees until, losing its temperature differential, the thing that gave it life, it disappeared, mingling with the air in the room and becoming indistinguishable from it.

As the spiraling, weaving vapor rose into the air and vanished, it became to Ricci her life's physical manifestation. Tomorrow morning, machines would take her personality, her quirks and idiosyncrasies, her memories and passions and smooth them over until the person she was—Mei Ricci, pilot and adventurer in search of lost treasure—vanished, subsumed into the vast Burthen commercial empire and indistinguishable from it.

In the past two days, Ricci had begged and pleaded with whoever was listening and watching to let her keep herself. She had planned and schemed, frantic to discover an escape. She had threatened to kill her body and deprive her mother's machinations of success. No one had listened. Her plans— such as they had been—had come to nothing. Twice she had attempted suicide, the attempts thwarted by an AI able to predict her every move.

She'd given up now. Nothing remained but to go with her escorts tomorrow and disappear. Eyes drawn to the balcony, she fought her lethargy, trying to find the energy for her nightly ritual. But what was the point now? At the close of each day, losing herself in the heavens for hours imagining Mitsumi and the rest plotting her salvation had provided hope, but giving into the inevitable now had led her to a sort of peace. Did she want to disturb it with vain dreams of eleventh hour salvation?

Perhaps not, but at least on this last night she could look back, reminding herself that, for a while anyway, she had lived her dream of independence and adventure. Her chair scooting backwards as she rose, Ricci grabbed the now lukewarm cup and moved to the balcony. After lowering herself into the reclining chair, Ricci leaned back and blotted out the present with memories.

"Mei." Her eyes flew open, and she sat up abruptly, searching for the source of the whisper in her ear, wondering what torture her mother had prepared now. She was alone on the balcony and saw no obvious mechanism for producing that whisper. Eyes narrowed, she shook her head. The wait must be affecting her. A deep breath and she settled back against the chair's cushion once more.

"Mei." This time she jumped from the chair and whirled around, her pulse racing. She hadn't imagined that voice. Still, nothing appeared to explain the sound. *That's enough, Mother*, she thought and turned toward the door to the apartment, then paused. Why would her mother go to such elaborate lengths to freak her out? She'd won. Everything she wanted would happen tomorrow morning, and Ricci could do nothing to stop it. But if not her mother, then who? She lifted her head to the sky; tiny sparks of orbiting ships caught her eye and then her breath. That voice had a familiar ring. Thoughts racing, wondering how they could pull it off, Ricci stepped back to her chair and eased into it, grasping the arms to still her trembling hands, trying to control a rising excitement from scattering her thoughts.

"Don't move." With a huge grin, she smacked the arms of the chair. That voice! She knew he hadn't abandoned her. But how was the captain doing it? As she shook her head in amazement, the voice came again.

"Yo—kee—movin—"

She moved her head; Mitsumi's voice faded in and out. She clamped down on her fierce joy and fought to keep her head still. They hadn't forgotten her! They were coming to her rescue; everything would be fine.

"That's better, Mei," Mitsumi said. "Lift your right arm if you can hear me."

Ricci lifted her arm and waved it in great arcs at the sky. How stupid she'd been to doubt them. Of course they'd been working madly on a solution, and now they'd found one.

"Calm down, Mei," Mitsumi said. "We don't want your AI to sense anything amiss."

With an effort, she lowered her hand to the chair's arm and struggled to control her breathing and heart rate. *Can't let my little buddy know anything unusual*, like being rescued *is about to happen.*

"Obviously, I can speak to you. You'll have questions, but those will have to wait. We have a plan. With this orbit we'll be out of communication range in ten minutes, so listen up. I'll tell you how to acknowledge after each step. Drum the fingers of your left hand on the chair arm if you understand."

Ricci responded.

"Okay, good. Do you have access to a way to tell time? If so, scratch your nose."

Ricci shifted in her seat, trying to keep herself from jumping up and cheering. She brought her left hand to her nose for a scratch and stared at her wrist just to assure herself that the skin display on her watch was working.

"Perfect. Now, the plan we've come up with will require that we are on the same time scale, so I want you to adjust your watch to match our clocks. We'll synchronize at 20:02 on my mark. If you're ready, change your watch to that time."

Ricci brought her trembling left hand in front of her and manipulated the display so it froze on 20:02, ready to start on the mark.

"All right, Mei, coming up on five, four, three, two, one, mark."

Ricci stabbed at the activation button as Mitsumi said the word.

"If you were successful, lower your left hand and flex your fingers."

Ricci complied. They had a plan—that was good. As part of her exercise in breaking Ricci's spirit, Mother had described in great detail the security measures surrounding Ricci. Her eyes flicked around the balcony as she recalled how extensive those measures were. She couldn't imagine what the crew had come up with to defeat those precautions. Sweat prickled her forehead. She was certain Mother wouldn't let her come to harm, but Mother would obliterate without mercy anyone trying to foil her plans.

"Sentaa wants to be the one to pick you up."

What did that mean, someone will pick her up? And for it to be Koning. Koning. She clenched her jaw, anger at Koning's betrayal warming her blood. Koning had violated Ricci's trust, after Ricci saved her life, and now she wanted to be the one to rescue her. Couldn't anyone else do it? Did she think this gesture could win Ricci's trust back? Ricci saw again in her mind her last glimpse of Koning. On the bed head bowed, tears flowing, Koning had been miserable at the turn of events. Perhaps she'd never expected that outcome. Perhaps she'd acted early before the events on Planet Quest. If Koning wanted to risk her life in an attempt at finding absolution, maybe she should let her.

"If you're okay with Sentaa being the one to pick you up, run your right hand through your hair.

Ricci stared at the city's twinkling lights spread out before her, unable to calm her swirling emotions. She shouldn't let Koning off that easily. She should make her work and sweat for Ricci's forgiveness if she was ever to receive it. She should teach her a lesson. But she didn't want to teach anyone a lesson, she wanted life to return to what it had been before, and she wanted to forgive Koning. Forgiveness—that was another trait her mother had chided her for and wanted to dissolve from her recalcitrant personality. So, in a way, allowing Koning back into her life was a blow against her mother. *Imagine that*, Ricci thought, *forgiving as an act of defiance.*

Mouth lifting in a satisfied smile, Ricci ran her right hand through her hair.

CHAPTER 30

Her orbital drop had been...interesting.

She'd descended in an anti-grav harness, one of two Mitsumi and Chandra had cobbled together from the prototypes Alloran had allowed them to keep.

"It's simple," Chandra had explained, gesturing at an elongated black box with two sets of straps on the bottom and one set on the top. "The straps around your legs and butt form a seat when the device lifts you. This controls it," he said, pointing to the rounded pyramid handle rising from one end. "This toggle switch," he pointed to a switch set in the pyramid where her thumb would fit if she wrapped her hand around the control, "moves you up and down. You move in every other direction by moving the control forward, backward, or sideways."

They had pre-programmed the drop from orbit into the gizmo. That worked fine until, arriving at the end of the program, Koning hung three klicks above the city. But it turned out descending was easy. The maneuver had been uneventful, exhilarating even, and according to her most recent contact with Mitsumi, she'd arrived undetected. But Quest had selected the descent corridor for its paucity of sensor coverage. The building she was now attempting to penetrate was much more thoroughly monitored.

Her hands trembled at the controls. Even though a remote spider drone was performing the actual insertion and she would intervene only as an emergency backup if everything went seriously pear shaped, Koning couldn't stop the tremors. This was the most delicate part of the operation, inserting the fiber cilia.

"Looks like it's going well," Chandra said in her ear.

On the screen in front of her a schematic showed the building. An exaggerated curved line depicted the progress of the cilia in its deep dive before rising toward the building's lobby.

"Yeah, thanks for that, Aber," she subvocalized. Four klicks from her target, squatting in an alley behind overflowing trash bins stinking with rotten, discarded food, Koning didn't need useless "encouragement."

They gambled that monitors from underneath were more scarce than if they'd attempted to insert the cilia through the side of the building. Watching the line creep up to the surface through the foundation, Koning licked her lips, and her breath quickened as the action window approached.

"Nice job, Sentaa," Mitsumi said. "You're almost there."

With gritted teeth, Koning bit back a retort. Everyone was on edge; they were only trying to help.

On the ship, safely in orbit it had been so simple. Wait for the AI to reboot, nab Ricci, and take off—no problem. But on the ground the timetable seemed horribly compressed. Forty-five minutes they'd given her from orbital drop to rescue— their best guess of how long she could remain undetected on the planet. And the opening during the security AI's reboot was next to nonexistent—two minutes and forty-eight seconds. How could she fly to Ricci, pick her up, and escape in such a short time? If she missed that window, the building's beam weapons would toast her. And, if she wasn't five klicks away from the building at the calculated dead spot after snatching Ricci when the AI came back on line it would detect her, vector nasty weapons to her, and once again it'd be Koning toast.

"Almost there, Sentaa, just a few more seconds," Chandra said, breathless with excitement.

"Would you just shut the fire up?" Koning whispered viciously. Her whisper broke security protocol, but damn they were irritating.

She closed her eyes and running a disobedient hand through her hair, held her breath, struggling to enforce calm. Ricci needed her; failure was not possible. She checked on the cilia's progress. It had emerged from the ground and now sat flush with the floor of the lobby. On the screen, a view from the cilia into the lobby replaced the schematic. A timer in the upper right-hand corner counted down to implementation. They'd also given Ricci a spread of forty-five minutes in which to expect rescue. If that window closed, Koning's orders were clear she was to abort the mission because by that time she would have been detected and in danger. They told Ricci that if the window closed without rescue, no one was coming.

As the numbers on the implementation counter descended toward zero, Koning held a finger poised over the actuate button on the laser/computational suite that everyone had assured her would launch Mantor's miraculous tangible hologram. Koning would be able to observe the AI's reaction —calling in a human strike force—through the cilia. Before the strike force's arrival she would shut down the tangible hologram.

Mantor had assured her that, at most, it would take three false alarms before someone would decide the AI was acting up and rebooted it. When pressed though, he admitted that he was guessing.

"I...I can't imagine security will put up with more than two false alarms," he'd said with a shrug.

Quest had been charged with breaking into their coms so she would know when the AI was rebooted. Mantor had assured them that the reboot had to be done off site. "Someone in the group of responders will have to order it," he had said.

"And I'll hear them when they do," Quest added.

Seeing more holes than assurances, Koning had voiced her concerns. "What happens," she said "if Tai can't break in or if our connection fails? How will I know they've called for a reboot?"

Mantor cut his eyes toward Quest, spots burning on his cheeks. "We, uh, haven't gamed out that result, so I guess, watch for someone who calls in after the all clear's been declared. He'll be the leader of the group and the one who will ask for the reboot. Once he calls in the report, he'll stick around with his team if he orders a reboot otherwise, he'll take off."

Inwardly, Koning cursed them for fools. They had a plan calling for precision timing and coordination and, if one little thing went wrong, they wanted her to *guess* when to start the action?

After a lengthy silence, Mitsumi said, "Do you still want to do this, Sentaa? Tai's willing to take your place." Quest nodded acknowledgement.

Koning swallowed hard and declined the offer. She had then decided on her own approach to testing the issue if something went wrong, but wouldn't tell the others for fear of being vetoed. Her idea would narrow the rescue slot, but increase the chance she came out of this alive. She refused to think about her plan's downside.

Back in the present, the counter hit zero. Koning stabbed the activation button. The first part of the plan succeeded as in response to the tangible hologram, the air filled with flechettes, sensors showed focused microwaves, and alarms blared. Right on schedule, human guards screamed toward the building and stormed into the lobby. Just as they wrenched open the doors, Koning hit the end button.

"Tai," she subvocalized, "where are we on accessing their coms?" Nothing. "Tai? I need that access."

Guards burst into the lobby waving their guns in search of the reported threat. Nothing in sight, they lowered their weapons and searched the room for something that had triggered the alarm.

"I'm encountering some difficulty, stand by," Quest said.

Panic. Her whole body quivering, Koning swore. "What

difficulty?"

"Stand by," Quest said.

"Wow, that's sooo helpful." She closed her eyes and with a deep breath tried to still her hammering heart. *I'm on my own,* she thought. *I guess I'd better pay attention.*

After a search turned up nothing, the guards milled around while someone, the leader evidently, turned from the group and held a conversation, with his superior, she supposed.

"Are you getting any of this, Tai?" Koning said hoping he'd fixed his "difficulty" and could help at last.

"Negative," Quest said. "They changed up the encryption when the alarm sounded. You're on your own."

With her lip painfully between her teeth to avoid screaming in frustration, Koning focused on the screen trying to decide whether the leader was ordering a reboot. They had counted on the fact that no reboot would be ordered after just one false alarm, but now doubt flooded her mind. She had to be right.

Koning couldn't hear either end of the conversation, but could imagine the accusations and excuses exchanged. After a few minutes, the leader gestured to the others and marched from the lobby. Koning decided that he had not ordered a reboot.

"I don't think he ordered a reboot," Chandra said.

Blood rushed to her cheeks, anger flaring. "If you geniuses don't *shut up*, you won't have to worry about the Consortium —I'll kill you myself. Not another word, unless you can tell me when the reboot's been ordered."

Koning started the timer. Five minutes. Five minutes for the guards to travel well away. Once again the counter ticked down and at zero Koning hit the activate button. Guards and guns, the prior scene repeated itself with Koning ending the projection just before the guards' entrance. The conversation was even more heated this time, if the leader's red face and emphatic gestures were any indication. Finally, the leader stalked out of the lobby, the rest of the guards trailing after him casting puzzled and annoyed glances around the lobby.

Had he ordered the reboot? The leader's actions gave Koning pause. If he had ordered the reboot, time was ticking away. No, she decided. They needed one more. Again after a five minute pause she activated the holo. The guards took their time and in marked contrast to their first two responses sauntered into the lobby, weapons drawn but not raised, faces weary. After another fruitless search, the man whom Koning had identified as the leader sagged visibly and holstered his weapon. *Now*, Koning thought, *now he'll make the call.*

As she tapped out a rhythm against her thigh, Koning fizzed, her thoughts buzzing. This was it. The leader had to be making the call now. *Will I bet my life on that?* No, she wouldn't. After adjusting the settings on the holograph generator, Koning touched the activation button. The hologram flashed into existence well away from the guards who had their backs turned on the projection.

"Sentaa, what are you doing?" Chandra said, his voice raised in alarm. Koning ignored him.

In the next second it disappeared when Koning pushed end. After glancing at the sensor readings, Koning stiffened and her throat clenched. A focused microwave pulse had been directed at the hologram during the second of its existence—the AI was still active.

"Oh," Chandra said, "that's clever. But won't it take too long?"

The scrum of guards in the room's center was not giving up its secrets. Koning grimaced and tried to guess what was happening. Had he done it now? Once again the hologram flickered into existence and disappeared. With a check of the sensor readings, Koning stifled a scream. Another pulse. What was he *doing* in there?

"Five minutes, Sentaa," Mitsumi said.

Eyes flicking to the clock, Koning groaned inside—her forty-five minute window to snatch Ricci had narrowed to five. After that, Ricci would conclude the rescue wasn't coming because they'd told her it was over. She'd give up and leave the balcony, and Koning's odds of discovery skyrocketed.

The leader must have ordered a reboot by now. In the lobby, the guards broke up and wandered around. One guard took up a position right where the hologram was programed to project.

"Time's up," Mitsumi said his voice weary, "Let it go, Sentaa. Don't get yourself killed."

Koning shut down communication with the ship. "Can't do it, Captain," she muttered and fumbled with the controls to adjust the location where the hologram would appear, but what had been effortless a moment ago was a monumental task under the time pressure.

A guard abruptly stepped into the new location she'd programmed. Jaw clenched to dam a flood of profanity, she worked the controls yet again. After what seemed eons, she tried once more. This time an alert guard spotted the fleeting figure and discharged a beam weapon.

Koning focused on the microwave sensor. Success! No microwaves; the AI was down. She grabbed the controls to her anti-grav harness and shot into the air, her last glimpse of the clock burned into her vision—her window had closed five minutes ago.

Eyes fixed on her wrist, Ricci sagged and closed in on herself bit by bit with each advancing second until, when the time expired without the promised rescue, darkness crowded out all other emotion and she slumped against the railing. They weren't coming. Anything could have put an end to their plans which, in her quieter, more thoughtful moments since contact, had always seemed outlandish. About to turn and reenter her apartment, she stiffened. How could she give up now? Maybe the schedule had slipped a little despite Mitsumi's assurances. If she left the balcony now she was sealing her fate. There was no downside to waiting on the balcony even through the night until Mother came for her in the morning. *Only the pain of hopes dashed*, she thought. And those were agonies indeed.

No. She gripped the balcony railing with both hands the tendons on her forearms standing out. She would not give up. If they wanted her, they'd have to pry her hands from this railing and drag her to her fate. Until then, she would not give up hope. Her gaze fixed, staring into the darkness, Ricci searched for signs of rescue.

Koning was having trouble controlling the harness.

Her only practice session with the device had been on the way down from orbit. After the ease of her descent, she'd supposed that zipping around the planet would be a snap. It turned out that doing anything but rising or descending was seriously difficult. Sensitive to the point of skittishness, the controls reacted to her hand's slightest motion. As if to validate her observation, she plunged toward the ground in response to a twitch she didn't recall making. Despite her instinctive reaction to yank back the control (bitter experience had taught her how even a small movement shot her upward), Koning rotated her hand. The resulting swoop drove her stomach toward her toes, but she missed the ground by a good three meters and put herself back on course.

Mitsumi and the others had been adamant. If time expires —abort. "You'll have been detected," Mitsumi said, "and your chances of survival small. I don't want to lose two crew members today. We've told Mei not to expect us if we miss that window. She won't stay past that deadline."

Six minutes past the deadline and still a klick out, Koning hunched her shoulders against an expected strike. Certain she'd been spotted and vulnerable, she should be on her way back to the ship, but couldn't give up. Ricci wouldn't leave, wouldn't give up on the crew just because they were a few minutes late. At the sight of the building, Koning called up magnification on her helmet's visor. There. On the balcony, Ricci stood gripping the railing. She knew it! She knew Ricci would still be there.

Vectoring toward Ricci, Koning increased her speed then yanked herself to the side just avoiding a flashing beam weapon, and juked the other way narrowly escaping another. Eyes wide, her breath coming in gasps, Koning whipped her head around trying to spot the shooters while keeping up her random feints and turns. There! Guards from the lobby.

One kept firing while the other motioned for his compatriots to join in the attempted barbeque. Koning couldn't approach Ricci from this direction—the guards would have their fried Koning before she could even get close. A building rose from a line of two-story structures behind the guards. Koning threw herself into an impossibly tight turn.

She grunted as she fought off a blackout from the high g turn that would take her behind the building—with any luck before the guards tracked. Two seconds, one—a searing pain in her calf, and she zipped behind the building. Despite the fire on her leg, Koning yanked back on the control to cut her speed and put herself into a steep dive to descend behind the two-story structures before she emerged from behind the larger building.

She just made it. Muscles bunched in her jaw, Koning forced the pain from her mind and willed her gorge not to rise as she choked on the aroma of seared flesh. Hidden from the guards behind the two-story buildings, Koning reached the backside of Ricci's building and rose up to the penthouse level. Ricci's balcony was just around the corner. Was Ricci still on that balcony? And how long had that AI been rebooting? Her leg throbbed but, on the bright side, an energy weapon had hit her and they were pretty efficient at cauterizing the wound; at least she wouldn't suffer significant blood loss.

No time for more thought, she whipped around the corner. Ricci stood at the far end of the balcony looking back to where the guards had been, leaning over the railing watching action on the ground.

Koning activated the exterior speaker on her helmet and screamed, "Mei." Ricci bounced up and whirled away from the scene below. At the sight of Koning floating at the other end of the balcony, Ricci sprinted toward her just as the railing and the balcony where she had been standing disintegrated. *I guess they decided Ricci dead was better than alive and untamed.*

Behind Ricci, another section of balcony disappeared and time slowed. The next shot would take the balcony and Ricci with it. Koning saw everything in excruciating detail as Ricci reached the end of the balcony, planted her right foot and leaped. Koning's breath caught, and she went cold. Ricci wouldn't make it. Her left foot cleared, but the right would hit the railing. She'd spiral to her death. Impossibly, Ricci lifted her foot at the last second, cleared the railing, and slammed into Koning as the rest of the balcony disappeared. Koning managed to wrap both arms around Ricci keeping her from plunging to her death. Koning didn't dare free up a hand to engage the quickset harness or to work the controls which would soon become necessary because, with the balcony's destruction, the guards had a clear line of sight to them.

As if understanding the dilemma, Ricci threw her arms around Koning's neck. Even through her suit, Koning felt Ricci's desperate grip.

"You're late," Ricci said, her voice picked up by the outside suit mike sounding tinny in the suit's speakers.

Sweat ran down Koning's face and burned into her eyes. "You're welcome—less attitude would be good right now."

"Apologies," Ricci said, sounding unapologetic. Ricci turned her head toward the building where the firing had come from. "Now, can we leave?"

Blanking the vision of impending death, Koning released Ricci, engaged the quickset harness, grabbed the control, threw them back behind the building and raced away toward the calculated dead spot because the AI should be coming back on line any second and—a flash of light seared into her right arm. In agony, screaming at the fire on her arm, Koning lost control of her hand. She and Ricci plunged toward the ground, gyrating out of control.

"No," Mitsumi said, raising his voice, in the face of Chandra's glare, "we're not leaving."

"They're two hours past the rendezvous time," Quest said evenly, floating next to Chandra. "They haven't made it back. It's time to admit they aren't coming."

Mitsumi stiffened. Unlike Chandra, Quest wasn't pleading, wasn't arguing—just stating facts, and the facts were that they'd cheered Ricci's desperate leap only to watch the defensive systems come online again and fire at the pair. Their last view had been of Ricci clinging to Koning, both spiraling toward the ground. A hollowness in Mitsumi's gut resonated painfully with Quest's declaration.

Chandra's voice was heavy with reluctance and sorrow. "You know Tai's right, Holtz." He lowered his head. "Sentaa and Mei are gone. Every second we remain in orbit increases the possibility the Burthens will connect the failed rescue attempt to us." Raising his head, Chandra met Mitsumi's gaze and opening his arms wide said, "Holtz, don't throw our lives away after theirs."

Regardless of what his gut and intellect told him, he would not abandon members of his crew when the slightest doubt remained as to their fate. He couldn't abandon them. But he couldn't deny his decision put them at risk. "You three can take the shuttle and the Ark. I'll transfer what few funds we have left to your accounts. They should be enough to buy a ride out system. If I make it, I'll come looking for you. If I don't make it," he shrugged, "you'll have the Ark and your freedom. That should be enough for you to live long, prosperous, peaceful lives."

Chandra drifted to Mitsumi and clapped him on the

shoulder. "Thank you, for that, Holtz. But I wish you'd come with us."

Mitsumi returned Chandra's gaze, but didn't speak. Now that he had decided, he wanted them gone.

Chandra broke eye contact and, pushing off to leave the mess, gestured to Quest and Mantor. "Come on, Tai, Viram, let's not waste anymore time."

Quest, rather than moving to follow Chandra, stared at Mitsumi. "I'm not going."

Chandra grabbed at the doorway before he drifted through and turned to Quest in puzzlement. "What do you mean? Hadn't you decided they weren't coming back?"

Turning to Chandra, Quest said, "They're not, in my opinion. I expressed my view to Captain Mitsumi, and he has decided the ship is staying. I'm part of the ship's crew and will not abandon it or my captain."

Incredulous, Chandra looked to Mantor. "Viram?"

He squinted at Mitsumi then shrugged and sighed. "This ship needs an engineer. I know Captain Mitsumi thinks he can handle it alone, but he's wrong."

Chandra eyed the others and muttered something unintelligible. With a cutting glare, he turned to Quest. "I can't fly the shuttle, Tai, you know that." Quest returned his look without speaking. Outmaneuvered, Chandra struck the doorway with the flat of his hand, sending him wheeling. When he managed to control his tumble, Chandra headed out. "I'll be in my quarters. When Burthen security shows up, tell them I'm unarmed and harmless."

CHAPTER 31

Surprised to be alive, Ricci evaluated her injuries. Lots of bruises and bumps, but nothing hurt like it was broken. Satisfied that death wasn't in her immediate future, she opened her eyes to inspect her surroundings. Her last memory was of spinning out of control, clinging to Koning with every ounce of strength. With a groan she attempted to sit up, closed her eyes against a wave of nausea, and sank back to the ground. *Better take this slow*, she thought. After a moment she tried again, inching herself upright. She looked for Koning. Her suited legs extended from behind a mound of trash. Concerned for Koning's condition, Ricci moved to stand up and grimaced. As Ricci struggled to her feet, Koning stirred. By the time Ricci had made her way over to Koning, she had sat up and was removing her helmet. Face pinched, Koning inspected Ricci. "You're okay?" she asked.

Ricci nodded, then gasped as she glimpsed Koning's blackened suit at her arm and calf. "Better than you. Does it hurt much?"

"Yeah," Koning gasped, "it hurts much." Koning moved as if to rise to her feet.

"Hold on for a minute. Just sit tight and let me inspect the damage." Koning nodded, then weaving unsteadily lowered herself until she lay on the ground once more. Not giving in to the urge to turn away, Ricci kneeled by Koning's leg. At the sight of the suit's scorched edges, and the chunk vaporized from Koning's calf, Ricci became light-headed and the ground lurched under her. Hands on the ground to steady herself, Ricci closed her eyes and fought the dizziness until everything stabilized.

"You okay there, Mei?" Koning asked with an arched eyebrow as Ricci opened her eyes. "'Cause I can look myself if you're having too much trouble assessing wounds I got saving your butt."

Ricci shot a look at Koning, checking to see if the expected wry expression was present. Pleased that it was, Ricci smiled wanly. "I've never done well with injuries." Steeling herself for the sight, Ricci turned her attention back to the leg. As with most energy weapon injuries, this one looked worse than it was—if you survived the beam, you could heal with time. The beam had struck muscle and sealed off the damage. Blood leaked from the burned crust, but a day in the auto doc would see it healed.

With Koning's arm, the story was much the same—time and the auto doc was all she required. The real problem was damage to the suit.

"So, how am I?"

Ricci lowered Koning's arm to the ground. Koning's face tightened, and she winced. "You'll live, more's the pity."

Koning's eyes shot open and a different pain shadowed her face. Ricci laid a gentle hand on Koning's arm. "You deserve everything you got and more, pulling that silly stunt. Tai was the logical one for this job."

Koning closed her eyes, her body relaxing into the ground. "I couldn't let anyone else take the risk, not after..." Koning's face colored. "Can you ever forgive me?" She cracked her eyes open, as if afraid of what she might see.

Ricci wanted to be angry, to blame Koning for everything she'd gone through these last few days, but couldn't raise the ire, not in the face of Koning's sacrifice. "That depends," Ricci said coolly.

Koning opened her eyes wide. "Anything, you name it."

"Whether you have a plan for our escape."

At this, Koning struggled into a sitting position. She nodded toward a box on the ground. "That unit over there is an anti-grav device we cobbled together from prototype units Alloran Combine gave us. It's how I flew to your rescue." Koning knitted her brows and craned her neck, searching for something. "I was strapped to it in a harness. The straps must have come apart when we landed."

Ricci frowned in confusion. "Wait, isn't Alloran manufacturing devices using the plans from the Ark? What happened?"

"The Consortium happened, then you happened—or rather I happened to you." Puzzled, Ricci moved to the unit Koning had indicated and dragged it over while Koning explained. "So, the Consortium tanked our deal and is looking for us."

Tears pooling in her eyes, her thoughts in turmoil, Ricci stared at Koning. Why would they give up so much for her?

Koning grabbed the unit Ricci had brought over, dragged it to her side, and undid a latch to reveal the back panel. Inside, a smaller box wrapped in straps, sat next to an emergency vacuum suit. Koning pulled both items from the box and refastened the back panel.

"There's your ticket out," Koning said.

Ricci's stomach knotted, and she whirled on Koning. "What do you mean *my* ticket?"

Koning picked at something invisible on her space suit, refusing to meet Ricci's eyes. After a moment she said, "The plan is to rendezvous in orbit using the anti-grav units to lift us and match velocity. We don't have another way off planet." With a nod at the holes in her suit, she said, "Up there, I'm dead in this suit. So, I guess I'll be cheering you on from here and hoping I can avoid the Consortium and your family. But that's not even the worst part." She lifted her head and locked eyes with Ricci. "The worst part is we're two hours late for the rendezvous. Mitsumi's jumped out system by now. It's what I would've done instead of waiting for the Burthens and the

Consortium to find me."

Ricci stared at Koning not believing her ears. It wasn't possible; Mitsumi must have waited. Ricci reached out and grabbed Koning's shoulders, shaking her. "That is not the way it's going down, Sentaa. Call the ship. Tell them we're still here; tell them to send the shuttle. It'll be dangerous, but—"

Koning shrugged off Ricci's grip, pain from the movement pinching her face. "I *can't* call the ship. I've tried. One of your guards must have directed an EMP on me."

Ricci shook her head. "An EMP would've done more damage. It—"

"The radio's out, Mei," Koning yelled, slamming the ground with her good hand. After a moment, she continued. "It doesn't matter why it's not working."

Ricci's thoughts jumbled together. With only one functioning suit, the crew's original plan wouldn't work. They needed another way to leave the planet. Or they had to make one suit work for two or repair Koning's suit.

"Your unit is pre-programmed to take you to the ship— if it's still there. Once it puts you close, the programming releases control to you to do the final tweaking to meet the ship yourself or if they've gone, you can come back to the planet." Koning looked away. "If the ship's gone and you have to come back, you shouldn't try to find me—your family might be using me as bait." Koning gave a wry smile. "But most likely they'll just kill me, unless the Consortium catches me first. I only hope there's no torture involved."

Her lips a flat line, Ricci considered Koning. There had to be a way to give them a chance to meet the ship without killing her. Anything, no matter how risky, was better than leaving Koning here, because either the Consortium or Ricci's family would kill her, no probably about it. As she swept her gaze around the area, Ricci focused on the straps that had formed the harness for the unit Koning had used. Her forehead creased, and she ran a hand through her hair, sticky with dried sweat as she worked through possibilities and risks. It might do the trick. Koning would suffer and her current injuries would be nothing compared to what would happen, but Ricci was almost certain Koning would survive the ordeal.

Ricci heaved herself to her feet, clapped her hands and rubbed them together. She gathered up the straps from Koning's harness. Puzzled at Ricci's actions, Koning said, "What are you doing? You can't mess around. You need to leave before someone comes to investigate."

Ricci stood over Koning, the harness straps gathered in one hand. Koning wouldn't like this, but Ricci wouldn't give her a choice. She tossed the straps into Koning's lap and shook her head in mock dismay. "That's a problem with you I've noticed." Open mouthed, Koning shook her head clearly wondering what was happening. "You give up too easily and just can't think outside the box."

Worrying at a loose thread on his jumpsuit, Mitsumi blinked his eyes trying to keep them moistened. In the zig that could be an issue if you tried not to blink too much which might happen if you were, say, staring at several screens trying to pick out a light flashing against a backdrop of millions of stars.

For the last five orbits, Mitsumi, Mantor, Chandra, and Quest had engaged in the same exercise. Koning and Ricci's anti-grav units were programmed to deliver them within ten klicks of the ship at this point in its orbit. Ricci's emergency suit would flash an irregular light pulse configured to be highly visible. They had started their search with hope, but continued failure had a way of dampening enthusiasm and dulling the senses. Mitsumi yawned and shook his head. He forced his eyes wide trying to keep his mind from wandering.

They'd rigged up screens in the mess—each crew member taking ninety degrees split between two screens.

"I've got 'em," Chandra shouted, pounding the bulkhead beside his head. Mitsumi and the others crowded behind

Chandra and there it was—flashing red at random intervals—the emergency suit's beacon.

"Have they spotted us?" Mitsumi asked. They had configured the exterior lights to flash as well because it would be up to Koning and Ricci to meet the ship.

"How would I know?" Chandra snapped. "You can see as well as I can."

Mitsumi sighed; Chandra had been prickly ever since Mantor and Quest had decided to stay, forcing Chandra to go along with their choice.

"They've changed direction," Mantor said. "They must have seen us."

"Can you magnify, Aber?" Mitsumi asked.

Chandra entered a command, and the image jumped closer. It took Mitsumi a moment to decide what was wrong with the picture.

"Is Mei towing Sentaa?" Mantor asked.

It looked like that to Mitsumi, but Koning's right arm and left leg were odd. Chandra must have seen the same thing because the image jumped closer again. Mitsumi went rigid. Koning's suit gaped open at her right arm and left leg. A tourniquet had been applied just above the two rips. As the pair moved closer, what appeared to be droplets became visible trailing from Koning.

"Tai," Mitsumi said, but didn't need to complete the thought because at the mention of his name, Quest shot away from the group and ricocheted expertly off the opposite wall heading out of the mess to the airlock. He would bring them in.

"I'll prep the auto doc," Mantor said following Quest. Eyes fixed on the screen, Mitsumi hung behind Chandra and gripped a handhold, his nerves jangling as Koning and Ricci moved closer. After forever, Quest appeared in the picture trailing his tether. He grabbed Ricci and attached a line from his suit to hers. Ricci held a strap in her left hand that attached to Koning's mangled harness. Quest took the strap from Ricci and actuated the winch for the tether.

With a tug on the handhold, Mitsumi launched toward the opposite wall, flexed his knees to absorb his momentum and pushed off through the entrance to the mess on his way to the main airlock. He arrived as the lock completed its cycle. His body taut and trembling, Mitsumi's thoughts cycled between wondering what had happened and rehearsing what he had to do as soon as the lock opened. Koning's lower right arm and lower left leg had been exposed to vacuum. The makeshift tourniquets couldn't maintain the atmosphere, so she'd probably also been oxygen deprived. Her suit had to be stripped from her on her way to the auto-doc to shave as much time as possible from her transition between the lock and the doc.

With his eyes closed, Mitsumi focused on what he needed to do to keep at bay the sight of Koning's blackened limbs. What a terrible tradeoff to make. A life for an arm and a leg. Federation medical technology even at its most advanced hadn't begun to approach regeneration of lost body parts and Koning's limbs were past saving. He groaned in frustration at the thought that if this had happened two decades later, technology might have provided an answer.

His eyes flew open, and he scrambled for a communication panel. Mitsumi slammed the actuator and yelled at Chandra. "Aber, the Ark. Have you searched it for medical information?"

Mitsumi fumed, waiting for Chandra's response. "I've seen the highest level heading for biology, but haven't…oh. What does she need?"

Mitsumi bowed his head and let out a deep breath. "Limb regeneration."

"Uh, you know medicine's not my specialty, right? I might not—"

"Aber," Mitsumi growled.

"I'm on it, Captain," Chandra squeaked.

Mantor appeared at the room's entrance. "Doc's ready."

A green light flashed on over the airlock and the inner door ground open. Mitsumi and Mantor grabbed Koning before the door had finished opening. Mitsumi worked Koning's helmet free. She was unconscious. Mantor ripped open the suit. Mitsumi tore off the strap from Koning's right forearm then, following Mantor's progress, yanked the suit off. When he pulled the suit from Koning's injured arm, flesh on the part exposed to vacuum sloughed off and hung in the air drifting in the currents toward Mitsumi's head. Mitsumi gagged and swallowed repeatedly, trying to keep the contents of his stomach where they belonged. Quest approached the three of them and pushed the entire group from the room toward the medical bay.

By the time they entered the bay, Mitsumi had stripped Koning's suit and clothes from her and as gently as he could, Mitsumi slammed her into the auto-doc unit. Just before the lid closed, Koning's eyes fluttered open and the corner of her mouth twitched as if she were trying to smile. "I always knew..." she said, her voice a husky whisper, "you wanted...to get me...naked."

It isn't possible to slump to the ground in the zig. You can't even collapse in on yourself, but somehow Mitsumi's posture conveyed both attitudes. Little globes of sweat separated from his forehead and floated in front of his eyes. Mitsumi snatched at a cloth and blotted his face. They didn't need anymore bodily fluids in the filters.

Mitsumi glanced at the doc's readouts. The display flashed red. Koning was alive, but her condition was so precarious that the doc hadn't completed its initial evaluation. Mitsumi turned from the unit. Puffy faced and red-eyed, Ricci floated in the entrance to the medical bay. With a nudge, she drifted into the room and opened her arms wide. They met in the center in a big hug. After a long moment, Ricci drew back. She shot a look at the auto-doc and her face crumpled. "How is..."

Mitsumi shook his head. "She's alive for now, but the doc hasn't completed its evaluation.

Ricci drifted to the machine and rested a hand on the case, staring as if it were transparent. "She was late for the meet-up."

She ran her hand along the case, caressing it. "Her orders, she said, were to abandon me if the time window closed."

Mitsumi exchanged uncomfortable looks with Quest and Mantor. "We...we were sure we'd given ourselves enough time. We," Mitsumi paused. It had been no one else's decision. He'd made the call, being decisive. But being decisive also meant taking the heat for choices that didn't work out. After swallowing hard, Mitsumi continued. "*I* didn't think you would stay on that balcony once the time had passed. The risk was too great if you weren't going to be there." He extended his arms toward her. "I was wrong. I'm sorry."

Still staring at the auto-doc, Ricci shrugged away his apology. "It worked out. For me at least." Ricci lifted her hand from the case and twisted to face the others almost squinting at them. "Why did you send Sentaa, anyway?"

"She insisted," Mitsumi said. "She persuaded us she was best for the job because she knew you better than the rest of us. Even though Tai was stronger and faster. Had more experience. She thought knowing you was more important. I suspect she also wanted to prove something."

With a smile that didn't quite reach her eyes, Ricci said, "She was right. She knew I'd stay no matter what."

"Captain," Chandra said over the intercom. "I've found something."

"It's a series of steps," Chandra said pointing at the translation Professor Aten's program produced from the Ark, his eyes gleaming with excitement, "for forming the correct epigenetic environment." In front of the display, Mitsumi, tugging on his knot of hair, squinted at the screen, as if seeing the characters more clearly would aid his understanding. Not wanting to appear too ignorant, he muttered encouraging noises as if he were following along.

Chandra gave Mitsumi a sideways look and changed his

approach. "The auto-doc can synthesize everything required by this formula and already has the growth acceleration factors we need. All we have to do is input these instructions into the doc's program and we're there."

Mitsumi straightened, bringing his hand from his neck and clapped Chandra on the shoulder. "Great news, Aber. How soon can you start?"

Chandra smirked. "I've already input the changes to the doc. The process is underway."

That's one problem down. Mitsumi punched an intercom. "Tai, can we jump?" He wasn't confident in their ability to remain unconnected with what had happened on Charlotte. The Burthens might not trace anything back to their ship, but they would look and, between them and the Consortium, they would be found. Once they jumped they'd figure out what to do with Ricci. She was safe for now, but an alert would be out, probably with a substantial reward. Ricci would be at a serious disadvantage. She could change her appearance again to avoid visual identification, but she could do nothing about her DNA.

"We can, Captain," Quest responded. "But we've just received a request from Charlotte traffic control not to alter our status."

Mitsumi's eyebrows knit in concern. But he forced himself to relax. No need to jump to conclusions—lots of reasons traffic control could want to talk to them. Everything was probably just fine.

"And an armed Burthen corporate security vessel has just lifted," Quest said.

Mitsumi's breath quickened, as concern returned and ramped up to full blown worry. Again he swatted the emotion away. *I will not borrow trouble*, he thought. Burthen had a large presence on Charlotte. At any given time, plenty of its ships would be lifting.

"Charlotte traffic control is vectoring the Burthen ship to rendezvous with us," Quest said. "The ship has a public manifest listing Kantic Burthen and Domenica Fylan among the passengers."

His stomach clenching as worry built to fear, Mitsumi could no longer deny the truth. Burthen suspected a connection to Ricci's disappearance. But she might not know their true identities—their ship was still broadcasting a false signature, and they'd been disguised on Charlotte. Fylan's presence must mean they surmised their connection with Chandra.

Twisting to look at Mitsumi, Quest posed the question that was no doubt on the crew's mind. "Three random jumps, Captain?"

Mitsumi closed his eyes and rubbed the bridge of his nose trying to force his fear-jumbled thoughts to order. Prudence dictated what Quest suggested—go lick their wounds and figure out what's next. But in that moment the future stretched in front of him—an endless series of deceptions because when they jumped, the Burthens would have good reason to believe they were behind Ricci's rescue. With the Consortium and the Burthens after them, they would all be Ricci—hiding forever. Something hardened inside him. His fear receded before a fixed determination. No. He wouldn't run. He opened his eyes and gripped the arms of his acceleration couch. This ended here. He'd find a way to deal with this. Freed from fear's paralysis, his mind raced, reviewing everything he'd learned of the Burthens, the Consortium, and their surprising connection.

And an idea appeared in his mind complete and gleaming with possibilities. And risks, he admitted to himself, reviewing the implications. Always risks. But life was risk. Nothing worthwhile was gained without risk—that's just the way the universe was constructed. Eyes fixed on Mitsumi, Quest waited impassively for an answer. They would have to discuss this— this was a gamble the others had to agree to. But he would bring them around.

"No," Mitsumi said. "Don't jump." He punched up a ship wide communication. "Assemble in the mess, please. We need to talk."

CHAPTER 32

"They are hailing us," Quest said. Mitsumi pressed his lips into a grim line and cinched his crash webbing even tighter. The rest of the crew looked at him, waiting for his word. Although they had all agreed, it was his show and up to him to sell the story.

After adjusting his expression to what he hoped was pleasant, open cooperation, Mitsumi nodded at Quest. "Let's see 'em Tai."

Kantic Burthen appeared on the main view screen and, off her right shoulder with a smile of pure, hungry malice, Fylan floated. He ignored Fylan for the moment and studied Burthen wondering how she managed it. Even through the view screen with her head raised in arrogant disdain, Ricci's mother projected intimidating power. Maybe he was only allowing her wealth and influence to sway his opinion. Maybe it was because, with her smooth, unwrinkled skin, she didn't look a day over thirty standard years though she was over seventy. She smiled. Warm and genuine, her smile relegated the sense of intimidating power to the background, though it didn't disappear. In the face of that smile, Mitsumi recalled an aphorism he'd heard: once you learn to fake sincerity, you've got it made.

"Captain Mitsumi," Burthen said. Fylan's eyes cut to Burthen and narrowed. "I've heard so much about you and your fascinating past. It's a pleasure to make your

351

acquaintance at last."

His hands spasmed, clutching the arms of the crash couch. Despite having prepared himself for this moment, her words struck a gut punch. They'd been identified. Cala, Riga, and their current husbands were the most likely sources of information on his "fascinating" past. *Get ahold of yourself*, he thought, *you should have expected no less.* His grip on the couch loosened. Mitsumi hoped his expression had not betrayed his emotion. "Ms. Burthen," Mitsumi inclined his head. "It is a pleasure to meet you. I am honored that the head of the Burthen Combine would grace us with a visit, although I cannot imagine what could prompt it." Mitsumi stifled the urge to lick his lips and squirm in his chair. "And bringing guests. The subject must be important."

Burthen's smile hardened and faint lines appeared at the corners of her eyes. Her aura of daunting control reasserted itself. A bead of sweat trickled from his armpit along his side. With every ounce of control he could muster, he kept his eyes locked on hers and reached deep for his earlier resolve.

"Ah, yes, Domenica. You are acquainted, perhaps?"

For a second, Mitsumi froze. Did Fylan know who they were? Had she identified them from the planet where they found the Ark? No. If she knew who they were, this chat would have no point. She suspected, but she wasn't sure. Chandra and the Ark, those were the only identifying markers. "I haven't had the pleasure."

"You have heard of the Consortium, though?" Burthen said, smiling with amusement.

Mitsumi nodded, not trusting himself to speak.

"Domenica heads up that concern. She and her organization are valuable assets in the Burthen Empire, even if the connection is discrete. On my behalf, she and her employees have sought a man named Aber Chandra who stole information Domenica and I are anxious to recover. Do you know this Aber Chandra?"

Now that was interesting. Burthen hadn't mentioned the

Ark. *Have you been keeping secrets, Domenica?* Mitsumi thought. Mitsumi opened his mouth. "No," he managed to say without croaking, "I can't say I do."

Fylan cocked her head, and her eyes drilled into his. He held her gaze for a moment, trying to project honesty and openness, then shifted his eyes to Burthen. "Now that we are all acquainted," Burthen said, "I have a permit from Charlotte port authority to inspect this vessel." Burthen lifted her hand and an official-looking document appeared in the screen's lower right-hand corner. "It grants me access to your ship to conduct a search."

Mitsumi didn't bother to examine the permit or question its authenticity. Given Burthen's power, it would be authentic and authorize what she described. He allowed sorrow to cloud his expression. "Those formalities aren't necessary, Ms. Burthen. You only had to ask. I feel a personal responsibility for harboring your daughter on my crew, unwitting though it was. Had I known her real identity, and that you were looking for her, I would have cooperated in a flash. Out of curiosity, though, what are you looking for?"

For a second, Burthen's control faltered, and Mitsumi flinched from that raw emotion.

"Someone took her, Captain. Someone with access to heretofore unknown First Civ tech swooped in and kidnapped Folami. And Aber Chandra is hiding on some prospector's ship."

Mitsumi swallowed hard, hoping his reaction wasn't visible. This was it. In the brief time he'd had and with varying degrees of success, he'd practiced different expressions he thought he might need in this interaction. He allowed the corners of his mouth to droop and his lips to part and lifted his eyebrows in what he hoped was a reasonable facsimile of sympathy. "I'm sorry to hear that, Ms. Burthen." *Okay, puzzlement now*, he thought. "But what does that have to do with us? I think I speak for the rest of the crew. We wanted what was best for M...Folami." He shrugged. "We'd have no interest in keeping her against her will. And as to this Chandra fellow, as I said we don't know him."

"The tech used in her abduction," Burthen said, responding to his question and ignoring his protestation of innocence, "appears to bear a striking resemblance to tech rumor says you were on the cusp of having Alloran Combine manufacture on Charlotte."

Mitsumi shook his head. "'Appearing' to have a 'resemblance' to tech that 'rumor' says we are involved with is a slender reed to support a weighty accusation like kidnapping, Ms. Burthen. We visited Charlotte to break up a long and so-far fruitless prospecting run. By the way," Mitsumi said, in what he hoped sounded like a breezy aside, "what ransom have the kidnappers demanded?"

"Who said anything about ransom?" Burthen snapped.

Innocence—a shrug, raised eyebrows, mouth parted. He'd practiced that one extensively, knowing he'd have to call on it frequently. *Butter wouldn't melt in my mouth, Kantic,* he thought. "I can't think of any other reason to kidnap a Burthen heiress and bring the might of its commercial empire down on one's head."

With narrowed eyes and through gritted teeth, Burthen said, "Ransom is not your concern. We're thirty seconds from docking, Holtz. Prepare to be boarded."

Now this one he'd had trouble with. He pursed his lips and lifting a hand to his chin, he averted his eyes for a moment. Was that thoughtful? "Sentaa Koning, who knew Mei best and was with her when you came for her, told us Mei wasn't too happy going with you." A lifted finger—surprised realization. "Perhaps it wasn't a kidnapping. Maybe someone was rescuing Mei from a fate she was trying to avoid."

Burthen glared at Mitsumi and closed the connection.

Burthen security was as good as its reputation. After the

Burthen ship docked, their search was exceedingly thorough. In the end, Burthen and Fylan floated in front of Mitsumi on the bridge. Wrinkling her nose at the tang of their inefficient recycling system, a smell that for Mitsumi had long ago faded into the background along with the bridge's torn fabrics and worn fixtures, Burthen surveyed the bridge, something sour on her tongue. "And Koning you say is in the auto doc for a few cuts from helping your engineer?"

Innocence. "Yep," Mitsumi said. "Sentaa can be clumsy."

With her eyes on Mitsumi, Burthen said, "Because if that's true and my security didn't burn chunks out of her while she was taking Folami, she should be out any moment." With a gesture, Burthen caused a few enlarged frames from a video of Ricci's escape to appear on the main screen. The blackened edges of two holes in Koning's suit were clearly visible.

Mitsumi winced at the sight, but schooled his features before turning to address Burthen. "Yes, she will and, with those holes in a suit, whoever that was couldn't have reached orbit without a ship even if this miraculous tech could somehow boost a single individual out of atmo." Mitsumi extended his arms in a gesture including the ship. "Your search hasn't turned up anything. No M...Folami," Mitsumi looked at Fylan, "no Aber Chandra." With a sour look Fylan pursed her lips. "After Sentaa's released, and you see she couldn't be Folami's shadowy abductor, will you let us leave?"

Before Burthen could answer, Koning appeared at the bridge entrance accompanied by two Burthen security personnel. "You sent for me, Captain?" she said.

"I did," Mitsumi said, then gestured toward Burthen and Fylan, hovering by the pilot's couch. "You're acquainted with Ms. Kantic Burthen, head of the Burthen Combine and Folami's mother?"

Quest was to have filled Koning in on the situation as much as possible after her emergence from the auto doc. Apparently, not much had been possible. Koning's eyes widened, and her mouth formed an O. Her surprise turned to hostility bordering on hatred. "We've met," Koning said.

Quest had been more successful in persuading Koning to dress in a pair of shorts and a short-sleeve shirt that allowed a clear view of her intact, unscarred left leg and right forearm. Mitsumi turned to a scowling Burthen. "Do you have questions for Sentaa? As you can see, she's not the one you're looking for."

Eyes riveted on Koning, as if trying to reproduce the burns with her stare, Burthen shook her head once. Her focus shifted to the guards bracketing Koning. "Report."

"They're not on board," a guard said. Burthen lowered her head and laid her forefinger across her lips and chin. "Are they outside tethered to the hull?" she asked the guard with a pointed look. Cheeks reddening, the guard activated his com. "Check the hull," he said.

Burthen turned to Mitsumi inspecting him. Seconds ticked by. Mitsumi yawned. *Nothing to see here, Kantic*, he thought. *See how bored I am?* The guard perked up, bringing a hand to his ear. "Nothing on the hull, ma'am," he said, his relief evident.

Burthen considered him for a long moment. Mitsumi returned her gaze, straining to keep his mouth in a flat line and maintain a neutral expression against a rising desire to pump his fist. *Steady on*, he thought. *Don't open the airlock before you've docked.* They'd cleared the first asteroid field, but the next one loomed larger.

Burthen allowed her mouth to lift in a smile. Though Mitsumi knew it must be contrived, even close examination revealed no cracks in the manufactured sincerity. *How* does *she do that?* "My compliments, Captain. This set was well played. I don't know how you managed it, but this round has gone to you." Burthen pushed against the pilot's station and drifted toward the bridge access, Fylan following right behind.

With a deep breath, Mitsumi stilled his racing thoughts and concentrated on the opening lines of the next gambit— lines he'd memorized and rehearsed, not trusting himself to extemporize something this delicate.

"Ms. Burthen," Burthen caught the edge of the bridge

entrance and rotated to face Mitsumi, Fylan following her lead. "We became fond of Me...Folami over the course of our travels. Now we know someone abducted her against her will, we will bend every effort toward finding her."

Burthen did not repeat her performance with the smile, but considered Mitsumi, as if waiting for the other shoe to drop. Into Burthen's silence, Mitsumi continued. "Should we find success and free her where your forces have failed, we will of course inform you right away."

Burthen's expression remained flat, but she drummed her fingers against the entrance.

Mitsumi cleared his throat. "But, if on finding her we determine that the alternate scenario I alluded to earlier seems more likely, and she was being aided in an attempted rescue, then—"

Burthen closed her eyes and sighed. "Everyone thinks they're an operative."

Thrown off his script by the interruption, Mitsumi could only stammer in response. "E...Excuse me?"

Burthen opened her eyes and fixed them on Mitsumi with a determined stare. "Jump to the find, Holtz. I don't know how you did it," she shot a look at Koning, "and I can't prove it, yet, but you snatched Folami, and you've stashed her somewhere we can't find her. You think this is a negotiation now, don't you?"

Something inside Mitsumi relaxed at the thought of everything being out in the open. Subtle by-play was not to his liking.

"Tell you what," Burthen continued, "why don't I let Domenica here torture you until you tell me where she is? I know she wants to because she doesn't believe you either. Then we can all live happily ever after." She pursed her lips. "Well, not all of us." She shrugged. "You and your crippled crew will suffer residual pain the rest of your lives, but that's what I call 'creative destruction.'" She cocked her head and with a sly, cruel smile said, "Not quite the negotiation you had in mind is it, Holtz? So, what'll it be?" Fylan's eyes gleamed in expectation.

His skin burned as he imagined its excruciating removal in long strips. On the other hand, Mitsumi thought, ambiguity has its advantages. Mitsumi tried to gauge Koning's reaction. Her lips were pressed out of existence and her glare was deadly. *Okay, Sentaa's with me.* He reached deep inside, dredged up his memory of innocence, and plastered it on his face.

"You're mistaken about our role in Mei's disappearance and our knowledge of Mr. Chandra. No torture will change that fact. But knowing your determination and persistence, I have arranged that everything happening on my ship is being transmitted to a secure storage facility on Charlotte to be released to Charlotte's constabulary tomorrow, unless I transmit medical scans showing me and my crew to be in the pink of health. I'm pretty sure not even Burthen Combine's resources can purchase escape from charges of torture."

Burthen pushed away from the entrance to the bridge until she approached Mitsumi, halting when they faced each other. His threat had no effect. Completely at ease, her face untroubled, she considered Mitsumi for a moment.

"You'd be disappointed," Burthen said, shaking her head in mock disappointment, "at what my Combine's resources can purchase, but," she shrugged, "the paperwork can be a bitch. So. Well played again. Let's return to the make-believe world where you're looking for my daughter. You find her and decide she wants to divest herself of her family. What then?"

Mitsumi kept himself from sighing. He still needed that bluff. Anything giving it away would be deadly. "I was less than forthcoming earlier when I described our voyage as fruitless. In fact, our recent voyage has not been without success."

Burthen rolled her eyes. "You can't be serious. My daughter for a few First Civ tech baubles?"

Mitsumi firmed his grip on the pilot's couch stilling a tremor. This was it. It was everything they had. Would it be enough? "Did you catch wind of the aborted trade on Support?"

"You mean the one where a prospector said he'd stumbled

across the ultimate storehouse of First Civ tech Elstone Combine thought it had purchased until Domenica here stopped all sales?"

Mitsumi returned her stare without responding.

"That was you?" She looked from Koning to Mitsumi. "Huh, we heard the so-called find was a worthless black box scam. Certainly, if it had been authentic, it would have been worth much more than Elstone offered." She cocked her head, her eyebrows almost meeting above her nose. "Are you telling me the find was real?"

Mitsumi shifted his eyes to the image still on the screen. "It was a First Civ data Ark. If it were real, the information it contained might enable someone to pull off Folami's kidnapping without leaving a trace, even if a participant had been seriously injured."

Burthen followed Mitsumi's eyes to the screen and the picture of an injured Koning that remained there. Burthen's eyes gleamed and her tongue darted across her lips. "Our scientists have concluded that whoever snatched Folami used impossible anti-grav tech that might allow someone to fly to and from orbit with just a pack on their back."

To Mitsumi's eyes, Burthen appeared to be nibbling the bait, tasting the possibilities, the sweet, tantalizing savor of unlimited profits tempting her. Time to set the hook. "The biotech possibilities in such a store may be as great, or greater, than things like anti-grav devices. Think limb regeneration, for example." Burthen swiveled to inspect Koning's flawless leg and arm. Turning to Mitsumi, Burthen narrowed her eyes, calculating. Even in the zig, Mitsumi felt a weight lift from his shoulders. Burthen was hooked.

"I assume," Burthen said, trying for nonchalance but unable to disguise her avarice, "such an unprecedented find would fetch an unprecedented price, yet the sellers were willing to let it go to Elstone for a relative pittance. Maybe this item isn't worth what the seller thinks it is."

"Elstone's offer might have reflected its inability to test the knowledge cache before purchasing it and, perhaps, the sellers' inability to offer sufficient evidence of authenticity. It was a huge gamble—sensible only because of the possible unlimited upside. Now, recent events might have demonstrated that authenticity and reduced the odds of failure while the upside remains unlimited."

"Still," Burthen countered with an undertone of menace, "the sellers may find they have wandered into waters deeper and more troubled than they are equipped to navigate."

Mitsumi spread his hands. "Which is why I'm certain the sellers would accept a reasonable offer, one trivial to the mighty Burthen Industrial Empire, especially considering that a major component would be non-monetary compensation."

Burthen considered Mitsumi with hooded eyes. "Credits invested yield a return. People are unique. If you're hinting at my giving up Folami for a price, it may be a price I'm unwilling to pay."

"Remind me again. Who comes out of your personality adjustment program?"

Burthen's expression remained unreadable, but Mitsumi was certain her resistance was a negotiating tactic. Mitsumi continued. "Isn't the purpose of the program to produce a different person with the same body? And isn't the point to manufacture someone who will advance Burthen fortunes in a way the old, discarded person could not or refused to do? Your willingness to employ personality adjustment on Folami demonstrates you already see her as an asset to deploy in the Burthen Empire's service. The question then is simple economics: do you benefit from trading one asset for another?"

Burthen glanced again at the screen. When she met Mitsumi's eyes once more her face reflected defeat. "What's your price?"

Sadness dampened the exultation Mitsumi should have felt. He didn't know what emotions and thoughts had warred within Kantic Burthen. Perhaps she'd resisted thinking of her daughter only as another resource, but could not break through the paradigm. Perhaps her defeat stemmed from recognizing a reduced negotiating position. He couldn't decide which was more dispiriting. Mitsumi ticked off his requirements keeping an eye on Koning because she hadn't agreed to these conditions. "Agree to allow Mei to live her own life and not dragoon her into service in the Burthen Empire. You may even find that, released from her obligations, she returns to the fold and is more of an asset than she would otherwise have been.

"Give us a license to employ Ark technology, but only for our own use not for sale or lease to anyone else. Pay us ten million credits." Mitsumi paused. Here's where it was dicey. In forming their plans, they hadn't factored in Fylan's presence in the negotiation. They had counted on Burthen wanting to deny her controlling interest in the Consortium. With Fylan here the dynamics were different. He cleared his throat. "We, uh, were not entirely truthful before."

Burthen closed her eyes and sighed. Fylan who had been floating off in a corner of the bridge perusing Koning's station without interest turned to Mitsumi.

Eyes fixed on Burthen, Mitsumi said, "Aber Chandra *is* part of our crew."

"I knew it," Fylan shouted. "*You're* the ones who left me for dead and stole that artifact." With a snarl, she launched herself at Mitsumi. Burthen nodded at one of her security men who intercepted Fylan mid-flight. They sailed past Burthen and Mitsumi into the arms of another security man.

Restrained in the grip of two security men, Fylan glowered at Mitsumi. Burthen cocked her head and considered Fylan. "I don't recall any mention of a confrontation in your reports regarding Chandra, Domenica," Burthen said, her voice heavy with menace. "Nor do I remember any suggestion you were chasing Chandra *and* a valuable First Civ asset." As Burthen's comment penetrated her anger, Fylan lost her glare and turned to Burthen with trepidation. "Have you been withholding information, Domenica?"

Eyes wide, Fylan shook her head once. "I can explain."

Her voice cold, Burthen said, "Yes, you will." She tilted her head, and the security men hauled Fylan from the bridge.

"I didn't know, Kantic," Fylan pleaded, "about the data. It was just a box. And Chandra was gone so there was no point..." Her voiced faded away.

Turning to Mitsumi, Burthen sighed. "I suppose you want me to keep that one at bay and let you keep Chandra."

Mitsumi nodded. "Yes, the Consortium and that other group that attacked us on Zong. That's our final demand."

Puzzled, Burthen said, "What other group?"

Confused in turn, Mitsumi said, "You know, the ones you had kidnap us." Burthen shook her head. "The ones with the funny accents?" Mitsumi said. Burthen's expression remained quizzical. "On Zong. The ones we escaped from."

Burthen huffed in exasperation. "I have no idea what you're on about. After you slipped away from us on Support, we didn't know where you'd gone. No one under my control kidnapped you on Zong or anywhere else." Burthen cocked her head and she smiled coldly. "How many people *have* you pissed off, Captain?"

Mitsumi surveyed the rest of the crew looking for help, meeting only blank stares. *Who* were *those people?* he wondered. That problem could wait, and he set it aside for the moment. "But the Consortium, you can order them to back off?"

Burthen's lips flattened. "I want the coordinates Chandra recovered."

With a silent curse, he hoped those would be off the table, Mitsumi said, "Aber has clean title to those. He did the work on his own time on paper Domenica let him have."

Burthen's face hardened. "Captain Mitsumi, you have grossly overestimated your leverage and my patience. I will pay you and your crew a million credits. You get to keep Folami and Aber, and I'll give you a license limited as specified. In return you will hand over the Ark and Aber's coordinates, and you will forfeit rights to any tech recovered from those coordinates."

Mitsumi opened his mouth, "We want—"

"That was not an invitation to bid." She glanced around the bridge. "In thirty seconds, I'll instruct my men to round you up and, before I discipline Domenica, I'll let her amuse herself with you and your crew until you disclose what I want to know or you're dead."

Mitsumi looked for Quest and Koning's approval. They both nodded. His spirits sank as the prospect of repaying Corban and Jonta and his expedition to return the Artifact and claim unimaginable power vanished like a false sensor return. This was not how it was supposed to end. He sighed. "We'll take it."

The money was just enough to pay for Pari's treatment, if the rest of the crew agreed to give up their split. Mitsumi wouldn't be able to repay Corban and Jonta the five hundred thousand credit principal amount they had invested in Mitsumi's busted venture, not to mention the interest. He wouldn't have enough credits to find the Artifact's world. Mitsumi still had to support himself somehow.

Their agreement reduced to writing and attested, disbursement of the credits awaited the Ark's transfer to Burthen custody. Five hours after Burthen and Fylan had come aboard, Mitsumi opened a channel. "Mei, Aber, you can come in now."

Puzzled, Burthen said, "Where did you have them stashed? My crew was thorough. We should have found them."

"We gave them the anti-grav units and told them to move away from the ship and wait for our signal. If we'd taken too long, their instructions were to drop back down the well."

Burthen shook her head. "But our scans didn't pick them up."

Koning smiled. "Nope, it turns out the plans for these units included an efficient stealth system." With a pointed look, she glanced at Mitsumi, "Something I wish I had known when I was flitting around on the planet."

A few minutes later, Chandra and Ricci, who was carrying the Ark and the translator, wafted onto the bridge. Chandra had removed his helmet; Ricci's still covered her head. Burthen directed one of her men to secure the Ark. Stoney faced, Ricci glared at her mother.

Burthen's face softened into what might almost have been a loving look. "I'm sorry it turned out this way, Folami. I only ever wanted what was best for you." Ricci's glare remained unrelenting. Mitsumi couldn't tell whether Ricci had heard her mother's declaration. Burthen waited for a response. After an uncomfortable two minutes, Burthen turned to Chandra and pinned him with a stare. "Mr. Chandra, your captain and I have reached an agreement which will allow you to purchase a cure for your daughter." Chandra's eyes rounded in surprise. "Yes, I know about your family, Mr. Chandra, but that payment is the limit of my charity. You will never work for any enterprise within my reach which I assure you is exceedingly long." Chandra opened his mouth to protest. "It's that or your life, Mr. Chandra. If you object to my choice, I'll change it." Chandra's mouth snapped shut, and muscles bunched around his jaw. "You stole from me, Mr. Chandra. That cannot pass without consequence." Chandra held her eyes for a heartbeat, then lowered his gaze.

Burthen gestured for her men to follow and floated off the bridge on the way toward the main airlock where her ship had docked. A few minutes later, Mantor spoke over the com. "They're gone."

Visibly relaxing, Mei Ricci removed her helmet and ran hands through her hair until it expanded into her trademark fuzz ball. Mantor and Quest floated onto the bridge.

"Please tell me you geniuses took a copy before giving away the most valuable data store in the universe," Koning said, addressing the group.

Mitsumi bristled at Koning's attack. If he hadn't acted as he did, they'd have been fugitives and dead within the year.

Mantor nodded. "We found a function that let it duplicate itself," he said. "Fed it energy and materials and bam, just like that," he snapped his fingers. "We had another Ark."

Mouth turned down in a scowl, Mitsumi responded to Koning's accusation. "We didn't give anything away, Sentaa," Mitsumi said. "We bought our lives and Mei's freedom. Isn't that enough?"

With a sidelong look at Ricci, Koning compressed her lips and stayed silent.

Eyebrows knitted with concern and fidgeting, Chandra asked, "How many credits did we come away with? She said we had enough to save Pari."

Mitsumi lowered his head unable to face Chandra. "A million credits," he said with sorrow. "That's what Burthen paid us."

Chandra squeezed his eyes shut and put a hand to his forehead.

"But I'm willing to contribute my share toward your daughter's treatment," Mitsumi said firmly. He surveyed the rest of the crew.

"I as well," Quest said.

"Count me in," Mantor said with a smile.

Koning huffed and looked at Ricci. "I suppose you'll join the party?" Ricci nodded. Koning swallowed hard. With her eyes fixed on Chandra, Koning said, "I hope the treatment works."

Chandra looked a question at Koning. She closed her eyes and sighed. "Don't make me say it. The pain would be too much."

Confused, Chandra glanced at Mitsumi. "That means yes, Aber. Sentaa will give up her share too."

Joy lit his face and Chandra pushed himself toward Koning, wrapping his suited arms around her in an awkward hug. "Oh, thank you, Sentaa."

Koning pushed him away. "Okay, that's enough."

Turning to the rest of the crew, Chandra said, "Thank you. I can't... Words can't..." He shook his head unable to speak.

Swollen with pride, Mitsumi surveyed the crew, his crew. His bitter disappointment at losing the credits to fund his search for the Artifact's home and find the means to save his brother dissolved in the glow of satisfaction at being able to do this for Aber and in the realization that he didn't need the funds. Everything he needed was right here. "C'mon, Aber, shed the suit and let's transfer those funds."

Quest cleared his throat. "Captain, where do we head now?"

They had just completed the credit transfer. Chandra had composed a message for his wife and children that would be delivered along with notification of the credit transfer when the messenger drone reached Del. The rest of the crew had assembled on the bridge to watch as Koning dispatched the drone.

Now, all eyes turned to Mitsumi. Mitsumi considered the question. He knew where he had to go. In the aftermath of their adventure, enticement at the prospect of obtaining the power to rescue Tuan and pressure from the Artifact had reasserted itself. One way or another he had to embark on that search. And here was the perfect opportunity. They had planned a year for the expedition, but had only been out three months. With the voyage's original purpose eliminated, he could search for the Artifact's home and pursue the mystery of its connection with the strange alien sheet.

Mitsumi wondered if they would come along, then decided that if they didn't, the galaxy would go right on spinning. He'd welcome whoever joined him but, as to the rest, he'd wish them well and not look back.

He cleared his throat. "I have a proposition, but first I need to tell you a little story."

He related his tale of the Artifact, the vision, and the sheet, leaving out any mention of the feeling that absolute power would accompany the Artifact's return. When he had finished, he said, "So I am off in search of an uncharted star outside the galaxy. Who's with me?"

Mantor grinned. "I don't have anything better to do for the

next year. Count me in."

Quest nodded his agreement.

Chandra shrugged. "Now that Pari's recovering, and I'm persona non grata in the Federation, I need to find something to do. Maybe if I disappear for a year, I can sneak back in under the scanners and reclaim my life."

Smearing a tear from the corner of her eye before it could float away into the filtration system, Ricci said, "I...I can't thank you enough for what you did—rescuing me, giving up your dreams to purchase my life." Koning moved to Ricci's side and snaked an arm around her waist in a hug. "I can't think of anyone I'd rather spend the next year chasing Andacks with."

In consternation, Koning shook her head with a frown. "I don't know. How will we make any money? And where would we even start?" Her eyes drawn to a flashing signal on the communications board, Koning made her way to her station.

"I'm not sure," Mitsumi said. "Maybe we should—"

Koning held up her hand, concentrating on the control board in front of her. Eventually, she lowered her hand and looked at Mitsumi. "That was a message burst from a Zongian messenger drone," Koning said. Mitsumi stiffened. That could be trouble. "It was from Professor Aten."

Mitsumi relaxed. The Zongian authorities still hadn't tracked them down. "Fine. Play it on the screen. Let's see what Mr. Aten has to say."

Mitsumi's head jerked back to avoid the nose that exploded from the 3D image. He'd forgotten what a beak that man had. "Newell, I want to update you on my progress." He frowned and shook his head. "Or lack of progress I should say. Even working with the two images—the one you gave me and the one the others left—I haven't made any progress on the only true alien language ever encountered in the history of the Federated Worlds, and I can say that with confidence because I'm—" Mitsumi twirled his finger signaling Koning to jump ahead in the message hoping to skip most of the self-congratulatory praise. "—Although the plates so far have

367

resisted my efforts, the plaque in the image you provided is another matter."

The plaque? Mitsumi thought. *Ah, below the metal plate they'd retrieved there'd been a plaque. It hadn't seemed important.*

"The plaque was written in a slight variant of First Civ standard, which is why I didn't recognize it right away and why the program I gave you wouldn't provide interpretation. Translation was trivial—for me, of course. For anyone else..." He shrugged. "The plaque states that the artifact, presumably the sheet you have, was found on a planet called 'Seldon' and it gives coordinates. I don't know if it's the planet where the plate was made or what. Anyway, I will keep plugging away at the alien language. I'm sure to make tremendous progress on this amazing find." *You're kidding me*, Mitsumi thought. *He's not going to give us the coordinates, is he?* "I'll keep you posted on any further developments. Good luck!" Aten reached forward to stop the recording then hesitated. "I don't suppose you're interested in the coordinates for this 'Seldon' place, but just in case, here they are."

The message ended. In the ensuing silence, Mitsumi shrugged. "I think that's as good a place to start as any, don't you?" Amid nods and sounds of agreement, Mitsumi said, "Okay then, all hands to stations." Mantor left the bridge, Ricci, Quest, and Koning strapped into their posts. As he surveyed his bridge, Mitsumi smiled. He still felt a pang of regret at not being able to repay Corban and Jonta, but he had a crew he could work with, command of a ship, and freedom. "My compliments to Charlotte guidance control," he said, "and request orbit breaking vectors to a jump point."

"Orbit breaking and jump vectors received and plotted," Koning said, "aaand transmitted."

"Vectors received and input," Ricci responded after a moment.

"Execute," Mitsumi said.

THE END

THE STORY CONTINUES IN *DAWN'S REACH*!

Who were those mysterious people who visited Lentar Aten on Zong and tried to kidnap Holtz Mitsumi? Where did they come from? What did they want with the metal sheet with the indecipherable writing? *Dawn's Reach* answers these questions and more!

Turn the page to read the first chapter.

DAWN'S REACH

On the day of her seventeenth birthday, Genia Calliot's life changed forever. No, that's not quite right. Oh, it has a nice ring to it—a ring that goes well with tales of adventure. And at the end of her life, she would indeed remember it thus, encouraged in this fiction by histories more interested in drama than in fact. But memory conflates and collapses events into nice tidy packages suitable for stories, rarely reflecting reality's messy edges. This day, in fact, was a day of celebration and enticing mysteries. It was not the day the snow cracked before the avalanche or the pebble rolled before the landslide. *That* day was a week in the future. No, *this* day was an exquisitely cut, sparkling gem. *This* day was perfect.

Pulse thrumming, Genia waited in the dark, holding her breath—a natural instinct to hide her location. *Silly*, she thought, the hard vacuum surrounding her interceptor, not to mention its centimeters' thick plasteel hull, meant that even if she screamed her prey would be none the wiser. With a mental effort, she loosed her breath and struggled to resume a normal pattern. The sensor panel showed only the asteroid she nestled against, waiting for her victim. He must have seen her disappear into this cluster and had to come investigate. "Come on," she muttered, "show yourself."

There.

At the screen's edge, a weak, but steady pulse nosed into range. Highly attenuated, the pulse meant the enemy had engaged his stealth protocol—a leaky one, fortunately for her. Her breath quickened, and a slow smile spread across her face. *Gotcha!* She flexed her hands on the weapons and flight controls. Just a *little* closer. At the back of her mind, an idea floated—there was something about that trace she should remember. Building excitement at her imminent kill pushed the thought away. A thousand more klicks.

Now.

The interceptor jumped, stooping on her victim at six gravities. She could have used her missiles, but she wanted this kill to be intimate. She only wished she could see the surprise on his face. But she'd have to settle for her imagination.

At ten seconds to weapons lock, she frowned with concern. Why wasn't he fleeing, or at least trying to evade? She had the advantage of surprise, but surely he'd seen her by now, even through her own stealth protocol. The nagging thought tried to break through as she acquired a lock and lit up her beams. Which stabbed through—nothing. The pulse remained on her screen, but the welcome sight of her directed energy beams lighting up space and melting metal remained absent.

"Oh Swarm," she said. The stray thought she had dismissed burst into her consciousness and her eyes darted to the screen sector showing the rear. Somehow her erstwhile target had come in behind her. In panic she corkscrewed away. Two missiles, ghostly traces with tiny cross sections, followed. Twenty seconds from impact, she plunged directly toward another asteroid, hoping to pull up at the last second and watch the missiles impact the asteroid instead of her interceptor. Forehead sheened with sweat, she waited until the last nanosecond to initiate the evasion. She flew a razor's edge between slamming into the rock and being spread across local space by the missiles.

Collision warnings blared and red lights flared as she grazed the rock and one of the missiles slammed into the asteroid. Where was the other one?

She only had a few seconds to realize with dismay that the

other missile was one of the new smart ones. It had anticipated her maneuver and bent its course to match hers as she came out of her dive.

The lights went out.

"You cheated!" Genia said bitterly.

"And how was that?" her father's rich baritone sounded in her cabin. Lights ramped back up, and the controls reset for another run. Genia removed her suit's helmet and mopped her forehead with a sleeve.

"We agreed no decoys and no smart missiles."

Giles Calliot chuckled. "No, you said, and I quote, 'I want to try this run without using decoys or smart missiles.' I merely agreed that you should try it that way. I never said *I'd* try it that way."

Genia ran through the conversation in her mind and found it exactly as her father had described. "You're such a politician," she muttered. She loved her dad, but his "lessons" were tiresome.

"Again?" Giles asked.

The answer to that one was easy. "No, four runs are enough. Besides, I'm starved and sick of losing."

"Okay, but you did much better this year. You almost won one of those runs."

Genia smiled, remembering a lock on her father's ship. He'd barely escaped that trap. "Next year, Dad. Eighteen is the magic number." She punched the exit button, and the simulator's door sighed open.

"You know if you put in more time between birthdays you'd improve much faster."

Genia stripped off the vacuum suit that was part of what made this simulation so realistic. "Those commercial simulations are garbage." She stepped from the simulator just as Giles emerged from his. Theirs were two of dozens of simulators scattered around the floor of a cavernous warehouse. The smell of grease and hydraulic fluid lifted her spirits. She supposed after nine years that smell had become linked with celebrating her birthday. Together they threaded their way through the machines quietly awaiting trainees from the first shift, their footsteps echoing in the huge space. Giles led the way to the control room where the lone operator stifled a yawn, then shot to his feet at Giles' appearance.

"Thanks again, Anfroy."

With a slight bow, Anfroy said, "It is as always my pleasure, sir. May I expect you again next year?"

Giles tipped his head toward Genia, a smile crinkling the corner of his eyes. "Ask her. She's in charge, apparently."

"Yep," Genia said. "I wouldn't miss it."

Giles expression turned serious. "Do you have any daughters, Anfroy?"

"Yes, sir. Three daughters."

Giles shook his head sadly. "Never let them get the upper hand, Anfroy. Once they understand their power, they'll twist you to their will without mercy; you'll be powerless to resist."

Genia's cheeks reddened, and she slugged her dad in the shoulder. "Stop it, Dad!" She marched through the control room toward the exit.

"Ouch," Giles said, clutching his arm and rubbing it theatrically. "Thanks again, Anfroy." With a wave good bye, he followed Genia.

In the car on the way back to their apartment building, Genia relaxed into her seat, drowsy now that her body had absorbed the adrenaline from the simulated battles. That too was a familiar feeling. They had to conduct their sessions early before normal operating hours. Still, she was lucky to be able to use the government facility on account of her father's position. Concern halted her descent into sleep. "Dad?"

"Hmmm?" Giles responded, concentrating on the road ahead even though traffic was light. One of her father's odd habits was insisting on driving himself rather than plugging into the traffic grid.

"Could you get into trouble using the training facility like that?"

The corner of his mouth ticked up in a half smile. "Then it really is true."

Puzzled, Genia shook her head. She couldn't think what he meant.

"Your seventeenth birthday *does* magically change you into an adult."

Sure, she was an adult now, but, "What do you mean?"

"You haven't worried about that before. You've always just assumed it was okay."

And he was right. She hadn't considered that anything might be wrong with their birthday tradition.

"Not to worry, Genia. I've ticked all the boxes for our outings. Now, it may be that as a Praetor who oversees Dawn's military and security apparatus, I received that permission where someone else wouldn't." He shrugged. "But hey, rank hath its privileges as they say."

This past year she had become increasingly aware that her father's high rank in Dawn's government was responsible for many of the things she enjoyed—their comfortable apartment in central Beton for example. As Giles steered the car under their building a chime on her Tab announced an incoming communication request. It was Kenric Toclive.

Her heart beat faster. She and Kenric had attended school together since they were nine. At their first meeting she'd crushed hard and never recovered. Violente Toclive, Kenric's mother, was a Praetor like her father. She was responsible for Dawn's economy—the second most coveted appointed position on Dawn beside her father's. So, in addition to being classmates, Genia had run into Kenric over the years at various governmental social events. Whenever they spoke, the atmosphere was easy, but their relationship existed in a weird borderland—more than acquaintances, not quite friends.

She had always hoped the connection would progress beyond that, but despite the hints she dropped, he never seemed interested. She consoled herself that he wasn't obviously interested in anyone else either.

But this year Kenric had returned from their six month upper class hiatus a different person. Oh, an unruly mop of black curly hair still topped his head and chocolate eyes still viewed the world with an amused twinkle. But he'd grown taller, his shoulders had broadened, his chest deepened and his face had lost baby fat giving way to a chiseled look that emphasized a strong, square, whisker-shadowed jaw. She wasn't the only one to have noticed his transformation from gangly, awkward boy to enticing young man, and he seemed to be enjoying his new role as a social singularity, drawing all the girls into his orbit.

Except Genia.

She had watched from afar while he flirted with the rest of their Instruction Center's female population. Although they'd crossed paths recently at several governmental soirees, their interactions had remained in that strange uncollapsed wave function. But now here he was, wanting to talk.

She debated whether to wait to talk to him alone in her room instead of in the car with her father. Caution thrust aside, she was an adult now after all, she accepted the request but positioned the camera to exclude any glimpse of her father.

Giles pulled into their reserved space as Kenric's face popped into the air above her Tab.

"Happy Birthday, Genia," he said with a crooked smile that dissolved just a little bit of her heart and caused her breath to catch.

"Thanks, Kenric," Genia replied, keeping her voice level and cool. She didn't need him to tumble to her raging emotional turmoil.

"I'm sure you have family plans today, but I was wondering if you'd like to grab a cold bulb with me tomorrow to celebrate."

Cold bulb, not her favorite treat, but...she fought back a silly grin and lost. "That'd be great."

"How about 15:30 after instruction?"

She nodded. "Sounds great."

"I'll meet you there then."

His face vanished. Giles raised an eyebrow.

"Not a word, Dad."

"Of course not, Genny. I just hope for your sake he's finally seen that enormous sign you've been hauling around."

"Sign?"

"Yeah, the one that says in huge flashing letters 'My infatuation with you knows no bounds, Kenric Toclive.'"

Genia groaned. Apparently she hadn't hidden that interest as carefully as she'd thought. "Am I that obvious? Because in my head my self-control was exceptional, and you were clueless."

Giles popped his door and headed to the lift. He grinned. "You forget, I read people for a living. Lots of folks think I'm pretty good at it."

"I should have known I couldn't keep it from you and Mom. What do you think?"

"Of Kenric?" Genia nodded. "Oh, from my exposure to him, he's a nice young man. You certainly could do worse."

That was not a ringing endorsement. He'd been more enthusiastic about other boys she'd seen. "But?" she said.

"But nothing." Giles shrugged. "You could do worse, that's all."

"But?"

Giles pursed his lips. "Kenric *is* a nice young man. His mother though," he grimaced, "she's another story."

Her father and Violente Toclive had sparred on several occasions over obscure, and to Genia meaningless, governmental details, but she'd never heard him make any comment about her.

"She's a very, and I emphasize that, *very*, political animal. She does everything with multiple layers of intention. You can never trust her obvious motive."

Genia bristled. She hated it when people assumed you could evaluate others on the basis of their friends or family, especially family. Kenric didn't choose his parents, so how could that accidental relationship tell you anything about him? "But he's not his mom."

Seeing her upset, Giles held out a placating hand. "You're right, of course. It may mean nothing. All I'm saying is that parents can influence their children and you should be aware of who his parents are." He shook his head. "Like I said, from my exposure to him he's—"

"A nice young man. Yeah, I heard that."

The door to their apartment slid open and lights sprang on in the entry hall. "Why don't you go shower," Giles said. "I'll wake your mom and start breakfast."

"Mmm," Genia said, "cakes and bacon and quarth juice?"

Giles kissed her forehead. "All your favorites as usual."

Genia smiled and headed to her room.

"Windows transparent," she said, and soft reddish light flooded her room. It was early yet, but the secondary star in Dawn's binary system was high in the sky. Triggered by the light, the holos on her walls sprang to life. There she was with her family at the Scissors and the Trewick Caldera and on the beach at Three Strike Bay.

She stripped out of her sweaty clothes and stepped into the sonshower, turning the setting up to allow the vibrations to penetrate sore muscles.

After her shower, spurred on by the enticing aroma of sizzling bacon, she drew on a pair of billowy light gray pants, threw on a blue shirt and drew her hair back into a ponytail. After a glance in the mirror to check the result, she marched from her room. Down the hall she emerged into the dining area where mother was just setting down a plate piled high with steaming breakfast cakes. Assorted fruit and a carafe of quarth juice were already set out. Genia's mouth watered and her stomach reminded her she had eaten an early dinner last night.

"Happy Birthday, Genny," her mother said with a warm smile and extended arms offering a hug. But the pained wrinkles around her eyes after she swept them over Genia's outfit spoiled the effect. True to form, her mother was dressed as if an intimate family breakfast were a State affair. To her mother's chagrin, Genia hadn't inherited her fashion sense or her need to demonstrate it. Genia's failings in that regard visibly disturbed her mother even seven years after Genia had rebelled and started selecting her own attire. Genia never had understood her mother's insistence on keeping up appearances. She wished just this once on her birthday, her mother would keep her disappointment in check. As if reading Genia's thoughts, her mother smoothed the pain from her face. Genia stepped into the offered embrace.

Giles walked in carrying a plate of perfectly crisped bacon. "Well, Mabot," he said addressing her mom, "seventeen years old. Can you believe this is our little girl?" He set the bacon on the table. "We're ready here; let's dig in."

When Genia couldn't fit another bite in her mouth, she sat back in her chair, eyes drooping as her early morning caught up with her. But Giles was having none of that.

"Now, Genia," he said and waved a hand in a sweeping gesture, "away with that sleepy look." He stood with sparkling eyes and a broad smile. "We have a seventeenth birthday to celebrate! First on your list, I believe was a hike and a picnic by the Firefall."

Genia smiled in return. Life ahead stretched brilliant, flat, and smooth to the distant horizon. "Is that where I learn this shadowy family secret you keep hinting about?" She was teasing. For three years now her parents had hinted that on her seventeenth birthday they would reveal what they called "The Family Secret." Although Genia had outwardly scoffed at the notion of such a secret, she was genuinely curious and looked forward to the revelation.

"All in good time, Genia," he said with an enigmatic smile.

At the Firefall, a torrent from a geothermal spring erupting from a shear mountainside burned before falling into a pool lost in the mist a thousand meters below. In the light breeze and blowing spray she shivered, but lost herself in the twin subsonic roars of the plummeting water and the burning, venting gas. Afterward, she toweled off, basked in the noon sun's warmth and munched on a sweet-sour algor fruit.

That afternoon, they attended the final installment of the holographic hit series *Swarm Destruction*, dined in her favorite restaurant, and ended the day at home with a few birthday presents.

Seated on the floor in their apartment's living area, after she'd opened the last present, disappointed again that it wasn't the promised secret, she eyed her father skeptically. "You were just kidding about the whole 'Family Secret' thing weren't you?" Her father smiled. She got to her feet and pouted. "It was only a joke, wasn't it?" Her father's grin broadened. She sighed. "Well, you got me good. That was some joke. You lied and I believed you. Ha. Ha."

With a chuckle, her father wrapped an arm around her shoulders and pulled her tight. "I would never, ever do something like that to a wonderful daughter like you." He looked at Mabot. "Would I, dear?"

Mabot closed her eyes with a look of extreme tolerance. "Just tell her, Giles. Genia has suffered enough."

Mouth sagging in a mock frown, Giles released Genia and pointed the way to the dining room. "No one has a sense of humor in this family anymore. But before we talk about the secret we need to recite the Preface."

Genia groaned. "Not that. Can't we just skip it? I'm sick of hearing it."

With a stubborn look, her mother shook her head. "Genia, we can't ignore the forms. They kept us together through the Cataclysm. Tradition saved humanity—brought it back from the edge of extinction. We should honor that."

The familiar argument grated. And regardless of what her parents said, she knew the real reason for their insistence on observing the forms. "But Mom," Genia said, her voice strained, "just because you and Dad feel guilty that I'm an only child doesn't mean you should punish me for your—" She stopped herself before the word came out because some things cannot be unsaid. But Giles completed her thought.

"Failure?" he said, and the pain on his face evaporated her frustration and impatience.

"I...I didn't say that," Genia said softly.

After a long, tense moment of silence, her mom reached out and patted her hand. "It's okay, sweetie. We know you didn't mean it." She looked at her husband. "Giles? The Preface?"

With an obvious effort, Giles smoothed the anguish from his face, lifted his mouth in a wan smile and repeated the ritual words. "This is the story of mankind's survival on Dawn. Three thousand three hundred and twenty-eight years ago, the Swarm appeared in Dawn's system and attacked without warning and without mercy. They rained destruction on Dawn and its people and in the course of ten horrifying days killed billions and demolished man's works on the land and in the skies. When the atrocity ended only five hundred remained hidden in caves high in the mountains."

Genia had said she knew the Preface and she did. It was taught every year in school and as her mom had said, the forms required its recitation on every child's birthday ending on their seventeenth. This was the last year of the ritual for her. The Preface had been adapted from the Book of the Lore, Dawn's earliest recorded account of the Cataclysm. In the last five hundred years, the Book of the Lore's more sensational aspects had been de emphasized.

"Darkness, literal and figurative descended on our ancestors. Factions arose and fought each other for food and clothing and land. Separated into five enclaves at continual war with each other, their conflicts threatened to extinguish human life on Dawn. To finish what the Swarm with its might hadn't accomplished.

"Until Farman. He was the one man with the courage to leave his faction's protection and offer himself weaponless to his enemies and plead with them to renounce war and remember their true enemy. After being tortured and killed, his death provided the spark that convinced each of the other four bands in turn to unite in cooperation. So, in honor of this great man, we recite the Preface to our children on their birthdays that they may remember our people have only two enemies—the Swarm that tried to destroy us and factionalism amongst ourselves that almost completed the Swarm's task."

Genia had heard the recitation in various forms all her life. In the last few years she had come to view the ritual narration with the mocking disdain common among her friends. But tonight the words carried more weight. It might have been sorrow at provoking her parents, or maybe it was residual emotion from the evening's entertainment. Whatever the reason, the loneliness and despair of five hundred people who had lost family, friends, a civilization, a world and fought for their lives so that one day she could enjoy everything in her life sank deep into her soul.

"And now, the moment you've been waiting for all your young life." Giles laid his Tab on the table and looked at Genia expectantly.

Genia shook off her melancholy. She wouldn't let the distant past ruin this moment. Her dad's statement was an exaggeration. But she *had* been anticipating the promised revelation ever since she'd learned five years ago that on her seventeenth birthday she would share in the family secret.

Giles activated his Tab's holographic display. A paper thin rectangular metallic sheet twenty centimeters wide and thirty long appeared floating above the table. It had strange writing on one side that looked like it was engraved on the sheet. Genia knew that it wasn't because just recently she had read an article about the Lamina. Of mysterious origin, it was only displayed to the public every few years. "We own the Lamina? That's the family secret?" She scoffed. "Some secret, everyone knows that."

"Do you know anything about its origin?" her father asked, ignoring her comment. She felt like not responding until he gave her the courtesy first, but decided she'd play his game.

She rubbed a finger on the bridge of her nose. "No, the little I've read about it said merely that an early exploratory expedition found it...in a crater or around a crater...somehow it's associated with a crater in my head."

"It was a thousand years ago. One of your direct line ancestors was exploring Agden's far northern reaches."

Genia whistled. "A thousand years. How many greats is that?"

"Thirty," her mother said. "Give or take. Have you ever counted them, Giles?"

Giles shook his head. "Does this ancestor have a name?" Genia asked.

"Estevenot," Giles responded. His face went stern. "Now pay attention and stop interrupting."

With wide eyes, Genia raised her hands, palms up. "Me? Interrupt? I was just—"

"Estevenot discovered one of the few crater's at the continent's far northern extremity. Not being the sort to merely report the crater's existence, he wanted to visit the crater's floor. From the rim, it was obvious that the floor was bare ground. None of the rest of his party wanted to go exploring. They were afraid, with reason, that the ground was ice and snow free because it sat above an awakening volcano. Not to be deterred by fear of molten lava and deadly gases, our intrepid ancestor ventured alone to the crater floor.

"At the crater floor, wandering around among building sized boulders, he came upon a domed structure. He said it was built of a smooth dark gray substance that had the feel of neither stone nor metal. He couldn't tell how old it was because in his words 'nothing about the building looked weathered or worn.' There was an entrance, but again in his words 'it was shrouded in darkness'—a darkness he described as tangible."

"Ohhh," Genia said, mocking, "sounds scary."

Giles shot her a warning look, but kept going. "When he shone a light on it though, it parted. When he stepped inside the interior became brightly lit and he saw the building was a single space. In the middle of that space was an altar."

"An altar?" Genia said. "Like where people used to sacrifice animals? Eww."

"On the altar," Giles continued ignoring Genia, "he found a small metallic sheet covered with unfamiliar characters. He examined the space in this building, but found nothing else of interest.

"His report of finding an intact building in the middle of a crater was met with ridicule even in the face of the 'Lamina,' as Estevenot christened the sheet, especially since his companions couldn't corroborate his story. He spent years trying to raise funds for another expedition to vindicate himself. Eventually, he scraped enough money together, but was never able to find the crater. In a fit of pique over his treatment, he kept the Lamina and handed it down with explicit instructions that it was never to be displayed in a museum and was only to be examined under strictly controlled conditions. Our ancestors obeyed those instructions long after they had lost any force. That was partly out of habit and partly because it was a source of pride to keep such a valuable object in their exclusive possession. But two hundred years ago, the family finally decided that enough was enough and such a find should not be kept from the public. We started to allow it out for exhibition every few years."

Genia yawned. About two minutes in to that drawn out explanation, she concluded that she and her dad had completely different ideas of what amounted to an exciting family secret. As her adrenaline level dropped, an overwhelming lassitude weighed her limbs. Now, she just wanted to climb in bed. "That's great, Dad. I'm glad our family's civic impulses finally won the day." She pushed to her feet, stifling another yawn. "I'm beat. I think I'll—"

With a shrug, Giles said to Mabot, "I so wanted our daughter to carry our family's legacy, but if she's not interested, I guess I'll have to find someone else to do it."

Thick headed with fatigue, Genia stared at her father then at her mother trying to figure out what he was talking about.

"Stop playing with her, Giles," Mabot said. To Genia, she said, "You haven't heard the family secret yet, dear. But your father will tell you right now," she glared at Giles, "won't he?"

Giles lifted his hands in surrender. "Have a seat, Genia." Genia sat. This new twist blew the cobwebs from her mind. She hoped this addition to the story would live up to its advance billing.

Eyes lit with excitement, Giles leaned across the table and lowered his voice. "The family secret is that over the centuries we have been able to piece together part of what's written there." He paused, unable to keep himself from making the dramatic reveal. "It's one of four such sheets scattered throughout the galaxy. When assembled, they lead the holder of the Key to a source of unlimited power."

Okay, Genia thought, *unlimited power, that sounds interesting, but how would anyone go about finding these other Laminae and what was that about a Key?*

Her father stopped, looking at Genia, apparently expecting her to gasp or squeal or do one of those other things associated with intense surprise. Her straight face and lack of audible response evidently came as a disappointment because he frowned. "Unlimited power," Giles said again with more emphasis and in a deeper voice like a villain in a holo melodrama.

Genia fought a yawn into submission. "Yeah, I heard you the first time, Dad. But what does that mean exactly? Are we talking about an inexhaustible supply of electricity? A never-ending source of heat? Because those tiny lights up there," she waved at the ceiling indicating the unseen stars above, "fit that bill for all practical purposes. Once you get close enough, that is."

Mabot gave a low chuckle. Giles drummed fingers on the table. "No, not that kind of power. The word used as close as we can tell means omnipotence—as in the ability to do anything imaginable."

Omnipotence. Genia turned the word over in her mind. Her fertile imagination had started assembling a list of things to do—right every wrong she had ever heard of, immortality for her and her loved ones, banish disease and poverty for everyone else, instantaneous travel to anywhere in the universe. The list kept growing, and as it did the idea of omnipotence insinuated tentacles into her mind's every nook and cranny and gripped.

She wanted that power.

Surprised as she was at that realization, because she had never imagined herself as power hungry, it was undeniable—she had to have it. Hot behind her realization, fear slithered in. What if someone else seized this power first? What harm could that person wreak?

"Yes," Giles said, dragging Genia from her reflections. "Now you understand the implications and why it is a secret."

Right, a secret because someone else might venture into the galaxy and uncover the other Laminae and the Key. In an effort to relax desire's tentacles clutching her mind, she switched to what she thought of as her analytic mode and began to compile a list of objections. "Do we have any clue what the Key is or where to find it?"

Giles shook his head and his eyes lost their fire. "No."

"How about the other Laminae? Are they on Dawn or somewhere out there in the universe's trillion trillion trillion cubic parsecs of space?"

"Over the thousand years since the Lamina's discovery we've scoured Dawn with no success."

"And do we have any prospect of ever leaving Dawn's system to explore that space and in an act of extreme improbability stumble across these other Laminae and the Key?"

"No," Giles said, shaking his head. "We have no such prospects."

That should have worked. It should have extinguished the

fire the Lamina had sparked in her mind. She had no hope of seizing the prize her father had described. It should have worked, but it didn't. With the recitation of each obstacle, her resolve had only hardened. She didn't know how or where or when, but she vowed to find the Laminae and the Key and take that power for herself.

ACKNOWLEDGEMENT

Many thanks to April Clausen for invaluable insights into Ricci and Koning's interactions. I know you apologized for yelling, but really there was no need. As with the proverbial mule, sometimes a two-by-four is the only way to get my attention. My editor Michelle Millet of Write on Editing again did marvelous, transformative work on the manuscript. And to the lovely Marianne without whom none of this would be possible and many commas would be misplaced, my everlasting thanks and undying love. For the many mistakes and infelicities I have only myself to blame.

ARTIFACT

Prospector's Run

Holtz Mitsumi is desperate.
Mitsumi gambled everything to find lost tech on the First Stellar Civilization's dead, shattered worlds. Massive riches were his if he won.

He lost.

Instead of wealth, he was saddled with a mysterious alien artifact that invaded his mind and instilled an iron compulsion to find its origin. But the artifact did not communicate with anyone else and appeared to be common manufactured diamond—as common as dirt and worth as much.

Broke and in debt, but driven to get back to the stars, Mitsumi is stuck. Mounting an expedition to find the object's origin is impossible.

Then an enigmatic stranger corners Mitsumi. He claims to have solid leads to fabulous lost tech and offers to let Mitsumi captain a prospecting run, in exchange for a share of the voyage profits.

After scraping a crew together, Mitsumi embarks on one last run to finance his search. But the crew has secrets, some of them deadly. Before he knows it, Mitsumi picks up the perfect accessory for a struggling prospector—an implacable foe. Chased across the galaxy, Mitsumi wrestles with his unruly crew in an impossible bid to survive and find the artifact's secret.

Dawn's Reach

The Swarm is back to finish off humanity.

Three thousand years ago the Swarm left Dawn's five hundred survivors in the stone-age. But in all the long years as humanity clawed its way back from the brink of extinction, the Swarm never reappeared—until now.

Or at least that is what many on Dawn feared. Genia Calliot is not so sure. The mysterious interstellar visitor to Dawn's system sparks a crash program to investigate. Genia vows to be part of it to learn the truth and not incidentally uncover the origins of an ancient alien artifact that is part of her family's legacy.

But enemies without and within threaten Genia and the entire human race.

Prospector's Choice

What would you sacrifice for omnipotence?

On the trail of ultimate power, Holtz Mitsumi and Genia Calliot run a gauntlet of danger and deception only to discover a truth that might destroy the entire human race.

BOOKS BY THIS AUTHOR

Quarantine

Hunzuu is desperate to find the One World.
The world on which the Son of God, the Anointed One was born and lived as a human. Hidden from the Commonwealth of Worlds' trillions of inhabitants, the One World's location is unknown. While working as an engineer aboard the star freighter Sittace, Hunzuu stumbles on a shadowy plot involving the One World. Vowing to find the One World and protect it, Hunzuu embarks on a journey that will lead him to dangers he could never imagine and a contagion that threatens the Commonwealth.

Even If By Fire

You've washed the blood from your hands. You're sick of shooting at your neighbors in self defense.
Where do you go?

It's 2057. Violence in the United States is an all-consuming cancer. Nowhere is safe. Well, almost nowhere. The Lost Land is a possibility, but not an attractive one. In the end though, there is no choice. If you can get there. The border to the Lost Land is closed and safety means a trek through the Rocky Mountains.

Peter Gillen must flee there to avoid unjust accusations, but he falls in with a shadowy group. Rose Horne is drawn there by the lure of peace, but she and her family are hunted in the mountains.

Then the U.S. sends in the army. And launches nuclear missiles.

Fans of Tom Clancy thrillers and alternate history timelines will love Even If By Fire.

Made in the USA
Las Vegas, NV
16 October 2024